THE LIST

ALSO BY STEVE BERRY

NOVELS

The Amber Room

The Romanov Prophecy

The Third Secret

The Templar Legacy

The Alexandria Link

The Venetian Betrayal

The Charlemagne Pursuit

The Paris Vendetta

The Emperor's Tomb

The Jefferson Key

The Columbus Affair

The King's Deception

The Lincoln Myth

The Patriot Threat

The 14th Colony

The Lost Order

The Bishop's Pawn

The Malta Exchange

The Warsaw Protocol

The Kaiser's Web

The Omega Factor

The Last Kingdom

The Atlas Maneuver

The Medici Return

WITH GRANT BLACKWOOD

The 9th Man

Red Star Falling

WITH M. J. ROSE

The Museum of Mysteries

The Lake of Learning

The House of Long Ago

The End of Forever

THE
LIST

STEVE BERRY

GRAND
CENTRAL

NEW YORK   BOSTON

Grand Central Publishing
Hachette Book Group
1290 Avenue of the Americas, New York, NY 10104
grandcentralpublishing.com
@grandcentralpub

First edition: July 2025

Grand Central Publishing is a division of Hachette Book Group, Inc. The Grand Central Publishing name and logo is a registered trademark of Hachette Book Group, Inc.

The publisher is not responsible for websites (or their content) that are not owned by the publisher.

The Hachette Speakers Bureau provides a wide range of authors for speaking events. To find out more, go to hachettespeakersbureau.com or email HachetteSpeakers @hbgusa.com.

Grand Central Publishing books may be purchased in bulk for business, educational, or promotional use. For information, please contact your local bookseller or the Hachette Book Group Special Markets Department at special.markets@hbgusa.com.

Library of Congress Cataloging-in-Publication Data has been applied for.

ISBNs: 9781538770870 (hardcover), 9781538770894 (ebook), 9781538774557 (large print)

Printed in the United States of America

LSC-C

Printing 1, 2025

For Richard L. Daley
Thank you

What good is it for a man to gain the whole world, yet forfeit his soul?

—Mark 8:36

TWO YEARS AGO

PROLOGUE

KILLING OLD PEOPLE WAS LIKE SHOOTING BOTTLES OFF A LOG.

So little to hold one's attention.

Even worse, the Priority was late.

Like clockwork, the old man arrived every Friday between 6:00 and 6:30 A.M., as the file expressly noted. Predictable as the squadron of yellow flies that had swarmed in half an hour ago and had been aggravating him ever since.

But not today.

Of all Fridays, the old coot decided to be late today.

Of course, if there had been any real anticipation—that thrill-of-the-hunt-ecstasy-of-success bullshit—the hour just spent in sweltering August heat wouldn't have been so bad.

He lowered the binoculars and focused on the quiet, pastoral scene. The woodbine bushes, palmettos, and sand pines of the lake's northeast shore provided thick cover for him, his camouflage fatigues blending perfectly. Brooks Creek meandered ahead, Eagle Lake beyond.

Hopefully, just a few more minutes and this would be over.

THE OLD MAN GRIPPED THE THROTTLE AND POWERED THE SKIFF across Eagle Lake. His wife called the fourteen-hundred-acre basin his meandering mistress. Apt. It'd been nearly thirty years since he watched bulldozers and front-end loaders carve its banks, soil that once supported pine trees and soybeans carted all over

Georgia for fill dirt. The remaining massive borrow pit eventually filled with water, becoming a readily identifiable blue splotch on the state map.

He'd been one of the first to test its virgin expanse, hooked from the start, and he hoped one day the last sight for his tired hazel eyes would be the comforting taupe of Eagle Lake's tranquil water.

He inspected the early-morning sky. It would be at least another hour before the sun crested the tallest pines rising from the eastern shore. No clouds lingered in sight, a tight clammy blanket of humidity the only reminder of the nasty thunderstorms from the past couple of days. But the birds and tree frogs didn't seem to mind. Nor the insects.

Nor did he.

Ahead, he spotted the familiar break in the shore.

He released the throttle.

The outboard wound down, slowing the skiff to a crawl. He knew most Woods County fishermen avoided Brooks Creek for four practical reasons. Limited space—only fifteen feet from bank to bank. Full of mosquitoes and yellow flies. Unbearably hot and sticky most of the year.

And the gate of limbs.

Thick water oak branches corkscrewed a barricade over the entire expanse. The space between the bark and water was limited, about four feet, yielding only to a certain size and shape of boat, like his flat-bottomed skiff, bought three years ago specifically for Brooks Creek.

He allowed the outboard to die, then inched ahead using a half-horsepower trolling motor mounted to the bow.

The limbs approached.

Thirty years of visits had taught him precisely when and for how long to duck. Beyond the barrier, the creek snaked inland another twenty yards until bulging into a secluded pool, where he knew the best fishing in central Georgia waited.

He spotted the old man.

About damn time.

Miserable heat. Bugs. Poison ivy. At least yesterday there'd been air-conditioning, though that seventy-year-old pain in the ass squirmed the whole time. He liked it, though, when they resisted a little. It added to the sport. Made for a challenge. But not too much. Bruises, cuts, blood, DNA, fingerprints. All were evidence that could definitely ruin a good thing.

He shook his head.

People were so damn predictable.

Living their whole life by precise agendas, never realizing the risks associated with regularity. Take this Priority. Every Friday, no matter what, he plopped his boat into the water at the county ramp and powered straight for Brooks Creek. Even his path across Eagle Lake was never in doubt. Like an invisible highway to the northeast, always right after dawn, staying till lunchtime. Usually, he'd take back four or five bass. Sometimes a catfish. It looked like he'd vary the routine once in a while. Maybe try the southwest shore or the east bank. No. If it's Friday, then this must be Brooks Creek.

Damn how he loved creatures of habit.

The old man cut another glance at the early-morning sky. Orange and yellow hues were being rapidly replaced by azure. What a great-looking summer day. Nothing beat morning fishing, weekdays, just after dawn, all alone.

He reached over and gripped his favorite jigger pole. Years ago he'd taken a month to whittle one from cane. Now they could be bought anywhere, professionally manufactured out of lightweight flexible nylon. Slowly, he tied the special double-reverse spinner knot learned from his father, assuring that the sinking Rapala at the tip was tightly secured. It was shaped and colored like a small bream, the perfect temptation for a near-blind, greedy-gut bass.

5

He tested the treble hooks fore, aft, and abeam.

Sharp. Ready to snag.

He extended the black pole from the boat and ever-so-gently lowered the plug beneath the quelled surface. Brooks Creek was best fished early. By midday, after the sun steamed the tepid water, warmth drove the fish into the cool lake bottom. Right now, just after dawn, the environment was perfect and he stared hard at the black crevices in the creek's east bank. Twice, when he'd won the Golden Angler award from the Woods County Bass Association, the snagged bigmouth bass came from those crevices.

The plug submerged.

Ever so gently he added to the allure by jiggering the pole up and down, the splashing piece of plastic now appearing like a fingerling bream casually investigating the surface. It wouldn't take long. Never did. The trick was knowing how to splash. Too hard would scare the bass off. Too soft would never get any attention.

The line knocked hard.

He tightened his grip and hung on, allowing the hooks to tangle deep. Jerk too soon and all he'd have left was an empty lure. When he sensed the hooks were set, he swung the frantic fish up and into the boat.

Hell's bells he loved jigger fishing.

He pinched his boot down on the thrashing bass and thrust a finger into the gills. Carefully, he removed the hooks and admired the catch. Four pounds. Maybe five.

It would make excellent fillets.

He was ready.

Occasionally he wished he could simply snap their necks. It'd be so much simpler and a thousand times less trouble. Unnoticed deaths took imagination, thought, and creativity. A flair for the expected mixed with the unexpected.

Like an art form.

The scene needed to be set perfectly in the Priority's mind.

THE OLD MAN DROPPED THE BASS INTO THE CATCH COOLER, THEN leaned over the side and rinsed the fish coat off his hands. He then reached into another Igloo for an apple. He'd overslept and left home in a hurry, not taking time to have his usual bowl of shredded wheat and coffee.

Overhead, swallows and mockingbirds twittered from tree to tree in search of their own breakfast. A welcome waft of honeysuckle accompanied bees filching nectar. He should have bought a lot here years ago, back before the price of lakefront property skyrocketed. But even now the lack of adequate water and sewer lines and paved roads kept the number of dwellings to a minimum. Especially here, on the northeast shore. Nothing but loblolly pine all around for miles.

He gnawed on the apple and, as always, tossed the spent core into the pool where he was about to replace the lure.

It never failed to draw a fish.

Pole in hand, he extended the lure back over the water.

HE SEARCHED HIS JUMPSUIT POCKET AND FOUND A PACK OF Doublemint. He folded a stick into his mouth and rejuvenated his palate. It was almost a conditioned response. Death and dry mouth.

A habit?

He grinned at the irony.

Then he relocked his eyes on the old man sitting in the boat fifty yards away. A minute went by. He flicked his wrist and the associate standing beside him understood what to do.

Timing was so important.

Nothing unusual except—

THE OLD MAN HEARD THRASHING AHEAD IN THE DENSE SCRUB ON the far bank, beyond the point where the creek left the pool snaking inland. People rarely frequented those woods, so he wondered if the visitor might be a deer, hog, or brown bear. Fifty feet past the pool the foliage thinned to a tiny beach. He gazed into the woods beyond and saw the orange of a hunter's vest.

"Hey," a male voice said. "You there. I need some help."

He whirled the jigger pole back into the boat.

"Please don't go," the voice said.

A man emerged from the thickets cursing after becoming entangled on a thorny dewberry vine at the water's edge.

"What's the problem?" he asked.

"It's my friend. We were huntin' hogs and he tripped. Damn palmetto root. I think his foot's broken. I can't carry him all the way back to the truck. I was thinkin' maybe you could take him in the boat and I could meet you wherever you put in."

He studied the hunter. Mid-thirties, square jaw, clean-shaven. A stranger. But a lot of people traveled from all around south and middle Georgia to hunt Woods County. He was certainly dressed appropriately. Crew-neck shirt beneath a fluorescent-orange vest. Camouflage pants covering stumpy legs. Mud-encrusted boots. Black gloves.

"Can he walk?" he asked.

"Barely," the hunter said, panting, trying to catch a breath. "But I think I can get him here if you'll help me get him into the boat."

"Go ahead. I'll come over."

The hunter retreated into the woods.

He shifted the two coolers, tackle box, and spare gas tank toward the stern, then reached for the paddle and inched the boat toward the clearing where the hunter had just stood.

He beached the bow and climbed out to wait on shore.

A couple of minutes later the hunter he'd just talked with

approached, supporting another man dressed almost identically. The other man appeared older, larger, and even with the first man's help he had a tough time walking, crying out several times as they plowed through the underbrush. He waited by the boat until they emerged from the thickets, then moved forward to help.

The hunter with the bad foot seized him by the hair.

His neck arched back.

Pain seared down his spine.

Another hand came across his face. He felt cold cloth and smelled something sickening, like fish guts dried in the sun. His eyes locked onto the hunter's. Steel-gray with a swirl of indigo, casting a gaze of pleasure that terrified. The grip tightened. The smell turned dizzying. His knees softened, then buckled. He crumpled to the soft soil and stole a final glance upward.

Then the light faded.

HE FISHED THE WALKIE-TALKIE FROM HIS BACK POCKET AND reported, "Got him. Move in."

Though it wasn't visible, at the mouth of Brooks Creek he knew another boat was drifting into position, its occupant there to keep watch with an unbaited line cast into the brown water, walkie-talkie ready in case a warning was needed. He yanked off his black leather gloves, exposing latex ones. His associate did the same. Together they lifted the old man and placed him in the skiff. Then they splashed water on the bank, the sodden soil smoothed with dead palmetto fronds erasing any trace of their presence.

He climbed over the old man's body into the skiff and sat astern. His associate followed but stayed near the bow. He paddled the skiff into the pool and, using the landing net, scooped the apple core from the water. He looked fleetingly to see if a good bite might be left, but the old fool had devoured the pulp down to the seeds. He stuffed the core into the old man's mouth, then maneuvered the skiff into the creek toward the lake.

He negotiated the protruding limbs and drifted toward the creek mouth. His other associate was now in sight and he stared toward the boat. A discreet signal confirmed that everything was fine. He tossed the paddle aside and cranked the skiff's fifty-horsepower outboard.

The engine shot to life. Rpms increased.

Oil billowed out in a noxious cloud.

Another hand signal ordered his associate toward the bow to prop the old man upright on the center seat. To keep the limp body high his associate supported the old man's head from under the chin, crouching down in front. He looked behind once more, again assured by his other associate that no eyes or ears were nearby. Seeing all at the ready, he twisted the outboard into gear.

The boat shot forward toward the pool.

His associate supported the old man, keeping him steady.

The outboard hummed at full throttle.

The limbs rapidly approached, the old man's head directly in their path. In the instant before the two met, he popped the throttle to neutral and rolled out of the stern.

The tepid water felt good.

A welcome rinse for the sweat and grime that had cooked his camouflage fatigues since dawn.

He surfaced shoulder-deep and swept back his gray-streaked hair. His eyes dried and focused just as his associate released the old man's skull, which slammed into the overhanging branches, the body pounding into the transom, reverse momentum sending what was a few seconds before somebody's husband, father, and grandfather tumbling into the creek.

Which was exactly where he wanted it.

If the blow to the head didn't kill, the water certainly would.

Drowning, boating accident, or any combination would each be an acceptable cause of death.

It really was like shooting bottles off a log.

His associate rolled out of the boat into the pool. The skiff settled into a slow cruise, finally lodging in thick brush farther down Brooks Creek, motor humming in neutral.

He surveyed the scene.

Everything was according to the processing criteria.

He signaled his associate, who treaded water until finding the shallows of the creek beyond the limbs. The old man's body floated facedown in the murky water, apple core nearby. He waded over and laid his fingertips on the carotid artery.

No pulse.

Confirmation.

He and his associate pushed through the creek toward the lake. Approaching the mouth, an increasing depth forced them to swim the remaining distance to the other boat. Their clothes quickly turned to anchors, but the distance was only a few yards. Once there, they climbed in, jerked off their gloves, and then sped away as the old man's body floated farther down Brooks Creek.

THE PRESENT

DAY ONE
TUESDAY, JUNE 6

5:50 P.M.

BRENT WALKER HATED REDNECKS.

Not all, of course, but most, though by the most commonly accepted definition he probably was one too. They were a peculiar breed, locally born and bred, with their own language, moral code, and pecking order. To understand them took time and patience—two commodities he'd found himself in short supply of recently. Making matters worse, the scrawny little pissant standing behind him was particularly annoying, complete with the trademark sunburned neck.

"Thought you were gone, lawyer," Clarence Silva said.

"I'm back."

"Lucky us."

He quit sliding the plastic tray across the stainless-steel grid and stopped before the desserts spread out behind a glass partition. He faced Silva, one of the last divorces he'd finalized ten years ago before leaving Concord for Atlanta. Silva had been an electrician's helper at the mill, who then had a wife and three kids.

Brent had represented the wife.

He reached for a slice of cherry pie and continued down the serving line.

The restaurant was rapidly filling with a dinner crowd. Day shift at the paper mill had ended two hours ago. Allowing for enough time to drive home, shower, and hustle the wife and kids into the

15

car, six to seven had always been rush hour at most of Concord's dinner establishments.

And there weren't many.

The two motels had restaurants. In addition, there was a café downtown, a country buffet on the Savannah highway, Andy's Barbecue near the mill, Burger King, McDonald's, Wendy's, and, his choice for the night, Aunt B's Country Kitchen. Being the first Tuesday of the month didn't help with the crowd. The Woods County Rotary Club was holding its monthly gathering just off the main dining room. He once was a member, one of three lawyers.

"Pansy," Silva said.

The idiot had crept close into Brent's personal space, the aroma from Silva's dingy clothes, like spilled milk, strong. A familiar waft. It came from eight hours at the paper mill. A mix of heavy bleaching chemicals and copious amounts of sulfuric gases. The smell of money, everyone called it.

He knew part of the unofficial redneck code was never to walk away from trouble—not now, not ever—so he turned and faced his past. "You got a problem, Clarence?"

His voice rose, the tone intense enough that it caught the attention of the people behind Silva. Good. He wasn't the same man who'd left this town a decade ago and everybody might as well learn that on his first day back.

"Thanks to you, lawyer, I lost everythin'."

He surveyed the fool. Not much had changed. Black oily hair down to the ears. Still thin as a sapling. Same long neck, like one of the pileated woodpeckers that built nests among the pines around Eagle Lake. In contrast, Brent was six-one, a fit 190 pounds, every muscle toned from a steady regimen at the gym. He liked working out. Sweating seemed to take the edge off, much like alcohol, tobacco, or drugs did for others. Thankfully those three vices had never really interested him.

"As I recall," Brent said. "You didn't have much to lose."

"You almost cost me my job."

16

"Bullshit." And he pointed a finger. "*You* almost cost you your job."

Ten years in Atlanta prosecuting criminals for the Fulton County District Attorney's Office and he'd thought the middle Georgia in him gone. Nope. Not a bit. Still there. Ready for a fight. And though he hadn't had a fisticuffs in years, he didn't necessarily want to brawl right in the middle of Aunt B's. Bad for his new image as an assistant general corporate counsel. A fancy title he was still trying to digest.

So he tried a diversion. "What happened to the wife?"

Silva smiled. Both front teeth were gone, and what remained looked like rotten corn kernels. "Married her again, six months after the divorce."

Why wasn't he surprised. The redneck code allowed a wide latitude for forgiveness, no matter the offense, provided a man's pride had not been too soiled. Which seemed the case here.

"Got another young'un too, after."

"How you must be proud."

His sarcasm was clear, so he turned back and started down the serving line.

"Guess she just couldn't go without it," Silva said to him.

Another mantra of the code provided that no matter what the problem, sex was always the answer. Whether good or bad, real or not, didn't matter. He knew he shouldn't, but he couldn't resist. "Killed any rabbits lately?"

He recalled during the divorce the wife's testimony of how Silva liked to buy the children cute little Easter bunnies for them to play with. Then he'd fatten them up, twist their necks, and cook them for Memorial Day. Grillin' Thumper, he called it. Needless to say the whole experience was traumatic on the kids and highly effective on the judge. Silva's visitation rights had been severely restricted.

"How 'bout you and me goin' outside?" Silva said. "I always wanted to twist your neck."

He stopped, turned, and considered the challenge. Why not? He wouldn't mind beating the crap out of this idiot. Might be a good way to finish turning that page on his new life. Unfortunately, common sense cautioned otherwise.

"Since you got the wife and the kids back," he said, "go get a life, Silva."

"Got one. I'd just like to screw your face up. How about it, lawyer? You up to it?"

"I don't think so," a voice said from behind him.

Brent turned.

Hank Reed stood planted, all five foot nine inches of him, head jutted forward projecting that famous look of stern determination, like a face from Mount Rushmore, glaring at Clarence Silva.

"This ain't got nothin' to do with you, Hank," Silva said. "Never liked this lawyer, and you know that."

"I'm not here to argue. Get your food and move on," Hank said.

He knew Silva wasn't about to mount a challenge. Silva surely remained only an electrician's helper at the mill, while Hank was the most senior of the senior day electricians and president of Silva's trade union. Messing with that would bring nothing but a mountain of trouble. So Silva moved on, shuffling past, angling for a table. Good thing, because Brent was just about to head for the parking lot and crush the little bastard.

But he didn't really want a bruised face tomorrow.

His first day on a new job.

New life.

No matter how much pleasure he would have derived.

6:05 P.M.

THE ASSOCIATE ENTERED THE WOODS COUNTY CONVALESCENT Center. The single-story building sat just outside Concord, near the regional hospital. It had been built five years ago, replacing a facility that had far outlived its usefulness. Its stats were impressive. Seventy-eight beds, a staff of fifty-one, its equipment state-of-the-art. The average age of a resident was seventy-nine, the current population divided sixty/forty, women to men. Everything was geared toward comfort. There were morning-coffee socials, craft classes, movies, video games, even candlelight dinners and birthday celebrations. As the center's promotional brochure noted, *We work together with the family to provide ongoing therapeutic programs that meet every resident's needs.*

Sounded great.

But he was a long way from retiring and, when he did, it would be to a beach somewhere warm where he could enjoy the fruits of his many labors.

After all, he was a pro.

He'd timed his visit to coincide with the evening shuffle. The file had indicated that 5:00 to 7:00 P.M. each day was not only a shift change, but a time when family members came and went, many dropping by either on their way home from work or after supper. Nearly all the elderly residents were locals, most born and raised in Woods County, men and women who'd worked their whole lives either at the paper mill, or for the county, or in the school system. Those were the top three local employers. The first convalescent center had been built in the 1960s, fully funded by Southern Republic Pulp and Paper, which owned the local paper mill. It was eventually remodeled twice. *The company's way to give back,* was how it had been billed both times in the press.

The file he'd studied on the Priority had contained photographs, license plates, and physical descriptions of the nearest relatives, but none of those faces had arrived during the past three hours of his surveillance, and none of their cars were parked in the nearly empty lot.

He knew the building stretched a little over twenty thousand square feet under roof, spread across two acres of flat, wooded land that had also been donated by Southern Republic. The Priority resided inside Room 46, in the building's east wing. His name was J. J. Jordon, seventy-four years old, suffering from severe blood clots in his legs, aggravated by gout and kidney failure. He should have died three weeks ago when another Associate had paid a visit to Jordon's home and switched out medications. That was a common method for processing, since the only question it raised was the liability of the pharmacy that had filled the prescription.

Which wasn't his problem.

In fact, the whole idea of the Priority program was to make a death somebody else's problem.

He'd studied Jordon's medical records, to which he had easy access, and noted that the old man's condition had stabilized. His family had chosen to admit him to the local convalescent center since they were no longer able to care for him on a twenty-four-hour basis. The incident with the bad pills had taken a toll, aggravating things, but not to the point of being fatal. So far, nineteen days of constant care had racked up quite a bill, the amount growing every day, with no end in sight.

This was not his first visit to the convalescent center, so he knew its layout. Thankfully, they'd caught a break with the family choosing here as the place to admit him. An outside facility would have only complicated matters. Medical records indicated that Jordon was being fed a constant supply of nasal oxygen. He was also heavily sedated, sleep being deemed the best medicine. That might explain why there were no visitors this evening to Room 46.

Information was so important.

It could be your best ally, which was why the files were prepared with such detail.

He walked down the carpeted corridor and bypassed the residents' rooms, heading instead for a closed door at the end of the hall. He was dressed in a suit and tie, one of the facility's security badges draped around his neck, which identified him as a physician from Savannah. He carried a small black bag. Medical professionals with regular business at the center were issued the badges, which allowed them to come and go as they pleased. Those from Savannah or Augusta were commonplace.

He stopped at the door and glanced around.

No one was in sight.

Security cameras had intentionally not been installed. The governing board that ran the facility, comprising seven Woods

County residents, had thought the measure unnecessary. This was a place where people came to live their final years in peace. Nothing nefarious about that.

So why spend the money.

He inserted the key that he'd brought and freed the lock. Inside was a mechanical room. He flicked on the light switch then relocked the door. His internal clock began ticking. He could not stay here long. Every second increased the risk of exposure. Processing this Priority, in this manner, was not standard operating procedure. But correcting the mistake of three weeks ago had demanded that more risk than usual be taken.

He opened the black leather bag and removed a small cylinder. He then approached a bank of tubes and valves, all leading to the center's respiratory generator. From there, pure oxygen was sent through the walls to each of the rooms, available if needed.

And currently, Room 46 was in need.

Actual processing decisions were always left to the Associate's discretion, though the final choice had to be approved before implementation. Once he'd learned that J. J. Jordon was here, the choice had been a no-brainer. Years ago, in central Alabama, an eighty-year-old woman had died in the bathroom at a nearby McDonald's. Police ultimately determined that a bleed line used to carbonate the drink dispenser had disconnected and flooded the bathroom with carbon dioxide. Levels built to a lethal dose, killing the elderly woman when she entered. Talk about a freak occurrence. How many people died going to the bathroom?

When the convalescent center was remodeled, this particular oxygen feed system had been purchased because of its quick-release valves. Normally there for purging, they also made for an excellent entry point. It had been three years since they'd last been utilized—by him then, too. That Priority had been easily eliminated, and this one, tonight, should be the same. The cylinder he'd brought already had a short span of flex-tubing leading from its valve, the male counterpart to that female attachment on the oxygen line leading to Room 46. The cylinder contained diosogene.

Colorless, but with a slight odor that resembled cut hay or grass. It, along with phosgene, was used as a chemical weapon in World War I, but had fallen out of favor in the time since. The great thing about it was that it didn't take much to kill and it left no residual traces, dissipating quickly.

He snapped on latex gloves, then disconnected the oxygen line for Room 46, connecting the cylinder and opening the valve, flooding the line. But instead of life-giving oxygen, J. J. Jordon was now breathing poison. Being heavily sedated helped, as there should be no convulsions. Unconsciousness would be nearly immediate. No heart or breath monitors were attached to Jordon. Instead, the file stated that he was checked several times an hour by the on-duty staff.

He kept the gas flowing.

Two minutes.

Three.

Five.

That should do it.

He disconnected and reattached the oxygen, which would quickly flush the line clean. He then deposited the cylinder and the gloves into his bag and prepared to leave. Back in the hall he worked his way toward the main entrance, blending in with people coming and going from the rooms.

No one paid him any attention.

Normally, he was required to confirm physically with the Priority that the processing had been successful, but that mandate had been waived for tonight because of the prior mistake. In the morning, he'd check and be sure.

Right now, he had other appointments.

6:20 P.M.

HANK REED WAS GLAD TO HAVE BRENT BACK. HE'D MISSED HIS BUDDY more than he would ever openly admit. Almost twenty-five years of age separated them. Brent was a college graduate and a lawyer—white collar. Hank barely made it out of high school, trained as an electrician, blue collar all his life. But in many ways Brent was the son Hank never had. They understood each other. Always got along. No pretending existed between them. He liked that. Nobody else had ever been that close to him. Ten years ago, when Brent left town, it had hurt.

But that was something he kept to himself.

Thankfully his "son" had returned.

He watched as Brent dissected a medium-rare T-bone, the table's location right smack in the middle of Aunt B's main dining room.

Exactly where he wanted it to be.

"Back one day and already in trouble," he said to Brent. "I didn't realize Clarence still carried a chip for you."

"People get real emotional about lawyers. Especially one who takes your kids away. I'm used to it." Brent pointed. "What happened to your hair?"

His trademark mane had always been coal black, razor-cut, layered to perfection. A bit unusual for a blue-collar guy, but he liked to look good. It was no real secret that dye accounted for much of the tint, but a few years ago he'd finally allowed silver to invade.

"I got tired of foolin' with it. Besides, it's time I start looking my age."

He was sixty-four, but prided himself on looking and acting like a man much younger.

"Damn, Hank. You growing up on me?"

"And it's good to see you too, fella."

Brent smiled.

He'd always called him fella, buddy, or counselor. Only when it was something serious had he ever used his first name.

"You get in today okay?" he asked.

"Left Atlanta this morning and drove in right after lunch."

"The district attorney sad to see you go?"

"I actually think he was. Doesn't feel like ten years have passed since I left here."

"You ready to become a company man?"

Brent shrugged. "I never thought I'd be one."

"Me either. But I think Southern Republic's glad to have you on the payroll."

"I'm surprised, considering what we used to do to them."

"I think that's what did it. They were afraid we'd re-team."

They'd made quite a pair. He the union head, Brent the hotshot local lawyer who knew no fear. Together they'd wreaked havoc with Southern Republic and, along the way, forged a reputation for them both.

"You got here just in time," he said. "Contract negotiations are right around the corner. It's going to be tough."

"More than usual?"

"The paper industry is in the toilet. People are using less and less of the stuff. Everything is goin' paperless. China is killing us with exports and lower prices. Health care and retirement costs are through the roof. It's a struggle, and life's a bitch."

Over Brent's shoulder, past the dinner crowd, he noticed a van wheel into the parking lot, CHANNEL 8 ACTION NEWS, SAVANNAH stenciled to the side beside a colorful NBC logo. Two men emerged and pushed through the restaurant's front door. One shouldered a small video camera, the other carried a spiral notebook. They looked around and Hank motioned for them.

They headed straight toward the table.

Brent noticed his interest and turned. "I should have known when you picked here to eat supper. These guys friends of yours?"

He smiled.

"Not yet. But they're going to be."

7:20 P.M.

BRENT STOOD IN THE BACK OF THE UNION HALL AND WATCHED HANK take to the raised platform at the far end, like an actor entering a stage, perfectly at home in front of a crowd. On the way over from the restaurant Hank had complained bitterly about the imbecile reporter from the Savannah television station. When he'd arranged for the news story last week, Hank assumed the same woman who'd come last time would be dispatched. Older and aggressive, she knew what it took to get her name noticed. But apparently she'd left the station, moving on to bigger markets. Consequently, instead of Lois Lane, the station sent Jimmy Olsen.

Brent knew the game.

Hank was softening the company's underbelly, feeding stories to the press, starting a PR battle to place them on the defensive before the real war over a new collective bargaining agreement began. For a guy who barely made it out of high school Hank had a talent with the press, knowing exactly how to deliver the perfect ten-second sound bite. *Make it short, sweet, and backbreaking.* Tonight's story, gathered from listening to the interview, which happened right in the middle of the restaurant, dealt with the upcoming contract negotiations and the continuing downward plight of the blue-collar worker.

"How about everyone take a seat," someone called out.

Hank was dressed in a short-sleeved checkerboard shirt, starched khaki pants, cordovan leather belt, and penny loafers shined to perfection. The usual garb he'd seen his old friend wear a million times. He was impressed, though, with the union hall, a handsome masonry building that reflected the 1920s-style architecture of Concord's downtown. Years ago, monthly business meetings had been held in the aged community center. But he knew that, a few years back, during the last collective bargaining negotiations with Southern Republic, Hank had negotiated for half an acre of company property and enough financial assistance to erect the building.

Three unions dominated Southern Republic Pulp and Paper's workforce. United Paperworkers International, UPIU Local 567, was the largest. The International Association of Machinists, IAM Local 893, stood next. Hank's International Brotherhood of Electrical Workers had always been the smallest. But by any measure that mattered, IBEW was the most influential of the three.

"I call the June 6 meeting of Local 1341 to order," Hank said.

The room quieted down.

Attendance wasn't mandatory but at least fifty men were there, including Clarence Silva, who threw him an icy stare that seemed to renew the earlier offer of a rumble.

How surreal it was to be back.

When he'd closed his law office, packed his clothes, and driven north to Atlanta, he doubted he'd ever return to Concord, Georgia. That was the whole idea about running away. You never went back. But a lot had happened during the past decade. His father died. His mother had grown lonely, her health deteriorating. And he missed home. Concord was where he'd been born and raised. He knew every nook and cranny. He'd practiced law there for five exciting years. People knew him, and he knew them. Only thirteen thousand populated the county, many living there all their lives. A quiet spot in rural middle Georgia, its sole claims to fame were Eagle Lake and a prosperous paper mill.

"As you're all aware," Hank said, "on July 1, this local's collective bargaining agreement with Southern Republic Pulp and Paper will expire. Its five years are up."

"Remember that," came a shout from the rear of the hall. "No five years this time."

"He's right. That was bullshit," another voiced said. "Five years is too damn long to restrict things."

Thankfully, during his exile Brent had never allowed his subscription to the *Concord Record* to expire, so he knew what had happened. Three years was the usual length of union agreements. But last time Southern Republic had lobbied hard for five and, to get it, conceded to Hank's demands for an extra percentage increase on wages—and financial help with the union hall. But that move turned out to be unpopular. A rare miscalculation of union sentiment on his old friend's part.

"I get it," Hank said, "no five years. But if the company knows we're not, under any circumstances, going to approve another five-year deal, what concessions do you think I'll be able to get? How will I bargain if they know, up front, our no-deal points?"

Brent noticed it was never *we*, or *us*, or *the local*. Always *I*. This was Hank's union. Plain and simple. Some shook their heads in opposition, but others nodded in agreement. Something Hank taught him long ago came to mind. *Logic is your friend. Use it.*

"Look," Hank said. "I'm a few days away from entering contract negotiations. I agree, five years in duration is long, but I have to have some bargaining room to make things happen. Cut me some slack here, and have a little trust. Have I ever let you down?"

Hank was perhaps the most interesting person Brent had ever known. He'd seen him be absolutely ruthless, showing no compassion at all to a perceived enemy. Yet he taught a Sunday school class at the First Baptist Church that was so popular, a waiting list had always existed to get into it. Hank had worked at the mill since he was nineteen. For the past twenty-five years he'd headed Local 1341 and for sixteen of those years he served as mayor of Concord. But when voters decided they'd rather have a full-time city manager than a part-time mayor, he obliged them by not seeking a fifth term. Inside the mill he carried the designation of senior day electrician. As best as Brent could recall, only five people had ever accumulated the requisite thirty years necessary to reach that level, Hank currently at the top of the seniority. Company management respected Hank. He had a talent for stirring up trouble when things didn't go his way. Some might call that terrorism. Hank liked to think of it as *active persuasion*. He was quick to file a grievance, and even faster at supporting what he filed with indisputable evidence. Where the other two union presidents could be bullied or charmed, Hank was susceptible to neither. He was a dealer. Pure and simple.

"You goin' to look out for us this time?" one of the men asked.

He stared across the hall at Hank, who smiled back like a father would to a wayward child. The usual response would be some feelgood platitude said for the benefit of a friendly crowd. A shallow reassurance of the obvious.

But Hank knew his audience.

"Do fat babies fart?"

9:25 P.M.

THE ASSOCIATE NOW WORE JEANS AND A PULLOVER SHIRT. HE'D LEFT the convalescent center around seven, stopping only long enough on the side of the road to change clothes. Light traffic on Highway 56 north from Woods County allowed for a leisurely pace. Darkness had enveloped only thirty minutes ago, daylight lengthening as the first day of summer approached in two weeks.

He slowed the Ford Explorer and crept into Dixie Pond, Georgia, a tiny, unincorporated community ninety miles north of Concord. It wasn't really a town, more a convenience store, gas station, and post office—a smudge in the trees between Savannah and Augusta. He'd come in search of what the locals called Barlow's Trailer Park, named after the elderly woman who owned and operated it. It sat on a wooded site a couple of miles off Highway 56, part of a ten-acre tract—forty-three lots rented by the month, well and septic tank hookups included.

The park's one claim to fame came two years before when a tornado uprooted three trailers. Miraculously, no one was hurt, but the mangled metal and snapped trees made for great video on all the Augusta newscasts. That event, along with all the other relevant information, filled the file lying on the passenger seat.

He veered off the asphalt, the utility vehicle's shocks working hard from powdery lime rock the consistency of a washboard. He threaded down the winding path between two walls of shadowy trees. Occasionally a house or trailer was betrayed by window lights. Deeper, he passed a set of nasty dumpsters, headlights exposing dogs roaming the warm night in search of food and companionship. The approaching row of forty-three mailboxes signaled the entrance to the park.

But he didn't turn in.

Instead, he drove on and stopped in the first pocket off into the woods.

No interior cabin light betrayed his exit. He'd switched off the bulbs earlier before leaving the hospital. He stood next to the open driver's-side door and calmly slipped on a black denim vest, the same one he always wore, zippered pockets full of the special items he'd need.

He rolled his right wrist and checked the time, then sauntered back toward the trailer park's entrance, confining his steps to the grassy shoulder. His eyes oscillated like a cat on the scent of nocturnal prey as he mentally began to supplement what the file contained.

Just a few window lights glowed. Only one trailer burned an outside light. Spidery antennas and satellite dishes jutted skyward, obviously no cable television lines had made it this far out. No natural gas lines either, LP tanks squatted beside most. Few external adornments, like porches or skirts, signaled not much in the way of money or permanency. According to the file many of the park's residents were blue-collar manufacturing workers employed throughout nearby Augusta. Most needed to be at work by seven the next morning. None were noted as night owls.

His destination was Lot 23.

There, except for an occasional one-night stand, Brandon Pabon lived alone. Twenty-eight years old, Pabon supported himself solely from the weekly workers' compensation benefits paid by Southern Republic Pulp and Paper Company. This was the third claim Pabon had pressed against three separate employers over the last ten years. On the first he received a mere $18,000. The second brought him $85,000. Now the latest was being milked for a solid six- or a possible seven-figure settlement. Already, almost $167,000 in medical bills had accumulated from chiropractors, neurologists, physical therapists, and vocational rehabilitative specialists—all from a supposedly devastating injury received when Pabon lifted a bag of cement from a wheelbarrow. The latest escalation, the one that generated tonight's visit, concerned the severe depression Pabon now allegedly experienced.

In pleadings filed with the State Board of Workers' Compensation, excerpts of which he'd read in the file, Pabon's lawyer had passionately argued that the depression proximately resulted from his client's "forced unemployment." Psychiatrists and psychologists supported that assertion, their prognosis calling for prolonged hospitalization—which meant more skyrocketing of the already astronomical medical expenditures. All total bullshit, for sure, designed by a clever workers' comp lawyer to milk the company for a massive settlement.

Thankfully, the file also reported reality.

Surveillance reports documented Pabon's regular barroom dancing. The manual labor he performed every weekend lifting things far heavier than a bag of cement. And the fistfights he seemed to love, mostly over women. The reports also described Pabon's hopeless addiction to heroin. Not so amazingly, none of his doctors had made any mention of the dependency. Certainly Pabon, an experienced injured worker who'd filed workers' compensation claims before, knew enough not to volunteer it. And since the doctors he'd been sent to apparently knew drug abuse was not a "compensable injury" under Georgia's workers' compensation law—which meant no insurance company would automatically pay their bill for services—no danger existed of them ever asking. As far as the doctors were concerned Pabon had a back problem, caused by a "compensable on-the-job injury," one fully covered by the employer's workers' compensation insurance.

Unfortunately for Brandon Pabon, he was another creature of habit. By nine o'clock nearly every night, especially on days after receiving a benefit check, he would be totally high.

Like tonight.

The Associate marched into the trailer park, turned left, and headed toward the rear of the wooded lots. Pabon's single-wide waited dark and quiet. Never losing a step in his determined stride, he found the gloves in a vest pocket. Not the same pair used earlier at the hospital—those were in the car along with the suit he'd worn, ready for incineration when he returned to Atlanta—these were new. He stretched the squeaky latex tight, then slipped a lock pick from another pocket. The file noted that Pabon's trailer door came equipped with only a flimsy cylinder lock and no dead bolt.

He stepped up three concrete blocks doubling as stairs.

He liked to time himself on how long it took to trip a lock. His personal best? Twelve seconds. Twenty-one were needed to open Pabon's front door.

A little slow tonight.

He slipped inside.

A miasma of coffee, alcohol, nicotine, urine, and sour clothes greeted him. Stuff lay scattered including opened cans of pears, chili, and soup. Lots of fast-food containers. Trash. Newspapers. Even greasy auto parts. So much that he found his penlight and used the beam to thread a path back toward the bedroom.

Pabon lay sprawled on the bed, mouth open, breathing heavy. No shirt, socks, or shoes, only a ragged pair of blue jeans, unbuttoned and unzipped, crotch soaked. He surveyed the cramped cubicle. On the Formica table beside the bed lay the remnants of the night's drug trip. None of the heroin remained, only an empty syringe.

Where were the medicine bottles?

He slid open the pocket door to the bathroom.

The tiny sink was a collage of grease, hair, dried toothpaste, and caked soap. The toilet lid stood up, its bowl muddy from a recent use without being flushed. A row of prescription medicine bottles lined the porcelain tank top. He held his breath, approached close, and studied each until finding the partially filled bottle of Valium that Pabon's medical records said he possessed a prescription for. It had been ordered for muscle spasms, but all it really provided was a legal supply of the barbiturates that, along with heroin, Pabon's body desperately craved.

Plastic bottle in hand, he returned to the bedroom. He tossed the pills on the sheets, and from another vest pocket found the hypodermic. It had been gathered a few days ago from a trash can in Atlanta by another associate. What it previously contained was anybody's guess. What it now held was enough heroin to kill. And to ensure Pabon didn't wake before the drugs took effect, he'd thoughtfully laced the depressant with Valium.

31

A couple of squirts. Air gone. Ready.

He set both the penlight and syringe aside, then gently grasped Pabon's arm, prepared to react if the young man suddenly woke. He didn't want to snap the neck—the processing criterion called for a nonviolent death—but if necessary he would. Luckily, Pabon stayed deep into his heroin-induced sleep, apparently enjoying the ride.

He clamped the penlight between his teeth, found a vein, then inserted the needle. Pabon flinched, but the heroin already streaming through him kept his brain subdued. He emptied the barrel then stuffed the spent syringe into the hand, pressing the appropriate fingers hard to leave sufficient residual fingerprints where they would be expected. Next, he laid the syringe on the night table, dropping the one already there into a plastic bag for later disposal.

Even with all the talk about the dangers from needle sharing, junkies routinely used one another's syringes. Any subsequent autopsy would find Pabon's blood full of heroin. The addition of the Valium would be chalked up to pure stupidity. No one would think twice about the overdose. Nothing to pique any investigator's curiosity.

He stood at the foot of the bed and surveyed Brandon Pabon. Long-haired. Scruffy beard. Acne-worn face. A residual scar, most likely from a knife wound, decorated a scrawny chest. His initial estimate hadn't changed. A worthless piece of crap good for only one thing—playing along with some clever workers' compensation lawyer who knew exactly how to manipulate the system. But others understood the system too and knew exactly what needed to be done to eliminate a claim. Pabon's demise would come from a totally non-compensable, non-work-related injury. At death the disability checks would stop, including every fourth that, by law, went to his lawyer.

Pabon's breathing became sporadic.

The chest heaved.

He checked for a pulse.

Faint and waning.

Just a few more minutes and one less claimant would be around to milk the system.

9:30 P.M.

BRENT PARKED AT THE CEMETERY.

St. Mark's Lutheran Church loomed dark beyond a curtain of oaks, the swan atop the whitewashed wood building barely visible in the glint from a half-sickle moon. After the union meeting he'd taken Hank back to the restaurant to get his truck, and they'd said their goodbyes. It had been years since he'd last attended one of Hank's monthly union revivals, and it had been nice to see things hadn't changed.

He climbed out of the Jeep and noticed the sky, flashing with distant lightning, rumbles of thunder in the distance.

A storm was coming. Fitting.

He wandered through the graves, the tombstones providing a vivid testimony to the area's rich history, markers dating back to colonial times. Hard to believe it had been eleven years since Paula drove away.

An hour later his wife was dead.

A one-car accident on the Augusta highway. Her vehicle had slammed into a steel electrical pole, ramming the engine through the passenger compartment, killing her instantly. He'd known the sheriff's deputies and the highway patrolmen who'd worked the scene, and appreciated what they did afterward. In the box marked CAUSE they checked ACCIDENT.

But nothing was further from the truth.

That highway was lined for miles with towering steel, electrical poles, spaced 150 feet apart, twenty yards off the shoulder. The tire tracks from Paula's car bore into the turf in a straight line from the pavement to one of the poles. If she'd fallen asleep, or become distracted, or passed out, the tracks would have been erratic. Instead, their intent was not in doubt. She killed herself. In a horrible, violent way. No note, no warning, no explanation.

Just dead.

If he could relive that last day with her, would he have done anything different? That question had tormented him for a decade. They'd been married for two years and thought they were in love. But he'd been wrong. He'd tried to make things work and had remained faithful. Finally, he decided to take the advice of every relationship counselor on the planet and be honest, telling her it was over. No more. They were through.

"You love her? Don't you?" Paula asked.

It had been the question he most dreaded, but he decided to be honest there too.

"I think I do."

"You sorry bastard."

Those were the last words she ever said to him.

God, how he wished he'd lied.

He found her grave. A few chickweeds had sprouted near the white granite headstone. He stared down at the darkened grass and studied the lettering that summed up her life.

DAUGHTER SISTER WIFE.

A part of him died that day too. No question. His life changed after the funeral. He'd lingered for a while in a daze, then closed his practice in Concord and found a new job 300 miles away in Atlanta. He went from being a small-town street lawyer to a metropolitan prosecutor. He'd been good at his new job. Made a name for himself. Tried to forget his mistakes and do his best.

More thunder rolled through the air.

Now he was back home.

To finally face his demons.

9:50 P.M.

BRENT LEFT THE CEMETERY AND CRUISED THROUGH DOWNTOWN.

Concord had been designed by practical men two hundred years ago with little imagination, its streets laid out in parallel grids that once served as an orderly transition from thick forest to town proper. A blue water tower remained the tallest structure. Brick row buildings with turn-of-the-century façades dominated, most the result of an extensive remodeling that occurred during Hank's tenure at city hall. Persecuted Lutherans, who fled Germany for Georgia in 1734, first settled the area. His father's family, the Walkers, were direct descendants of those Salzburgers. Every kid at Concord Elementary was taught about the two Revolutionary War battles that had raged nearby, the county named for General Robert Woods who led the local militia against the British. During the Civil War, Sherman miraculously spared most of it from burning on his way to Savannah, its tranquil laziness offering his soldiers a rest before their final assault to the sea. First Street was part of the old Quaker road James Oglethorpe himself used to connect his colonial towns. It was once home to a cotton gin and gristmill, and a railroad depot eventually came. Now all three were local museums, the depot's centerpiece a historical marker commemorating George Washington's visit in 1791.

He turned off First Street onto Live Oak Lane.

Another right and two blocks later he was home.

His parents bought the two-story Victorian home thirty years ago, its front façade dominated by a generous covered porch, its side by a detached two-story garage. The neighborhood had been part of Concord for decades, the homes first constructed when the old Republic Board moved people into the area sixty years back. Once a haven for managers and superintendents, the solitude now provided comfort to retirees, or families just starting out with the time and energy to tend to a demanding old house.

He turned in at the brick mailbox marked 328. His hybrid Lincoln was parked in the drive, his mother's Prius nestled behind. He wheeled around both vehicles and deposited the Jeep in the garage, then he walked back toward the front porch and noticed someone standing in the driveway.

A woman.

Dressed casually. Her empty hands at her side.

In the penumbra of light from the street he saw she was about his age, short-haired, her face a mask of no emotion.

Like a ghost.

If he was still in Atlanta he would be much more cautious. But this was Concord. Home. So he approached her. "Can I help you?"

"Are you Brent Walker?"

The voice was low, nearly a whisper, as if someone might be listening.

He considered lying, but decided not to. "I am."

"We don't know each other, nor is it important that we do. But I came to tell you to watch yourself."

He was surprised. "From what?"

"Your job. Be careful. It's not what you think it is."

Now he had questions. Lots of them.

But without another word she turned and walked toward a Tahoe parked across the street at the curb, beneath one of the streetlights. He hustled after her and reached for her arm.

Which he gently grabbed. "Excuse me."

She did not resist or cry out as he turned her around. Instead, her eyes bore into him. "Heed Proverbs 22:3. And may God have mercy on you."

He was stunned.

She wrestled her arm free, climbed into the vehicle, and drove off. He watched the Tahoe turn the corner down the street and vanish.

What in the world?

He stood there a moment and gathered himself, then walked back to the house, the sweet aroma of the nearby white magnolias nearly overpowering. Inside, he found his mother in the kitchen cleaning up. Hard to believe she would be sixty-six on her next birthday. Her silver hair was close-cropped, her eyes a sparkling sapphire. Bean-pole-thin and perpetually happy, she would always be, in his mind, a woman who could never sit still.

He decided to keep what just happened to himself, as he really did not know what to make of it. Instead, he told her about dinner and the union meeting, finishing with, "It's good to see some things never change. Hank is still the same."

"Most people around here fish or hunt as a hobby. Hank plays politics."

"And he's good at it." He sat at the bar. "Rain's coming."

Moths teased the light outside the window over the sink.

"Are you going to miss Atlanta?" his mother asked.

Not really. The Fulton County District Attorney's Office had been an adventure. For sure. Lots of twelve-hour workdays and eighty-hour workweeks prosecuting every kind of crime known to man. He'd started out handling burglaries, but graduated to violent crime and then spent the last few years trying nothing but murders. He hoped he never saw another bloody corpse again.

"I never thought I'd work at the paper mill."

"Neither did your father."

He could still hear the lecture, delivered at least once every few months. His father had been a self-taught machinist who worked all his life for somebody else, punching a time card and collecting a paycheck every other Thursday. Three weeks of vacation a year, sick days accrued, health benefits guaranteed, and a retirement check waiting when he finished.

A good, decent living.

Just one thing, though.

He didn't want his only child following in his footsteps.

"Under the circumstances," his mother said. "I'm sure he'd approve."

But neither of them voiced what they both knew. His mother was sick. She'd noticed it coming on for a while, but had said nothing to him until three months ago. Her mind was slipping. Enough that she'd seen a doctor who confirmed the early onset of Alzheimer's. Medication had been prescribed, which could only delay the inevitable, so his place was back here with her.

His demons be damned.

"I shouldn't complain," he said. "I've got a decent salary, medical insurance, retirement plan, and a title. Assistant corporate counsel to a multi-billion-dollar corporation. Who knows? Maybe even corporate counsel one day."

"What about Hank, he okay with that?"

"I was waiting for him to mention something at dinner. But nothing. I know he's going to expect things, though. Inside information. A heads-up for trouble. In the old days I'd spend an hour or two every day tied down with him plotting and planning something against the company. Contract negotiations are just around the corner, so I'd say he's going to become a problem."

"You don't forget who you work for now."

"I know. I only hope Hank won't either."

Strange, really. Ten years ago he was a young lawyer in a small town hustling a living from courthouse to courthouse. Then he became a criminal prosecutor in a big city. Now he was an assistant general counsel for a paper company. Forty years old and already with three different careers.

Who would have thought?

"Are you going to be okay?" he asked his mother.

"I don't know, son. I truly don't."

"You scared?"

"I'd be a liar if I said I wasn't."

"I'll be here. All the way."

He caught the loving look on her face that expressed her thanks better than words.

"Southern Republic's a good company," she said. "They're lucky to have you."

He stared out the window.

Rain started to fall.

He hoped she was right.

Brent readied himself for bed, still troubled by the visit to the cemetery and the stranger who'd clearly sought him out. The sad, forlorn look in her eyes had jarred him.

And what she said.

Proverbs 22:3.

He was no scripture scholar, though he'd once been a regular and dedicated church member. Not so much since Paula died. He wondered if his childhood Bible was still there, so he opened the drawer of the nightstand.

There it sat.

A gift from his father long ago.

He lifted the book out and opened to the page where his father had written, I PRAY THIS BIBLE WILL BE A BLESSING AND COMFORT TO YOU. DAD.

He gently caressed the page above the ink, as if somehow that would connect him to his father. Hard to believe he was gone.

He then leafed through the thin pages and found the cited passage.

A prudent man sees danger and takes refuge, but the simple keep going and suffer for it.

He'd been around ten when his father had given him the Bible. It was an annotated study edition that contained a multitude of footnotes explaining the various passages. The notes on Proverbs 22:3 pointed out that

God in His mercy has denied man the knowledge of the future. In its place He has given man hope and prudence. By hope man is continually expecting and anticipating good. By prudence we derive and employ the means to secure it. There are many evils, the course of which we can neither stem nor divert. Prudence shows beforehand the means to be used to step out of their way, and hide oneself. The simple, the inexperienced, the headstrong, giddy, and foolish, they rush in without prudence to regulate, chastise, and guide them. Thus they commit many faults, make many miscarriages, and suffer often in consequence.

He considered the words and warnings.

What was the woman trying to say?

And why direct the message at him?

Both were good questions.

10:35 P.M.

HANK NAVIGATED THE DARKENED STREETS OF CONCORD AND HEADED for the paper mill. He had one more errand to run before the night was done.

One he preferred to keep private.

Marlene Rhoden made no secret of her affections for him. She was a year older, a robust woman with curly crimson hair, ample breasts, and an unabashed personality to match them both. She was company management, in charge of Southern Republic Pulp and Paper Company's thirty-two data entry clerks. Which gave her extraordinary access to an enormous amount of information. They'd quietly dated off and on for the past few years. She'd hinted often of her desire to formalize the relationship with a ring and a wedding. He preferred the current arrangement, since his one and only experience with marriage had not ended well.

No more wives for him.

He parked in the paved lot behind one of the administrative buildings. She'd left the rear door wedged open with a folded magazine. He found Marlene in her office. No one else was around. She routinely worked late and alone. What was unusual was his presence.

She released her hold on the keyboard and stretched her long fingers, wiggling out the stiffness.

"No kiss for me?" she asked.

He knew the drill and stepped around the desk, pecking her on the lips.

"That it?" she asked.

"I'm tired, Marlene. Just had a long meeting. I want to go to bed."

"Great idea. Let me finish up here and I'll join you."

"Alone."

She smiled. "Can't blame a girl for tryin'."

No, he couldn't. And try she did. Every chance she got. Which, if the truth be known, he liked.

Who didn't want to be wanted?

"My right leg from knee to ass is dead asleep," she said. "Ergonomic chair, angled keyboard. Right. None of it's worth a damn."

One thing loomed in her fault column—she was a bit of a hypochondriac. What had he read about carpal tunnel syndrome? Supposedly data entry clerks were in the high-risk category. But what the hell. Every job had its problems. He routinely dealt with enough voltage and amps to fry the body to a crisp.

She stood and gathered up a stack of files. A drawer across the room hung open and she squeezed the manila folders back inside. He knew company policy. Hard copies were retained for six months then discarded to make room for new paper, all of which would eventually have to be entered into the computers too. Southern Republic was not the most modernized when it came to record retention. Old school still prevailed.

She popped the joints in her back and worked her legs. Beyond the lime-encrusted windows the night sky loomed dark and threatening. Storms had been creeping in for the past hour. Now the worst had arrived. Rain began to smear the panes. Lightning crisscrossed the sky. The building vibrated from a roll of distant thunder. It had been a dry spring, the usual late-afternoon thunderstorms few and far between. A thorough soaking wouldn't hurt a thing, and his tomatoes could use a good watering.

They engaged in this ritual from time to time. He would come to her house and she would provide a tour through the company files, which she could remotely access. She'd come to learn what interested him most. Sales reports. Workers' comp claims. Litigation. And anything and everything that had to do with the owners. Was it corporate espionage? Probably. But he didn't see it that way. More a familiarization with the enemy. A gathering of intel. Nations did it every day. You could learn a lot if you knew where to look. And together they did. His thirty-six and her twenty-one years at the mill more than enough of an education.

She came close and wanted another kiss.

"Can we do that after?" he asked.

"Nope. You owe me a big one."

He was curious about that debt, but he paid it anyway.

They were both divorced with grown children and grand-children. Never had she stayed over at his house. But he had been known to spend a few nights at hers. She could be a pain in the ass—pushy women came with that liability—but most times she was a jewel. Even more important, she knew the company's computer network like the grocery shelves at the Piggly Wiggly. And there was nothing better, sex included, than good information.

The kiss ended and she handed him a flash drive. "All there. Lots of facts and figures. Some interesting emails. And a memo I think you're going to love."

Tonight's bounty.

He smiled.

"Everything you might need to prepare for the upcoming contract negotiations," she said.

"So what is the debt I owe you?"

"I made some progress...on that other matter."

He caught the conspiratorial look in her eye.

For the past few months, ever since she'd first noticed the anomaly, they'd tried to gain access to a particular section of the company records. But a thick firewall had been intentionally erected, one that could not be breached by her finely honed computer skills. Not knowing something always irked him, particularly when it was being deliberately hidden. So it had become a challenge for them. Now he realized why she'd wanted to meet here tonight.

"I've piddled with it some, off and on," she said. "And I made it past the first security level. You want to see?"

He motioned to the computer. "Give it a whirl, baby."

She grinned at his term of affection as she sat at the terminal. A few keystrokes gained her access into Southern Republic's central banks. A few more and she found the main directory.

More lightning flashed outside.

The building's power momentarily flickered.

"You better hurry up," he said, "before the whole thing goes to backup generators. There are surge protectors that will shut things down."

Which his electricians had installed. The company's main servers sat just down the hall in a room kept at a perpetual fifty-five degrees.

She scrolled through a long list of folders and positioned the cursor over one nondescript entry titled PRIORITY. She pressed the VIEW key and requested an index be displayed. The cursor blinked ONE MOMENT PLEASE then announced in flashing letters, PASSWORD REQUIRED.

"We've never gotten that far before," he said.

"I know. Any ideas what the password could be?"

"I assume you tried all the obvious ones?"

She nodded. "Names, dates, places. Anything I could think of. But that would be too simple. It's surely a long, complicated mix of letters and numbers. Totally unique."

He agreed.

More thunder and lightning came from outside. It sounded like the center of the storm was directly overhead.

She leaned back. "That's a bugger bear. Nothing else in the system has that kind of heavy restriction. Especially from me. I know every password into the central files." She pointed at the screen. "Except that one."

"Maybe they don't trust you?"

She chuckled. "Look at us, Hank. Are we trustworthy?"

He grinned. "Absolutely."

He'd suggested a few months back that she ask the main office for more information, but she was told to leave it be. *For owners only,* had been the explanation. Which made him want into it even more.

"Somebody has to input data into that folder," she said. "God knows the owners aren't doing it themselves. But no one in my department, or anyone at the main office, has ever been inside there."

He glanced at the wall clock.

10:44 P.M.

He should leave before plant security made their rounds at the top of the hour. Last thing he needed was to be seen here, with her, at this hour.

More lightning strobed the room, which caused a momentary break in the power. The overhead fluorescents flickered and the computer screen faded in and out.

Just as he predicted.

Marlene reached to shut off the terminal. "You're right, we need to—"

Suddenly, the screen changed. The password request page had been replaced with a menu labeled PRIORITY.

"We're in," she said, astonishment in her voice.

Forgetting about the storm, they both scanned the index. Not much there. Which made its security even more puzzling. She opened the first file, scrolled through its contents, and printed a copy. Then did the same for the other three. None were long. He retrieved the hard copies from the printer.

"Get out of that file," he said. "Now."

She exited the central banks and switched off her terminal.

"Does that get me another kiss?" she asked.

"Honey, that gets you whatever you want."

11:54 P.M.

THE ASSOCIATE MADE SURE BRANDON PABON DIED, THEN LEFT DIXIE Pond and drove north until finding Interstate 20. There, he started back the 130 miles west toward Atlanta. Halfway he exited, turned south, and entered Reeling, another tiny middle Georgia town.

One last appointment before the night ended.

The Priority, Tim Featherston, took an early retirement from Southern Republic at sixty-two and spent the last six years doing nothing but visiting doctors. Five years ago it was his pancreas. A year after that his heart. Then Featherston became convinced he'd contracted lung cancer, the end result of being a pack-a-day smoker. But test after test revealed nothing. Just recently, stomach cancer had become his latest obsession, and Featherston spent days trying to convince various specialists he needed an operation.

Those doctors, though, were not privy to the fact that Tim Featherston learned an awful lot from the latest edition of the *Concise Encyclopedia of Modern Disease*. So when he showed up at their offices and vividly described symptom after symptom, all consistent with known and identifiable afflictions, it was perfectly understandable why they covered themselves on a possible malpractice claim by performing test after test.

To a medical insurer Featherston was an expensive nightmare. To a medical provider he was a godsend. And no legal way existed to stop his extravagance. In fact, with all the changes in health care laws over the past few years, it had become even easier for Featherston to abuse the system. Even worse, vested retirement benefits and guaranteed health coverage assured Featherston of full coverage, and myriad federal laws protected him from cancellation. A seemingly never-ending cycle of Featherston satisfying his psychosis, and the medical providers their greed.

But all that ended tonight.

Unlike the files on J. J. Jordon and Brandon Pabon, the one on Tim Featherston bulged with extracts from an extensive medical history. So deciding how best to accomplish the appointed task had been difficult. Virtually every part of Featherston's body had been repeatedly examined and thoroughly tested, so a medical death would require imagination. Violence was out of the question. That always attracted attention. But one little tidbit buried deep in the background report had provided enough to spark his imagination.

Thankfully, Featherston lived alone. His wife left him years ago and his children never visited. No girlfriends or female companionship were noted.

All of which greatly aided in the decision-making process.

He followed the directions in the file and parked on a dirt road about a quarter mile beyond Featherston's home. Before climbing out he changed shoes, replacing his boots with tennis shoes so that he left no tracks that could be linked back to Barlow's Trailer Park. He then slipped on the vest, grabbed a canvas bag from the back seat, and slowly backtracked up the dirt road.

Featherston did possess one legitimate medical concern. He was highly allergic to bee stings. The records noted that he'd had two prior incidents of anaphylactic shock, both dealt with immediately with minimal issues. Worldwide, only a tiny portion of people ever experienced full anaphylaxis. Of that, less than 0.3 percent died from it. Epinephrine was the recommended treatment, and Featherston possessed a prescription for a pen, which he refilled each year.

He approached the darkened house and quickly tripped the two locks that secured the back door. The file had indicated that Featherston had no alarm system. *Too expensive.* And no animals. *Too much trouble.*

He stepped inside and carefully eased the door shut. The air was cooler and carried the waft of cooked food. He eased toward Featherston's bedroom, the roar of a window air conditioner masking his approach. The man slept hard, the snoring competing with the window AC. He stepped over, set down the canvas bag he toted, and found the syringe in his pocket.

Pre-loaded. Ready.

Featherston lay on his back, mouth half open. Carefully, he peeled back the comforter and exposed the right leg, sheathed in thin pajamas. He positioned the needle above Featherston's thigh. The injection point could be anywhere since, as noted in the medical files, over the past two days Featherston had been subjected to several injections.

One more would not matter.

He plunged the needle into the skin and injected the concentrated dose of bee venom. Featherston roused from his sleep, eyes wide, but the venom worked its magic in an instant and the body went limp. The symptoms should be immediate. Throat swelling. Shortness of breath. Low blood pressure.

Featherston's chest heaved as his breathing went shallow. The injection was meant to speed the allergic process along and leave the right residuals for any competent medical examiner. The venom itself, while reacting with Featherston's cells, was rapidly metabolizing and being absorbed into the tissue, working its fatal effects, then dissolving away.

A bit more theater was needed, though, for this scenario to become sufficiently innocuous.

He lifted the canvas bag up to the bed. Inside was a clear plastic container. It held four wasps that he'd managed to catch yesterday in preparation for tonight's visit. He unscrewed the lid and held it in place with one hand, while the other righted the container. He brought it down close to Featherston's fleshy bare chest and slipped the lid away, hovering the open top above Featherston's stomach, applying no pressure to leave an outline mark.

The wasps became agitated.

Surely for a variety of reasons, the most important of which was the fact they were contained within a small space and desperately wanted out. Everything around them was a barrier and non-resilient, except the soft flesh.

Which they attacked.

With vigor.

Stinging Featherston repeatedly.

He egged them on by tapping the sides of the container. When they seemed finished stinging he removed the vial and they fluttered away.

The scenario seemed perfect.

A few wasps had made it inside and stung Tim Featherston, who hadn't been able to defend himself. No time had existed to find his

EpiPen. The wasps should still be flying around the trailer by the time the authorities arrived.

He sat on the edge of the bed and waited for verification.

And it came ten minutes later when the man died.

He turned to leave.

It had been a productive trip.

An aggravating mistake corrected. An expensive workers' compensation claim eliminated. And a costly medical abuser stopped.

He'd certainly earned his pay for the night.

DAY TWO
WEDNESDAY, JUNE 7

7:25 A.M.

BRENT WAS IN SHIRTSLEEVES, HIS SUIT JACKET STREWN ACROSS THE Jeep's passenger seat. The lack of air-conditioning under the ragtop made the drive steamy, so he'd slipped the coat off at the first stop sign.

The Jeep had been his father's mill car. Everybody owned one, since the daily dose of caustic precipitants from the smokestacks destroyed a paint finish. To save the trouble of having to wash something of value every day, people either carpooled, walked, rode a bicycle, or bought an old clunker that a few blemishes wouldn't hurt. The Jeep's corroded maroon paint and faded roof still bore the scars from years of daily exposure. It was strange even driving it. But his mother had insisted, saying it was doing nobody any good rusting away in the garage.

Southern Republic Pulp and Paper Company's only mill occupied a picturesque bend on the Savannah River three miles east of Concord, with South Carolina in view on the opposite bank. The tract once supported nothing but stubborn palmetto bushes and crabby sand pines, a haven for deerflies and gnats. Now only helter-skeltered patches of that remained, the rest a sea of concrete and asphalt.

His father used to say paper mills needed four things to survive. Tons of pulpwood, lots of energy, around-the-clock manpower, and clean flowing water. Brent's teenage indoctrination had included several tours of the hot, filthy, calamitous place. He'd always thought it akin to a living entity, one that produced paper by the hour and paychecks once every two weeks.

Three brick buildings the size of football fields stood ten stories tall, one for each paper-making machine. Steel and masonry tanks of varied shapes and sizes dotted the spaces in between. Highways of pipe, wire, and tubing connected it all, everything iced with a coat of white lime, the thickness depending on height and location.

Smokestacks spewed a scalding combination of steam and precipitant. A steady procession of trucks trekked in and out throughout the day hauling tons of cut pine, all methodically sorted and stacked in towering mounds. Off to one side rose a mountain of chipped bark. Farther on sprawled acres of black ponds, places where water borrowed from the Savannah rested until, according to EPA standards, it rid itself of enough impurities that had invaded during the process of converting pulp into paper. Another legion of trucks moved eighteen hours a day to and from the ponds, carting the viscous sludge away for disposal so more water could drain, yielding more sludge.

The company's administrative buildings rose inside the plant gates but outside the heavy production areas. They comprised four shoeboxes, three stories each, built at varying times. The only noticeable difference was that the air-conditioning compressors for the two built in the 1960s were bolted to flat roofs, while the two from the 1980s were cooled by compressors on the ground. Each rectangle was a tasteful combination of brick, stone, and glass, white lime coating the exposed surfaces. Brent had learned that, thanks to a corporate restructuring four years ago, the buildings now housed not only the mill's but Southern Republic's entire accounting, payroll, industrial relations, computer control, human resources, land management, forestry, building products, and engineering departments, along with the chief executive officer, two vice presidents, the comptroller, and the office of general counsel.

He followed the morning procession of cars off the parkway and down the tree-lined main entrance. Ahead, white smoke fumed into the sunny morning, the roar of machinery clear more than half a mile away. He passed the same sign that had been there for years. SOUTHERN REPUBLIC PULP AND PAPER COMPANY—BUILDING CONCORD'S FUTURE—6,345 MAN-HOURS SO FAR THIS YEAR WITHOUT AN ACCIDENT.

He shook his head.

Brent Walker. Company man.

What had he gotten himself into?

7:45 A.M.

HANK HEARD THE FRONT DOOR OPEN.

He sat at the kitchen table finishing off one of his monstrous bowls of cereal. Heap in half a box of cornflakes, nuts, raisins, sliced bananas, whatever berry was in season, and two percent milk, and the result was a meal easy to fix, eat, and clean up.

Ashley paraded into the kitchen.

His daughter was a carbon copy of her mother, and equally impetuous with an alley cat nerve and quick mind. It was the only thing about her he wished were different, as he did not like reminders of Loretta. Eight years ago she'd left him for another man, leaving only a note lying on the same table he sat at now.

I found someone else, so I'm leaving. Divorce me and be done with it. I want nothing but my clothes, which I've taken. I don't want us to fight and I don't want us to be angry, though I suspect you will hate me. Good luck with your life and be happy. If it matters at all, I will be. Finally.

It took a long time for him to deal with that rejection.

And for the most part he had.

But reminders of it were not appreciated.

Marlene had taken him back to her place last night so he could bestow upon her a proper reward, and he'd done good. He'd stayed

51

out a little too late, though. He wasn't twenty-five anymore. He actually needed sleep. But he was in a good mood. Thanks to Marlene, on all counts.

His daughter looked upbeat too. She used her size, not much over a hundred pounds, to disarm people unaccustomed to her brashness. But growing up in Concord as the mayor's daughter had come with advantages that she'd learned to maximize. From the refrigerator she found orange juice and poured herself a glass. Every morning, after dropping Lori Anne at school, she stopped by on the way to work at the post office. He knew, though, today's visit was going to be different.

She sat at the table. "Okay. How is Brent?"

"Other than wanting to whip Clarence Silva's butt, he seemed fine."

"Silva needs his butt whipped. But that's it? Fine? You know I hate that word. You were in politics twenty years. I heard you give a zillion speeches. And all you can muster for me is *fine*?"

"What do you want me to say? Brent is ready to get married and you two ought to be pickin' out the china pattern?"

"You know what I mean."

"He's only been back one day. Give it time, honey. This is not going to be easy. There are a lot of things to consider."

"You don't think I know? Paula has been dead and buried a long time, yet she's still in the way."

"I hope to hell you don't talk like that around other people."

One thing he'd learned from politics was that sugar always worked better than salt, unless salt was all you had to work with—which usually wasn't the case. Ashley seemed oblivious to the difference.

"Who am I going to talk to about this?" she asked. "You're the only one who knows anything."

He looked at her. "You both made a lot of mistakes. They're not going to get fixed in a day. You know, I could talk with Catherine—"

"No. Absolutely not. He never wanted his mother involved then, and I'm sure not now either. Leave her out of this."

He sighed. "You two are some piece of work. Do either of you have any idea what you're doing?"

She finished her juice. "Not really or I wouldn't have screwed things up to start with."

And that she had. Big time.

He knew about Brent's breakup with Paula. And he was one of the few to know it had been suicide. No one blamed anybody. Sure, there'd been talk of something between Brent and Ashley. But when Brent left for Atlanta alone, the talk left with him. People moved on to other gossip.

Now he was back.

He said, "Little one, you have to give this time."

Her eyes were watery. He could tell this was hard.

"I'm trying, Daddy. I really am. But I love him."

8:02 A.M.

CHRISTOPHER BOZIN GAZED UP IN AMAZEMENT. AT THIRTY STORIES, compared with the monstrosities surrounding it, the Southern Republic Tower rose puny into the Atlanta skyline. But what the structure lacked in stature was more than made up for in elegance. The building was a relative newcomer, there less than a dozen years. An unusual hexagon shape, its architecture gradually smoothed until culminating in a point, appearing from the ground like a gigantic sharpened pencil resting on its eraser. The exterior was all glass, tinted in a classy dark-blue hue, and provided both solar insulation from the constant Georgia heat and the building's more common, and simple, name—the Blue Tower.

Southern Republic occupied only the twenty-ninth and thirtieth floors. The remainder was leased commercially. In years past the company dominated more of the tower, but that changed four years ago when most of the corporate departments were moved three hundred miles south to Concord, only the sales force and owners themselves remaining in Atlanta. The salespeople were kept because, along with satellite offices in New York, Chicago, and Los Angeles, Atlanta proved a more convenient access point for the worldwide purchasers of the company's main products—paper, lumber, bags, and building supplies. The owners stayed because none of them wanted to live full-time in the heat and humidity of middle Georgia.

He entered the busy mezzanine and rode the elevator to the twenty-ninth floor. His two-room suite of offices faced northeast and befit his status as a co-founder and one-third owner of Southern Republic Pulp and Paper Company.

"Good morning," he said to his admin assistant. "Beautiful out there today." He kept walking into his private office and Nancy followed. "What do we have on tap this morning?"

"It's not going to be that easy," she said. "How are you feeling?"

He stood at his desk. "You know I don't like you mothering me."

"Any pain?"

"Not yet," he said, before adding, "but thanks for asking."

He knew she cared far more than either of them would ever admit. He'd never married and she was divorced. He'd often thought himself the cause of her marriage ending, though neither one of them ever discussed it. His own bachelorhood at nearly seventy years old was, perhaps, the only overtly odd thing about him, a fact that repeatedly sparked gossip, some even suggesting he was gay. But Nancy knew better.

"Could you try and not let Mr. Lee get you worked up?" she asked.

"That's much easier said than done."

"You want me to make a doctor's appointment?"

He smiled. "Determined, aren't you?"

"Just concerned, Chris."

She was much more informal when other people were not around.

"I appreciate it. But no, I don't need a doctor. I'm truly fine."

"You don't look fine."

He'd hoped she wouldn't notice what he had an hour ago while dressing. A gaunt look had invaded his face, noticeable from the tired eyes and sallow skin. Something more than just old age or stress was happening.

Something bad.

"I'll let you know when I have a problem."

She shook her head. "Like hell you will. So I'll keep asking."

8:40 A.M.

CHRIS FOLLOWED NANCY OFF THE ELEVATOR.

Her low heels pounded the carpet as she headed toward a locked mahogany door. The thirtieth floor accommodated only the company boardroom and a conference center used for large gatherings and occasionally leased out to third parties, the view from its glass walls and observation deck worth the high rent charged.

He watched as Nancy unlocked the boardroom door. The three executive secretaries alternated preparing for the monthly board gathering. Hamilton Lee's handled January, April, July, October. Larry Hughes' February, May, August, and November. Nancy was responsible for March, June, September, and December. Company rules required that one of the owners always witness the preparations.

Five other rules also governed.

First. Switch on the overhead fluorescents. Though the space was less than three hundred square feet and a morning sun enveloped, the ceiling lights were always lit. A Bohemian crystal chandelier, imported from the Czech Republic, dangling from the center, was more for decoration and remained unlit.

Second. Prepare the windows. A wall switch mechanically retracted a set of ivory sheers across the tinted glass. Their opaqueness still allowed the bright morning to filter through but shielded the interior from any curious viewers. For night meetings, another row of retractable lined curtains was available that allowed no light in or out. Both the walls and the glass were soundproof.

Third. Activate the signal jammer that prevented any cell phone reception or remote eavesdropping from outside the room.

Fourth. Prepare the stations. The conference table had been crafted by a north Georgia cabinet shop, carved from Honduran mahogany, its unique shape, like a cog from some intricate machine both circular and individual, with no added prominence given to any one side. The fusion of the boomerangs formed three individual workstations, each equipped with a leather blotter, four drawers, a computer, and a high-backed chair. Nothing identified who used which side. Only within the drawers, which stayed locked, did the personalization of each station become apparent.

Nancy withdrew a chamois from a drawer and swiped the table clean of dust. The shiny surface matched the mahogany façade of the room's polished walls. The floor was covered in a royal-blue carpet the consistency of a Turkish rug, which likewise helped contain sound. She straightened each chair and blotter, then switched on the three computers.

Chris glanced at his watch. 8:59 A.M.

Fifth. At no time, once prepared, was the boardroom left unattended.

So he stepped to the door and waited.

9:01 A.M.

CHRIS WATCHED AS THE BRASS ELEVATOR DOORS PARTED AND THE remaining two-thirds of the corporation stepped onto the thirtieth floor. Larry Hughes and Hamilton Lee each wore a tailored business suit. The only variations in their dark conservative theme were their individual choices of tie, cuff links, and jewelry. Together, the three men owned the entire company and had since the beginning. For organizational purposes the everyday responsibilities had been subdivided years ago. Chris was the moneyman and oversaw accounting, payroll, purchasing, billing, and accounts receivable. Lee's realm was production, managing the paper mill, the sawmills, the bag plant, and the building products and forestry divisions. Hughes got all the rest. Sales, land acquisitions, land management, human resources, and industrial relations. Within their individual areas, each ruled supreme. Only together, as the board of directors, could they establish company-wide policy.

Lee smelled of his usual cologne. Hughes of cloves from the gum he habitually chewed. Chris offered only the expected pleasantries with minimal civility. He despised being confined in a room with them, and knew the feeling was mutual.

Nancy left.

He watched her stroll away. She would return to her office, locking access to the thirtieth floor. The elevator only moved between the two floors, installed solely for company use, and the building's main elevator array had already been barred from access.

The thirtieth floor was now secured.

He closed and locked the boardroom door.

Lee and Hughes headed for their respective side of the conference table. No one spoke. He watched while Lee unlocked the drawers at his workstation and removed a spectrum analyzer. A brief sweep of the room confirmed no electronic listening devices. A check was required by the board itself both prior to and after any meeting. No cell phones were ever allowed.

Lee replaced the monitor in the drawer. "The room's clean."

Chris wedged himself into the high-backed chair and rolled close to the table. The other two men did the same. For this calendar year Lee served as designated chairman. The job rotated annually in a set order and carried no additional aura or duties except to chair the meetings.

"This June meeting of the board of directors is called to order."

Chris slipped a gold watch from his vest pocket and noted the start time on a pad. 9:06 A.M. The task of serving as secretary likewise annually rotated. He would make notes in his own form of shorthand. Later, Nancy would generate a polished version of minutes, to be approved at the next meeting, for the official record.

Lee glanced at Hughes. "Item one. Projected third-quarter production figures. Update us, Larry."

Hughes tapped the keyboard in front of him. Chris watched in silence, remembering last month's meeting where escalating raw material costs at the paper mill had become a major concern.

"The price of chlorine and natural gas continues to rise. At present, we're looking at over $2 million for the quarter in new costs that we can expect to be permanent, though the wholesalers swear chlorine should come back down by December."

Lee shook his head.

"I'm negotiating with the natural gas people," Hughes said. "We're their number one customer in Woods County. I've told them biomass as a fuel is looking better for the long haul."

It took an enormous amount of electricity, oil, coal, and natural gas to keep the Concord mill operating—a constant battle to stock an available and affordable supply of each. Coal had long been their number one energy source. Cheaper by far. Six years ago, at Chris' urging, they'd spent $35 million to add a coal fire boiler to help reduce costs. But coal prices had steadily been increasing and that boiler was looking more and more like a bad investment.

Lee turned toward him. "Chris, are revenues still holding?"

He stopped note taking and tabled his gold pen, a gift from Nancy last Christmas. He turned to his monitor and found the relevant information. A push of a button and he transferred the data to the other two terminals.

"On your screen is the projected flow sheet for the next quarter. What concerns me are timber prices. They're fluctuating wildly and will definitely affect the bottom line."

He'd made no secret of his dissatisfaction with Hamilton Lee's handling of the forestry division. Timber was the main staple in the mill's daily diet. Nearly two thousand cords of wood were laboriously cooked into pulp every twenty-four hours. The equation was simple—no wood, no paper—so a steady, affordable supply of trees had to be assured. Company timber from company land helped. But outside trees were the bulk of it, the open market price changing by the hour. Which meant it needed constant attention. Something Hamilton Lee rarely provided.

"The damn timber owners seem intent on milking every dime

they can," Lee said. "And the bioenergy people are buying up trees as fast as they mature, driving the prices up for manufacturers."

"How about our reserves?" Hughes asked.

He winced at the question. Hughes' answer to everything was to dip deeper into the company cookie jar. Southern Republic owned or controlled, through long-term leases, thousands of acres of pine trees. But that wood was designated *reserve* for a reason, to be used only in emergencies to keep the mill running. The idea being to negotiate and buy other people's trees as cheaply as possible, not indiscriminately harvest timber that cost money to grow.

"For now, I'd rather just pay the open market price," Lee said. "It's cheaper than cutting and replanting our own trees."

Chris smirked. This was the same point that had sparked last month's heated argument. He wondered again how Lee would even know the costs, as most of the memos circulated on that point came back uninitialed.

"None of that sounds good," Hughes said. "Chris, what's the bottom line?"

9:20 A.M.

BRENT TAPPED THE NAILS INTO THE SHEETROCK AND RE-FORMED HIS ego wall. He'd removed all the frames a few days ago from his downtown Atlanta office. The bachelor of arts diploma from nearby Georgia Southern University. Law degree from the University of Georgia. His Georgia State Bar admission. Certificates of acceptance before the Supreme Court of Georgia, Georgia Court of Appeals, and United States District Courts. All had made the journey from Concord to Atlanta and back.

Building B was one of the older of the mill's admin buildings. Its walls were papered with a fading mauve vinyl, the nicotine-stained acoustical ceiling tiles a reminder from the days when smoking had been allowed. The stairs were Georgia granite, the handrails slick brass from all the friction, the hallways sheathed in thin tile glued to hard concrete. His office was lined with a row of dingy aluminum windows, a set of dusty venetian blinds bisecting the morning sun across the newly hung diplomas in alternating rows of light and dark. The overhead fluorescents hummed enough to be annoying. His steel desk was a gunmetal gray with a laminated Formica top, the chair upholstered in a cracked dark-green vinyl. A plain black metal table supported a computer terminal. The floor, like the rest of the general counsel's space, was carpeted with a tight woven pile in a dirty shade of gray. His new boss, Southern Republic's longtime general counsel, told him earlier that first and foremost this was a manufacturing plant. Luxury didn't last long around there.

And the man was right.

"You going to miss prosecuting all those criminals?"

He turned.

Hank stood in the doorway dressed in his standard mill uniform. Short-sleeved shirt, stained khaki pants, lime-bleached work boots. Old clothes, for sure, but degrees better than the tattered overalls and blue jeans most of the other workers sported. His old friend wore the same hard hat he had for years—BOARHOGGER written in black marker above the company logo. It was a label IBEW members had bestowed on him years ago, referring to his unwavering attitude toward management.

"What brings you by?" Brent asked.

Hank shrugged. "The company expects me to appear sooner or later. So, for their benefit, I thought I'd make it sooner."

"I'll never understand how you work all day and never lose the crease in those pants."

"Lots of practice. Now answer my question. You're going to miss it, aren't you?"

"Who wouldn't? It was a great place to work. Lucky for me the Fulton County district attorney wanted to break with the norm and hire someone with no prosecutorial experience. I remember the two days I went for the interview. Going from office to office, meeting the other prosecutors, trying to small-talk my way in." He shook his head. "So unfamiliar. Surreal. Quite a change from my usual daily life as a solo practitioner."

"You must have made a good impression."

"I was so naïve. It's another world up there. Totally different from anything around here."

But he'd succeeded, rising to a supervisory position and over-seeing other prosecutors. The DA had been sorry to see him leave.

"You going to be okay?" Hank asked, concern in his voice.

He looked at his old friend. "I think I am."

"Ashley is anxious to talk to you."

He hesitated, then said, "I'll probably wait until tomorrow. I can only handle so much excitement in one day."

"The question is, will she wait. How about some unsolicited advice from a battle-scarred old friend? Go easy. Be sure."

"Seems that was the mistake I made once-upon-a-time ago."

"Probably so. But you actually have the luxury of time here. Use it wisely."

It was good advice. "I've missed you telling me what to do all the time."

"As if you ever listened."

"You were right about Paula," he said.

"That's one I wish I'd been wrong about."

Hank had told him early on that she seemed unstable. Her grand-mother had committed suicide and her father tried once when she was a little girl. He hadn't listened, thinking she was different. He'd been so wrong. But he knew why Hank had really come, so he got to the point. "You goin' to cut me some slack here?"

"What do you mean?"

"You know. Southern Republic signs my paycheck now. I want to do a good job for them."

"And I want you to do a good job. But what's wrong with help-ing an old friend out a little?"

"Don't you think it'd be kind of dumb for me to funnel you infor-mation? The company's not stupid. They know we were once a team. Hell, it's probably the reason they hired me. To stop us from reteam-ing. Besides, I won't have anything to do with contract negotiations. They'll have me buried up to my ears in workers' comp cases."

Which had been made clear at his interview for the job.

Hank shook his head. "I thought I taught you how to hedge a hell of a lot better than that."

Maybe he had. Hank taught him a lot through the years. Especially about loyalty and friendship. To him the man was a brother, father, and friend—all combined into a vociferous personality that many found offensive. But not him. He'd learned that there was a surprising degree of empathy and affection hidden deep inside that gruff exterior. Nothing overt ever. Just a look. A gesture. Unspoken, but understood. One that said, *I'm there if you need me.*

"You didn't answer my question," Brent said. "Are you going to give me a break?"

Hank turned to leave. "We'll talk again. Soon."

But he did want to know, "How is Ashley?"

"Screwed up," Hank said, as he walked away.

9:40 A.M.

CHRIS STARED ACROSS THE TABLE AND ANSWERED HUGHES' question. "Our financial situation is okay. But not good." He stared hard at Hamilton Lee. "It could be better."

"Meaning what?" Lee asked, taking the bait.

"Meaning if you spent as much time in the office as you do on the golf course, we'd all be a lot better off."

"I resent that."

"I don't give a damn what you resent. This is a business, Hamilton, not a hobby. This industry is contracting inward by the day. Everybody is going paperless. Tariff barriers and protectionist subsidies offered to our foreign competitors have made for a totally uneven playing field. Export duties and taxes on wood exports are increasing annually. None of this is good."

"Aren't we compensating with making packaging and sanitary materials?" Hughes asked.

"To a point," he said. "People ship everything today, and that cardboard we make helps. Paper towels and cleaning supplies are solid too. But they are not enough. We're definitely feeling the pinch."

"I do my job," Lee declared. "But unlike you, I have a life outside this tower."

"Lucky for this company I don't have a life, or we'd already be in Chapter 11 bankruptcy."

"Why don't we turn our attention to the union negotiations," Hughes said, clearly trying to diffuse the tension. "Are we ready?"

He resented the interruption. But it was typical of Hughes, who had no guts for a fight. He was a follower, and of late Hughes had hitched his horse to Lee's wagon more often than not, resulting in lots of two-to-one votes.

"We're ready," Lee said. "Our new assistant general counsel is on the job. Brent Walker started this morning."

"Has Hank Reed been by to see him yet?" Hughes asked.

"He will, before the day's out."

"Industrial relations assures me we have enough leverage with the paperworkers and the machinists to get five-year deals," Hughes said. "Of course, getting the electricians to agree with that will depend on Reed and how agreeable he wants to be."

"Hank will work with us," Chris said. "He always has."

"It could be different this time. Five years was tough to get last go-round. We had to give an extra percent on wages and even help build that union hall. This time Reed will probably want a swimming pool."

"Hamilton, these guys are just trying to scratch out a living. We pay them good for the area, but five years of locked-in wages is a lot to ask. Hank knows how to play the game. We should not underestimate him."

"But that's why Brent Walker is there," Lee said, his tone mocking. "Your idea too, wasn't it?"

"Thank God one of us was thinking."

"Hiring Walker was good business," Hughes said, breaking the moment again. "We all agreed on that. He'll be a valuable asset. But this negotiation is going to be tough."

"I think we should be prepared to make some concessions," Chris said.

Lee bristled. "Like what?"

"An adjustment in the medical deductible. Maybe assurances on guaranteed overtime. Perhaps some additional vacation or sick time. Small, relatively inexpensive things to us, but big to them."

Lee shook his head. "Reed will throw those bones right back in our face."

"Damn right," Hughes said. "He'll want solid wage increases and twist our arms hard to get 'em. I hear he's already talking with the machinists and paperworkers, getting ready for us."

"I've heard that too," Lee said. "But I don't think those discussions will be a problem."

"Why's that?" Hughes asked.

"I tell you what," Lee said. "Why don't we address the collective bargaining negotiations at a special board meeting next week. I'll send a memo on the date and time. Right now, we have to talk about the Priority situation."

Chris laid down his pen. No minutes were kept on this topic. No votes recorded. "Did we not authorize five Priorities out of the eight candidates at the last meeting?"

"We did and they've all been processed. But a problem developed. One of the five survived the first encounter and had to be reprocessed."

He was surprised to hear that.

"Thankfully, the Priority ended up in the Woods County nursing home and was easily handled," Lee said.

"What of the error?" Hughes said.

"I have a meeting on that subject after we adjourn. The issue for us is the other three from the list."

"Why is it necessary to authorize more?" Chris asked.

Lee stared across the conference table. "You just told us times were tough. Every dollar counts."

The tone mocked him, but he knew how Lee liked to jerk his string. Lately, the length of that string had progressively shortened, particularly on the subject of Priorities. He decided not to take the bait and simply said, "There's no need to authorize more."

"But there is. We were going to authorize eight last time, but stopped at five."

Lee turned toward Hughes.

"Raise the list, please?"

10:08 A.M.

CHRIS WATCHED AS HUGHES PUNCHED THE KEYBOARD, INPUTTING an access code known only to the three owners, which changed every few days. Once into the secured directory, Hughes opened the PRIORITY file. Instantly, all three screens displayed a column of eight sets of numbers.

034156901
456913276
343016692
295617833
178932515
236987521
492016755
516332578

"This is the list from May's meeting," Hughes said. "The first five were authorized Priorities, the last three were not."

"Who are the last three?" Lee asked. "We didn't discuss them."

Hughes opened another file and double-clicked the mouse. Background information windowed onto the screens.

"Number 6 is Melvin Bennett. Sixty-four. He took early retirement two years ago. Medical records show good health, except diabetes that's under control. Assuming no serious complications he should live another fourteen years according to the mortality tables. Our projection on total retirement benefits, if Bennett lives the full fourteen years, is right at $590,000. That's not counting any medical bills, and surely there'll be some. Right now, our average retiree incurs about $48,000 in medicals a year. If a Priority is authorized, be aware we'll have a $50,000 death benefit to pay. But the residual savings, excluding medical bills, will be pushing $600,000."

Chris' gaze soldered onto Lee.

"What about Numbers 7 and 8?" Lee asked.

"Number 7 is Paul Zimmerman. Currently on our payroll at the mill in the powerhouse. Good worker. Been with us seventeen years. His file is clean. But he has five children and medical expenditures for those dependents have run nearly $500,000 over the last two years. One child is handicapped, another has a growth problem. The hormone shots are $3,000 a pop—with four a month required. Medical records indicate these will continue for the next two years. Our estimate is over a million in medical expenses for his dependents over the next twenty-four to thirty-six months."

Hughes paused.

Chris took the moment and studied the background information on Number 7, as the man would be referred to from this point forward. The obvious did not have to be voiced. At Zimmerman's death there would no longer be any medical benefits available for his dependents. "I'd suggest simply terminating his employment. Firing would solve the problem and realize the savings we're looking for. He can apply for government-mandated health care then and receive the subsidy. That's what the Affordable Care Act was designed to do."

"True," Hughes said. "But there'd be a union problem and grievance fight. Though I'm sure something adequate could be concocted to support our decision."

He pointed to the death benefit on the screen. "The widow can't live on $50,000 and feed five kids. Severing his employment would be more than sufficient for our needs and still let the man support his family somewhere else."

"Which union?" Lee asked.

"Electrical," Hughes said.

Lee shook his head. "That's Reed. He'll be all over us demanding that job back along with lost wages. Probably even a few days off with pay for the trauma the man went through. I've seen that movie before. No way. Feeding five kids isn't my problem. What about Number 8, Larry?"

"Michael Ottman. Seventy-one. He retired six years ago. Has a bad heart and bone cancer. Cost estimates are between $1 and $1.5 million for the chemotherapy and cancer treatments, then another $200,000-plus in terminal care cost, depending on how long he lingers. The numbers here are obviously fluid, but any way you look at it they're substantial. There's also a death benefit we'll have to pay."

The death benefits were a nuisance. Part of a collective bargaining agreement negotiated in the early 1990s, they required the company to pay money to a worker's heirs based on a formula that took into account length of employment and amount contributed by the employee to the fund. It was a form of life insurance that had proved costly to finance. In the late 1990s, at Chris' insistence, the benefit was removed from all three collective bargaining agreements. Some of the older employees, though, still possessed vested rights to payment.

"The bottom-line savings from all three, after paying death benefits, would be nearly $3 million," Hughes said, "and that's depending on how bad projected medical expenses on Numbers 7 and 8 turn out actually to be."

"Perfect," Lee said with a satisfied smile. "Those savings would be welcomed. We can redirect those moneys elsewhere."

He was disgusted with the whole topic. More and more Lee, aided by Hughes, resorted to the list to make up the dollars lost from either loose management or downturns in the market. The Priority program had never been intended as that sort of redemption.

"Have files been prepared on these three?" Hughes asked.

Lee nodded. "When they were preauthorized in April, background work was done in anticipation of a May Prioritization. They are now ready for immediate processing."

He knew the procedure. No one was Prioritized without first being preapproved and the appropriate background file generated. That way any issues or problems could be dealt with early.

"I move we Prioritize the remaining three from May's list," Lee said.

Hughes gave the motion life with a second.

"I'd offer an amendment to Number 7 of 'firing only,' not full processing," Chris said.

The suggestion was not out of order. Not everyone was fully Prioritized. Occasionally, criteria were set—conditions imposing specific hows and whens on the manner of processing.

"Will you accept the amendment as offered?" Lee asked Hughes.

"No."

"Neither will I. Any more discussion?"

He sat silent. Further argument was pointless.

"We'll vote on the motion as offered by a show of hands. All those in favor? All opposed?"

Motion carried two to one.

10:30 A.M.

BRENT KEPT ORGANIZING HIS OFFICE, FINDING THE THINGS HE NEEDED in a supply closet down the hall. He didn't have an assigned assistant. Instead, he and the general counsel shared the services of three ladies, all supervised by an attentive older woman named Martha Riddle, who'd worked at the mill for nearly a quarter of a century.

"We're so glad to have you here," Martha said to him. "I knew your father. He was a lovely man."

He heard that a lot. "He definitely was."

"We all miss him."

As did he.

"How is your mother doing?"

"I think she's glad to have her son back home."

He and his mother had both decided to keep her medical condition

68

to themselves. Nobody's business. He was curious, though. "Was this my predecessor's office?"

She nodded. "It was. Peter was an excellent lawyer. A really hard worker."

"How long was he here?"

"Five years. We all enjoyed working with him."

He knew the man had died tragically by suicide. But beyond that he lacked for details.

"Was he troubled?" he asked.

"He was...quiet. Sullen. For him to smile or laugh was a rare event. He was a joy to work for, though. But I always thought him bothered by something. I never sensed he'd take his own life."

He understood that observation perfectly. "It's hard to see sometimes."

"Peter was a good lawyer. He worked the files with expert precision."

"It sounds like I have a lot to live up to."

She grinned. "I'm sure you'll do just fine."

"I bet you've seen a lot of people come and go from this office?"

"You could say that. We're like a two-man law firm with only one client. But it's a big client."

She was right about that. He pointed at the stacked file boxes, which had been delivered a few minutes ago. "How many active workers' comp cases do we have?"

"Two hundred and thirty-one," she said with no hesitation.

He nearly smiled. This woman struck him as someone who knew every detail. A lot like his mother, who didn't miss much either.

He mentally counted the boxes. Twenty-two. A lot, for sure, but not much different from his active cases at the DA's office, or when he practiced law. Back then he'd handled pretty much whatever walked through the door. Small fees. Large fees. Sometimes no fee at all. He'd employed two assistants and together they'd run the office. When he closed things down it had been easy to find them new jobs. Their excellent reputations had preceded them. Now here he was, not as a boss, but as a mere employee. One small cog in a really big machine.

"I'll leave you to become better acquainted with all your new clients," she said, pointing at the boxes. "These are the active cases. The retired files going back ten years are downstairs. Anything older is in off-site storage."

Good to know.

"One question," he said. "Where did these boxes come from?"

"After Peter died," she said, "we sent them to an outside firm in Savannah, and they've been temporarily keeping everything current. Now that you're here, we're back in business, so I had them returned. That firm is also available to us, if we need them, for any help on the files. But that has to first be approved by the general counsel."

"Got it."

She left and he decided to get the hard part over with. So he opened the first box and started transferring files to the three metal cabinets that lined one wall of his new office. Thankfully, the boxes were alphabetized and he used the time to note the names on each file. He kept emptying the boxes, filling the metal drawers, closing them with an annoying screech. He was working up a sweat, the building's air-conditioning not all that efficient when it came to ridding heat and humidity.

Two cabinets were full.

He worked on the third, stacking the files on top, transferring them to the drawer one at a time and noticing the wide variety of thick and small. He was not looking forward to reading all that paper. But he would. He'd have to. No other way to be prepared. What had Confucius said? *Without preparation there is sure to be failure.*

Yep.

He filled the second drawer in the third cabinet and slid it shut a bit too hard, causing the stack of remaining files atop to slide back toward the wall. He managed to stop the avalanche, but not before one of the files fell behind the cabinet.

Just great.

He removed the pile from the top and stuffed it into the next drawer. Then he slid the half-empty cabinet out and spotted the file—which had miraculously dropped spine first, keeping its contents intact. He retrieved the folder and noticed something else lying on the floor, propped against the dusty wall.

A small frame.

He lifted it out and saw that it was a family picture. A woman and two small children standing in front of Cinderella's castle at Magic Kingdom. A typical tourist shot that millions of families possessed. His parents had taken him there twice as a kid.

But this one was different.

The woman.

She'd come to his house last night.

10:40 a.m.

HAMILTON LEE WAS NOT IN A GOOD MOOD. "CHRIS'S BECOMING A major pain in our ass."

Bozin had left just after the meeting adjourned. He and Hughes had lingered. The boardroom was one of the few places they could talk freely with assured privacy.

"It used to be amusing to see how far I could push him," he said. "Now it's just tedious. I really think the old bastard's losing his nerve. I think he'd like to retire, but he's afraid to leave things with us."

"Has he suggested anything about retiring?" Hughes asked.

He shook his head. "But I've picked it up from the office gossip. He's had a long-standing thing for his secretary. She wants him to quit and marry her. But he listens to her about as much as he does us."

"Chris hasn't looked all that good lately. Perhaps we should suggest retirement? Money can't be a problem for him. Even so, the severance payment is in the millions."

Hughes was referring to their shareholder's agreement that

specified a multi-million-dollar cash payment in the event any one of them died or retired.

"Maybe you should make that suggestion," Lee said. "He'd tell me to stick it. Something needs to be done, though. We need Priority capability—without all the arguments. I really don't see why Chris has so many reservations. He harbored little hesitation in the past."

"I agree, especially considering what's at stake."

"Exactly. All those employees in Concord have a great life. They get paid well. Have the best health care in the business. When they retire, we give them a solid pension. They are taken care of from cradle to grave. We bust our asses providing that financial security for them. It's not easy."

He could see Hughes agreed.

"One thing I do agree with Chris on," Lee said. "The paper industry is in trouble. China's killing us. The environmentalists are driving us crazy. Times are tough, and we're going to have to be a lot smarter to survive."

"I caught what you mentioned earlier about Hank Reed's contact with the other two union presidents," Hughes said, "and how that wouldn't be a problem this time around. What do you know that I don't?"

He grinned. "I decided to stay a step ahead of our little busybody."

"That can be pretty tough. Reed's got eyes and ears all over the mill."

"I made sure when the bastard goes snooping into our computers, he finds some especially enlightening material."

Hughes chuckled. "What is it?"

"Special memos I wrote just for him. He's going to love them."

"Has he got them yet?"

He rolled his arm and glanced at the white-gold dial of a Boucheron timepiece. Twenty thousand dollars. A gift to himself.

"I'll know that in about ten minutes."

11:00 A.M.

JON DE FLORIO WOUND HIS WAY THROUGH THE REVOLVING DOORS into the Blue Tower. He wore a single-breasted Brooks Brothers suit tailored to a perfect fit. His shirt was handcrafted, encasing his thick neck and long arms far better than any store-bought variety ever could. He chose his dress clothes carefully to not only project the right image but also camouflage his muscular legs and sinewy arms. He was only forty-three, but his hair had already grayed. A fact that didn't bother him in the least. His face stayed clean-shaven, his hair cut short, his green eyes constantly studying everything around him.

He'd worked for Southern Republic Pulp and Paper Company twelve years. In the beginning he was anonymous, but now he carried the title chief of security. Officially, he supervised the ninety-two guards the corporation employed across the paper mill, bag plant, sawmills, wood yards, railroad, and warehouses. Unofficially, he managed the company's Priority program. His corporate biography that appeared in every annual report had been precisely drafted.

BACHELOR OF ARTS FROM SOUTHERN VIRGINIA INSTITUTE. OWNED AND OPERATED DE FLORIO INVESTIGATIVE AGENCY FOR 7 YEARS. HAVING STARTED WITH THE COMPANY AS A CONSULTANT, JON BRINGS A UNIQUE BRAND OF EXPERIENCE, APPLYING THAT EXPERTISE TO ENSURE OUR PEOPLE AND PRODUCTS REMAIN SAFE.

But almost none of it was true.

He held no degree. Southern Virginia had been chosen simply because the state abolished the college years ago and no enrollment records still existed, the diploma that hung prominently on his office wall a forgery. He'd never owned or operated a detective agency either. But the biography purposely did not specify where that agency had existed. He did, though, start with the company a dozen years ago and in a loose way worked as a "consultant" since he'd interned for two years as an associate under his predecessor, who'd run the Priority program from its inception. When that man decided he'd made enough money and wanted to take some time and enjoy it, De Florio was promoted as his replacement. Eventually, he was given an official title and office simply as a way to explain his presence since the board came to find it more convenient to have him nearby and instantly available.

Southern Republic owned facilities all across the southeastern United States, though its two largest revenue producers, a thousand-acre paper mill and a two-hundred-thousand-square-foot paper bag manufacturing plant, were in Concord. Annual revenues were in the $2 billion range, the threat from lawsuits, theft, and fraud constant. So much so that, in years past, the company perennially contracted with an outside security firm for protection. Eight years ago the service was internalized and placed under his direct supervision, publicly for cost-saving reasons, privately to accommodate the growing expansion of the Priority program.

He'd timed the start of his workday to coincide with the completion of the June board meeting. He knew the three owners had gathered, but the Rule was clear—anytime Priority orders were completed an immediate report of the outcome must be made to the chairman.

He rode the elevator to the twenty-ninth floor and confidently strolled off. Marble floors, paneled walls, and an arched coffered ceiling surrounded him. He crossed toward the management corner where suites accommodated the three owners. Chris Bozin was strolling out into the hall as he approached.

"Good morning, sir," he said, as they passed.

Bozin acknowledged the greeting with a nod.

The man was not a chitchatter. Generally, only business had ever passed between them. Bozin was a somber, paternal soul with a genteel face centered by a sharp, Roman nose. Tall, upright, distinguished in appearance and bearing, with thick glasses magnifying his scrutinizing gray eyes. The wavy silver hair remained thick and accounted for the nickname trade journals and the press sometimes used when referring to him. The Silver Fox. A play on words that also referenced Bozin's sly knack for business. He was by far the superior of the three owners in brains and guts, responsible for a majority of the company's success.

De Florio kept walking and turned a corner, arriving at Hamilton Lee's suite just as Lee and Hughes stepped off the private elevator from the thirtieth floor. He and Hughes exchanged pleasantries before Hughes excused himself.

Lee then led him into the office and closed the door.

The prodigious space commanded a panoramic view of downtown Atlanta. He knew all about the décor. The desk was a French antique shipped over from the Languedoc. The sofa and chairs nineteenth-century English. The small conference table an art nouveau dining room set converted to business use. Lee liked to take credit for the look, but he knew it had all been professionally coordinated by a north Atlanta interior designer. Truth be told, he never really cared for its obviousness and, while visiting, felt more like he was in a museum than in a working office.

"Have a seat, Jon. Some coffee?" Lee asked, parading over to the wall bar.

He declined.

Lee filled a china cup, then stepped to his desk that angled catty-cornered before two outer glass walls. He was already comfortable in one of the open-armed, Georgian chairs in front.

Lee sat. "All right. Proceed."

"All five Priorities from May's list have been processed. Number 1—heart failure. Number 2—kidney failure. Both deaths verified by associates at the scene. As you're aware, a problem occurred with Number 3 but that was corrected last evening. On-site verification was impossible. But I checked this morning. The convalescent center's computer acknowledged death during the night, time undetermined. Though I have no independent confirmation on Numbers 4 and 5, death was confirmed by my associate's personal observations."

"The causes being?"

"Number 4 was a drug overdose. Number 5 anaphylactic shock caused by a bee sting. All five processings were consistent with the criteria placed on each."

Lee sipped his coffee. "Any more problems?"

"Everything went smoothly, without incident."

"I'm always amazed at your creativity. How interesting it must be to innocuously orchestrate so many varied results."

"That's what I'm paid to do."

"Why did the problem occur with Number 3?"

"The criteria specifically called for a medication switch—"

"There was a good reason for that."

He realized that the availability of life and car insurance benefits sometimes figured into the board's decision making. Double indemnity for an accidental death was occasionally used as a means to financially aid a Priority's dependents. But the gesture was not entirely altruistic. Rule required processing methods be varied, and medication errors were an explainable variation that led nowhere back to the company. Instead, third parties would be implicated in any possible liability.

"How did the mistake in processing happen?" Lee asked.

"The associate managed to change out the prescription, but his choice for the change was not powerful enough to induce death in this individual. That was an unacceptable miscalculation on his part."

"And what of the mistake?" Lee asked.

"Corrective action will be taken."

"As I knew it would," Lee said, adding a tip of his cup.

He didn't acknowledge the compliment. Flattery meant little to him.

"The board has just Prioritized the remaining three from May's list. No criteria were placed. They've already been prechecked, correct?"

He nodded. "Their files are prepared and ready."

"Process at will."

"As I recall, last month I voiced an objection to the timing of these."

"That was last month, this is now."

"But the processing of the five from May's list has only just been completed."

"Caused by the mistake incurred with Number 3, in not getting it right the first time."

He felt the slap, but said nothing.

Lee seemed to sense his hesitancy and turned conciliatory. "I have no doubt, Jon, you'll handle things efficiently, as you have so many times before. The board has the utmost confidence in you. Now, on another subject, has the bait been taken?"

He nodded. "Last night. The file was accessed from Marlene Rhoden's terminal in industrial relations. The back monitor we installed showed a copy was made too."

Lee shook his head. "Marlene is making some poor choices. She's worked for us a long time. Just shows how shallow people's loyalty can run these days."

De Florio knew that Rhoden was divorced, was the mother of two grown children, and wanted to be the next Mrs. Hank Reed. She made no secret of that fact among her co-workers. And she'd apparently decided that offering Reed unlimited access into company files might accomplish that goal.

Which they had used to their advantage.

"At least Reed is both predictable and determined," Lee said. "He prides himself on staying a step ahead of us. He thinks we're too stupid to know what he does."

"Why do you tolerate him?"

"Because he can also be quite helpful. He's an effective inside weapon that's kept our labor relations amicable. And he works cheap. All he asks is a little help with his image and a favor or two now and then for his people, which we're happy to provide. And the employees listen to him. But this time the deck's stacked." Lee shook his head. "Reed will come to us, like he always does, wanting to make a deal. But this time he'll be trying to bargain with information that *we* provided. Rather clever on my part, if I do say so."

He was tired of the self-promoting, which was another glaring difference between Hamilton Lee and Chris Bozin. "Is there anything else you need from my department?"

"No, that'll be all except for the immediate processing of the remaining three from May's list...without mistakes."

2:00 P.M.

BRENT TOOK A LATE LUNCH IN TOWN ALONE, STILL BOTHERED BY his discovery. He'd shown the photograph to Martha and she'd explained that it was of Joan Bates, the wife of his predecessor, Peter Bates, and their two children. It had been taken a few years ago, both kids now teenagers. When they'd cleaned out the office somehow the frame had been overlooked. But no one had moved the file cabinets. Okay, he now knew who'd taken the time to find him to deliver a rather cryptic warning. The mystery of the day, though, was why. But he hadn't shared anything with Martha or questioned her further so as not to draw any attention.

Yet the whole thing was odd.

He decided that now was as good a time as any to stop by a local bank and open an account. He needed to transfer his money from Atlanta back to Concord. There were three to choose from, but prior to leaving ten years ago he'd done all his business at Capital Fidelity & Trust. So he stopped there and opened checking and savings accounts, moving all his funds into them. He didn't have much. Nearly $70,000 in savings and another $5,000 in checking. Three CDs he'd taken out a few years ago had yet to mature, so he left those alone. He'd deal with them as they came due. He carried no debt, his car was paid for, and he satisfied his one credit card in full every month. Living with his mother reduced his overhead, but he'd already worked out with her the contribution he would make to the monthly expenses. She was debt-free too, living off both her own and his father's Social Security benefits and the monthly retirement check that still came from Southern Republic's pension fund. His father had worked his entire adult life at the mill and managed to garner the maximum in yearly benefits, which included health care for his mother until she died.

He left the bank and headed back to the Jeep, parked down the street.

"Brent Walker, as I live and breathe," a voice said.

He turned to see an old adversary. Doris Dunn. Curvy. Leggy. Attractive. And knew it. She capitalized on that with billboards and print ads that included a full-color headshot with her long blond hair, beside it the words PRETTY. TOUGH. He'd seen them over the years on his visits back home and always thought the periods after each word should not be there. To him, the whole thing sent the wrong message. Or, knowing Doris, perhaps it had been the one intended all along. Years ago they went toe-to-toe in court, mainly in divorces. She'd been the first female lawyer in town. But now a couple more had set up shop. They exchanged pleasantries and talked a few minutes about old times. Finally, he told her he should get back to work since, "I'm not the boss anymore."

"You also don't have to hustle fees every month, anymore."

He grinned. "Which I don't miss."

She turned to leave.

But he decided, what the heck. "Doris."

She stopped and turned back.

He stepped closer. "Did you know Peter Bates?"

"Not all that well. I don't do workers' comp cases. But he always came to the monthly bar association lunch."

"Does it still meet?"

She nodded. "Second Tuesday of every month. You should rejoin."

He'd probably do that. He'd actually once liked the gatherings. All the lawyers coming together to talk shop and visit. At his interview, the folks at Southern Republic had made it clear that they wanted him involved locally.

"Do you know the circumstances of Peter's death?"

"It was awful. He drove out to Eagle Lake, took a shotgun, and ended it. They found him a day later, after his wife reported him missing."

But what he really wanted to know was, "Any indication why he did it?"

"No one knows. But he was a quiet man. Always friendly and no one had a bad word to say about him. But he wasn't the life of the party, if you know what I mean."

He did. "What about his family?"

"From what I heard, the widow moved away from here after it happened."

If he asked *to where* the signal would be that he was far more interested than he was letting on, so he stayed coy and said, "That makes sense. Probably wanted to get as far away as she could."

"I know I would."

As would he, since that had been exactly what he'd done. "Thanks for the info, Doris. I'll see you in the trenches."

4:48 P.M.

JON SHIFTED THE TRANSMISSION OUT OF OVERDRIVE AND PUMPED the gas. The SUV popped into gear and handled the tight curve, steadily climbing the steep road. He looked ahead at the A-frame perched indiscreetly on the side of a craggy incline. Redwood and cedar sanded smooth, stained dark, the oblong walls indistinguishable from the surrounding dense pines. There were neighbors, but none close, with each lot spanning at least two acres and carrying a high price tag for both the privacy and the view.

The elevations north of Atlanta were not really mountains, more part of the Appalachian foothills. Many were inaccessible, but the A-frame sat on the side of one of the more populated inclines, the road leading up curbed, paved, and well lit, winding its way through an enveloping canopy of maple and sycamore, passing driveways that led both up and down to expensive homes.

Title to the house officially lay in a nondescript corporation created first in Alabama, then purchased by a Texas company that was wholly owned by a Tennessee corporation, itself owned, through surrogates, by Southern Republic Pulp and Paper Company. The trail was intentionally complicated and difficult to follow, particularly if full access to all relevant documentation was not available, which it wasn't. The house was not used officially by any of the corporate entities in its chain of title. Occasionally, it provided a place of privacy for Hamilton Lee and Larry Hughes and their mistresses. But mainly the Priority program used it—though not regularly or predictably, no place had that distinction—as one of several locations where De Florio could discuss face-to-face with his associates their specialized business.

He rolled up to the paved drive and stopped.

In his briefcase he found the remote control. The iron gate swept back on command. Like all the company's secured locations the A-frame was fenced, alarmed, and routinely patrolled by a private home security firm. He wound his way down the drive toward the house and parked in front, but intentionally left the gate open.

Guests were expected.

And even before he climbed out of the vehicle, a ruby Chevy Blazer motored through the gate and parked beside him.

He grabbed his briefcase and locked the car, then pressed the controller closing the gate. Using his key, he opened the front door and walked inside.

Three men from the other car silently followed.

All wore dark suits, nothing flashy or trendy, just traditional blue, charcoal, and gray, white shirts, matching ties, and black leather shoes. He rigidly applied a dress code to all associates and also conducted meetings in a precise manner. Two of the other men fully understood. The remaining man was attending his first gathering.

The two who understood were Milo Richey and Frank Barnard. He'd personally recruited both after a recommendation from several long-standing criminal contacts. Richey was twenty-nine, Barnard thirty. Nothing about either stereotyped them with their profession.

No scars or readily identifiable marks. No beards, mustaches, or fancy hairstyles. No flashy jewelry, earrings, or gold chains. A watch was required, but it need only be accurate, not expensive. Just plain faces, on plain heads, attached to plain bodies with personalities to match. All difficult for any witness to later recall.

Both Barnard and Richey were professionals, thoroughly schooled in the techniques of murder for profit. Richey had worked as a payroll killer for a south Florida drug cartel, Barnard a freelancer used by a variety of West Coast organizations. Both came highly recommended, his offer of steady employment and good pay a powerful inducement.

The new man was Victor Jacks. Earlier, he'd specifically instructed Barnard to bring Jacks along. He was recruited three weeks ago, the Priority program expanding to the point that, simply to keep up, additional help was needed. Jacks was older than the other two but possessed a similar plain appearance and nothing personality. He was also experienced, previously working for a Chicago organized crime family. But just as with Milo Richey and Frank Barnard, the lure of regular work and steady pay finally enticed him to make a trip to middle Georgia.

Rule required that all associates be single with no dependents. Less complication and less chance of a breach in security. It also made them instantly available without the need for explanation. Girlfriends were tolerated. Anything steady or serious discouraged. One-night stands were much more common and preferred.

Though he maintained a public presence within Southern Republic, no one, including the board, knew anything of his associates' identities. It was better that way. He exclusively hired and fired them, solely responsible for their actions, both good and bad.

"Gentlemen, have a seat. If you'd like anything to drink, the bar is over there."

He gestured across the great room.

Overhead, the ceiling pitched to a point, a second-floor loft bedroom overlooking downstairs. The south wall was all plate glass that opened onto a cedar deck. Beyond the railing loomed the hazy skyline of Atlanta twenty miles to the south, illuminated from the west by the evening sun.

He switched on a couple of lamps.

No one accepted his offer of a drink. Instead, the three men situated themselves on the sofa and chairs. He slipped off his coat and loosened his tie. He carried no weapon. Guns were forbidden. Another Rule imposed on both himself and his associates. Rarely were they used in processing, the presence of one only drawing unnecessary attention. He settled into one of the cushioned chairs, extracted the manila folders from his briefcase, and tossed them on the coffee table. "We have three new Priorities. I'll allocate those in a minute. Did all of you get acquainted on the way up?"

They nodded.

"Victor will be joining us as a new associate. I've already oriented him generally on our operating procedures, but I wanted to add some further instruction by revisiting the mistake made earlier this month."

He stared at Richey.

"Milo, please review the facts surrounding what happened with Priority Number 3 from May's list."

5:05 P.M.

BRENT'S FIRST DAY ON THE JOB WAS DRAWING TO AN END.

Both at the DA's office and as a private practitioner, rarely had the day ended at five. Long hours were not only necessary, but also expected. The same seemed to be true here. There were a lot of people and departments for only two lawyers to service. But as Martha had noted, the company also contracted with several outside firms, who assisted on the more time-consuming endeavors. The coming contract negotiations would definitely require longer days.

Today had been all about organizing. Not much else. Martha and the others had already left for the day, the secretarial space down the hall quiet. The general counsel himself had been gone since midafternoon for an off-site meeting. So he was alone.

Time to be nosy.

Earlier, Martha had showed him around the company's virtual world. The general counsel's office had full access to all personnel, medical, and retirement records, information needed in order to do the job. So he found the main search engine and typed in PETER BATES. The screen lit with Bates' employment application, performance reviews, and various medical claims, then ended with a termination of employment and pension account. He decided to check the medical claims and learned that Bates had incurred some substantial psychiatric bills. He scanned a few of the reports and saw a consistent diagnosis of clinical depression, compounded by bipolar disorder. Bates had been prescribed, and was taking up to the time of his death, a strong regimen of antidepressants. Which certainly explained the sullenness.

He clicked on PENSION.

The record that appeared noted the date of death. Nearly four months ago. Cause? Gunshot wound, suicide. A notation indicated that the company had specially extended health insurance coverage to the dependents, a wife and two children, for a period of two years, at no cost.

Extremely generous.

What he wanted was the contact information and he found it on the fourth page. A change of address form. Joan Bates now lived in Statesboro.

Not far away.

Good.

They needed to talk.

5:10 P.M.

JON WAITED FOR AN EXPLANATION.

Milo Richey was openly uneasy. He should be. The associate had made a mistake, his first since joining the team two years ago.

"The file specified a substitution of medication as the sole criterion for death. I made the switch, upping the milligram dosage to a level that should have proven fatal."

"But it didn't," De Florio said.

"I thought it more than adequate," Richey said.

"And your source for making that determination?"

"I obtained the information on non-recommended doses from the pharmaceutical company's website."

"Why not verify death at the scene?"

"I assumed the dosage was more than sufficient to achieve the desired result."

"Was anyone around? Any risk of detection?"

Richey shook his head. "The Priority was alone for the night. His wife was out. I broke in and made the switch earlier. He takes his meds at 7:00 P.M. every day. He should have been dead by 9:00."

"Then why not take the time and be sure?"

"It was an error on my part."

"That it was. For Victor's benefit, being new here, I'll finish the report. Last night I had Frank revisit Priority Number 3 from May's list. Death was induced by toxic gas poisoning, which accomplished the processing."

He rose and stepped across to the bar.

"Milo, I thought you understood the Rules under which we operate."

"I do," Richey said. "It's my first mistake in two years."

He poured himself a glass of mineral water, adding a couple of ice cubes from the refrigerator beneath. "Frank, for Victor's benefit, please explain the *proper* procedure."

Barnard turned to Jacks. "The file establishes the criterion for processing. If no criteria are established, then death is at our discretion. Of course, it has to be undetectable and raise no suspicions. That's why we pre-work a Priority to learn lifestyle and habits. A lot of the information we need can be found in company records, or in the records of companies under Southern Republic's control. We have access to a wide variety of bank, medical, and insurance records. Most times, it's the pre-work that will reveal the most appropriate method to be used for processing. Usually, it's a chemical inducement. We have plenty of agents that cause instant death and leave no residue. Most generate biological failures. A derivative of acetomorphine is our most common compound. It induces heart failure with no residue. Berylanhydride does the same to kidneys. Chlorohydrate to the lungs. And all of those metabolize away as they work.

"Accidental deaths are risky. But they're used when necessary to be consistent with the processing criterion. Mr. De Florio encourages variations. We don't want to draw attention by establishing a pattern. To ensure diversification, all processing decisions, including the actual means of death, have to be cleared prior to implementation. Once processed, death must be verified and then promptly reported."

"Please repeat the last part," he said.

"Death must be verified, then reported."

"And why is that?" he asked.

"Because the risk of detection is increased beyond acceptable limits if more than one attempt at processing is needed."

He drained the mineral water in one swallow, banging the glass on the marble bar top. "Like here. The risk of detection at last night's second encounter was great. Frank had to get in and out of the convalescent center without being noticed. Thankfully, the Priority was housed in a facility that we control." He paused. "At the first encounter we have the advantage of planning, surprise, and expertise. A second encounter, even though nothing may suggest foul play, narrows our area of operation and confines the field. It takes away options. In short, we lose the advantage."

No one said anything.

"And there's another point. In the case we're discussing now, the Priority survived the first encounter and had to be treated medically, which adds to our cost since now those additional medical expenses will have to be paid by the company because of our mistake. That's unacceptable. This is a cost-savings program, not cost-generating. The bottom line is clear. We have to get it right the first time, period."

"I understand, Mr. De Florio," Richey said. "I assure you I won't make that mistake again."

De Florio reached down beneath the counter and gripped the pistol. He brought up, aimed, and fired. The bullet passed right by Victor Jacks, who seemed momentarily startled. A rivulet of blood instantly streamed from a hole in the left side of Milo Richey's head. The bullet exited out the right, splattering blood onto the sofa. Richey's head cocked to one side, the body settling into the cushion, eyes frozen wide in death.

"No, you won't make that mistake again," he said, lowering the sound-suppressed pistol and returning it under the bar.

No one moved. He assumed Frank Barnard had expected it and Jacks, as the rookie, was surely professional enough to understand.

He motioned to the coffee table.

"The top two files are yours, Frank, and the bottom is for Victor. It will be your debut. They're self-explanatory. Please act immediately. And I don't want to have this discussion again."

DAY THREE
THURSDAY, JUNE 8

8:05 A.M.

ASHLEY REED CLIMBED INTO THE MAIL VAN AND DROVE OUT OF THE parking lot, heading for her daily route. She'd been a letter carrier for fifteen years, starting back when she was called a mailman, to her indignation. The job paid great and came with the advantage of getting her home before four o'clock so she could be there when Lori Anne climbed down off the school bus. The benefits helped too. Medical insurance relieved the worry of doctor bills, and the retirement plan was first-rate. The only thing about the job she didn't particularly care for was the uniform. A dull blue and tight fitting, but at least it forced her to keep to a diet, along with regular exercise. Overall, her life was good. No appreciable debt. Excellent job. A wonderful daughter. Lots of friends. A perfect life.

Except for Brent Walker.

He'd first been a problem in high school, becoming more of one years later, the memories of him constantly interfering with her three marriages.

If she hadn't changed her name after each divorce, she would now be Kristen Ashley Reed Mathis Simmons Evans. But thanks to an express provision in the third divorce decree, she again became simply Ashley Reed. Never had she used Kristen. Too formal. She preferred her middle name. Lori Anne carried a different last name. Manley Simmons, Husband Number 2, was a good man from a local family, but the marriage failed after only three years. He paid a modest amount of child support, all his idea since she'd asked for none, and he stayed perpetually behind—but she never pressed the point legally. Husband Number 3 hadn't fared much better, only two years from courthouse ceremony to divorce. Another good man from a good family. And her first marriage, to Kyle Mathis, was so short and unmemorable that she still generally regarded herself as having only been married twice.

Even though each marriage was unproductive emotionally, the second had produced Lori Anne and the third a three-bedroom split-level house she occupied and Chevy pickup she still drove, the debts on both in her name only. She remained friends with all three ex-husbands. No need to part enemies, as the relationships never stood a chance.

She loved Brent Walker.

And realized now she always would.

He'd changed little since they were teenagers. A pleasant face centered by an engaging smile that always made her feel better. She went to great lengths, though, to avoid his hazel eyes, their stare able to penetrate straight to her heart. His eyebrows, like his hair, were a chestnut brown, but the brows flared at the end, making him appear perpetually curious. He stayed muscular, and she could still see him scooping up ground balls at the Woods County High School baseball games.

They'd barely stayed in touch while he was in Atlanta. A handful of calls, a letter or two, an occasional face-to-face when he was in town. Neither one of them was much on social media. Two months ago he'd called and told her about his decision to return home. Trying not to repeat mistakes from the past, she hadn't encouraged him one way or the other. But she was thrilled he was finally coming back. They'd come close to being together several times, the last attempt happening eleven years ago, but his guilt and her immaturity nixed both that and every other opportunity. The past few years had been the toughest of her life. At least before he'd been nearby. But for so long now he'd been nearly nonexistent.

Live Oak Lane was not on her usual route, but yesterday she'd detoured and driven past. Just seeing his car parked out front in the Walker driveway was comforting. She'd almost stopped but decided against it. What was the rush? They had all the time in the world.

Or did they?

Patience had been one of her former mistakes, as had an indifference that came with consequences only the years since had taught her to appreciate. She did not intend on repeating either error. So she started toward the first house on her route and resolutely decided that if she hadn't heard anything by 5:00 P.M. she'd find Brent before nightfall.

8:18 A.M.

HANK PARKED IN THE DRIVEWAY AT 328 LIVE OAK LANE, CLIMBED out of his pickup, and studied the Walker homeplace. Forty years the rambling Victorian two-story had sat among tall pines and moss-draped oaks. The clapboards were an unadorned gray topped by a gabled tin roof. On one side rose a brick chimney veined thick with orange-flowered trumpet vines. All across the front alternating round and square bundles of sculpted shrubs backdropped beds of blossoming begonias, impatiens, and hydrangeas. The front yard was a dense carpet of Bermuda grass. The whole place looked like something out of *Better Homes & Gardens*.

Catherine Walker was busy working the front flower beds. She wore a pair of faded jeans and a button-down cotton shirt. A floppy straw hat protected her pixie-cut silver hair and pale facial skin from the June sun. Cloth gloves covered both hands.

"You're looking lovely," he said, walking over. "As always."

She stopped weeding and slapped the dirt from her gloves. "Still the charmer, Hank."

"Your impatiens are beautiful."

"I was afraid the lack of rain might keep them from budding."

"It has been dry lately."

"That storm Tuesday night helped. But I'm sure you didn't come by on a workday to admire my flowers and talk about the weather."

"I don't know. Seems like a good reason for a visit to me."

Catherine grinned. "Aren't you supposed to be at the mill?"

"One of the perks of being a union president is the ability to leave when I need to."

"Where are you supposed to be?"

"Not here."

"This must be important."

He sighed. "I'm afraid it is."

He followed her up the front stairs to a pair of white rockers. She offered him something to drink but he declined.

"I've thought about this for a while," he said, "and I finally came to the conclusion you and I need to talk. Parent-to-parent. I'm violating a confidence doing this, but I think it has to be done."

A crease laced her brow. "What's this about, Hank?"

"Ashley and Brent. They're in love."

He watched her reaction. But she said nothing. "You know?"

"Paula was not the love of his life. I could see that. There were a lot of problems in their relationship."

He nodded. "I was aware. Brent would talk to me about it."

"That's more than he did with me or his father."

"I hear you. I get the same cold shoulder from my daughter. She tells me precious little. What do they say about the preacher trying to save the souls in his own town?"

She smiled. "Children can be so difficult, can't they."

"When Brent lived here," he said, "I was more aware of the situation. But since he's been gone I've gotten next to nothing in the way of information. He used to tell me about the problems with Paula, as I said. He shouldered a lot of the blame for that himself. I was never a fan of hers. There were a lot of problems with her family. And I didn't realize how Ashley felt about Brent until about eight years ago. I'm ashamed to say I was too busy being mayor and running the union and didn't keep up with everything she did. Apparently both she and Loretta needed me, but I wasn't there."

"No need to be that rough on yourself, Hank. Ashley turned out fine. She's an excellent mother and well thought of around town. And Loretta. She was a grown woman and made her choices."

"I missed a lot of Ashley's growing up. That was back in my wild days. I wasn't a good father...or husband."

"I've never heard you speak like this before."

"We're gettin' old. Time to face the music."

He remembered the day Loretta left after thirty-one years of marriage. His extramarital affairs started when he was mayor. A clerk at city hall. Payroll clerk at the mill. Local insurance agent. Indiscriminate strangers that meant little to him beyond casual sex. All strokes to the ego that slashed, one by one, at his wife's heart. Characteristically, Loretta never said a word, keeping the pain to herself, only silently questioning why her husband needed the affections of another woman. Even on the day she left she'd said nothing. No point, really. The stupidity of his ways seemed apparent. And he couldn't blame it on alcohol, he never drank. Or drugs, he hardly downed an aspirin. All he could do was beg forgiveness.

Which was never granted.

Brent handled the divorce. Uncontested. Quick and quiet. Loretta moved to north Georgia and married a dentist. She'd always wanted to live in the mountains, but he'd refused. *Concord's my life*, he told her.

So she left him to it.

"You miss her, don't you?" she said.

Catherine and Loretta had been friends.

"It was all my fault. I ruined that marriage."

"Sometimes people just grow apart," she said. "You and Loretta were together a long time."

He shook his head. "I drove us apart. I was a fool. Now I live alone, which is the price for my idiocy."

"You've dated since the divorce. I know that for a fact."

"I wouldn't say women are beating my door down."

"You had no trouble before the divorce."

Only a friend of many years could be so blunt without offense. "Maybe that was the attraction for them? I was somebody else's."

"It takes two, Hank."

"I look back and wonder what I was thinking."

"Loretta could have forgiven you. She could have chosen to work it out. Instead, she decided to leave and marry another man."

He was surprised by her defense of him. "I thought you women stuck together."

"I'm not condoning what you did, only saying Loretta didn't necessarily have to do what she did, either."

"Turnabout's fair play."

"I don't think the Lord views it that way."

"Thou shall not commit adultery."

"Forgiveness is a duty. Luke 17:4, I believe."

He smiled. "I never realized you were such a biblical scholar."

"I have many talents you may not be aware of."

Catherine Walker had always been an interesting woman. But right now his daughter was the major concern. "One reason I think Ashley stuck with me was because of her own situation. She hadn't been the best wife to three men either. I think she understood what failure in marriage meant. That duty of forgiveness, as you say."

He'd often thought both he and his daughter were cursed with an inability to find what their hearts truly desired. Ashley had promised her mother that she'd look after him, Loretta grateful that her daughter would finish what she'd been unwilling to do. The minister who married them long ago had said, *"Till death do you part,"* yet religious fervor could not compensate for the toll deceit took on the heart. That point of no return when emotions gestated from love to hate, respect to loathing, caring to indifference. His former wife was now bonded to another man and another life. Every week he preached the gospel to his Sunday school class. Too bad he never learned to practice what he preached until it was far too late.

"I want you to know," he said, "that I don't think there's been anything sexual at all between Brent and Ashley for a long, long time. They're both better than that. But the feeling between them seems real. And Paula was aware of that situation."

"I know that."

He was surprised. "Mind if I ask how?"

"She talked to me once about it. Paula could be quite difficult. That much was clear. She was hard to please, and she never really concerned herself with anyone else's feelings. It's amazing she was like that at all. Small-town girl from a down-to-earth family. Her parents were good people."

"Except they killed themselves."

Catherine stared beyond the railing. "I often wondered about the pain I saw in Brent's eyes. He tried hard to conceal it, but I could see it there."

"Ashley had her share, too. I think she tried to forget with three husbands. Those were mistakes that should have never happened."

"But she has Lori Anne. What a darling girl. How old is she now?"

"Twelve, and she runs us to death."

"I bet her granddaddy spoils her?"

"Every chance I get."

He hesitated, deciding best how to finish what he started. Damn Ashley. This should have been done years ago.

He sucked a deep breath.

"There's something else."

10:37 A.M.

FRANK BARNARD STARED AT THE LOG CABIN, TWELVE HUNDRED square feet under the roof in the woods of west Georgia, the muddy Chattahoochee River in sight.

He knew the history of Priority Number 6. Melvin Bennett bought the property in his forties, made payments until his fifties, then built the cabin in his early sixties. Two weeks after retiring from Southern Republic Pulp and Paper Company, Bennett and

94

his wife packed a moving van and drove two hundred miles west from Woods County, across Georgia, spending the past two years quietly beside the Chattahoochee within sight of Alabama. He also knew how many and how far away Melvin Bennett's neighbors lived. He likewise knew the Harris County Sheriff's Department did not make regular patrols, and the nearest hospital was forty miles away.

He'd arrived last night and, to supplement the file, spent most of the evening doing on-site surveillance. Afterward, back in his motel room, he studied the information in more detail. Relatively healthy, Melvin Bennett was concerned only with a long-standing diabetic condition and a peanut allergy. Though he was insulin-dependent, no major problems presently existed from the disease. As for the allergy, he maintained a running prescription for an epinephrine auto-injector, which he kept nearby in case of emergency. De Florio's notes in the file suggested a processing consistent with that allergy. But devising a method to accomplish that, while at the same time not raising any suspicion, had taken thought.

He considered himself a consummate professional. Nearly five years he'd worked for De Florio, performing flawlessly. He'd traveled all over the country, twice to Canada and once to Mexico, processing Priorities under the most varied of circumstances. Only a small percentage of Priorities lived in and around Concord. Most moved away at retirement to be closer to family. Some sought the warmth of Florida or the coolness of the mountains. Distance aided processing and allowed for a diversified pattern. Rule expressly provided that people who lived in and around Woods County could be Prioritized only on a staggered basis so as not to attract undue attention.

He was well aware of De Florio's rise from associate to chief of security. He wanted to one day follow in that path. He certainly didn't want to end up like Milo Richey. But Richey had screwed up and, in this business, there were no second chances. Especially for an ambitious associate looking to get ahead.

But first things first.

Melvin Bennett's untimely death.

When he'd entered Bennett's cabin last night after the elder man went out, he discovered that Bennett's wife was out of town, her sister's telephone number tacked to the refrigerator door, a message on the answering machine checking on Bennett ending with love and *"I'll see you Saturday."* Knowing Bennett would be alone for the next two days, he'd finalized the method of processing, then telephoned De Florio and cleared everything, even receiving a compliment on his ingenuity.

Now he was back.

Watching from the thickets that engulfed the cabin as Melvin Bennett bolted out the front door carrying a fishing rod and tackle box.

Bennett headed straight for a small skiff tied to an aging dock. No time was taken to lock the front door. The file indicated that Bennett liked to say that if somebody broke in, he sure as hell wasn't going to have a door to fix too. So he never locked anything. The outboard roared to life and Bennett started upstream for what the file noted as *his usual Thursday afternoon of solitary fishing*. Once the man was out of sight Barnard immediately entered the cabin.

He went directly to the kitchen and popped open the refrigerator. Lining the shelf inside the door, exactly where the file said, stood four vials of insulin. Through gloved fingers he examined each. All full, their plastic seals intact—except one. Half full. Obviously the one currently in use. He carried the used vial to the sink, then removed an empty syringe from his pocket. Puncturing the rubber seal with the long needle, he worked the plunger, slowly siphoning a full syringe, expelling the medicine down the drain. He repeated the process two more times until the vial was empty. From another pocket he found a bottle of saline mixed with arachis oil.

Essence of peanut.

He filled the syringe and injected the contents. He repeated the process until the vial returned to its original half-full level. The only difference, now it contained salt water and poison instead of life-giving insulin.

He rinsed the sink thoroughly and replaced the tampered-with vial in the refrigerator. Eight hours later when Melvin Bennett injected himself he'd notice little. But within a few moments he should be in shock. The high concentrations would hit in an instant. To make sure there would be no heroics, he unplugged the house phone from its jack. There'd be no cell phone calls either, as he would be outside, close by, with a jammer working.

By morning Melvin Bennett would be dead.

All he'd have to do was maintain a vigil and confirm the inevitable.

12:04 P.M.

BRENT SCOOTED OUT OF THE MILL AND DROVE STRAIGHT INTO Concord. He had a general idea where to look, and it took only a few minutes to spot the boxy white van with its distinctive red, white, and blue markings. It was stopped in the opposite lane next to a dilapidated aluminum mailbox.

He pulled the Jeep up beside.

Ashley glanced to her left and instantly reacted, slamming the gearshift into park and jumping out of the right-hand seat. Without saying a word she opened the driver's door and climbed into his lap, kissing him long and hard, one of her Grand Canyon kisses as she liked to call them. Suddenly, he wasn't sitting in his father's Jeep on a tree-lined drive three blocks over from his parents' house. He was back in high school. Over twenty years ago. In the front seat of his '65 Ford Galaxy.

At Eagle Lake.

"Why'd you do that?" he asked, when they stopped kissing.
"You didn't like it?" Ashley said.
"I didn't say that."
"You worried about another girl?"

97

"Not particularly. I'm not going steady."

To emphasize the point, he displayed the senior ring still on his finger. "You, on the other hand, do have a problem."

He motioned to the chunk of gold and topaz held in place by a rubber band. It belonged to a two-letter jock who played center field in baseball and guard for the basketball team. Whom he doubted would appreciate having his girl kissed.

"You worried about him?" she asked, unconcerned.

He didn't want to be used as a way to make a boyfriend jealous. "Should I be?"

"I'm not."

She was hard to figure. They'd been friends since grade school. Riding bikes. Swimming in the lake. Playing as children and teenagers do. Only during the last year had they become close, spending most of their time only talking. Before tonight, there'd been no indication either wanted to burn the bridge from friendship to lovers.

She straddled his lap in the middle of the front seat, short shapely legs bent at the knees. He gripped her supple waist, his fingertips almost touching.

"What do you want, Brent Walker?"

She loved to ask questions like that, always more interested in others than herself. It was one of the reasons he found her so fascinating. She reveled in sharing dreams and aspirations. Their conversations always steered toward where they'd be twenty years from graduation. She was so different from other girls.

"I want to be a lawyer," he said.

"Since when?"

"Since a few days ago when I decided. You're the first person I've told."

"Going to defend the weak and protect the poor?"

He smiled, her dainty face only inches away. "Hardly. I'd like just to work in Concord and help out the people I know."

She wiggled closer, her smell intoxicating. Lately, he even savored it when she wasn't around. She kissed him again. Longer and harder than the first time.

"You know I love you." Her voice was matter-of-fact.

"No...I didn't know that."

"You should."

He wasn't even sure what love meant. He certainly loved his mother and father, his aunts and uncles, his grandparents, and his cocker spaniel. A few girls he'd cared for, but he'd never really considered the depth of his feelings beyond that. Toward Ashley he certainly felt different. Something about her he couldn't explain. Something he didn't want to explain. But if love meant being able to speak his mind unabated, opening his heart, and not feeling ashamed about expressing genuine emotion, then maybe he might love Ashley Reed.

He kissed her again.

"I ought to kick your ass," Ashley said, when they parted. "You've been home a whole day and not even one phone call."

He smiled. She was as light as ever, her smell still familiar, a faint floral scent, like roses and jasmine combined. "I didn't know postal regulations allowed wearing perfume."

"I wore it for you. Figured I'd see you before the day was through."

"You know you're nothing but trouble."

"Trouble you can't live without."

"You're cocksure of yourself."

She hopped down and stood on the street before him. "I'm staring forty-two dead down the barrel, but I've held up."

She raised her arms and twirled around. Yes, she had. Same happy eyes. Cheerleader freckles. And honey-colored hair cut boyishly short. She didn't look a whole lot different from when she used to flit down the halls of Woods County High, turning every head along the way. That, and later visions of her, had stayed with him for years. Now the apparition was live flesh and bones standing before him.

She stepped back close to the open car door. The smell returned, as certain as a new car and equally appealing. "I want you, Brent."

And, God help him, he wanted her too.

But the guilt from Paula still haunted him. He heard again what she said the last day of her life. *"You love her? Don't you?"* But before he could feel any worse, Ashley kissed him again, then asked, "So when do you plan to ask me out all proper and all?"

He smiled. Not a thing bashful about her. He vividly recalled the time, not long after college graduation, when they'd first made love. In Eagle Lake. Thrashing around like fish in heat. He'd worried the whole time someone would come along and catch them.

"You going to give me a chance to get situated?" he asked.

"Not much of one."

Hell, what choice did he have? And did he really want one? "How about lunch tomorrow?"

"You got it."

She backed away. "Right now, I gotta tend to my route. If I stay much longer we may end up in the back of that van." A twinkle in her eye accompanied the observation. "No lunch break today. I'm getting off early. Papa Evans is going to be buried at two."

"I heard Mr. Evans died."

"He was old and frail. No surprise, really. But still awful. Gary asked me to go. He's ripped up."

Gary Evans had been her third husband, his father, Fred, her father-in-law for the short time that the marriage lasted. Papa was the nickname, though, everyone called him.

They talked a few minutes more, then she kissed him goodbye and drove off in the van. He hated to see her go.

She made him feel so good.

And so guilty.

5:46 P.M.

"PLEASE BLESS ME, FATHER, FOR I HAVE SINNED, IT HAS BEEN A month since my last confession and these are my sins."

Chris Bozin paused.

"Eight times I let my greed dominate the brotherly spirit I should show others. And I practiced deceit more than I should have."

"Selfishness is a sin all of us are guilty of at one time or another," the priest whispered, the face on the other side a shadow through the stitched screen.

"I'm afraid, Father, my sins are of a magnitude more grievous than you realize."

"Neither Christ nor the church distinguishes among sins. To Our Lord the violation is identical, the penance the same."

"I'm also afraid, Father, my time may be short."

"In what way?"

"My health is failing."

The priest offered no salience. "If such be the case there's little you can do to affect it."

"But there may be something I can do for my soul."

"Do you do this simply because your time may be short?"

"I do it because my eternal soul deserves better than what my mortal consciousness has provided."

"You do realize that mortal consciousness is a measure of the eternal soul."

"But is not forgiveness the keystone of both the church and God?"

"Absolutely."

"Then I seek absolution in the name of the Lord."

"I absolve you of all your sins, including those of greed, selfishness, and vanity, you have committed during the past month. For your contrition please recite three Hail Marys and one Our Father. In the name of the Father, Son, and Holy Spirit, you may go in peace."

The priest slid the panel shut.

Chris reverently made the sign of the cross, said a quick Our Father, then slowly pulled himself up off his knees.

He was inside the Shrine of the Immaculate Conception, which sat in the shadow of the Georgia state capitol, an olden brick-and-stone structure topped with spires, towers, and bells, one of the first Catholic churches built in Atlanta. He'd been a regular attendee for over thirty years, turning to religion for some measure of serenity. Surprisingly, though, he'd found a degree of personal satisfaction.

And through the years he'd willingly maintained his membership, becoming a prodigious contributor, his tithes legendary, all the priests becoming close friends. The voice of the associate who just heard his confession was new, the young man obviously yet to hear about Christopher Bozin.

He slipped out of the confessional.

A young woman rose from the adjacent pews and approached. He held the oak door open until she was inside, then crept toward the main altar, his steps cushioned by the crimson carpet runner. High above, from the peaked central nave, murals of Christ and the Virgin Mary gazed down. To his left, rows of tiny candles flickered from a side altar. He knelt in the first row of pews and silently said the contrition of the four assigned prayers.

Then he sat, and quietly waited for the start of 6:00 mass.

7:05 P.M.

THE CADILLAC WOVE THROUGH EVENING TRAFFIC AND DREW TO A halt in front of the church. Slowly, Chris climbed into the back seat and sank into the soft leather. The car belonged to him, the driver one of four domestic aides he employed.

He lived in southwest Atlanta simply because Hamilton Lee and Larry Hughes lived toward the northeast, his home a three-story neoclassical mansion built to reflect a love of things Italian. He'd modeled it after country estates visited in Tuscany, the main house perched among ten lush acres surrounded by sycamore trees and an eight-foot-high brick wall topped by sharpened wrought iron. He'd incorporated all the required amenities. A halo-shaped swimming pool, fountains adorned with Roman statues, and a beautifully manicured Italian garden that had won four Coweta County Garden Club awards.

He possessed no immediate family, his closest relatives a few nieces and nephews he rarely heard from. Most people were nothing but passing acquaintances. Occasionally a friendship would mature, none ever reaching the point of being close, though. Only

Nancy. They'd been together a long time. He trusted her. Probably even loved her. But he could never do anything about it. How could he? Bad enough he lived with the knowledge of his evil ways, no way he could involve anyone else.

Instead, he opted for the solitude of his own thoughts and the occasional adulation others provided. He maintained a reputation as a respected member of the chamber of commerce, past Rotarian, longtime Mason, and active church member. Since he controlled Southern Republic's purse strings he was the contact point for countless charities. He gave yearly to the Heart Association, Cancer Society, and Juvenile Diabetes Research Foundation. His picture regularly appeared in newspapers, brochures, and magazines handing out check after check. All part of his crafted façade.

In reality, though, he was simply a cold-blooded killer.

Probably the most diabolical serial killer in history. How many Priorities had there been? Hundreds? At least. More like a thousand. How long had it been going on? Twenty years? No. Closer to thirty. So many lives indiscriminately ended to protect the bottom line. Where other companies laid off, scaled back, shut down, reorganized, went bankrupt, or simply closed their doors, Southern Republic murdered. How did it start? How had it gotten to this point? When had it become so easy?

The car inched through traffic.

His mood darkened like this after church. Something about the majesty of an omnipotent being implementing some grand design brought to the surface what tiny bubble of conscience he still possessed. He lost all sense of values years ago, somewhere between the first Priority and the five hundredth. But of late he'd found notions of right and wrong, good and evil, life and death, reentering his decision-making process.

And it frightened him.

Especially given the realization of his own mortality.

He reached over for the day's *Atlanta Constitution* lying on the back seat and tried to flush the disturbing thoughts from his mind. But it was hard to concentrate.

Instead, he remembered back thirty-plus years.

And how everything had started.

"I'm telling you, Chris, it's the deal of the century," Hamilton Lee said.

He and Lee were huddled in a tiny office in downtown Atlanta, four stories up in a ten-floor dilapidated building. The space was more desk than air. Hamilton Lee sat in one chair, a cracked-leather briefcase in the other. Lee was excited. He'd just returned from Concord, a tiny town, in a tiny county, in a tiny part of Georgia. A paper mill had been built there after World War II that was, at first, a moneymaker. Wholly owned by a family out of Massachusetts, not much had been done in the way of moderniz-ing or expanding. Premature deaths had claimed all its founders.

Now the heirs wanted out.

Since World War II, New England paper companies had steadily discovered the richness and relative cheapness of southern pine forests. The warm climate was ideal for growing trees. Water flowed plentifully. And the proximity of railroads, highways, and deepwater ports made the locale irresistible. One news account labeled the area "the wood basket of the world." Mills sprouted everywhere. But it was a volatile market, one that demanded a company either keep pace or be left behind. Republic Board and Paper, headquartered in Concord, Georgia, had involuntarily chose the latter.

"What's really great are the labor costs," Lee said. "The wage scales are a good dollar to a dollar and a half an hour less than anywhere else."

Lee worked for Roland Paper Company, a multistate conglom-erate that owned four mills. He'd been an assistant superintendent at their Savannah plant for nine years. Young. Bright. Energetic. His only fault was a perpetual impatience and a desire to be in charge. Unfortunately, that kind of ambition took time—time Lee had no intention of expending climbing a corporate ladder— so he'd been on the lookout for a company of his own.

How different they were.

Chris was a deputy chief loan officer for Georgia Merchants and Savings Bank. Lee a brash, arrogant entrepreneur. Timber had brought them together, Georgia Merchants a sprawling institution that financed much of the booming pulp sales market. It had evolved slowly. Landowners needed to sell their wood. Companies needed to buy. Cash was not always available and the investment was risky since trees could burn, attract disease, or be devoured by insects. So banks had stepped in and assumed the risk, providing capital in return for an above-market rate of interest. Georgia Merchants maintained a wide portfolio of timber loans from all across the state, regularly doing business with Roland Paper.

"Chris, we can buy this mill for pennies on the dollar. I talked to one of the heirs and all they want is out. They have a note due at a New York bank that's gobbling them up in interest. They just want the principal paid. These people don't know anything about the paper industry."

"I agree, Hamilton. It sounds good."

And it did.

Damn good, in fact.

He was tired of loaning money and watching others make a fortune. He wanted to try his own luck in the business world. Wanted out of this cubicle of an office. Wanted more than a two-room apartment on the east side of Atlanta. A big car would be nice. Maybe a butler and a housekeeper. Visits to Europe. Lots of dreams. And there was nothing wrong with dreaming.

So long as it didn't interfere with sound thinking.

He'd often wondered if what they were planning was foolish. Particularly for a twenty-eight-year-old assistant mill superintendent and a thirty-eight-year-old deputy loan officer, neither of whom had ever owned a business before.

"Can you get the money, Chris?"

"How much we talking about?"

Lee told him. "That's enough to buy and renovate."

The amount surprised him. He'd actually figured on more. "I can get it."

A smile formed on Lee's face.

Together they dreamed of forming a company, resurrecting a town, building a skyscraper, and becoming millionaires a hundred times over.

"We're going to need some expertise in sales," Lee said. "I don't know beans about selling paper. But there's a guy who works in our sales department that can sell like nothing you've ever seen. Larry Hughes. I think I can get him to go in with us."

He recognized the wisdom in that. "That's smart."

Lee's smile got broader.

"It's the deal of the century, Chris. The deal of the century."

7:35 P.M.

A KNOCK CAME FROM OUTSIDE CHRIS' BEDROOM DOOR. HE AMBLED out of the walk-in closet as his butler entered. He noticed the change in jackets, the navy one worn to drive the Cadillac replaced with white, which he required to be worn inside the house.

"Would you like dinner in the study or the dining room?"

Home only a few minutes, he'd gone straight upstairs to change. He really hadn't given dinner much thought. His cook was talented and he used to genuinely enjoy her meals. But not so much, as of late.

"I'll eat in the study."

He omitted the *I'll try.*

His butler excused himself and left.

His bedroom was his favorite place. Priceless murals of Susanna and the Elders highlighted the walls. Two original Biedermeier pedestal tables sat next to nineteenth-century tapestry chairs. A Jacopo Brustolon crucifix bought in Rome hung over his bed. The decorating costs alone were more than he'd earned in all his years as a deputy loan officer at the Georgia Merchants and Savings Bank.

But money was no longer a concern. His worries now centered on things that couldn't be readily controlled, like the pain in his abdomen that had steadily increased over the last hour. It started just before he left the Blue Tower, becoming uncomfortable during church. Kneeling in the confessional had aggravated it. Lately, almost everything seemed to have that effect.

He shuffled back into the closet and slowly peeled off his suit, shirt, and tie. He loosely draped the clothes over a brass valet. The steward would come later and hang everything. He carefully slipped on silk pajamas and a monogrammed paisley robe. He switched off the light and started across the carpet toward the bath.

The pain became unbearable.

Like a fist rammed into his gut.

His eyes teared and he doubled over, resisting hard the urge to cry out. He gritted his teeth, crept into the anteroom, and carefully settled into a leather chair at his writing desk. He waited a moment, hoping the agony would subside. He switched on the lamp and reached for his cell phone, dialing the number stored high in his FAVORITES.

A pleasant male voice answered on the third ring.

"I delayed calling as long as I could," he said. "But I think I need to see you."

"Have there been more problems?" his doctor asked.

"The pain is becoming regular. I've been feeling...different."

He reported the blood in his urine, a difficulty in peeing, weight loss, and how the pain had settled in his abdomen. Then, he said, "I was hoping for a little more time."

"Call my office first thing tomorrow and we'll arrange for tests. Chris, you've put this off long enough."

"Could they be done over the weekend?"

He was hoping his old friend would understand.

"You don't give up, do you? I'll arrange it."

"It's my nature. And thank you."

He hung up.

Amazingly, the pain had all but disappeared.

But it did that. Showing little rhythm or predictability. Coming and going. Seemingly dictated only by the deterioration occurring uncontrollably within him. Yesterday, when Nancy had quizzed him, he'd lied about how he felt. The truth would only worry her, and he didn't want to do that.

He pushed himself up and inched toward the bathroom. He might even be able to eat a little. He hadn't eaten all day and the food at least sounded good when his butler mentioned it.

So he washed his face and hands, then cautiously made his way downstairs where he knew dinner was waiting.

7:50 P.M.

CHRIS TRIED TO FINISH THE MEAL BUT COULDN'T, LITTLE MORE THAN picking at most of it. Finally, he shoved the cart away from the chair.

He was watching *Jeopardy!*, as he did most nights. He enjoyed the game. And it definitely beat those exposé newsmagazine shows or sitcom reruns that dominated most of early-evening television. He enjoyed seeing how many questions he could pose. The only annoying thing about the half hour was how much the new host looked like Hamilton Lee.

Both were tall and thin with grayish-brown hair. High furrowed brows led down to deep, full eyes. Each sported a graying mustache and was swarthy-complexioned, though he knew Lee spent a lot of time in a tanning bed at an expensive men's salon where he also had his hair styled, mustache trimmed, and nails manicured. Lee even dressed like a game-show host. Double-breasted suits, no vent, wide lapels in the European style, a splash of silk puffed out of a jacket pocket that matched at least one color in his usually loud ties.

"European Castles for $800, please."

"It's the smallest of Ludwig II's three Bavarian masterpieces."

"What is Linderhof?" he whispered before the contestant dinged and echoed the same thing. He knew that only because he spent one July in southern Germany touring the castles and enjoying the Alps.

His brief interlude without pain ended just as the Double Jeopardy round drew to a close.

He shook his head in disgust.

It was going to be another long, sleepless night.

Upstairs in his bathroom, hidden away so the staff couldn't find them, were the few remaining pain pills prescribed months ago when the last attack occurred. There'd been no need of them for a while.

He sat like a statue and waited for the agony to subside.

He thought again about his two partners and the rift that had widened between them. There no longer seemed any practical way to erect a bridge. He was the oldest of the three at sixty-eight. Hamilton Lee the youngest at fifty-eight. Larry Hughes in between at sixty. Their respective ages, though, carried no associated seniority. The articles of incorporation were clear. Each shareholder controlled an identical one-third interest. Yet the two younger men had, of late, effectively teamed to freeze him out of any real say in company policy. This was particularly true regarding Priority decisions where, in recent years, he'd become reluctant to authorize the number Lee and Hughes routinely favored. But what could he do about it? Turn them in? Make a deal with prosecutors? Give them Lee and Hughes in exchange for immunity?

Hardly.

His crime was too great for any show of mercy. No prosecutor would even consider a deal. And he had no desire to spend the rest of his life in prison. So what could he do? Vote no? That's about it, though the gesture seemed meaningless. People were still going to die, since two-to-one would always be a majority.

He glanced around the study.

Bookshelves lined one wall, fashioned from what used to be a choir stall imported from a convent in northern Italy. The walls themselves were part goffered velvet, part fresco. The décor was all original Italian antiques. He loved the room. It was where he read his paper in the morning and watched television in the evening. All beautifully coordinated. Detailed. Like his life. A neatly organized package surrounded by calculated extravagance. He'd come a long way from a deputy loan officer and had no desire to retreat. But he could also still hear the priest's words from the confessional.

Mortal consciousness is a measure of the eternal soul.

That it was.

11:38 P.M.

FRANK BARNARD GLANCED AT HIS WATCH. MELVIN BENNETT'S CABIN had been dark nearly two hours.

Time to move.

He entered through the front door, now locked since Bennett was home for the night. But the tumbler was ridiculously easy to pick.

The cabin's central air-conditioning engulfed him with welcome relief from the stifling humidity of the west Georgia night. His clothes were soaked with sweat from the last few hours of waiting, now transformed into the feel of a cool wet rag.

Bennett lay sprawled on the floor, where he'd fallen after being seized by an attack. Considering the high concentration, the symptoms would have been nearly instantaneous. Tightening in the throat. Shortness of breath. Wheezing. Abdominal cramps.

Then death.

He checked for a pulse.

None.

He opened the refrigerator and checked the insulin vial. The level was definitely lower. He knew each contained four injections and he estimated a quarter of the saline was gone.

He deposited the vial into a baggie.

From the floor he retrieved the spent syringe and dropped it in the baggie too. An autopsy would reveal the allergic reaction.

110

The oil that had caused it would still be there, but in a much lower concentration thanks to the allergic reaction. How would it be explained? Who knew? Cross contact most likely. People like Bennett would avoid anything and everything related to a peanut. But a knife or a fork may have some residue on it. Traces could have made their way into other prepackaged food. It didn't take much to stir a reaction. Certainly, there'd be nothing to suggest foul play.

His watch read 11:46 P.M.

The file said Bennett medicated himself every night with the insulin before the 6:00 news.

So he'd been dead awhile.

He plugged the phone back in, then left.

Job done.

DAY FOUR
FRIDAY, JUNE 9

9:45 A.M.

BRENT STOOD OUTSIDE THE DOUBLE DOORS AND STARED THROUGH the small glass window into the courtroom. The Woods County courthouse was a familiar place. Five years he'd practiced before the same oak dais. Criminal cases, car wrecks, breaches of contract, divorces. Battle after battle that grew his practice, made him a living, and forged a reputation.

The two-story building had been erected after the war in the 1940s. Tall pecan trees dotted the lawn in front, the architecture distinctive in its neoclassical style. Sherman burned the original building to the ground while his soldiers cheered. In defiance, a life-sized marble statue of a Confederate soldier was later erected that remained until two years ago, when it was finally removed.

"Good to see you again," a voice said.

He turned to see a familiar face. Kelvin Williams. The old deputy had worked bailiff duty a long time.

"It's good to see you too, Preacher."

They shook hands.

Everybody referred to Kelvin as Preacher since he spent Sundays in the pulpit of Concord's Church of God spreading the gospel. Williams was an amicable man with a reputation for generosity. Brent turned back and stared through the window, beyond the rows of empty seats, toward the front of the courtroom. Inside the bar two lawyers were arguing to a judge.

"Is that S. Lou Greene in there?" he said, referring to the tall man who stood to the right of the judge's bench.

His old friend approached the window in the other door. "Yep. That's Cue Stick himself."

Preacher had a name for everyone. "How's he rate?"

He knew the scale. "Okay" meant Preacher had read a newspaper during most of the trial. "Good" was worth his attention about half the time. "Damn good," he'd sit and listen to every word.

"Good. Don't take no crap off nobody."

He recognized the other lawyer, a man from Savannah who, in years past, had done a lot of insurance defense work. Neither of the two judges of the Ogeechee Judicial Circuit were present, just an administrative law judge today who appeared once a month to resolve workers' compensation claims.

Greene seemed about mid-forties, ramrod-tall, like a pool cue, his noticeably square face made even squarer by tortoiseshell-framed glasses. His thinning auburn hair hung long and was bundled into a ponytail that draped past the shoulders. He sported a powder-blue seersucker suit, white pinpoint Oxford shirt, daffodil-yellow tie, and brown-and-white patent-leather shoes.

"Interesting outfit," he said.

Preacher was still looking in through the window in the other door. "Calls it his Atticus Finch look. Swears when they colorize *To Kill a Mockingbird*, Peck's seersucker'll be blue."

Brent wore the typical south Georgia lawyers' work uniform. Khaki trousers, button-down white shirt, miscellaneous tie, navy-blue blazer, and loafers. After moving to Atlanta he quickly discovered suits and wing tips were the rule there, so his blue blazer and khaki pants had been relegated to the back of the closet, and penny loafers to the weekends.

He stepped away from the door. "What's the scoop on Greene?"

"He came here about four years ago. Built up clients fast. All comp cases. Got offices all up and down the Carolina line. Word now between Savannah and Augusta is after an on-the-job-injury, see your doctor first and Greene second."

"Amazing he could build a practice that fast."

"You know the program. His clients don't just walk through the door. He's got a whole platoon of runners who stay on the lookout. Most of 'em ex-clients. And he spends a fortune on advertising."

Scattered all along the Georgia–South Carolina border were a sugar-processing plant, a trailer manufacturer, a textile weaver, a carpet yarn plant, lumber companies, three paper mills, a bag plant, a meat-processing facility, a peanut producer, and a concrete plant. Not to mention hundreds of retail businesses. All with employees. Fertile grist for a workers' compensation lawyer's fee mill.

"What's Greene pay on a referral?"

"Some of the runners get just $50 to $100. Got a cousin who made a couple thousand on a big one, though."

"Surprised the state bar hasn't gotten him. They'd pull his ticket for that."

Preacher chuckled. "I'm sure Cue Stick's got it covered. Real clever fellow."

Greene seemed both comfortable and knowledgeable standing before the judge, the disheveled image not out of character with the specialty of workers' compensation. There were no juries to impress, only an administrative law judge who rode circuit hearing appeals in the morning then played golf or tennis in the afternoon with the same lawyers who'd appeared before him that morning. The system was fueled entirely by greed—that of the insurers for high premiums, defense lawyers for billable hours, plaintiffs' lawyers for settlements, and employers for convenience. Skill was not nearly as important as knowledge of the fine print. It was paper pushing at a highly profitable level. And though short on physical appearance and courthouse image, careful managers like S. Lou Greene could make a lot of money.

"What you got there today?" Preacher asked.

He gestured to the files he held. "Comp cases for the company."

Preacher shook his head. "Like watchin' clothes dry."

"It pays the bills."

"You need to get back in front of a jury. You had a talent."

He smiled. "And it's good to see you, too, Preacher."

He pushed through the doors and noticed that the hearing had ended. He walked to the front and introduced himself to Greene, who shook his hand.

"Welcome to the fray," Greene said.

"It's good to be back. I think we have four cases together today. Where would you like to start?"

"How about the quickest."

Greene turned to the administrative judge, a stodgy, salt-and-pepper-haired man who looked half asleep behind the dais.

"Your Honor, *Brandon Pabon v. Southern Republic Pulp and Paper* was scheduled for hearing today, but Claimant Pabon died Tuesday night of a drug overdose. Which is unfortunate for both Mr. Pabon...and myself."

12:48 P.M.

HANK WANTED HIS RELATIONSHIP WITH S. LOU GREENE KEPT private. Ten years ago, when Brent Walker left for Atlanta, he'd agonized through a couple of tough years, attempting to use some of the other local legal talent. But none possessed the quickness of mind and innate skill he'd grown accustomed to with Brent. Greene's arrival brought an ally with both brains and flamboyance. He met him one week and they teamed the next, both seemingly understanding the benefits to be derived from some mutual cooperation.

The main office of Greene's legal network was once the old Concord National Bank. The Depression claimed that institution a long time ago and another never took its place. The building fronted First Street, a façade of carved granite that included fluted columns and a set of nasty gargoyles that glared down on everyone who entered. It stood a full two stories and provided more than enough room for Greene, his two paralegals, three secretaries, and an array of computers used to process the hundreds of workers' comp claims he regularly maintained.

Hank had checked out of the mill ten minutes ago, noting the usual *union business* on his time card. As a local president he was allowed flexibility in dealing with union affairs on company time, federal law even mandated such, but one of the unwritten perks he'd acquired from years of cooperation and confrontation was the privilege to leave the plant virtually unchecked and unquestioned.

He parked behind the office in the rear lot and quickly stepped toward the back door. Habit forced him to look up. Flying proudly, like every day, the flag gently rustled. He knew the story. On a vacation through Germany, atop a castle on the Rhine, Greene had spotted a black eagle, talons extended, splashed before a yellow background. The sight enchanted him, so Greene bought the banner, brought it back, and it soon became tradition to hoist it every time a claim was settled. For the past five years few days had gone by when it had not flown all day.

Inside, he marched past the row of secretaries and heard a groan. He knew his visits weren't popular. Normally he needed some paperwork prepared immediately, which required them to stop what they were doing to accommodate him. It was a nuisance, but he expected Greene to cater to his demands. In return, he used contacts at plants all over the area to channel workers' comp claims this way. But unlike other runners who shared in the proceeds, he took nothing financially for the effort.

He trudged up the granite stairs and into Greene's spacious second-floor office. The lawyer was perched behind an oak desk.

"Look what the cat dragged in," Greene said.

"That any way to say hello to a buddy?"

"My buddy doesn't come by unless he needs something."

He sat down. "So nice to be appreciated. Have you had a chance to look those company memos over I brought the other day?"

Greene reached across the messy desk for a clutch of paper. "This is pretty confidential stuff, Hank. Where'd you get it?"

"Somebody with connections."

On the flash drive Marlene had supplied him had been an array of sales and cost figures. Most of it useless. Some, though, quite informative. There were also emails and memos among various departments. Anything from the three owners themselves was considered the Holy Grail, and Marlene had managed to snag a few.

Especially one.

An email from Hamilton Lee to Southern Republic's industrial relations manager.

> On the collective bargaining session just around the corner, per our meeting of last week, I wanted to confirm our position about five-year contract deals. During the last negotiations an effort was made to secure a five-year duration on the labor contracts. But costs associated with that, particularly with reference to IBEW where a percentage increase in wages was conceded, were high. Such efforts are not necessary this time. Of course, request five years in our initial offer but bargain that away in return for concessions. Each union will surely not want to agree to any long-term deal. It should be easy to secure three years in duration without any major concessions on our part. I wanted you to know that you have the board's authorization to negotiate in this manner. Please keep me informed.

Greene held up Lee's email. "Seems the company isn't interested in five years this time."

"And that could be a problem. Those two years were my only bargaining chip. Without 'em, all I can hope is just to keep what I already have."

"You think they're going to want takebacks?" Greene asked.

That was a dreaded word, one that required him to return benefits he'd sweated to acquire in years past. Like a slap in the face, where the company reacquired what it had never wanted to give in the first place.

Talk about murdering his image.

"They sure look like a possibility," he said. "What else do I have to offer them?"

"Not a whole lot. These negotiations might be a disaster."

He didn't want to hear that.

"On a brighter note," Greene said, "I met Brent Walker this morning. In court."

"You be good to him, Lou."

"Is he going to help you with the negotiations?"

"Brent won't let 'em blindside me."

"He may not be involved in the negotiations. New kid on the block and all. He told me today he's got three filing cabinets full of workers' comp cases."

"He's still on the inside. So you never know what he might come across. What do you think about those health care costs mentioned in the stuff I left with you?"

"That's the company's number one expense, bar none, growing every year by the millions of dollars. They're self-insured, which comes with good and bad. If I were you, Hank, I'd expect proposals upping the yearly deductibles, raising the employee premium contribution, cutting some benefits, that sort of thing."

He shook his head. "That'll go over real big with the membership."

"And it won't help your image as a hard-nosed negotiator."

No, it would not. "I've got to at least hold on to what I have—and try to get a little more."

"And what do you have to offer in return?"

He thought about the two extra years he once believed his ace in the hole.

"Looks like not a damn thing...right now."

12:17 P.M.

MOODY'S BARBECUE WAS BRENT'S FAVORITE PLACE TO EAT. IT WAS located east of town on Old Post Road, right outside Concord's city limits, a wooden farmhouse hauled across the county years ago just before Eagle Lake was flooded. For the past fifteen years it had housed a restaurant, owned and operated by a retired paperworker, its rustic feel and down-home quality intentional. The menu varied, a choice among beef, pork, or chicken, all served on paper plates wrapped in tinfoil, with two slices of fresh white bread. The sauce, a mustard-based spicy mixture, was what made the place extra special. Just the right blend of sweet and sour. People traveled all the way from Savannah sometimes just for lunch, the mouthwatering aromas strong from the instant customers parked outside.

He met Ashley there a little before noon. She was on her thirty-minute lunch break before beginning afternoon deliveries. He bought them each a quarter-pound plate with mild sauce and RC Colas and they took a seat at one of the picnic tables inside. Each was encrusted with etched carvings and initials, the tabletops long ago evolving into works of art. All part of the charm, like barbecuing in your backyard without the gnats.

"You took your time texting," she said.

He'd waited until nearly ten last night before confirming their date. "I figured you were still at the funeral."

"I left there around eight. It was all so sad. A lot of people came. Papa Evans was well liked. The whole family's pretty ripped up." She spoke with surprising emotion for an ex-wife and ex-daughter-in-law.

He could sympathize with the Evanses. He knew how it was to suddenly lose a father. They ate a few moments in silence.

"You know," Ashley said, "no matter how hard you try, you can't keep avoiding it."

He stared at her as a memory returned.

Those same words, but a different voice.

"You can't keep avoiding it," Paula said again.

He'd driven over to tell her the wedding was off. They were sitting on her parents' front porch, a waft of honeysuckle in the air. Paula looked her usual perfect self. Slacks and blouse. Hair combed and sprayed. Nails lacquered pink. Earrings. A single brooch. The invitations had all been sent, the ceremony scheduled for three Saturdays away. A modest affair with a reception afterward.

But he was having second and third thoughts.

Ashley Reed the main source of his confusion.

"*I assume you're in love again with Annie Oakley,*" *Paula said, like a parent scolding a naughty child.*

"*Does it really matter how I feel?*"

She angled her head toward him. No reverse gear for her, just barrel straight ahead. "*It doesn't matter one bit. What matters is here.*" *She pointed to her washboard tummy.* "*You should have thought about that before you decided to get me pregnant.*"

But he doubted that had been his call.

Their relationship had dragged on two years. They met right after he returned home from law school and opened his practice. A local girl, born and raised, who taught third grade. Ashley had been a continual presence, but her inability to commit never allowed her to be anything more than a momentary diversion. He'd delayed things as long as he could. Finally, two months ago, Paula told him he could stall no more.

A child was on the way.

"*We're going to have a family, Brent. And isn't that more important than Annie Oakley?*"

She was taunting. Seeing how he'd react. A game they played more and more. Paula pushing, he absorbing. Surely, she had it all figured out. The announcement would come after their honeymoon in Cancun. Returning hardly tanned from a week in the Mexican sun, she predicting for her family and friends, with a smile, that the trip may have been productive. It would be her parents' first grandchild, another honor he knew she was intent on snaring from her younger sister who'd just recently married.

"*You can't keep avoiding it,*" *she said.*

"*No, I can't.*"

"*Oh, come on, Brent. It's not a prison sentence. I'm not so bad. You enjoy yourself when we're together.*"

"*I never said I didn't.*"

"*You just want her more.*"

He caught the edge in her voice. "*I never said that either.*"

"You didn't have to." Then she added, *"From what I hear your little pistol is hot after a new husband anyway. And it's not you."*

He'd heard that too. One source of gossip confirming they intended to marry. Characteristically, Ashley had said nothing. She never did. Probably because she really didn't know herself.

"That'd certainly solve your problem," he said.

"I don't have a problem. I'll soon have a loving husband and a baby on the way. We have a beautiful wedding planned and we're going to have a wonderful time in Mexico. What more could a girl want?"

He wanted to say, How about a husband who loves you? But decided silence was better. His choices were limited. And it was his own fault. They weren't kids anymore. Maybe it was time he faced reality. No child of his was going to grow up fatherless.

For once Paula might be right.

He couldn't keep avoiding it.

"I'm not avoiding it," he told Ashley, not exactly sure whom he was answering.

"Then what are you doing?"

"I'm trying to readjust to being back home. To giving up a good job. To pleasing a new employer. To—"

He caught himself. That last one—about helping his mother—he could not talk about.

"To making up for what happened with Paula?" she asked.

He said nothing.

"It can't be done, you know."

He wasn't so sure. But he reminded himself that one of the reasons he'd returned was to give it a try. While in Atlanta he'd thought about Ashley. A lot. That he could not deny. No more obstacles existed between them. If it was going to work, this might be their last chance to try.

"So where are we going Saturday night?" she said.

He swallowed a mouthful of sandwich. "I didn't know we were going anywhere."

She gave him a mischievous smile. "Lori Anne's going to be with her granddaddy. I have the night free."

Why run anymore? He wanted her. She wanted him. Perhaps the debilitating effects of guilt passed with time?

"Then I guess we'll be at your place."

Another smile from her. "My thoughts exactly."

2:15 P.M.

VICTOR JACKS GAZED AT THE CORPSE SLUMPED ON THE WOOL SOFA. His first assignment in his new job as an associate had brought him to rural southwest Georgia and a double-wide belonging to Michael Ottman.

Priority Number 8 from May's list.

He'd read the file yesterday. Ottman, a seventy-one-year-old widower, had both a diseased heart and terminal cancer. After retiring from Southern Republic he'd moved two hundred miles away from Concord to be closer to his daughter, who lived down the dirt road in another double-wide. His retirement benefits were meager but, coupled with Social Security, were enough to allow a solitary life in relative comfort.

Number 8 drew the attention of the board because of an extraordinary number of medical expenses looming on the horizon. During orientation De Florio had explained that retiree health benefits were the most troublesome area for the board to manage. There was literally no way to predict them. Pay-as-you-go was the only course for handling them, and that amounted to financial Russian roulette. Terminal care was particularly expensive. An almost bottomless pit. And Number 8 hadn't helped matters by telling his doctors that he intended to take advantage of every single benefit available.

De Florio had explained about the nearly constant battle that ensued to provide adequate benefits while at the same time ensuring the company's insurance reserve fund remained solvent. There was only one way to succeed. Costs had to be controlled. And in the case of Michael Ottman, a Priority decision seemed the easiest way to avoid the massive out-of-pocket expenditures sure to come, while simultaneously generating savings that could be used on other, less costly, claimants.

Pretty clever, he thought.

He'd fit right into the Priority program. Killing was his profession and De Florio had offered more than enough money to make his devotion to a single employer profitable. Yet that wasn't the only lure. Finally, no more worrying about the next job, concerned whether a client was legitimate or a setup. No more looking over his shoulder, protecting himself from retaliation or retribution.

Now he could simply kill.

But he remembered the lesson De Florio had graphically illustrated yesterday with that bullet to the head of Milo Richey. No mistakes. Everything had to be done precisely according to Rule.

His first assignment had been easy.

A knock on the door, then a squirt of gas for instant unconsciousness. He'd cushioned Ottman's fall to avoid any bruising. A single injection and the heart failed. With Number 8's history no one would think twice about the cause of death. The injection point, deep in the ear canal, would never be noticed by any medical examiner.

De Florio's array of toxins was impressive. The one he'd just used an excellent example. Odorless and tasteless, producing a fatal heart fibrillation in nearly an instant, leaving nothing in plasma or tissue other than a whiff of fluoride that would be attributed to either the local water supply or the last time the decedent brushed his teeth. Nothing for any toxicology tests to discover. And that was assuming any tests would be run, which was unlikely.

Older people just died.

He checked for a pulse through a gloved hand.

None.

The settling of the body and rapid color change provided further corroboration.

Death was verified.

DAY FIVE
SATURDAY, JUNE 10

10:15 A.M.

BRENT WAITED UNTIL THE WEEKEND TO MAKE THE FORTY-MINUTE drive west to Statesboro. He'd wanted to go sooner, but work had commanded his undivided attention all week. What had Joan Bates said? *The prudent sees danger and hides himself, but the simple go on and suffer for it.* He'd done a little more research and learned that the biblical passage was generally thought to mean that clever or sensible people could see trouble coming and avoid it. But the gullible? Or the childish? They just went ahead and suffered the consequences. He wasn't sure which category he supposedly fell into.

Or how those words of wisdom even applied to him.

He hadn't mentioned anything about Joan Bates' visit to anyone, especially his mother or Hank. The woman had sought him out specifically, gone to a lot of trouble actually, so he'd decided to fully investigate before sharing any information. That caution came from being a prosecutor. He'd learned in Atlanta that things worked best when kept close.

Statesboro sat in neighboring Bulloch County. For a long time the town wasn't much. As the story went, during the Civil War a Union officer asked someone for directions to Statesboro. Reportedly, the answer he received was, *"You're standing in the middle of town."* After the war the whole area grew, becoming a major

124

center for cotton and tobacco sales. Today thirty-five thousand people lived and worked there at various manufacturing and distribution centers. But its biggest employer, and main claim to fame, was Georgia Southern University. His alma mater. Twenty thousand students. Home to the Soarin' Eagles. Six-time national football champions. He'd loved going to those games, which he'd continued to attend long after graduation.

A sea of middle-class neighborhoods ringed busy central downtown with a mix of single- and multifamily homes, many of the dwellings rentals catering to students. During his four years at college he hadn't availed himself of the local housing, as he'd lived at home and commuted back and forth. The address he'd obtained from the company records was for one of the newer subdivisions east of town, just off the highway from Concord. The Bates residence was a single-story ranch-style home that filled a wooded lot. He parked on the street and walked toward the front door, passing the same Tahoe that had sat parked in the driveway on Tuesday night. Sprinklers irrigated the front yard.

He pushed the doorbell.

A few moments later the door was opened by the woman who'd confronted him. She was dressed in a button-down shirt and jeans, one hand holding a dish towel. Her manner remained stoic, except for a momentary glimmer of recognition and a brief smile of welcome.

"Good morning, Mrs. Bates," he said to her. "I thought it best you and I talk further."

She stared at him with eyes that almost seemed born to worry. He'd seen that look before in the eyes of victims, along with a severe consternation that flowed across her every feature that signaled only one thing. Pain. She motioned for him to come inside and they sat in an oversized living room with exposed wood beams and a brick fireplace.

"My children are out," she said. "So we have privacy."

He wondered how much this woman had cried during the past four months. She made no attempt to hide her solemnness. None at all. He gave her a moment to compose herself and took in the room, noticing the large crucifix on the wall and an array of family photos framed on a side table. Many with her husband.

"I'm sorry for your loss," he felt compelled to say.

She nodded an acknowledgment.

"Why didn't you just introduce yourself the other night?"

"I thought it best not to."

"Why did you find *me*?"

"I was told you would be replacing Peter at the mill."

"That's the how. I asked why."

"You sound angry."

"I'm confused. Help me understand."

"My husband gave that company many years of his life. He worked hard. He took care of me and our children. He did what a good husband and father was supposed to do."

Again, not an answer. But it seemed there was a lot inside her that needed to bubble out. And he could relate. Plenty of bubbles were percolating inside him too.

"Did you read Proverbs 22:3?" she asked.

"I did."

"A good husband will repair his house while the weather is fair, and not put it off till winter," she said. "A careful pilot will take advantage of wind and tide, and put out to sea before a storm arises." She spoke in a cold monotone. Like someone on some serious medication. "We must make every day the day of our repentance. To make good use of our time, so that when we come to die we may have nothing to do but to die."

She was speaking as if to someone far off. He stayed quiet and let her talk.

"Your new job will kill you," she said.

And her sad eyes hardened even more.

He had to ask, "In what way?"

"Are you married?"

He shook his head. "I was. But she killed herself."

He hoped that commonality might drop some of the barriers between them.

"Then you know exactly what I'm feeling."

He nodded. "It was eleven years ago. And I still feel the pain."

"Did you have any idea she might take her life?"

Not a question he'd ever been asked before, by anyone. Mainly because only a few knew the truth about Paula's death. But he'd certainly asked himself that a thousand times. The truth? "I had no idea at all. But the tendency ran in her family."

"Peter's too. He was so strong in many ways, and so weak in others. But I never thought he'd leave me or his children."

He decided to try again. "What did you mean by Proverbs 22:3? *The prudent sees danger and hides himself, but the simple go on and suffer for it.*"

"It's not always smart to be headstrong. Sometimes the smarter course is to avoid a bad situation altogether."

"Why does any of that apply to me?"

"My husband was a fragile man who refused to seek solace with Christ, and chose instead to rely on the perils of man."

"So you learned my name and address and came to see me on my first day back in town to warn me that unless I seek the Lord, my job will kill me?"

"I prayed hard first. Then God told me I should do it."

He could see she believed every word. "What else did God tell you?"

"To give yourself freely to heaven. To allow Christ to lead you. My husband could not do that. Can you?"

He didn't answer her. Because his beliefs were none of her business.

"You don't have the Lord in your life?" she asked.

Apparently, what he'd at first thought was a genuine warning about something unknown was nothing more than a grieving widow trying to find some semblance of peace wherever she could. Be that with the Bible, God, or attaching herself to a total stranger.

He'd seen it before in the faces of clients looking for something or someone to blame.

This had been a waste of time.

He stood. "I should go."

She reached out and gripped his arm. He froze and stared down at her, suddenly realizing that being alone here with this woman was not a good thing. This could take a bad bounce. So he told her, "I believe."

"Then pray with me. For my husband. And for you."

He felt for her. How could he not. And he understood the shock, anger, guilt, despair, confusion, and rejection. All those emotions had been triggered inside him by Paula's death. He'd never sought any professional help. Instead, he'd used time and the isolation of moving hundreds of miles away to get through the aftermath. This woman had tried the same with her own move.

But what else could be done to help her?

Not much, probably.

So what would it hurt?

"I'd be honored to pray with you."

12:15 P.M.

HANK DRIED OFF.

He'd added the swimming pool a dozen summers ago, eliminating just enough of the pines and live oaks so the screened enclosure now swallowed the majority of his already compact backyard. A luxury, and definitely out of character for the blue-collar image of a working stiff he went out of his way to perpetuate. But given the length and intensity of the Georgia summers, what he called *the twenty thousand gallons of chlorinated water held in place by a kidney-shaped concrete hole* became an understandable necessity.

He tossed the towel aside and slipped on a terry-cloth robe. He swam every evening after getting home from work and many times on the weekend. Living alone came with the privilege of doing what he wanted, when he wanted. Loretta had loved the pool and used it far more than he ever did. But after she was gone he came to enjoy it too. A day late and a dollar short. Which seemed the story of his life.

He sat and grabbed the clipboard off an adjacent table. Attached to it were hard copies of the documents Marlene had been lucky enough to snag from the company records. The memo from Hamilton Lee was downright shocking. Southern Republic's lack of interest in any five-year deal was totally unexpected. He'd surely thought the company would again want those extra two years. His plan all along had been to trade for things like a percentage increase on wages and more benefits, then force a five-year agreement onto his membership. What was he going to do now? Take his people out on strike? Hardly.

In all the years of Southern Republic ownership no local had ever walked. That was bad for the company. Bad for the members. Bad for Concord.

He heard a car motor into the driveway. The screen door opened and Brent walked onto the pool deck. He was dressed in shorts and a Georgia Southern T-shirt. Tennis shoes protected his feet.

"What brings you by?" he asked.

"Did you know Peter Bates?"

"I had a few dealings with him. Not all that much. He did little with the unions. The general counsel handled us."

"Was there anything at all suspicious about his death?"

"That's an odd question. Should there be?"

"I'm just asking."

He shook his head. "He shot himself. The sheriff told me it was clear as a bell. Nothing about anything raised any questions. Why the interest?"

He listened as Brent told him about the visit from Joan Bates and his own visit, earlier, with her.

"Now, Joan I did know," he told Brent. "She was a regular at church. A real Bible thumper. Peter? Not so much a churchgoer. But her? Everybody knew Joan was one of the faithful. If you didn't, she'd remind you every chance she got."

"As she did with me."

"You prayed with her?"

"I knelt with her. She got intense. I think she was speaking in tongues for a little bit."

He chuckled. "That's Joan. She's been known to do it with the pews full. I think it may be one of the reasons she moved away, after Peter died. Don't let her get to you. She's harmless."

"The whole thing was a little weird," Brent said. "But I had to check it out."

He nodded. "I agree. And as long as you're in an inquisitive mood, take a look at this."

He handed over the clipboard, the pages peeled back to the odd list of numbers he and Marlene had retrieved Tuesday night.

034156901
456913276
343016692
295617833
178932515
236987521
492016755
516332578

"What do you think they are?" he asked.

Brent studied them for a moment. "Couldn't be phone numbers, too many digits. Might be zip codes. The new ones are longer." Brent counted. "There are enough numbers for a zip code. Where'd you get these?"

"Off the company computer."

"They just dropped into your lap?"

"Actually, that's exactly what happened. Fluke of nature."

Brent smiled. "In another words, don't ask, don't tell."

"Something like that."

"In that case they could be company ID numbers, file numbers, computer access codes, even passwords. God knows they change them enough. I was told that happens once a week." Brent looked at the list again. "They also could be Social Security numbers? But no hyphens. Social Security numbers are always broken apart. So are the new zip codes."

He came to the point. "Can you do me a favor and see what you can find on 'em?"

"Hank, you're putting me in a bad place. I owe the company loyalty. And confidentiality. You know that."

He held up his hands. "I know. I know. But you have access to personnel records, medical records, all sorts of things. It's probably nothing. But could you take a look so I can be sure." He paused. "For old times' sake."

He could see that Brent knew he was holding back. Just asking for this level of favor was enough of an indication that there was more involved.

"Tell me the truth," Brent said. "How did you get these numbers?"

"Or else?" he asked.

"Or else."

He had no choice. But there was no one he trusted more. "They were behind a firewall in an ultra-secure file. It was a fluke my person got in. They'd been trying for weeks, without success. So you can see why I'm so curious."

"Marlene?"

He nodded. "It could cost her job, if she's caught."

"Then why put her in that position?"

"It's her way. She loves the intrigue."

"And she's a little sweet on you too?"

"Has my daughter been tellin' you things?"

"Her and others. You're quite the topic of the local gossip."

Always in the past they'd been a team, delivering a solid one-two punch. One leading, the other following, depending on the fight. But things had changed. Brent worked for the other side now. And no matter how much he hated that fact, he had to respect it.

To a point.

"Look, they could be nothing at all," he said. "Just some mumbo jumbo that's irrelevant to anything I need to be concerned about. But the level of security protecting them makes me curious. Do this. Take a look. If what you find crosses any ethical line with your newfound position as a company lawyer, then don't tell me a thing. Keep it to yourself. But if it's nothin' at all—just some crap—you can tell me that, can't you? To put my mind at ease."

Hank could see that he'd gotten to his old buddy.

Logic is your friend. Use it.

"Sure," Brent said. "I can do that."

DAY SEVEN
MONDAY, JUNE 12

8:05 A.M.

CHRIS MARCHED ACROSS THE BLUE TOWER'S TWENTY-NINTH FLOOR, away from management's corner, to the cadre of offices that accommodated the company's sales force and chief of security.

Jon De Florio's office didn't share the prestige he, Lee, and Hughes enjoyed, but it was respectable and the position came with two subordinates and an administrative assistant. More than enough help to accommodate the meager responsibilities the official position actually entailed.

He noticed the assistant's desk was empty. He and De Florio were often first in every morning. So he stopped at the open doorway to the private office.

"You've come a long way," he quietly said.

De Florio, framed by an overcast morning filtered even grayer by the tinted glass, looked up from what he was reading.

"It's been, what, fifteen years? You've done a lot here."

"The Priority program is on a steady course," De Florio said in his characteristic low voice.

"Not like in the beginning, huh? Prioritizing was so haphazard. We never considered pattern, variation, or verification. Those little things that make all the difference. But you fixed that, Jon. The Rules you fashioned have proven sound. The program's success is directly attributable to your efforts."

"I appreciate that, Mr. Bozin. I've tried to do a good job."

He stepped inside. "Do you like your position, Jon?"

"This office, my title, yes, they're measures of respectability my actual profession never enjoys."

He liked that there was no pretense between them. No secrets either. "I've noticed that you spend more time in here than you used to."

De Florio nodded. "I've been devoting more attention to my public position. My associates are competent and handle the Priority orders efficiently. They don't need me standing over them. That's one reason I requested the third associate earlier this year."

"I understand you're back to two again?"

"Unfortunately, I had to terminate the employment of one."

"Will the loss be a problem?"

"I'm already looking for another, and should have somebody in place by August. Luckily, background files on the three new Priorities approved a few days ago were generated in April. It's the pre-work that consumes the time. On-site surveillance. Records review. My associates devote about eighty percent of their time to file generation and twenty percent to actual processing."

"But that eighty percent is time well spent."

De Florio nodded. "There's a proven correlation between a successful processing and a thorough file."

He was impressed with how effortlessly the man sitting across from him discussed murder.

"And," De Florio said, "with union negotiations approaching, I assume there will be a one- to two-month lull in any new Priority approval, as in the past."

"A safe assumption. Negotiations tend to consume everyone's attention, at least for a while. Realistically, it will be July before any new names are added to the list." He motioned to the mail and files stacked on one corner. "You seem to have a lot to do."

"I haven't gone through this stuff in days. I've been busy with the processings from May's list and overseeing the training of the new associate."

He smiled. "I'll let you get back to your work. Didn't mean to interrupt."

He left the office and headed back to management's corner, satisfied with what he'd learned. De Florio and only two associates.

Until August.

Perfect.

8:20 A.M.

JON TURNED HIS ATTENTION TO THE STACK OF PAPER ON HIS DESK, realizing that was perhaps the longest conversation he'd ever had with Christopher Bozin.

He wasn't fond of the administrative prattle associated with his job, usually passing most of that on to his assistant. Some things, though, couldn't be delegated, simply for appearances' sake, and he started shuffling through the various memoranda that required his initials.

Most were reports from his two subordinates. He gave a few a cursory glance. One concerned the resolution of a troublesome theft situation at the Concord bag plant that had cost the company thousands of dollars. Half a dozen more involved personnel changes that required his approval. Since the fiscal year expired on June 30, the security department's budget submission, prepared by his admin assistant, was there for review. But a memo at the bottom of the stack captured his undivided attention.

```
TO: J. De Florio
FROM: Computer Systems at Concord mill
DATE: June 9
RE: Power Surge / Security Breach?
A routine check of main computer core revealed
electrical damage to the secured access circuits.
Power interruptions were reported during
thunderstorms this week. No specific damage was
noted but a circuit board was found charred.
```

```
Perhaps from a lightning strike. Power surge
protectors did trigger and are thought to have
insulated the system. However, there could have
been a drop in the secured access system allowing
entry into the secured files for a short period
(approximately 1 to 2 minutes). Time of day
makes any actual access unlikely. Most storms
peaked after 9:00 P.M. when the vast majority of
terminals with potential access were not in use.
Wanted to make you aware of the possibility.
```

What day of the week had this happened?

The memo was dated last Friday and did not specify anything except *this week*.

He grabbed the phone, dialed Concord, and got the sender on the line, keeping his voice calm and cordial. "I received your memo on the possibility of a secured file access. You talk about power interruptions during storms last week. Exactly what day of the week was that?"

"It's hard to say, but the worst storm occurred last Tuesday, the sixth, which probably accounted for the damage. But there were storms on Wednesday and Thursday also."

"Any evidence of entry into the secured files?"

"Not from our end. But there wouldn't be. We rely on the secured access system for protection. Of course, the individual terminals would keep a record in their directories of any file entry."

"Do we know which terminals were operating during the storms?"

"We didn't go that far. And I really wasn't going to. No maintenance requests came from any department. We don't even know if there was a breach. Even if there was, it would have lasted only a minute or two at most. The odds of access at that time of day are pretty slim."

"I'm sure you're right," he said for his listener's benefit only, "and I appreciate your thoroughness. But why did it take a week to detect this?"

"No breakdown occurred and, for some reason, the backup system didn't trigger any control panel alerts. Which, by the way, may also suggest that the system itself never failed. That's why I said *could have* in the memo and put the question mark on the 're' line. The actual damage was found only when we physically went into the system on Friday to do some routine work. Once it was brought to my attention, I thought I should report it. Odds are, my people tell me, no access into the secured system occurred at all."

He thanked the man and hung up.

But he was not as convinced.

9:25 A.M.

HAMILTON LEE WAS CHANGING HIS CLOTHES IN THE MARBLE bathroom adjacent to his office, replacing his Armani suit with a knit shirt and Ralph Lauren golf slacks.

"What's the problem," he called out, as De Florio walked into his office and closed the door.

He stepped from the bathroom.

"The computer systems people have reported a possible breakdown of the secured access code that protects the board's personal files, including Priority. The breakdown may have occurred last Tuesday during a thunderstorm in Concord. The same day Marlene Rhoden worked late and stole the memos we left for her to find."

"And you believe she may have gotten into the secured files?"

"The thought crossed my mind."

"Any proof?"

"Not in our system. But her terminal could tell us for sure."

"What makes you think she even tried to access the Priority files?"

"Years of being paranoid."

137

He smiled. He wasn't as concerned as De Florio seemed to be, but he wasn't foolish either. "Check it out."

"My thought, too. Do you wish a suspension on the processing of the remainder from May's list in the meantime?"

"How's that progressing?"

"Numbers 6 and 8 are fully done. Seven will be shortly."

He considered the request, but he had an 11:30 tee time and had to be finished with golf by four. His wife had made that clear. It was the start of the summer social season and she did not want to be late for the first event this evening. And he did not want to lose the dollars gained from that last Priority.

Every penny counted.

"Go ahead and finish."

12:55 P.M.

CHRIS WAS DRESSED IN A POLKA-DOT GOWN, OPEN IN THE BACK, identical to one he'd worn most of the weekend. He was in his doctor's posh downtown Atlanta office, on the fifteenth floor of a medical building adjacent to Crawford W. Long Hospital. He'd spent the weekend having tests. Today a couple more were required. But thankfully, they could be performed in the office.

It had been two years ago, during a routine physical, that another doctor first noticed the mass. A subsequent biopsy confirmed that his prostate harbored cancerous cells. At his insistence a conservative treatment had been employed involving a drug combination designed merely to check any spreading. He'd vetoed surgery, not wanting to draw attention. Luckily, the drugs were somewhat successful and subsequent tests confirmed that the cancer seemed contained. But that situation had changed over the past few weeks.

"I'm not going to bullshit you, Chris. The tests confirm that the prostate-specific antigen is in your blood at disturbing levels. The physical exam and X-rays show radical enlargement. The cancer's back and it's spread. Definitely to the bladder, the adjacent bone, lymph nodes, maybe further. It's not good. The unconventional approach you took gave it more time to metastasize."

"What are the survival odds at my age?"

"Unfortunately, it appears to be fast growing. The prognosis, at best, is no more than a year. Probably more like five or six months. A year ago we could have removed the prostate and testicles, but that won't help anymore. Too much spreading. There's radiation and chemotherapy, but the side effects can be worse than the disease."

He absorbed the death sentence. "You're telling me there's really nothing to be done."

"I'm sorry, Chris. Telling someone they're going to die is the toughest thing I do as a doctor, especially to a friend."

He'd heard enough. What more was there to say? He slid off the examining table and shook the man's hand. "I appreciate everything you've done. I'll be in touch if I have any problems."

Fifteen minutes later, after dressing, he left the office and shuffled toward the floor's elevator bank. He pushed the DOWN button and patiently waited for a car to arrive. He'd heard nothing he hadn't already suspected. He was going to die. And there was nothing he could do about it. Though he could not say the words, he'd chosen his course of treatment with the idea that he would ultimately die from the disease.

And fast.

He visualized the impertinent smirk Hamilton Lee perpetually wore, evidence of the perverse pleasure Lee seemed to get from thinking himself in charge. And Larry Hughes. That puppy-dog personality that allowed Lee the luxury of consistently outvoting him. He remembered the beginning. How he found the money while the one, not much more than an okay manager, and the other, only a moderately successful salesman, indiscriminately spent it. They were both total failures as executives. If he hadn't done what he did the whole venture would have bankrupted long ago. Now, thanks to his failing body, they could reap the full harvest from the seeds he'd so carefully sowed. That thought bothered him more than dying.

But what could he do about it?

Only De Florio and two associates. Until August.

That meant De Florio was shorthanded. Seemed ideal. He'd been thinking of what to do for weeks. No more.

Time to act.

He turned, reentered the doctor's office, approached the receptionist window, and asked to speak to the billing clerk. His name should be familiar, as he was one of the few patients her boss allowed to pay later. Everyone else either was covered by insurance or paid as they went, a sign tacked to the wall next to the window affirmatively proclaiming PAYMENT FOR SERVICES TO BE SATISFIED WHEN RENDERED.

The woman approached from the other side of the glass and he politely explained that he did not want either the office visit or the hospital time from the previous weekend billed to him.

Instead, for the first time ever, he handed her his Southern Republic insurance card.

8:36 P.M.

THE LEARJET LIFTED OFF THE RUNWAY AT ATLANTA'S HARTSFIELD-Jackson and climbed into the darkening sky. The ride started bumpy, summer thermals playing havoc, but the advantage of jet engines and a pressurized cabin allowed a quick escape above the cloud deck.

Jon settled into one of the comfy seats and enjoyed the flight, content with the luxury of a twin-engine jet that he knew cost millions of dollars. It was one of Southern Republic's many toys. This one particularly impressive. Cordovan leather interior, wraparound stereo system, digital television, and full, in-flight internet access. Two pilots were employed around-the-clock, the aircraft routinely used by the board and company officers for both business and pleasure. Hamilton Lee liked it as a way to impress a new mistress. Larry Hughes appreciated the speed in which he could get to his Smoky Mountain hideaway. It had proven particularly convenient for quick trips to Concord since the nearest commercial service was seventy miles south in Savannah. Yet Jon rarely utilized the amenity. His line of work called for a more covert form of travel. In and out, unnoticed. That was generally by car. But tonight he needed to get to Concord quickly, and didn't have time to drive the nearly four hours it took.

Forty minutes later the jet descended.

The Woods County airport was nothing more than two metal buildings and a single concrete runway. Even so, the facility was a vast improvement over the stretch of open field that had served the area in the years before Southern Republic's arrival. He knew that during Hank Reed's tenure at city hall the company had lobbied hard for the creation of the Concord Airport Authority to finance needed improvements, revenue bonds eventually issued that paid for upgrades, most notably the concrete strip, two hangars, a fuel depot, and lights to allow night use.

The jet's wheels kissed the asphalt.

Three minutes later the aircraft was nestled inside the hangar Southern Republic leased from the authority, engines whining down. He stepped from the plane and headed straight for the Ford F-150 the company kept on hand. He drove six miles east to the mill, Southern Republic Boulevard nearly deserted. Evening shift wouldn't end until 11:00 P.M. Then a procession of mill cars would cruise in and out, graveyard shift arriving for another night's work to morning.

He passed through the main gate. The night security supervisor was there and quickly provided a status report he cared nothing about. Ten minutes later he excused himself, ostensibly to take a walk around and observe. Through the years he'd deliberately fostered a reputation for liking to see his department's operation firsthand. Many times he appeared at the mill and bag plant, at all hours of the day and night. Twice he'd fired a guard caught sleeping. Tonight's visit would simply be chalked up to another one of his surprise inspections.

He walked straight to administrative Building A. Beyond, the mill blazed with light and smoke, its intricate combination of concrete and steel unaffected by time or weather.

And it wasn't a quiet beast.

The roar from three churning paper machines blared even from several hundred yards away. He'd often thought it akin to working inside an internal combustion engine running at full power. He stared up at the towering main smokestack piercing the night sky, a dark plume of precipitant rising that, despite multi-million-dollar scrubbers, wafted of sulfur.

Building A loomed quiet. Prior to leaving Atlanta he'd checked the overtime roster and learned that none had been authorized past 6:00 P.M. Which was exactly why he'd waited until now for a visit. He'd brought a master key, so it was easy to enter through the front doors.

Inside, he hopped the granite stairs two at a time.

The third floor was occupied almost exclusively by the industrial relations department. At the door marked DATA ENTRY he again used his master key. The shadowy room harbored four desks, computer terminals, and a row of filing cabinets. He switched on no overhead lights, more than enough illumination spilling in from the mill through the open blinds. He headed straight to Marlene Rhoden's workstation and jerked the plastic cover off her monitor. He switched on the machine and entered the appropriate commands to display the hard drive directory.

The screen lit up with a long list arranged chronologically.

He scrolled down for last week's dates. On June 6 the directory indicated that an access file had been created at 10:05 P.M. The next entry showed a copy made of UNION from the INTERCORP subdirectory in the central banks. He recognized UNION as the file containing the memos Hamilton Lee had planted, hoping Rhoden would find them. The next entry indicated that a copy had been made.

The notation immediately after was the problem.

At 10:11 P.M., the directory revealed that another access file was created. But this time from the SECURED FOLDER. He was aware that one of the files in the SECURED FOLDER, tucked deep behind a heavy firewall, was titled PRIORITY. Most disturbingly, Rhoden had labeled her own access file with the same designation. Unfortunately, the directory was not detailed enough to indicate if the entire thing had been copied, but the next entry confirmed that a copy of something had been made. So he assumed at least part, if not all, of the PRIORITY folder had been breached.

He'd seen enough.

Fear just became reality.

Maybe it was what Lee had told him about Hank Reed. Maybe it was just his inbred paranoia. No matter.

They now had a much more serious problem than a nosy union president trying to make a deal.

DAY EIGHT
TUESDAY, JUNE 13

7:03 A.M.

HUNTING IN GEORGIA REQUIRED A LICENSE. THERE WERE RULES. Regulations. Specific times of year when specific things could be killed.

And all with defined limits.

None of that mattered to Paul Zimmerman, who loved to roam the wetlands bordering Eagle Lake for hogs.

Several good reasons accounted for why Zimmerman loved to hunt hogs. First, they were unregulated, so there was no need to obtain a license just for the privilege of killing one. Second, there was no season, which meant he didn't have to worry about the game warden every time he got the urge to hunt. Third, and somewhat most important, the carcasses provided a bountiful supply of meat. And with a wife and five children to feed, Zimmerman made good use of fresh pork chops, sausage, and, his personal favorite, chitlins.

Provided, of course, that hogs could be found to kill.

According to the file, though, Paul Zimmerman, Priority Number 7, knew how to find hogs. He was skilled at spotting their tracks, scenting their droppings, and following their trails. He was also intimately familiar with the forests of northwestern Woods County and southwestern Screven County, particularly Solomon Swamp, where boars and sows loved to congregate.

And what hog wouldn't?

Plenty of trees, a bountiful supply of nuts and berries, and extensive wetlands fed by the nearby Ogeechee River. Paul Zimmerman spent at least a couple of days each month roaming the murky expanse.

Which Frank Barnard knew.

After returning from west Georgia and his successful rendezvous with Melvin Bennett, Barnard had checked the company personnel rosters over the weekend and learned that Tuesday was Zimmerman's rotation day. The twenty-four hours allocated so the body could readjust to the coming rigors of staying up all night. Zimmerman worked shift at the mill, particularly graveyard, the hourly bonuses paid for pulling all-nighters a big help with the family bills. He was scheduled to start back on graveyard shift tomorrow. Another week of working 11:00 to 7:00, sleeping all day, then stretching the evenings into chores around the house and time with his kids.

Barnard had been perched in the tree stand nearly an hour waiting on Priority Number 7. Summer engulfed the weathered boards in a wall of aromatic pine resin, the thick needles ideal cover, the stand sitting high among a cluster of tall pines in Solomon Swamp's higher ground. The morning air was stifling, the ground moisture only magnifying the discomfort. Luckily, he was high enough that the mosquitoes had yet to find him, but the yellow flies were out in force.

The file on Paul Zimmerman stressed several varied places the man loved to hunt, but Barnard had taken a calculated chance that Zimmerman would use his day off to head for Solomon Swamp.

Which was exactly what Number 7 had done.

An hour ago he'd discreetly followed when Zimmerman left his house in Concord. Fortunately, the Priority did not bring any of his dogs, as they would have added complications in processing. Once sure of Zimmerman's ultimate destination, he'd rushed ahead and stealthily made his way to the northern part of the swamp, hustling to take up a position in the stand. Per procedure, yesterday he'd cleared the method of processing with De Florio.

"A hunting accident is the only viable method that will not raise suspicion," he'd said.

"Is there no other way?"

The tone of De Florio's question had suggested he was considering his proposal.

"The man's healthy. No illnesses or afflictions. Anything medical would raise questions. Unfortunately, accidental is the only way, something related to hunting the most logical."

"All right," his boss finally said.

He felt he should add, *"Frankly, Mr. De Florio, this Priority should not have been approved with the rest. Too many risks."*

"I agree," was the only comment before the line went dead.

He caught sight of a bit of orange in the distance.

Through field glasses he watched Zimmerman push his way north through the vegetation toward the thicker swamp near the Ogeechee. He'd fully scouted the area yesterday. The wrinkled cedars and saw palmettos that thrived in the soupy soil close to the river would have provided him little cover. Farther east was where he'd discovered the deer stand and its convenient proximity to a defined trail. It was a gamble as to the ultimate choice of route and, if wrong, he would have to track Zimmerman down and shoot him on the ground. But with the Priority now in sight that risky venture wouldn't be necessary.

He set the binoculars aside and cradled the rifle, focusing through the telescopic scope. A high-pressure sound suppressor bulged at the long barrel's end.

What would happen afterward?

A hunting accident would be high on the list of possibilities. The local sheriff's department and the Georgia Department of Natural Resources would send people who would ultimately determine that the shot came from a certain direction and above. How could they not? He'd left more than sufficient breadcrumbs for them to follow. That was the thing about his line of work. Make it believable and plausible and most will go where you want them to go.

Zimmerman was a hundred yards away, the orange vest winking in and out among the ground cover.

Hunters sometimes shot one another.

Seventy-five yards.

It happened all the time. Especially in dense woods like this.

He brought the rifle level and aimed through the scope. Orange filled the center of the crosshairs. He waited until Zimmerman drew closer.

Fifty yards.

He squeezed the trigger. A slight jolt, then a faint pop accompanied the round leaving the barrel. An instant later Zimmerman's skull shattered in an explosion of blood and brains.

The body dropped to the ground.

He lowered the rifle.

Damn, he was a good shot.

7:15 A.M.

BRENT FELT A LITTLE STRANGE WITH THE TOPIC OF CONVERSATION.

"Did you spend the night?" Hank asked.

"No. But it was late when I got home."

They filled a booth at Billy's having breakfast. The diner was a downtown Concord landmark, a monument to glass, linoleum, and grease. Brent was working on the Split Rise Special—two eggs over easy, grits, toast, and coffee—and Hank wanted to know all about his Saturday night with Ashley.

"Aren't you supposed to be after me with a shotgun or something, defending the honor of your daughter?"

"Little late for that, isn't it?"

He chuckled. "You could say that."

"What did your mother say when you got in?"

"She was asleep. But she wouldn't have said anything."

"You need to talk to her," Hank said. "She might could help."

He'd ignored that advice once before, years ago, but couldn't resist saying, "I remember somebody else here who wouldn't listen to anyone either."

Hank seemed to instantly know what he meant. "You were right. I should have handled things with Loretta different. I screwed up. I admit it. And lost a wife along the way. But don't you make the same mistake."

He knew all about the regret Hank harbored, allowing selfishness to ruin his marriage. The only thing that eventually grabbed his friend's attention was when his wife told him she'd fallen in love with another man and was leaving. No anger. No hard feelings. No nothing. Just over. He recalled Hank coming to him dazed. Reality had hit home like the blare of an air raid siren. A week later he drew up the divorce papers that quietly ended their long marriage.

Hank was wrong about one thing, though. He really couldn't talk to his mother about any of this, not with what she was about to endure. The prognosis was not good. The doctors had said her mind would gradually slip away. It could take a few years, and medication could help, but there was little that could be done to stop it. He hadn't said a thing to anyone on the subject and debated telling Hank, but decided against it. So he simply said, "Mom doesn't need to be involved in this."

"You might be surprised. Give her a chance."

He wondered about the full court press. Hank rarely did anything without a thought-through purpose.

"I should have kept my ass in Atlanta," he said. "I knew this would happen with Ashley. It's really hard for me to shake things."

"You didn't kill Paula. She killed herself."

"I never should have said what I did."

"But it was the truth."

"It should have been said years before."

Actually it had been, in a variety of ways, but Paula never listened to what she did not want to hear. Only on that last day had her ears opened.

"May God forgive me, Hank, but a part of me was relieved when she died. Ending it with her would have been hell. She would have made sure of that. I still hate myself for feeling that way."

"Time to get real, Brent. Isn't that what you told me once? Paula was selfish. You two were always oil and water. That marriage was based on one thing, and you know it."

That it was.

Two weeks after they returned from the honeymoon, Paula lost the baby. He always wondered if that had been intentional or a true act of God. They resolved to try again but, thankfully, no success ever came.

They'd definitely been oil and water.

His idea of a night at home was like last Saturday. He and Ashley had curled under a blanket on the back porch and watched the stars, talking like they used to. Sure, every night couldn't be like that, but was it a sin if they happened along every once in a while? He could not remember a time when he and Paula shared such intimacy. Their relationship seemed more like roommates than spouses. Just making love became an ordeal of hygiene and etiquette. Most of their weekend nights had been consumed at functions where a room full of people small-talked their way to midnight. Paula had loved the social life. He'd hated it.

"You've got to let this go," Hank said.

"I never should have let things go that far."

"Don't you think the time for repentance is over? It's been eleven friggin' years."

He said nothing.

But Hank could see right through him. "Don't bullshit me. You came back here to let it go."

That's right. He had. But he still wasn't ready to openly admit that.

Not yet.

"On a different subject," Hank said. "Did you look into those numbers I gave you?"

He was hoping Hank had forgotten about them. "Not yet."

"I need you to do that. Per the terms we agreed upon."

He knew the right answer.

"Okay. Soon."

9:20 A.M.

JON CALMLY REPORTED WHAT HE FOUND IN CONCORD. HE WAS sitting in Hamilton Lee's Blue Tower office. He'd been waiting for Lee to arrive at work since 7:30.

"This is a problem," Lee said. "A big problem."

"I tried to find you last evening but was unsuccessful."

"I was out," Lee said, volunteering nothing more about his night.

"I could not suspend further processing without your approval, based on what you said yesterday."

"Is the list complete?"

"The final Priority, Number 7, was processed an hour ago."

"Any problems?"

"A hunting accident." While he was on the subject he went ahead and made a full report. "Number 6 was processed last Friday. Number 8 the same day. Only the hunting accident occurred in Woods County, the two others were scattered around the state. I'd like to point out that I was forced to okay two accidental deaths in one locale for the same month. That violates Rule."

"You worry too much, Jon."

And you worry too little, he thought.

He resented the cavalier attitude Lee took on Priority decisions. This was not something trivial. People were being murdered, and he didn't particularly want to be caught. Yet he realized most of Lee's nonchalance could be Jon's own fault. He'd made the program so efficient that success had come to be expected, no matter what the risks.

"Look, Jon, there's nothing connecting those two deaths. They're two tragic accidents, things that happen from time to time. The local funeral homes should be grateful. I think Hughes owns one of them in Concord, doesn't he? Right now, I'm far more worried about our immediate problem. Is there any indication what, if anything, was accessed from Marlene Rhoden's terminal?"

"The directory noted only from what folder in the central banks the information originated. I checked the SECURED FOLDER this morning. On June 6 it contained one file. May's list of eight authorized Priorities."

"Even assuming the file was copied, a list of eight numbers would mean nothing. It could easily be seen as some kind of work file."

"Until it's deciphered."

"Assuming someone cares enough to do that," Lee said.

"You told me yourself Hank Reed is clever. Maybe he's clever enough to want to decipher the list?"

"He may not even have it."

He detected a hint of hope in the last statement and couldn't resist. "As I recall, last week you were positive Reed had the memo we planted. If he has that, then he has the list."

10:00 A.M.

CHRIS SENSED HAMILTON LEE WAS AGITATED, AND THE SIGHT BOTH pleased and interested him. They were in the boardroom on the thirtieth floor, engaged in a special meeting, originally called to discuss the upcoming union negotiations, but another subject now seemed of greater urgency.

"We have a problem," Lee said.

Then he listened as his partner reported what De Florio had found.

"This is our first breach in the program," Hughes noted.

"Alleged breach. We have no idea if anyone actually has the Priority list."

"Why did you find it necessary to plant memos in the system for Reed to find?" Chris asked. "I don't recall us approving such a tactic."

"During the last negotiations it became obvious that Reed accessed the system and used our own cost projections against us. The idea of that happening again galled me, so I decided to turn it around to our advantage."

"What exactly did you do?"

"I wrote a memo instructing our Concord people that we weren't interested in a five-year deal. I told them it wasn't worth the trouble and to take three years when offered, but try and get takebacks for the concession."

He understood. "You figured if Reed knew that, he'd come to us and offer five years on a silver platter. Those two years are his strongest bargaining chip."

Lee nodded. "And when he made that offer, the cost would be far less than last time."

"Since Reed would figure we didn't give a damn about five years to start with."

"Seemed like a good plan."

Actually it was, and Lee was clearly proud of himself for thinking of it.

"What if he doesn't offer to get those two years for us?" Chris asked.

"He will. I know Hank."

"Come on, Chris," Hughes said. "That whole move was damn smart."

"Maybe. But no vote was taken on that strategy."

"That's right," Lee said. "I made the decision on my own."

"And because of that somebody got into the secured folders and may have enough evidence to indict us all for mass murder."

"How could I know there'd be storm damage to the system at the precise time someone was trying to nibble on my bait?"

He wasn't backing down this time. "You invited someone to snoop in the computer. That comes with clear risk."

Lee shook his head. "Reed was going to do that anyway. I only left something for him to find."

"What's being done about the problem?"

"I've directed De Florio to find out whether Reed has the list and, if so, what he knows about it. I didn't ask how he proposes to do that, nor do I want to know. Jon will take care of it, like he always does."

"And what of May's list?" he asked.

"Fully processed, with no problems, including the three approved at our last meeting."

His mind raced, more pieces of the plan he'd conceived fitting into place. "Needless to say, I assume we're in agreement to suspend any further Prioritizing until this matter is resolved."

Neither objected, then Hughes changed the subject. "What about the negotiations? How are we going to handle things this time?"

Chris had been waiting for a mention. "I have to be at the mill for the close of the fiscal year. I thought I could put in the customary appearance by ownership."

"I have no objection to that," Lee said.

"Nor I," Hughes said.

No surprise on either count. Though industrial relations lay within Hughes' sphere of supervision, he routinely delegated all the responsibility to subordinates. Similarly, whenever negotiation time came around Lee looked for an excuse not to spend two weeks cooped up in Woods County. They both also probably figured the three hundred miles between Atlanta and Concord would get him out of their hair, at least for a while.

He knew what he had to say. "I'll get the five years, as cheap as I can."

"You should be able to get them for only agreeing to no takebacks," Hughes said. "Reed will be happy to settle for what he's got right now. The status quo is good for all of us."

"Assuming he doesn't have the list and doesn't know what it is."

Neither one of them said a word.

"I'll keep both of you informed as to my progress." But he had no intention of doing any such thing. What he did need, "Hamilton, have Jon report directly to me in Concord what he finds

concerning the list. I also want Brent Walker involved in the negotiations. I may need to use him with Reed. I want him close by.
Please arrange for that to happen."

10:50 A.M.

CHRIS STOOD ALONE BEFORE THE OUTER GLASS IN HIS OFFICE.

The meeting had adjourned a few minutes ago after more decisions on how to handle the upcoming negotiations. All three men
had promptly left the boardroom and returned to their respective
offices on the twenty-ninth floor.

It was not even noon, yet his abdomen ached. It seemed to start
earlier and earlier each day.

He gazed down over the morning traffic, thinking again about
the Priority program. A long time had passed since it started. Then
its victims were simply aggravations, problems that seemed to
constantly jeopardize a tenuous investment. The first one?

How could he forget.

Robbie Shuman.

"I'm sick and tired of hearing about Robbie Shuman," Lee said
again.

*They were in the middle of the monthly board meeting, crowded
around an oval table in a tiny conference room, part of the space
the corporation leased in one of downtown Atlanta's older office
buildings. The* Savannah Morning News *lay before them, its front
page headlined* PAPER COMPANY UNDER FEDERAL SCRUTINY, *the article anything but flattering.*

> Federal authorities have confirmed an investigation has
> been started into the air emissions and water discharge
> activities of Southern Republic Pulp and Paper Company.
> The Atlanta based corporation purchased the Concord,
> Georgia, paper mill six years ago. Since then, the plant has
> been undergoing a rapid expansion with the addition of

two more paper machines and extensive modernization. Allegations have come to light that the company may be violating its discharge permit into the Savannah River and air emissions may exceed federal standards. United Paperworkers Local 567 President Robbie Shuman said yesterday that Southern Republic is violating the law and called for an immediate investigation, offering documentation to support his allegations.

"That son of a bitch is going to sink us," Hughes said. "We've got millions invested and are about to invest millions more."

"Something has to be done," Lee said. "I'm in the process of buying three sawmills. We can't take this kind of publicity. It's tough enough squeezing money out of banks without this crap."

Shuman had been a problem from the start. He was a papermaker and president of the papermakers' union, the mill's largest. Southern Republic inherited him from Republic Board. He was a tough little man with wavy black hair, a bushy black mustache, and beady gray eyes. The two sets of contract negotiations since their purchase of the mill from Republic Board had both been ordeals, all thanks to Shuman. The third was about to begin in a couple of months, and no one was looking forward to it. Shuman stayed in the newspaper and obviously knew how to dial a telephone. In the last forty-eight hours they'd fielded questions from the Atlanta Constitution, Savannah Morning News, and New York Times, and yesterday a producer from 60 Minutes called to arrange an on-camera interview between one of the three shareholders and Mike Wallace.

"This is getting way out of hand," Hughes said. "We don't need this kind of attention. Shuman's got to go. Why can't we just fire him?"

"What good will that do?" Lee asked. "He'd just continue to raise hell and the union would grievance us to oblivion. We'd have every governmental agency there is coming down on us."

"So what are we supposed to do?" Hughes said. "Pay the son of a bitch by the hour to make our lives a living hell?"

"We could kill him."

Lee and Hughes both turned toward him.

"What did you say, Chris?" Lee said.

"We could kill him."

"You mean as in dead?" Hughes asked.

"That's exactly what I mean."

Lee was intrigued. "You've obviously given this some thought. What do you propose?"

"Reed and the electricians are easy to work with. York and the machinists even easier. Shuman and the papermakers will not cooperate. We've tried force, threats, bribery, favoritism, courtesy, even ass licking. He doesn't want to work with us. What he wants is controversy. He sees that as a way to heighten his image. You're right, Hamilton, we can't fire him, that'd make things worse. We'd be up to our butts in grievances and lawsuits."

"We're about to be anyway," Lee said.

"If no one's around to be a plaintiff, who's going to sue us? If there's no one left to file the grievance, who's going to fight us? Who's going to ride as the Lone Ranger for the environmentalists? Who's going to funnel documents and other crap to the press? Nobody but Shuman. If he's dead, that won't be a problem."

"Ever heard of a martyr?" Lee asked.

"He won't be one. It seems Shuman likes to gamble. Bets on almost anything. Plays the numbers. Ball games. Goes to the dog tracks down in Florida. He doesn't lose a lot, but what he does is steal our electrical instruments, tools, and scrap copper, then pawn the stuff to cover the losses."

"How did you learn that?" Hughes asked.

"A good PI can find out a lot, if given enough time and money."

"So we can kill and discredit him at the same time," Lee said.

"Exactly. He tries to fence stolen stuff and gets shot. The criminal element can be tough to deal with. Happens all the time. For appearances we plant more stolen items in his house to make the thefts clearer."

"Damn, Chris, you're serious," Hughes said.

"I've never been more serious."

Lee wanted to know, "Who's going to do it?"

"I have some friends who can put me in touch with the right person."

"And the cost?"

"Ten thousand dollars."

"What about getting caught?" Hughes said.

"It won't happen."

"I say do it." Lee seemed sure.

Hughes was in shock. "You two are nuts. We're talking about killing a man."

He looked at Hughes. "That man is jeopardizing everything. Like you said, we have millions at stake." He gestured toward the newspaper. "We don't need this kind of press. You want to be the lead story on 60 Minutes? How many lenders you think will do business with us after that? And without money you can kiss this whole thing goodbye. Shuman's a troublemaker and he's not going away. We've given him every opportunity. Tried everything possible. It's just too bad for him he's a thief. I say we take care of the problem. Afterward, his credibility will go to zero and I can assure you he won't make it to sainthood. In sixty days he'll be forgotten, then we can get on with building this company."

"I agree," Lee said again. "We're just starting to turn a profit. Our production is expanding by the day. The way things are going, in a few years all three of us will be rich. The last thing we need is bad publicity and a cold shoulder from prospective lenders. If one irritating, redneck union president is all that stands in the way, then we should eliminate the problem."

They stared at Hughes.

"Okay," Hughes finally said. "Do it."

He remembered how it was done.

Shuman was shot three times after leaving a Savannah pawnshop. An hour before an assortment of stolen tools and copper were planted in Shuman's garage, with more found at the pawnshop itself.

The police verified everything as part of the subsequent investigation, even locating other pawnshops thanks to an anonymous tip courtesy of the private investigator. The company ultimately issued a press release linking Shuman's activism to an ongoing investigation of him he was trying to stop. His recent activities in damaging the company were tied to a blackmail attempt Shuman had supposedly begun. It was plausible, believable, and accepted.

And Chris had been right.

Ninety days later all their troubles passed, smoothed over by a timely death.

His mind snapped back to the present.

It wouldn't be long before Lee and Hughes learned about his cancer, the die had been cast yesterday when he took step one and intentionally generated an insurance claim. Their reaction would be predictable. He'd have only one chance to stick it up their asses. Did Hank Reed really have May's Priority list? More important, could Reed decipher it? And Brent Walker. Could he handle himself? Was it right even to involve him? But what choice did he have? For his plan to work he needed their help, whether they wanted to participate or not.

Time for step two.

He stepped back to his desk, sat in front of the computer, and started to type. At first the words came with difficulty. Soon they flowed with ease, the pounding of the keyboard therapeutic—a release of the soul—partial satisfaction for what little conscience he had left.

An hour later he finished and copied everything to a flash drive.

He ejected the drive and switched off the machine.

But intentionally did not erase the original.

4:09 P.M.

BRENT FINALLY DECIDED TO DO WHAT HANK WANTED. WHAT WOULD it hurt? If the list of numbers was nothing, then no harm no foul. If it was something, then, as they agreed, he'd keep it to himself and not violate the confidence of his new employer. He'd known this ethical vice would happen, just not in week two of his employment.

He found the list Hank had provided and studied the numbers again.

034156901
456913276
343016692
295617833
178932515
236987521
492016755
516332578

The direct approach seemed best, so he faced the computer screen on his desk at the mill and typed the first set into the search line, then hit RETURN.

And got a hit.

William Mesnan.

Apparently, 034-15-6901 was the man's Social Security number. He clicked on Mesnan's name and was taken to a menu of various company records associated with the employee that dated back thirty years. The last entry caught his attention. DEATH BEN-EFIT. He clicked again and learned that Mesnan had died of a heart attack three weeks ago. He tried the next number and began generating a list of his own.

034156901 William Mesnan, May 23, Heart attack
456913276 Patrick Brown, May 21, Kidney failure

He was about to type the third set into the search engine when Martha tapped on the doorframe. "The boss needs to see you."

"I thought he was gone."

"He was. Now he's back and needs you."

A week on the job and he'd already learned that the general

counsel liked to delegate. A lot. Which was fine. At the DA's office he'd accepted more than his fair share of the load. He was the new kid on the block here, so he should act like it and not complain. Besides, any excuse to not do what he was doing was truly appreciated.

He exited from the screen. "Tell him I'll be right there."

She left.

He slipped the list of numbers and his notes back into the desk drawer and closed it with an air of finality, thankful that he could postpone snooping for Hank for a while longer.

Maybe forever.

He hoped.

5:45 P.M.

HANK SAT BESIDE THE POOL, LOST IN THOUGHT.

He'd led the electrical union for a long time. Many men had placed their trust in him. And never once had he betrayed that trust. On the contrary, he'd fought hard for every single one of them, friend and foe alike. No one could ever say that he hadn't done his best. He was reading some information supplied by the national union to locals designed to help with negotiations. It was good to know what others around the country were thinking and doing. The back door to the house opened and Ashley bounded out onto the deck. She was dressed in a pair of denim shorts and an Atlanta Falcons jersey. Flip-flops protected her feet. He was glad to see her.

"What brings you by?" he asked.

She walked over and sat next to him. "Lori Anne's at a friend's house. I have to pick her up shortly, so I thought I'd kill a little time here."

"When's my granddaughter's next softball game?"

"Next Wednesday."

"I'll be heavy into negotiations, but I'll be there."

He never missed a game.

160

She noticed what he was reading. "You going to have a big fight with the contract?"

"Like always. But nothing new. It's tough pleasing everybody."

"But you're going to try, right?"

He smiled. "Like always. How's it going with Brent?"

"You tell me. I haven't heard from him since Saturday."

"Give him time, little one. This is complicated. More so than Brent even realizes."

Ashley's face hardened. "Have you two been talking?"

"I promised you I'd stay out of it with him." His pledge, though, had not included any silence toward Catherine Walker. "But I wouldn't wait much longer. It's time *everything* between you two gets laid on the table."

"Don't I know," she said. "The first forty-two years of my life were utter turmoil. I don't plan to repeat that in the next forty-two."

"If you need help, I'm here."

She reached over and squeezed his arm. "And I love you for it. But I got this. Truly, I do. Now I have to go."

He watched her leave, hoping she would not make the same mistakes he'd made.

He thought again about what Marlene had found in the company computers, especially the mysterious list of numbers. They'd been intentionally secreted away behind heavy restricted access. What was it about these innocent-looking numbers that mandated such high security?

He stood and walked to his outside office.

When the pool was added he'd simultaneously enlarged the two-car garage into a three-bay carport. On the far end of the elongated building he'd built himself an office. Abutting one wall were a pair of four-drawer file cabinets where he kept his union papers. Among those were a list of current members, along with birthdays, wives' and children's names, and other information. He used it religiously to make sure all his members received a birthday and anniversary card, a personal touch left over from his political days, the gesture constantly solidifying the fifty-plus votes needed at reelection time.

He found the union roster and carried it over to a counter abutting the opposite wall. Brent could be right. They might be Social Security numbers. But he had no way of determining that for sure. His files did not contain Social Security numbers. Only union IDs. That's why he needed Brent. He could ask Marlene, and would if Brent didn't come through soon. But he preferred to keep her out of it. Every time she did something for him, she placed her job on the line. And she wasn't a union employee, protected by a collective bargaining agreement. She was terminable-at-will, with no recourse. And he did not want her to lose her job.

The house phone rang.

He yanked up the extension.

"Hank." The voice was his chief steward at the mill. "Paul Zimmerman's dead."

He was shocked. Zimmerman was one of his most loyal supporters, even serving two terms on the city council during his last term as mayor. A solid vote, loyal union man, and friend.

"They found his body near Solomon Swamp. He'd gone after hogs. Looks like a hunting accident."

He knew how Zimmerman loved to hunt. He talked about it all the time. In fact, the freezer in the carport still held the pork chops Zimmerman gave him a couple of months back.

"His wife and kids must be in pieces," he said.

"It's pretty bad over there. I just got back and thought you'd want to know."

"I'll head right over."

He hung up and immediately started toward the house to change, the list of numbers on the clipboard forgotten.

DAY TEN
THURSDAY, JUNE 15

8:45 A.M.

HANK OCCUPIED HIS USUAL REALM.

His spot filled the northeast corner of the football-field-sized building housing paper machine number three. A grimy plate-glass window lined one wall and overlooked the churning machinery two stories below. Officially, it was designated the electric shop's break room. But no one outside Hank's inner circle had actually taken a break there in years. Unofficially, thanks to a federal law that required company space be made available for union activities, the room served as Hank's office. And he used his designated locale to the fullest, converting what was once an employee break room into a fortified union stronghold. It even had a name. Affectionately dubbed the Boar's Nest by the electricians to go along with Hank's personal moniker, Boarhogger.

Two years ago, in a power-flexing move, the company foolishly tried to evict him, claiming the space was needed for expansion of an adjacent control room. In reality management was irritated with the barrage of grievances he'd recently filed. He responded to the challenge by arranging for calls to be made to a Savannah television station alerting them to supposed environmental violations being sent downriver to their viewers. The callers specifically encouraged reporters to contact Hank Reed.

And they had.

Two film crews were sent and the story was in production when management conceded and stopped the eviction. Which simultaneously stopped the story since without a union president to go on camera, stamping validity to the claim, there was nothing to report.

Talk about tit for tat.

The door to the Boar's Nest opened.

"Hank, we need two more helpers on that generator repair for paper machine number one," one of his guys said.

He was busy on the landline phone and waved the man in, motioning for the door to be closed, the roar from the paper machine deafening. He cupped his hand over the mouthpiece and said, "I'll get somebody down there. Tell 'em to sit tight and not get their panties in a wad."

The electrician nodded and left, quickly closing the door. Two minutes later another interruption came from his cell phone. Still talking, he checked the display. He quickly ended the call in his ear and answered his cell.

He'd been waiting patiently.

"Hank, they're headed to the main conference room."

"The big cheesers?"

"All of 'em. Even Bozin himself. And a surprise. Your boy Brent too."

That was a shock. But a nice one. "Hang around as long as you can."

"It won't be long. I can only unscrew and rescrew this power plug from the wall so many times."

"Be imaginative. Break something. Keep me posted."

He hung up.

The machinists and paperworkers outnumbered electricians nearly eight to one. But they were all confined to designated work areas. Electricians, because of their reduced number, were rovers, their assignments and locations constantly changing from day to day. He'd long ago forged that mobility into a network of eyes and ears that kept him instantly informed.

He knew management would gather. They always did right before negotiations. Too bad he couldn't bug the room. But why go to all that trouble? He had ears on the inside. Since no matter how much Brent protested, he knew where his loyalty lay.

Even if Brent didn't.

He shook his head, thinking again of the possibilities.

He always said he'd rather be lucky than good.

9:00 A.M.

BRENT FOLLOWED HIS BOSS INTO BUILDING A. THE COMPANY'S general counsel was a half-bald, middle-aged man, with a rotund M&M body. The weather-beaten face liked to sport a smile of permanent courtesy. That, and his archaic wire spectacles, gave the man a polite, resigned, timid look. Perfect for a company lawyer. A month ago, during his interview, Brent had immediately taken a liking to the man. The lawyer had been with the company fifteen years, hired from a Savannah firm where he'd been slowly inching his way toward partnership. The promise of a title, a steady paycheck, and excellent benefits had lured him away. He definitely thought he was going to like working for him. Comforting was the fact that his new boss dressed a little like his old one at the Fulton County District Attorney's Office. Dark suits, white shirt, silk tie, and suspenders. But unlike the DA, who always said he liked the look and feel of pants supported by braces, his new boss seemed to wear them more out of necessity.

Building A was one of the two newer administrative complexes, trendier since it housed upper management. There were newly carpeted floors, upscale wallpaper, and furniture more of wood than metal, the décor leaning closer to fashionable than functional.

"Why am I included in this meeting?" he asked, as they walked.

"Beats the hell out of me. I was told to bring you along."

"What's this about?"

"Contract negotiations. One of the owners, Mr. Bozin, is down from Atlanta and wants a rundown. Have you ever met him?"

"I remember seeing him at the Concord Fourth of July celebration a few times. But that's about it. What's he like?"

"They call him the Silver Fox for a reason. He's smart. Knows every dime this company has, and ever did have. Actually, I'm glad it's him this time. Mr. Lee and Mr. Hughes can be a pain. They're too impatient. Hard to get along with."

"But why me?" he asked again.

"I was told this would be a good opportunity for you to see the negotiating process." His boss then flashed one of his trademark Cheshire Cat grins. "From our side."

Apparently, his reputation had preceded him.

But he should not be surprised.

They strolled into the conference room. The walls were south Georgia pine, stained dark, and dotted with aerial photos of the mill and bag plant. Twelve goose-necked armchairs lined a coffin-shaped table. An overhead projector and screen angled from one corner, a chalkboard from another. He knew three faces among the men present. Southern Republic's chief executive officer, its industrial relations manager, and the head of personnel. He'd dealt with industrial relations and personnel during past battles between the company and IBEW, all while at Hank's side.

He glanced toward the far end of the conference table.

Christopher Bozin sat silent. He studied the gentle face of the older man, noticing its distinct lack of color. The eyes looked tired and the folds that lined his cheeks and neck were dry and brittle.

"I'll introduce you," his boss whispered.

They walked over.

Bozin stood and they shook hands, the grip clammy and light. After a few pleasantries, the older man said to the group, "Why don't we get started."

Everyone took seats around the table.

"It's that time again," Bozin said. "Hard to believe five years have passed since the last negotiations. Seems like just yesterday we were doing this. What is the substance of our first offer?"

"Two percent on wages. Slight increase on the medical benefits. An adjustment in the pension. But nothing on assured overtime, though we're willing to talk about some additional job positions," the industrial relations manager said. "On the non-economic side, the paperworkers have already asked for special consideration on their wood yard people. They say there's too much turnover and the problem is bad supervision. They've even threatened a grievance. They claim our supervisor is nuts."

"Is he?" Bozin asked.

"Wood yard people need a firm hand," the personnel manager said. "We've denied everything. Privately, though, we've conceded there is a turnover problem. Also, and again privately, the union has told us they'll be satisfied with a change of supervisors. We can even wait a couple of months for appearances' sake."

Bozin seemed pleased.

"As I understand it," the CEO said, "Mr. Lee told me privately that we're supposed to bargain away five years down to three to keep the final concessions down? Five years is not all that important this time."

"Correct," Bozin said.

"Are wage increases over and above our first offer on the table? I've pressed Mr. Hughes for an answer, but he's never given me one."

"There should be no need," Bozin said, "if we use the five years to our advantage. There'll probably have to be some wage increases in the final deal, the unions will never be satisfied with two percent, but we'll just have to see when we get further in. What about Hank Reed, any of you heard anything?"

"He's been pretty quiet lately," the personnel manager said. "He was in my office the day before yesterday ready to go balls-to-the-walls, as he put it."

Brent was fascinated to watch the other side at work. Not a whole lot different from what he and Hank used to do—plotting, planning, trying to second-guess what the company would do next.

"Where's Hank getting his legal help from these days?" Bozin asked.

"A local lawyer named Lou Greene does all his legal writing," the personnel manager said. "Hank speaks highly of him. Kind of like the way he used to talk about you, Brent."

He acknowledged the observation with a nod.

"We still allow Hank to come and go as he pleases?" Bozin asked.

"Best way to keep an eye on him."

The group chuckled.

"We can count on Reed to have all his ducks in a row," the CEO said. "He always does. We should be prepared for a fight."

"I agree," Bozin said with a nod. "Reed is at his best during negotiations. Let's not underestimate him."

The meeting lasted another half hour, the company's bargaining position finalized. Before adjourning Bozin said he needed to make a quick trip to Atlanta tomorrow but would be back Sunday, present at the negotiations when they opened Monday morning.

As everyone filed out of the conference room, Bozin called out, "If you would, Brent, I'd like to talk with you a moment. Alone."

They stayed in the conference room with the door closed.

Bozin started the conversation.

"I'm curious, how did you learn about our opening in the general counsel's office?"

"I saw an ad in the *Georgia Law Journal*. Just an accident, really."

Bozin nodded. "It was sad what happened to your predecessor. So sudden and unexpected. He was a fine man. We were lucky somebody of your caliber came along."

"Does that mean 'somebody who used to be connected to Hank Reed'?"

"I'd be lying if I said that didn't factor into the decision. But we also hired you because you're a good lawyer. The Fulton County DA spoke highly of you."

Always good to hear.

"But let's face facts. You and Reed once gave us fits," Bozin said.

He smiled. "Just doing my job."

"Good lawyers are a dime a dozen," Bozin said. "Good lawyers who understand politics are hard to find. Good lawyers who understand politics and Hank Reed are virtually nonexistent. In fact, you may be the only one on the planet. Though I would not tell him this to his face, Concord was never governed better than when Hank was mayor. He knew how to get elected, stay elected, and govern."

Bozin smiled at him.

Brent returned the grin and said, "I'll keep your secret."

"When I learned that you applied for the opening in our general counsel's department, I was the one who personally lobbied for your hiring."

That was news. "Why?"

"In all honesty, I thought it would be handy to have someone on the payroll who could reason with Reed. If need be."

First Hank came to enlist his help with the company. Now the company wanted his help with Hank. "I'm not sure what I can do."

"You can help us get him to an agreement."

"I'll do what I can. But Hank generally does what he wants, not what I say."

Bozin grinned. "I imagine Hank listens to you more than you want me to believe. And I'd be disappointed if you didn't still have some loyalty and connection to him."

More than this man realized, he thought. But he only said, "I owe him a lot."

"And if you thought we were deceiving him you'd tell him, wouldn't you?"

Bozin's tone had deepened.

Was this some kind of test? "I would hope the company would be honest in its dealings with all employees."

The older man grinned. "I see you have a quick mind, too."

He said nothing.

Finally, Bozin broke the silence. "I've requested that you sit in on the negotiations. I want you to get a feel for the company's side of the process. Who knows? You may be our general counsel one day. So you need to become familiar with the way *we* do things.

These negotiations come along only every few years, so we should take advantage of the opportunity. I also want your insights on Hank—without violating any confidences. Fair enough?"

He nodded. "More than fair."

Bozin pushed back his chair and stood, signaling the conversation was over. He rose too. Bozin extended his hand.

"It's been good talking to you. I want you to know that I'm pleased with our new assistant general counsel."

CHRIS WAITED FOR BRENT WALKER TO LEAVE THE CONFERENCE room, then followed. The young lawyer headed one way, he the other down the carpeted hall. Before turning the corner, he stopped and glanced back.

He'd told Brent a half-truth. Yes, he was pleased with his selection. But he'd also included the younger man in the staff meeting because he wanted him to know the company's bargaining position firsthand. Whether he told Hank Reed the details mattered little. Five years. Three years.

Who cared?

The death of the company's assistant general counsel, by suicide, had been both unfortunate and random. No Priority decisions were involved. Just one of those fortuitous events that could be parlayed into an advantage. The real question was whether Brent Walker was up to what he had in mind. Where before he'd been unsure, the critical assessment, the one essential to his plan for his partners—

Had just been made.

6:43 P.M.

JON ENTERED THE LOBBY OF THE BELVEDERE THROUGH BRASS-FRINGED revolving doors, the hotel an imposing edifice of stone, terra-cotta, and marble. It was one of downtown Atlanta's largest, a hub for both travelers and locals drawn to the many restaurants and lounges dotting its open interior.

A thirty-five-story panoramic interior rose above the lobby. Railed balconies draped with flowered vines lined the floors from ground to glass-topped ceiling. The central promenade rose three stories, each level accommodating swanky shops and opulent bars. Indoor plants and feathered palms abounded, the fall of water loud from flowing fountains, live music played somewhere in the distance.

A dinner crowd was just arriving, most of the gentlemen in suits, ladies in evening dresses. Jon fit right in, appropriately attired in the navy Hart Schaffner Marx suit he'd worn to work. Hamilton Lee had called an hour ago and caught him just before he left the Blue Tower. Lee wanted him to stop by the Cafe Carmón where Lee and his wife were due for dinner at six. It was important they talk immediately. He strolled to the maître d' stand and saw his boss socializing at one of the clothed tables. Lee obviously had been on the lookout and immediately excused himself.

"I appreciate you coming," Lee said. "Shall we?"

His employer led the way as they casually strolled to the other side of the atrium, commandeering a small alcove adjacent to one of the fountains.

"I wanted to give Mr. Bozin time to get to Concord and myself time to think everything through before we talked," Lee said. "The board concurs with what I've already directed you to do. Find out if Reed has the list. If he does, get it back but we need to know if he's deciphered it. Or even attempted to. We want this situation contained and kept quiet for now."

He nodded an understanding.

"Also, Mr. Bozin will be in Concord for the negotiations. He's asked that you report directly to him. Do it. But Jon, I want a report too, separate and apart—and first."

He nodded his further assent.

"Mr. Hughes and I want you to keep an eye on Mr. Bozin. Without going into a lot of detail, suffice it to say we have concerns about him."

He'd long sensed the tension among the three owners. Understandable given their differences. Bozin possessed a distinctly different philosophy from the other two. More cautious. Concerned with following procedures. He didn't take chances and didn't like others taking them either. Jon actually preferred that methodology.

"How involved should my surveillance of Mr. Bozin get? I don't like being put in the middle. I work for all three of you, without favorites."

"I wouldn't be ordering this if I didn't think it critical. Just monitor enough to know what he's doing, who he's talking to. We have a possible breach in our Priority system. A serious one. Needless to say, I don't want to take any more chances."

"Do I report the information on Mr. Bozin directly to you?"

Lee nodded.

"As to Reed, I have no authority to do anything other than observe and report?"

"Correct," Lee said. "For now."

DAY TWELVE
SATURDAY, JUNE 17

7:45 A.M.

BRENT WOKE AND FOCUSED ON THE CLOCK BESIDE THE BED. HE'D never needed an alarm, his body blessed with a self-contained chronometer that could wake him at the precise time intended. The trait had been a godsend in college and law school—he never missed an 8:00 A.M. class—and it came in handy for early court sessions too.

It was strange waking up in his old room after so many years away. He and Paula had lived in a house a few blocks over during the time they were married. He sold it just before leaving town. But lying alone, here, in his childhood bed, he imagined himself seventeen again. His first thoughts then were usually of breakfast, his mother, and the day of the week. Mondays were bacon and eggs. Tuesdays cereal. Grits and toast came midweek, French toast on Thursdays. Depending on her mood and the weather, Fridays were either oatmeal or eggs again. Saturday cold cereal. And Sundays pancakes and sausage, with church afterward.

But he remembered his father too.

Weekend mornings when the lawn mower or one of the table saws in the garage would wake him after a Friday night at the VFW playing pool or celebrating after a baseball game. Concord always seemed such a safe place. One he hoped that might, some-day, provide stability for his own children. Yet here he was, in his forties, with no wife and no kids. That longing had been another reason why he'd returned. It seemed his fate was inexplicably linked with this spot on the earth.

He rose, slipped on a pair of tattered gym shorts and an old jersey, and drifted downstairs. The house was quiet, his mother still asleep. After eating a bowl of cornflakes he headed out the back door toward the garage. The detached building was a full two stories, its second floor once his father's woodworking shop.

He gassed the lawn mower, an old two-cycle job that his father had tinkered with for years. Since he'd left, his mother had cut the grass. She'd always loved yard work. But he wanted to contribute toward the household chores and lawn care seemed the most productive thing for him to do.

The morning was trademark middle Georgia, June hot. A thick coat of dew licked the grass and made the cutting a little slow. An hour later he was in the garage searching for the gas trimmer when he heard a vehicle enter the driveway. He stepped out to see Hank Reed climb out of a pickup.

"You're up early," he said.

Hank wore his usual starched khaki pants, shiny penny loafers, and a cotton, button-down shirt.

"And seriously overdressed. Where you headed?"

"You hear about Paul Zimmerman?"

He had not.

"Somebody blew his brains out in Solomon Swamp." Hank shook his head. "A damn hunting accident."

He shook his head. "That's awful. Does the sheriff know anything?"

"I talked to him yesterday. They don't have much. The shot came from a deer stand. Paul had a vest on. Nice bright orange. Lot of good it did. They can't find a soul who was in the area at the time. No tracks. No nothin'. The funeral's tomorrow. I hate funerals."

He agreed. In the past eleven years he'd attended only two. First Paula's. Then his dad's. More than enough.

"What brings you by?" he asked.

"I need you to look at somethin' else and tell me what you think."

Hank slipped a sheet of paper from his back pocket and handed it over. He unfolded a memo from Hamilton Lee on the upcoming contract negotiations and an instruction about not seeking five years in duration.

"Hank, this deals with negotiations. I'm out of the loop on this one. I don't have any idea."

"Does the memo sound reasonable to you?"

"You know more about Lee than I do. I've never met the man."

Hank pointed a finger. "You're flip-flopping like a fish on a hot dock."

"And you're pushing things to the breaking point. I can't breach my employer's confidence. Maybe it's like the memo says. Going for five years is just not worth the trouble this time. How did you get your hands on this?"

"Same as that list of numbers. The company's computer obliged me."

He remembered Thursday's management meeting at the mill and decided to pick a little himself. "What do you want from this collective bargaining, Hank?"

"I need at least three to five percent on wages. My guys aren't going to be satisfied with two percent. There are several side issues on call-ins and sick days that need adjustment. And I've got a ton of retirees on my butt about medical deductibles. There's also a stupid point the members rammed down my throat on assured overtime. But the company's never going to agree to that."

"What do you have to offer?"

"Nothing, if they don't want five years. That's my problem." Hank paused. "Come on, help me out, have you heard any talk on this?"

No way he was going to breach confidentiality. "Like I said, Hank, my boss is handling the negotiations. I'm the new kid on the block. Workers' comp cases are my problem."

"Then why include you in that powwow Thursday with the big cheesers?"

He grinned. "I saw one of your guys tinkering at a power outlet when I went into the building. I figured you were keeping an eye on things. You know I can't talk about that."

"Without five years on the table, I'm screwed."

"Tough tour of duty for an old warrior, huh?"

"Have you got any ideas?"

"Doesn't Lou Greene have any wisdom?"

"Lou's good for drafting things, but useless on strategy. He's too accustomed to workers' comp, which for him is like shootin' fish in a barrel. Right now, I need finesse."

"What does Greene think of that memo?"

"He reads it just like it says. The company isn't interested in five years."

"Why don't you agree?"

"It just seems fishy, considering how hard they fought for that last time."

"Hank, you always think there's a sinister plot. It could be you just got your hands on something you weren't supposed to see. After all, I don't think the company expects you to invade their computers."

"You meant what you said? You wouldn't let them snooker me, would you?" Hank asked.

He owed Southern Republic loyalty. His inclusion at Thursday's strategy session had surely been a test, his discussion with Bozin afterward a message. But he and Hank had been through too much together. Not to mention Ashley. A paycheck was one thing, a friend another. Especially a close one. Even one who chose to put him in an untenable position.

"Hank, has the company ever been able to play you?"

"I like to think not."

"Then what are you worried about?"

"I don't know. Just a feelin'. Things don't feel right. What about that list of numbers? Anything?"

"Not yet. But I'm working on it. Have you met with one of the owners yet?"

The details were never explained, nothing about who, where, or when, but he knew how Hank really got things done at negotiation time. And it wasn't during the public show of the negotiations.

"Not yet. But the call should come any time."

"Find out then."

Hank snickered. "I already intended to do just that."

10:30 A.M.

BRENT CLIMBED THE WOODEN STAIRS TO THE GARAGE'S SECOND story, cooling off after removing the creeping Bermuda grass invading his mother's flower beds. The top floor was bare studs with a rough plywood floor. Two dormer windows provided light. There was no ceiling, never had been, only the open rafters supporting a pitched roof.

Years ago, two walls had been lined with benches supporting his father's woodworking tools, the saws and drills heard at all hours of the day and night. It was where his father built birdhouses. Intricate, beautiful works his dad had enjoyed giving away. The backyard was littered with them, and during the past week he'd noticed several still adorning the neighborhood.

All the pegboards remained, but the Swiss cheese panels where cold chisels, hammers, and rasps once hung were now bare. The table saws, sanders, and drills were also gone, everything sold when his mother held a huge garage sale. He understood why she'd been so willing to part with his father's treasured things, that need for distance and a sense of moving on. He'd been searching for the same thing for a long time.

The splintered surfaces of the workbenches now supported cardboard boxes, each meticulously packed by the moving company and delivered from Atlanta a few days ago. He hadn't kept a lot, most of what he'd owned had been sold during his own garage sale a few weeks ago, but enough remained to fill the musty loft.

He threaded his way through and looked up at the old shelves for the wooden container. It was not one brought from Atlanta.

This one had stayed in the garage since college. He recalled seeing it while moving in the furniture, an aged Florida grapefruit crate lifted from the throwaway pile at the Piggly Wiggly what seemed a zillion years ago.

He carefully slid it down and carried it over to one of the workbenches.

Inside were mementos from high school and college, tossed there one afternoon after cleaning out his room, the décor adjusted for a man no longer eighteen. But there were also things from law school and his time while practicing law in Concord.

Right on top was the press clipping from Paula's death.

She would have loved the funeral. So many attended that the crowd spilled outside the church and onto the lawn. Luckily, the day had been gorgeous, capped by an azure sky. The casket, a white bronze, had been draped in yellow roses, her favorite, but closed—the one thing she would have regretted—the windshield and steering column doing too much damage for the mortician to repair.

He could still see her as she was that last day of her life. Shoulder-length auburn hair. Inviting lips. Surprisingly warm blue eyes. But that pleasant façade hid an inner turmoil. One he never really understood. She was certainly dedicated. There'd been home-cooked meals every day. Not a speck of dust on the furniture. Not a weed in the flower beds. Everything in its place, orderly, like her life.

He'd tried hard to ignore his unhappiness by pouring himself into work. The demands of a private practice and his political maneuvering with Hank distracted him, for a time. But their problems only multiplied. Eventually, life became a simple toleration from one day to the next. Finally, it turned tragic one September day. Now he'd returned to somehow make amends. But to who? Himself? Paula? No way existed to satisfy both.

Fate?

It truly was fickle.

He lifted out his high school letter sweater, neatly folded inside a blue-tinted plastic bag, three pewter baseballs still tacked to the stitched gold *W*. He'd earned it during his sophomore year. Three graduation announcements lay underneath along with tassels from high school, college, and law school. The scarlet sash was still there, worn over his gown when he'd graduated as the history department's honor graduate in college.

His Little League trophies had tarnished with time. And on the bottom was the scrapbook of his baseball days, clippings yellowed and loose, the tape long since dried hard.

He thumbed through his annuals, noticing how much he changed during eight years of high school and college. His hair progressively shortened, then thinned. Black-framed glasses were replaced by gold wire-rims. Now he wore contacts. A happy, care-free appearance, seen through eyes that once carried a whimsical expression, became hardened by years of trying to make the grade.

His senior high school annual was full of messages. A close friend warning, *Don't get a big head. And can I hitch a ride to Statesboro every day for college?* Other friends recalling snippets that made him smile even now.

He lifted out a greeting card and opened it.

From Paula.

You know what you mean to me. We've had our ups and downs, but we endure. Even you can't argue with that. I think we're stronger now than ever. I want you to know I'm here for you. I'll always be yours.

Love, Paula

She'd given it to him the last Christmas they spent together. She loved cards. There'd been many between them over the years they were together. Yet he kept only this one. Why?

He could not remember.

It seemed predetermined they were at least going to try at a life together. He put off the wedding for as long as he could, even tried to get out of it weeks before, but Paula made sure it happened.

Oh, yes, she made real sure.

At the bottom of the box he noticed a single sheet of yellowed paper. He recalled how it made it into the box. He'd just returned from trying to tell Paula the wedding should be postponed. But she'd exploded the baby bomb. So he'd sat in his room and typed out a list, trying to decide what to do.

Paula Pros: Pregnant. Prudent. Dedicated. Loyal. Resolute. We have a history together. Would make an excellent mother. The perfect hostess, but also a wonderful guest. Great cook. Never have to worry about another man. Would always have a clean shirt. Great lawyer-wife. My child deserves a father. She wants to marry me.

Paula Cons: Pregnant. Obsessive. Stubborn. Possessive. No spontaneity. Vain. Inhibited. Hard to please. Can aggravate the hell out of me. Totally dependent. Cries a lot. Would I ever be able to pick out my own clothes? Be careful when I laugh.

Ashley Pros: Exciting. Always happy. Beautiful. Sexy. Spontaneous. Complex like a jigsaw puzzle and equally pleasing when figured out. Unpredictable. Not a jealous bone in her body. I trust her.

Ashley Cons: Unpredictable. Fleeting. Unable to commit to anything. Keeps far too much to herself. I'm never sure what she's thinking. How would she be with a room full of lawyers? She does not want to marry me.

"Son?"

He turned. His mother stood at the top of the stairs. He hadn't heard her climb up.

She stepped closer. "What are you doing?"

"Remembering." He showed her the sheet. What did it matter anymore? "I wrote that a few days before Paula and I married."

She looked the list over, her face betraying nothing. "Is that the only reason you married her. She was pregnant?"

He told her years ago that Paula had been pregnant when they married. "Looking back, I think it was. I made it clear it was over. The wedding was off. Then she told me she was pregnant. Where before I was simply confused, I suddenly became trapped."

"So you did the right thing for the wrong reason."

"That pretty much sums it up."

"You seemed to have had a real dilemma. I never realized you and Ashley were so close."

"She's always been special to me, in a different sort of way. When we were kids it was just friendship. But by the end of high school, it was a whole lot more."

"You want to talk about it?"

"Not yet."

"When you do, you know where I am."

He knew she wouldn't press. She never did, and he loved her for the trust she seemed to always show in his judgment. A thousand times she'd preached that experience was the best teacher.

She turned to leave, then stopped. "You going out tonight?"

"Ashley and I are having dinner. You mind?"

She reached out and gently squeezed his arm. "Paula's been gone a long time, son. Life goes on."

Forty-five minutes later he was dousing the front flower beds with water when a mail truck whipped to the curb and Ashley jumped out.

"What are you doing on this route?" he called out.

She traipsed through the freshly cut grass to where he stood with the hose. "Regular called in sick, so I offered to fill in. You're looking good."

His bare chest and legs were covered in sweat, grime, and grass clippings. "I'm filthy."

She handed him the mail. "Save some energy for tonight."

He caught the twinkle in her eye, which had always captivated him. "I hear you."

"Gotta get back. I have two routes to handle today."

"See you later."

She trotted back to the van, his eyes riveted on her.

His mother was right.

Life did go on.

1:35 P.M.

ALL WEEK BRENT PROMISED THE TWO YOUNG BOYS NEXT DOOR they'd go fishing Saturday. That's why he rose early and cut the grass. So right after lunch he packed the Jeep with fishing tackle, poles, and a cooler of drinks and they headed for Eagle Lake.

Only one of his father's three fishing boats had survived his mother's garage sale. A ten-foot, flat-bottomed skiff powered by an aging outboard and equipped with a bow-mounted trolling motor. It was the smallest his father had owned, the green skiff resting quietly under a mildewed tarp behind the garage the past two years. Starting last Monday he'd spent time scrubbing the hull and making sure the motors worked. A few of his father's rods and tackle pieces were still in the garage, more than enough to outfit all three of them. He was even surprised to find the rod he'd liked as a teenager.

He pulled the skiff to the public boat ramp at the southeast corner of Eagle Lake. It was the most popular spot for launching, three concrete ramps fading down into the gray-brown water, a large bait-and-tackle shop nearby along with rental cabins offering accommodations to the anglers who traveled from all over middle Georgia and western South Carolina.

He floated the skiff and gassed the outboard, then he and the boys powered out. Fifteen minutes later they drifted with baited lines cast in the mineral-rich water.

"Did you come out here when you were little?" Grant asked.

"All the time."

"With your daddy?"

"Sometimes. Sometimes by myself or with friends."

James tightened his line. "Did you like to fish?"

"I sure did."

The boys, James and Grant, ages twelve and thirteen, were the grandchildren of Grace Tanner, who'd lived next door all his life. Her husband, a local pharmacist, died years ago of cancer. Grace and his mother had been best friends forever. With both of them widows, they looked after each other. The boys were here for a summer visit. Grace's son and daughter-in-law lived in North Carolina. He'd been wanting to do a little fishing, so his mother had suggested bringing the boys along.

He looked around and admired the pristine lake, a perfect fit between tall stands of old-growth pine, birch, hickory, and oak. Its irregular shape had been intentional, designed to create coves and inlets that translated into marketable shoreline for landowners fortunate enough to abut the banks. He'd handled many real estate closings for lakefront property back in his days of private practice.

"Did my daddy ever come out here with you?" James asked.

"Not really. He wasn't much of a fisherman."

"Did my granddaddy?"

"Oh, yeah. He and my dad fished here all the time."

James sighed. "I miss Granddaddy."

"I miss my dad, too."

Grant tugged at his line. "They're in heaven. Right?"

"That's exactly where they are." He didn't like to think about it.

"Do people die like that all the time?" Grant asked.

"Every day, son."

"How is it you're chosen to die?"

This was getting heavy. "Hard to say. The only thing certain is everybody's time comes."

Some sooner than others, though.

"Your daddy's time came here on the lake, didn't it?" James asked.

He looked at the boy. "How did you know that?"

"Grandma told us."

"It wasn't out here on the lake. Happened that way, up in one of the creeks." He pointed toward the northeast.

"How did he die?"

"Nobody's sure. He was fishing alone and had an accident."

"Could we see where?" James said.

"Why would you want to?"

"I don't know. I just do."

It was an innocent request, like children sometimes made, but it bothered him. After Paula died he'd always avoided that stretch of local highway, never wanting to see that power pole again. Likewise, since two summers ago when his father's body had been found floating facedown, his boat stuck among the thickets, he hadn't thought of ever returning to Brooks Creek. Why was he like that? Reality many times was far less frightening than what the imagination envisioned. The concrete pole. Brooks Creek. Places where something awful had occurred? Or were they barriers that needed breaching? What had his mother said earlier? *"Life goes on."*

That it did.

Maybe a visit would do them all some good.

"Okay, let's take a look."

He reeled in the line. The boys did the same. He cranked the outboard and they chugged north. Thanks to high scattered clouds the hot midafternoon sun shone more peekaboo than direct. The lake lulled at almost a dead calm so the flat-bottomed skiff slipped easily across, a ribbon of dirty-brown foam unfolding behind them.

He studied the wooded shoreline. The trees seemed thicker with homes, cabins, and trailers than he remembered. Three years had passed since he'd last traveled across Eagle Lake, that day with his father for an afternoon of fishing.

Their last ever together.

Up ahead he spotted the familiar break in the shoreline.

He released the throttle and slowed the skiff.

"Where is it?" Grant looked ahead.

"Through that opening."

Both boys stared at the impenetrable shoreline dense with trees and bushes. Almost directly off the bow was a narrow break where the water disappeared inland. It could be missed if you didn't know where to look.

But he did.

The skiff inched toward it and he said, "This is Brooks Creek."

He clicked off the outboard knowing what waited. Almost immediately he saw the limbs, the sight forming a knot in the pit of his stomach. He'd earlier dodged James' question about how his father died.

But he knew what happened.

According to the police report his dad apparently misjudged the limbs' height. Blood and tissue samples found on the bark matched a corresponding contusion on his father's forehead. He remembered the autopsy report and pictures and would never forget the comment at the end of the report.

Death accidental.

But his father's demise had always puzzled him. Brian Walker knew every inch of Eagle Lake. Particularly the limbs that guarded Brooks Creek. It was one of his favorite spots. His skiff, the same one they were now using, came specially equipped with an electric trolling motor to allow maneuvering inside the tight confines. He and Paula had given him the motor for Christmas.

The skiff eased to the limbs, the oak six to eight inches in diameter, even thicker than he remembered. The branches still spanned the creek's entire expanse. Grant reached out and grabbed hold. He thought he should be honest, particularly since he didn't know how much their grandmother had told them.

"My dad's head hit those branches."

James looked at them in awe. "They're big."

The clearance from the bottom edge to the top of the water was about four feet. Just enough for the skiff to squeeze beneath. He glanced at the outboard. It should make it too.

"Grant, lie down in front. You too, James."

185

Both boys did as they were told and he paddled under the limbs, ducking as they passed overhead.

They came out the other side into a pool.

"This was one of my daddy's favorite spots."

"Are there lots of fish here?" Grant asked.

"Not this time of day. The water's too hot, so the fish head out to the open lake. Mornings and evenings are the best time to fish here." He only knew that because his father taught him.

"Was your daddy here in the morning time?"

"Just after dawn. He liked to fish then."

He glanced around the pool, its quiet shoreline still blanketed in dense forest, the water forming a narrow canyon between stands of tall vegetation. A tiny beach eased down to the water on the far side of the pool. The place was hot and eerie. A shudder shot down his spine.

"Let's fish here," Grant said.

"No, son."

And not just because the fish were in cooler water. Something else about Brooks Creek bothered him. Hard to describe. A strange feeling. "We'll go back out in the lake. Like I said, the fish are all out there this time of day anyway."

He turned the skiff around and paddled back toward the gate of limbs.

On the other side, before cranking the outboard, he glanced back past the limbs toward the pool.

And never wanted to see that place again.

6:15 P.M.

HANK SPED NORTH ON GEORGIA 16A. THE STRETCH OF HIGHWAY had been funded by the state as a way to provide four-laned efficiency to commercial traffic in rural, outlying areas, the route from Savannah to Augusta through Woods County, into Screven, then Burke, and finally Richmond County a much-welcomed addition. He vividly recalled its opening, how eighteen-wheelers that once regularly roared through downtown Concord started bypassing it, taking with them their noise and pollution.

Woods County was a near perfect rectangle of three hundred square miles and carried the distinction of being the smallest county of Georgia's 159. Down the entire length of its western boundary ran the muddy Ogeechee River. The more majestic Savannah River formed the eastern boundary of both the county and Georgia. Its northern and southern extremes were nondescript straight lines that, on maps, connected the two rivers and divided Woods from Effingham to the south and Screven to the north.

Highway 16A bisected north to south and County Road 30 spanned east to west, dividing the land into four distinct quarters. The southwest portion was dominated by farms and Eagle Lake. The northwest by Solomon Swamp. The southeast held Concord, the mill, the bag plant, and a majority of the population. And the northeast was almost totally owned by Southern Republic, the acreage gradually transformed over the past thirty years into a sprawling pine tree expanse. Interspersed among the huge company forests were private tracts, land owned by families who'd possessed title for over a century, perennially refusing to sell. Toward the extreme northeast corner, spilling over into southeast Screven County, lay a tract of old-growth timber that Southern Republic had intentionally saved from harvesting.

Hickory Row.

Hank knew all about the three thousand lush acres. They were originally bought for the hardwood and christened after the bushy trees that dominated the site. Ultimately, they were turned into a corporate playground.

Stables housed thoroughbreds for breeding and riding. A quail farm produced birds by the thousands, and manicured fields among the trees comfortably accommodated their slaughter. Four massive lakes dug into the sandy clay helped with drainage and were stocked for fishing around which wound nine holes of golf. Two lodges and many individual cottages quartered guests. Three impressive houses provided a residence for each of Southern

Republic's owners. A staff of 150 kept everything gorgeous and catered to both owners and guests. The entire acreage was fenced on three sides, the fourth protected by the Savannah River. To ensure both privacy and a perpetual view, the company bought all the adjoining acreage on the South Carolina side and left it dense forest.

Hickory Row, though, was more than a private refuge. It also served a corporate function, its lodges and cottages routinely filled with customers wowed with luxury then lured by the sales department into lucrative paper deals while quail hunting, fishing, playing golf, or riding the trails.

Hank slowed his pickup and approached the main gate. He provided the uniformed guard his name and was waved through. He declined a road map, as he knew his way around.

He'd made the call to Atlanta just after returning from consoling Paul Zimmerman's widow. The private phone number stayed safely stored in his address book, used only at negotiation time when he knew the call was expected. The man on the other end was cordial and agreed to be at his house in the Row by 6:00 P.M.

A series of asphalt roads spiderwebbed through the manicured forests and carried familiar names. Lee Trail, Hughes Drive, Bozin Way, along with the more descriptive Quail Run, Deer Park, and Hickory Boulevard, the widest leading in from the main entrance.

Mill electricians routinely worked at the Row, though the facility employed a private staff of three electricians on a separate payroll. Consequently, Hank was kept informed as to its daily happenings.

He followed Hickory Boulevard to the first intersection and turned left. Half a mile later he found the concrete drive lined with a knee-high stretch of trimmed hedges. The house beyond was an odd structure, specially designed to reflect the unique personality of its owner. There were no outside walls and at first glance it appeared all roof. The few walls that did exist, along with the roof, were sheathed in cedar shingles stained a dark green. Brick piers supported all sides forming a cloister at the main entrance.

Strategically placed windows were trimmed in dark green and blended indiscriminately with the roofline. It was every bit of five thousand square feet, the architecture severe, dark, and restrained, long shadows from the surrounding hickories and pines adding to its somberness. He knew the sense of drama had been intentional and accounted both for the house's notoriety and nickname the employees gave it.

Dracula's Place.

6:30 P.M.

FRANK BARNARD WORE A PAIR OF MAROON RUNNING SHORTS, A white Georgia Bulldogs T-shirt, and a pair of dingy Reeboks. He slowly jogged down the street, a block over from where Hank Reed lived. For more affect he sported earbuds and a phone strapped to his arm.

He casually checked his watch.

Reed was now twenty miles away at the north end of the county. De Florio had called two hours ago and told him when and what needed to be done. His boss had also briefed him on the layout of Reed's house, describing the list of numbers to be found and instructing him, while there, to place listening devices in the outside office and on the phones. A fairly simple operation and, given Reed's preoccupation and the fact that he lived alone, he should have a couple of uninterrupted hours to accomplish the task.

He rounded the corner, jogged to the next block, and passed directly in front of Reed's house. It was a split level, wood-sided, painted white with charcoal shutters and a walnut-stained front door. A thick brush of grass covered the front yard under a shady canopy of oaks and pines, the scattered beds full of ivy and summer flowers. No cars filled the drive, the double cedar gate leading to the rear of the house and the carport closed. But De Florio had said that wasn't unusual. Reed and most of his visitors used a rear entrance.

He jogged over to the next block and turned west, following

the curb until he found the narrow right-of-way that ran back south between two wooded lots. De Florio explained how Reed had paved the alley while mayor, claiming a municipal need for a rear entrance to his property.

He trotted down the shady lane. Another cedar gate waited open at the end. He stopped and spied the rear of the house. Reed's truck was gone, his mill car nestled in the carport. Only part of the house could be seen, the oversized carport and attached office blocking the majority of first-floor windows. Just the top of the screened pool enclosure peeked up from behind the carport. No sounds emanated anywhere. The second story likewise appeared quiet. He knew there were no external cameras.

He looked around. No one was in sight, though he heard and smelled what apparently was a barbecue a few backyards over. Quickly, he scampered through the back gate and headed straight for Reed's outside office.

He approached the half-glass door and removed the pick from his pocket. Fifteen seconds and the lock tripped. He gripped the knob through his T-shirt, opened the door, and slipped inside. De Florio had also told him that there was no burglary alarm wired for the office.

The space was quiet and smelled of chlorine and coffee. A makeshift Formica counter spanned one wall. Two filing cabinets abutted another. Open cardboard boxes resting on the linoleum overflowed with magazines. Paper was everywhere. Some bound to clipboards, some fastened in binders, most stacked loosely.

This was going to take a while.

A shrill ring pierced the silence.

His eyes shot to the phone on the counter. He froze and waited. After two rings it stopped. Strange. Suddenly, from inside the pool enclosure, a door opened then closed.

What?

The house was supposed to be empty.

Footsteps approached across the pool's concrete deck. He remembered what De Florio had said about the layout and knew the person could only be headed his way. De Florio also made clear that

190

detection in any manner was unacceptable. He needed to leave the office fast. He spun toward the door he'd just come through, a view of the driveway and subsequent alley clear through the open slats of the mini blinds covering the door's glassed half. He was just about to leave when a red Chevy rolled through the back gate.

Can't go that way.

He turned and stared across the narrow office toward the door at the other end. It too was half glass, the cobalt blue of the pool just outside.

Inside, directly next to the outer door, was a tiny bathroom. He shot straight for it and pushed the wooden door nearly shut as the outside door opened and someone stepped into the office.

He peered through the cracked-open door.

The visitor was a woman. Mid-thirties, blond, cute. He remembered what De Florio told him about Reed and assumed she was his daughter. What was she doing here? She shuffled through the paper on the counter, then lifted the handset for the phone.

"Sir, according to the court's scheduled amount, that bond will be $385. The bondsman's not here right now, but I can get in touch with him and have him stop by the jail tonight."

Reed had a sideline business as a local bail bondsman. De Florio had briefed him on that too. The woman stood silent, listening, while the party on the other end spoke. Then she said, "That's fine. He'll be in touch."

She hung up and immediately opened the outside door leading to the driveway. Two car doors opened, then closed.

"I'm in here," she called out. "Was Lori Anne any trouble?"

"Not at all. She and Shelby had a good time," another woman said.

"Is Granddaddy here?" a little girl asked.

"Not right now. But he'll be back soon."

The two women started talking away from the doorway, a car engine idling made it difficult to hear anything specific. But he heard when the little girl announced, "I have to go to the bathroom."

A second later flip-flops entered the office.

He tensed. The child couldn't be allowed to see him. If she entered the bathroom he'd have no choice but to snap her neck, then slip out the pool door before the women decided to check on her. He could escape through the front of the house and resume his jog.

The footsteps came closer.

No time to pull on latex gloves. He'd just have to be careful what he touched.

The door inched inward.

"Lori Anne."

The child stood just outside, a mere few inches of white pine separating them. Reed's daughter was still outside, at the open doorway to the drive. He hoped she didn't enter the office too. The situation could then gestate rapidly out of control.

"Not out here," the woman said. "That's Granddaddy's room."

"I have to go."

"In the house. Then change and go swimming."

The child pushed the door further inward.

He prepared himself to grab her the second she was inside, one hand on her mouth, the other snapping her neck before she could make a sound.

"Lori Anne, I said not out here."

"But—"

"I'm not going to say it again."

"Okay. Okay."

Flip-flops receded.

The door leading out to the driveway closed, its mini blinds clanging. A few seconds later he heard the car leave through the back gate and a door for the house open and shut.

He listened.

No one seemed to be in the office.

He slowly inched the door open. The room was empty. He realized the pool area was about to be occupied and he'd taken enough chances.

So he left.

6:50 p.m.

HAMILTON LEE STOOD OUTSIDE AND WATCHED THE PICKUP DRIVE in and park in front of his house. He knew what the staff and employees called it. Dracula's Place. A reference to both its stark architecture and his abrasive personality. But he didn't mind. A little fear from those who worked for you was not a bad thing.

"Good to see you, Hank," he said, as Reed climbed out. "Seems like we only talk to each other at negotiation time."

"You waitin' for me?"

"Actually, I came out to see if the deer had left any of the summer buds. We have a terrible time with them out here. They eat everything. My wife's coming down next week and she loves the flowers. Let's go inside."

He led Reed into the house and back to a spacious den. "Can I get you anything to drink?"

"No, thanks. I had dinner before coming over."

"We're alone here. Only one of the staff back in the kitchen. Bozin is in Atlanta for the weekend, I'm told."

"I appreciate you comin' down."

"Negotiations start Monday and I've been wondering when we'd talk. It's one of our rituals I so look forward to every few years. Luckily the company plane was available when you called."

"I should have called sooner, but I've been fairly busy getting ready and haven't had time till now."

Lee doubted that observation. More likely Reed waited to the last minute intentionally, thinking his aloofness could be used as a bargaining chip. Particularly after he read the planted memos.

They both sat.

"I assume you're going to want five years again?" Reed asked.

They never small-talked or beat around the bush. Probably because they really weren't friends. More necessary acquaintances. But he decided to keep up the pretense a little while longer. "That's right. Just like last time. We need those extra two years to keep things stable."

193

"I was afraid of that. So what are you willing to give to get 'em?" Reed wanted to know.

Set the hook. "The more critical question is, can you deliver five years?"

"I've talked to the other two union presidents. I can get 'em to give you five, but it'll cost."

"And what if we're not interested in paying those costs for five years?"

"Maybe I can get you interested."

He shook his head. "You amaze me, Hank. Last time it was like pulling teeth to get those additional two years on the contract. I had to pay extra on wages and help build that union hall of yours. Now you're saying you'll get them for me?"

"You know I can't take my people and walk. A strike would serve no purpose. You'd love those couple of years, you just don't want to pay through the nose for 'em. I can get 'em . . . cheap."

The plan was working. Not only had Reed found the memo, he'd believed every single word. But he decided to stall a bit more. "Why didn't you negotiate this with Chris Bozin? He's the one down here this time."

Reed shrugged. "I prefer to deal with you."

He paused and started to reel him in. "So what will those extra two years cost, assuming for the moment I'm even interested?"

"No takebacks on anything we have. Some adjustment on the medical deductible, particularly for retirees. And at least a modest assurance on overtime."

"What do you mean by modest?"

"Enough that I can tell the membership we won the point. If you want it to fade into oblivion a year from now, you won't get any flak from me."

All the internal memos he'd read lately warned against guaranteeing any overtime hours. So he liked that concession. "I think that would work. Now to the meat of the coconut. What about wage increases?"

"Four percent spread over five years."

"Two percent and you guarantee the other unions will join."

"Three percent up front and I'll deliver the other two unions."

"Deal." But he wanted to know, "How are you going to explain a five-year contract to the other unions? None of them were wild about that last time."

"I won't have to," Reed said. "As soon as you see our first offer your people are going to automatically revise their offer down to three. Probably claim too much expense, the unions have asked for too much, anything just to blame us. When that happens we'll be out of gas. Everybody knows there's not going to be a strike. What'll we have to bargain with? Those added two years are our only negotiating tool and they know it."

"What makes you think we're going to revise our offer down? We've never done that before. We like five years."

"Changing from five to three has been your plan from the start."

He told himself to play along. The fish was out of the water and in the boat, with the hook firmly in its mouth. Let the fool think he won. "And how did you know that?"

"I have my sources."

"Care to tell me who?"

Reed only smiled.

"No. I don't suppose you'd 'fess up to that." Lee shook his head and finished the performance. "Not bad, Hank. Good work, as always. It's pretty hard to pull one over on you."

9:00 P.M.

CHRIS DROVE HIMSELF DOWNTOWN, PARKED IN THE UNDERGROUND garage, and slowly made his way up into the Blue Tower. He'd returned to Atlanta from Concord last evening and spent a quiet day at home, mainly enjoying the splendor of his summer garden while waiting for darkness.

The building's mezzanine cast a ghostly quiet. The only person in sight was a lone security guard manning the ground-floor information desk. All visitors on weekends were required to sign in and out. But that rule didn't apply to one of the owners. So he ignored the guard and continued a slow determined stride to the elevator bank, the pain in his abdomen mounting.

On the twenty-ninth floor he walked directly to his office. He didn't switch on any lights, preferring not to announce his presence. Though he already possessed some information, more thoughts had occurred to him over the past few days. It took half an hour to extract the remaining data from his computer and make sense of it in the narrative. Finally, he transferred everything to the same flash drive used a few days ago.

He switched off the terminal and ambled toward the door.

He did not bother to check his mail or phone messages.

Neither mattered anymore.

The pain was becoming unbearable and he was glad for the solitude.

He gazed across the darkened room at his desk—hand-carved oak, topped with Italian leather, imported from London. An assortment of Victorian chairs, a small Chesterfield sofa, bookcases, and a mahogany library table rounded out the English décor. He'd come a long way from making loans and agonizing over $1,000 deals. His accomplishments were legendary. His companies profitable. His reputation was one of a savvy businessman, the Silver Fox, who'd supposedly made a fortune through brains and hard work. But he could no longer ignore the ghosts of those sacrificed along the way. Their voices screamed at him through the night. And only in the twilight of his life had he come to regret what he'd done. His soul was beyond saving, his eternal fate sealed. Yet there were others whom he could save. People who would grow old and die naturally. Priorities who'd never make it onto future lists. And at the same time he could deny Hamilton Lee and Larry Hughes any measure of satisfaction.

He savored one last looked around his office.

Knowing he would never see it again.

DAY FOURTEEN
MONDAY, JUNE 19

10:00 A.M.

BRENT WALKED INTO THE COMFORT INN, THE FIRST TIME HE'D visited the local motel in years. The two-story structure occupied a highly visible tract just east of Highway 16A on County Road 26, the spur into Concord, and was the largest of the county's three motels.

Fourteen years ago he'd handled the divorce that forced the husband, a Howard Johnson's franchisee, to close the doors. A year later the county foreclosed and took the property back for taxes. A year after that another franchisee bought the building, changed the name, and upgraded. Now it comprised forty rooms, a pool, plenty of cabbage palms, a nice restaurant, and two spacious meeting rooms used regularly by the Concord Kiwanis Club and the Woods County Lions Club, as a placard out front announced.

Off-plant sites for collective bargaining sessions became the norm years ago. A site away from the mill diffused any charge of over-reaching and allowed the parties to comfortably sit at the table on an equal footing. He'd been told that the Comfort Inn had played host to the last two bargaining sessions, the site provided free of charge, the hope being that most of the participants would eat lunch in the dining room.

He entered the meeting room just as Christopher Bozin stepped to the front and said, "Gentlemen, how about we get started."

It was a safe salutation since a quick survey revealed no women were present. Bozin gave everyone a moment to quiet down. Brent found a chair just inside the door at the back of the room.

"I want to welcome you to the ninth set of negotiations between Southern Republic Pulp and Paper Company and its three chartered unions. The company is here. We're ready to negotiate an agreement and we hope it'll be done in record time."

Light applause followed.

Bozin beamed a broad congenial smile.

Though Brent was attending his first set of negotiations, he felt he'd been there before thanks to Hank's graphic daily descriptions. About twenty-five men were present, each union sending a negotiations committee that varied from three to five people along with a representative from their respective internationals. The company had assigned two-man teams to bargain with each local, all from industrial relations. Brent and his boss would float among the three sets of talks, offering legal help where needed.

All the blue-collar hourly men seemed unaccustomed to being strapped into shirts, ties, and jackets. A white or white-striped short-sleeved shirt, with polyester tie and no coat, seemed the most prevalent ensemble, though a few sported what must have been their Sunday suits. As usual Hank stood out among the crowd with a French-cuffed white shirt, silk tie, and pleated navy-blue trousers supported by his trademark cordovan leather belt. The cuff links and tie tack were obviously supplied by the union since, even from a distance, the colors and shape of the IBEW international emblem were easily recognizable. Everything was shined, pressed, and tastefully coordinated. So much that it would be easy to mistake him for one of the owners rather than an hourly paid senior day electrician. Bozin finished his introductory remarks and everyone began to collate into their respective groups. Brent headed toward Hank, knowing that, as Ricky Ricardo would say, *He had some explainin' to do.*

"For a guy who's not in the loop you're sure right here in the middle of things," his old friend said.

"Me being here is as much a surprise to me as it is to you."

"How'd it happen?"

He motioned toward Bozin. "I received a special invite from him."

"I guess they figure you can't help with me unless you see the show for yourself."

"Sound familiar?"

Hank smiled. "Tough being a double agent, huh?"

"I don't like it." And he hoped Hank got the message.

"You going to be here for the whole thing?" Hank asked.

Brent nodded.

"I like it."

He shook his head. "You don't hear a word I'm saying, do you?"

"I try not to."

Arguing was pointless. So he whispered, "Have you had your usual chat yet with Hamilton Lee?"

"Saturday night."

He knew how things happened. "So this is all a dog-and-pony show."

Hank nodded.

"It's a done deal. These folks just don't know it yet."

10:20 A.M.

JON CASUALLY ENTERED THE CROWDED NEGOTIATIONS ROOM DRESSED in his usual business suit. His public appearances at company functions were rare, but he needed to survey the situation and speak with Bozin.

The older man immediately noticed his presence and walked over, asking in a low voice, "Anything to report?"

He stepped close and whispered, "An attempt was made to enter Reed's house on Saturday but was unsuccessful. Another attempt will be made soon."

"Please keep me posted."

"I will. I also wanted you to know I have a guard outside to help if needed."

"How thoughtful. I'll let the unions know."

He excused himself and left.

Outside, Victor Jacks stood next to the double doors, dressed in the uniform of a Southern Republic guard. No one, including Bozin, knew his true identity. Jon walked by and threw his associate a knowing look.

One that said to keep his eyes and ears open.

12:00 P.M.

THE LUNCH BREAK CAME AT NOON SHARP AND EVERYONE RECESSED to the Comfort Inn's dining room where a midday buffet of meat loaf, country-fried steak, snap peas, okra, corn, mashed potatoes, biscuits, and apple cobbler had been laid out. Chris watched while everyone piled their plates full. He then ordered a small salad from the menu with an iced tea. Upper management and Brent Walker joined him at a wall table.

"How's Reed?" he asked his industrial relations director.

The company reps for the other two unions had already informed him that things were going smoothly with the paperworkers and machinists.

"Being his usual pain in the ass. Already raising hell about the five years. Wants it dropped to three today."

"He'll get his wish in a couple of days," he said, adding a grin everyone understood.

Hamilton Lee had called last night and gloated about his Saturday meeting with Reed. He knew the two would talk. It had happened that way at every negotiation since the 1990s. A deal would be hammered out in private, the agreement being that Reed would surreptitiously convince the other two unions and his own members to go along. Not a practice federal labor laws would necessarily sanction, but one that worked. The company benefited. Employees benefited. And Reed benefited.

He turned to Brent Walker, assuming he was the only other person at the table who knew about Reed's secret meeting with

Lee. "Just remember, Brent, union negotiations are not always as they appear. Far more illusion than reality."

Brent grinned. "I'll try and keep that in mind."

Lunch ended at 1:00 P.M. and everyone slowly made their way back for the afternoon bargaining session. On the way out Chris saw Brent push into the men's room.

He followed.

Brent was towel-drying his face and hands when he stepped in and went straight to the urinal. They were alone.

"I meant what I said the other day. I truly want your insight on this whole process."

"I'm not sure what I can offer other than to help with what the company may need."

It took effort to pee and hurt, but he kept the pain to himself. He then flushed and stepped over to wash his hands. "I think you're just being coy. We all know that you've been involved one way or the other with negotiations in the past. Hank relied heavily on your advice. You understand the process. I'm sure you know Hank met with Hamilton Lee on Saturday night, as they always do before the negotiations. You and I are the only two here that know that. So I assume you know a deal has already been made, at least in principle, and we just need to convince everyone else of its wisdom. Right?"

Brent stayed silent. Which was a tacit admission.

He yanked a paper towel from the dispenser. "I need your insight. Your help to convince everybody. I'm not asking you to betray a friend, only help your employer." He tossed the crumpled paper into the trash. "I imagine Hank would even appreciate the help. It seems to be getting tougher and tougher to make these deals."

He adjusted his tie and faced his newest employee.

"I'd also like to talk with you a little more. In private. Do you think you could have dinner with me?"

"Of course," Brent said.

What else would the younger man say?

"Have you ever been to Hickory Row?"

"I'm afraid I've never made its guest list."

"You have now. Come, tomorrow night. At seven. Dress comfortably. I'll tell the front gate to expect you."

2:40 P.M.

ASHLEY WAS CLEARING OUT HER MAIL TRUCK FROM THE DAY'S RUN. Concord's only post office sat on Highland Drive, north of the central business district. It was a gray government rectangle of rough granite shaded by tall oaks. A fenced asphalt parking lot spread out behind it, the gate open, and she saw a familiar vehicle motor in and stop.

Catherine Walker emerged.

Ashley was surprised. "Nice to see you. It's been a while. What brings you by?" She tried to mask the apprehension in her voice.

"Something that needs to be done," the older woman said, as she drew close. "The other day Brent and I had a chat. I told him then that life goes on. I've thought about that ever since and decided to take my own advice." Catherine paused. "I have Alzheimer's."

Had she heard right? That couldn't be.

"It's in its early stages. But I have the disease."

She did not know what to say.

"I can see that Brent didn't tell you."

She shook her head. "Not a word."

"That's the lawyer in him. God knows both he and his father could keep a secret. Now, don't look so glum. It's early, there are treatments, and I have a few good years left. That's one reason I'm here. To tell you that. The other is that your father came to see me."

Another surprise, but she had to know, "What did he say?"

"He's concerned about you and Brent. As I am."

"He promised to stay out of this."

"He loves his daughter and is worried. I love my son, and I'm worried too."

"This whole thing is a mess, and neither one of us really knows how to fix it." She paused. "Brent and I love each other, Catherine. I think we have for a long time. We should have worked that out before a lot of other people were hurt."

"Like your ex-husbands? Paula?"

Her face tightened. "That's not fair."

"None of this is fair. Don't get me wrong, I'm not here defending Paula. She had her faults, and was obviously quite troubled. But Paula is gone."

"Not to Brent. He still feels guilty."

"I want you to tell me why."

She hesitated. "I think you need to ask him that. It's not my place."

"But it is. You're the reason he feels guilty. Look, I wasn't blind to the problems in that marriage. Brent was never happy. There always seemed to be turmoil. But I never realized, until recently, the full extent of *your* involvement."

"Brent never cheated on his wife with me."

"I would have expected no less. But you were still there. A presence. An obstacle. A competitor to her. In some ways it was worse than an affair. You had his heart."

"Paula was determined to hang on to Brent. I think she knew from the start he didn't really love her—like a husband should love his wife. He tried to stop the marriage, but she wasn't going to let go."

"So if you loved him, why did you let him marry Paula?"

A fair question, one she'd posed to herself many times in the years since. "I was so screwed up back then. I didn't know what I wanted. I never focused on anything. Brent was the only man I ever felt really close to. I trusted him, though at the time I didn't realize that. It's taken growing older to see the mistakes I made. You're right, I should have told him how I felt. He'd get so agitated with me. He tried to pin me down, but I wouldn't allow it. Paula, to her credit, never gave up. She stayed with him, got the ring and the wedding."

"But she needed a pregnancy to make it happen."

"It never would have happened otherwise."

"And all of this has been festering for how long?"

"For me? Fifteen years. It ruined my three marriages. And Brent's." She watched the older woman closely, gauging the reaction. "I want you to know, again, it wasn't like we were sneaking around all the time. Our relationship wasn't all that physical. When he moved to Atlanta, I thought I could finally get over him—"

"But you couldn't."

She shook her head. "It only got worse. My third marriage was a disaster from the start. But I didn't want her to die, Catherine. You have to know that. No one wanted her to die. Her killing herself was the last thing anybody considered. Brent, especially. He had no clue she was that unstable."

"Paula kept a lot to herself. Which became her undoing. What about you, Ashley, when do you plan to tell Brent everything?"

She stared at Catherine Walker.

And saw it in her eyes.

"Your father felt I should know the truth. Of course, he doesn't know about the Alzheimer's. He was doing what daddies do for their daughters. Help them out. I'm glad he did. I've thought of little else since he dropped by. I have a granddaughter I never knew existed."

Silence hovered over them.

Both women absorbing the magnitude of the situation.

Tears swirled in Ashley's eyes.

"Brent has to know," Catherine said. "It may draw him closer."

"It may also drive him away," she said.

"Deceit can do that, but it's a risk you'll have to take. At some point, the lies have to end."

Tears now filled Catherine Walker's eyes.

"I almost think you're on my side," she said.

"I'm on Brent's side. If you make him happy, and I think you do, then I'll support you a hundred percent. I don't want to see him, or you, hurt anymore."

"Paula was so difficult. He wanted to end things. He really did. But she didn't play fair."

"That's right. Including killing herself. I get his guilt. I really do. But what would he have done if he'd known Lori Anne was his daughter?"

"I've asked myself that a million times. It happened right before I married Manley Simmons. I immediately knew the child was Brent's. But I told everyone it was Manley's."

"Why didn't you tell him before he married Paula?"

"I don't know. It seemed easier to keep quiet. Say nothing. Go on."

"He would have married you."

"I know that now. Then, I wasn't so sure."

"Brent never asked about Lori Anne?"

"Once, years ago. But I lied. Manley suspects, but God bless him, he's never said a word. Lori Anne adores him. Telling the truth could be devastating for her."

"But lies are always worse."

Amen.

"In the divorce Manley agreed to pay child support. I went along just to keep up the pretense. But I've put every dime into a special account. I figured one day I'd give it back to him." She had to say, "I love Brent, Catherine. This time I'm not going to let him go."

"I came here today to say that I'm sick and getting old. I have to know my son's going to be all right. I'm afraid Brent's hesitant, thinking I won't approve of any of this. But it's not my decision to make. It's yours and his, not to mention Lori Anne's. Make this happen, Ashley. Fix it, while you can."

She never could have had this conversation with her own mother. Sadly, she was a selfish, narrow-minded woman who lived across the state. True, they were cordial, with calls on holidays, birthdays, and Mother's Day. But that was the extent of their relationship. No bond existed. Lori Anne barely knew her. They were both far closer with her father, but sometimes she wished for a mother.

"I really would like a granddaughter," Catherine said. "While I can enjoy her."

Tears flowed.

"I think she'd love that too."

4:45 P.M.

HANK LEFT IMMEDIATELY AFTER THE FIRST DAY OF NEGOTIATIONS ended, waving off an offer by his negotiations committee to reconvene at the VFW for a beer. For the next week none of the union delegations would report to work at the mill. Instead, the Comfort Inn would be where they'd toil from 8:00 to 4:30, until their respective locals concluded a deal.

Overall, day one went well. After pitching IBEW's initial offer, Hank preached all afternoon about the dire needs of his members. Which included assured overtime, new call-in procedures, health benefits, and wages. Each was debated in agonizing detail. The company countered with its initial offer and, as expected, asked for a contract five years in length. He'd feigned surprise and raised hell about the evils of long-term deals, all for the benefit of his negotiations committee and to further the perception of how tough and unrelenting he could be. He'd need a strong reputation later in the week when it finally came time to convince the other two locals, and his own members, to join in a five-year deal.

That and a little luck, he thought as he parked his truck under the carport.

He drifted inside the house and stripped off his shirt and tie, donning his bathing suit. He wasn't hungry, rarely did he eat dinner before seven, so he headed outside to the pool. The sun had already made its daily pass over the backyard, the late afternoon looming hot and humid. He plunged into the lukewarm water and began to relax. A few laps back and forth was the extent of his exercise program. He was in good shape. No appreciable health problems, and he was genuinely looking forward to a decade or two of peaceful retirement, living off his savings and the monthly check Southern Republic would send to supplement Social Security. He enjoyed the water for a few more minutes, then dried off and stepped into his office. He needed to make a few calls and remind some scatterbrains about their court appearances scheduled next week. The bail bonding business brought in a nice side income, one he'd also be counting on in retirement.

The phone rang.

Which happened at all hours of the day and night. He answered and learned that somebody was looking for bond money.

"What's the charge?" he asked the caller.

"Got myself arrested for burglary."

"How much is the bond?"

"Ten thousand."

Now for the real question. "Got collateral? Land, car, jewelry. Something I can hold to make sure you come back."

"Thought that's what the bond was for."

They all said the same thing. "The bond's for the court. I don't plan to pay out ten thousand of my dollars when you decide not to show. I need collateral, so I know you're serious."

The caller sighed. "I'll have to get back to you."

"Give me your name."

The caller did.

"You own any land in the county?"

The caller did and told him where.

"You're also going to need a thousand bucks for my fee. Ten percent, like the law allows."

"Didn't know that either."

"I guess you figured I was going to sign my life away just 'cause you're a great guy?"

"I'll call you back later."

"You do that."

In anticipation of a possible return call, he reached for the county tax roll. He bought a copy every January from the Woods County tax commissioner. That data allowed instant verification on what land a potential bondee, or their family, owned and to what degree it was encumbered. He thumbed through and confirmed what the caller said. He owned a half-acre tract near the mill assessed at $8,000, a $4,000 first lien in place to the Woods County State Bank. Now if the man called back there'd be no blind reliance on what was said. He'd know. And he liked knowing the answers before the questions were asked.

He slid the printout back on the plywood shelf.

Glancing down, he noticed the clipboard lying on the counter with the list of numbers. He hadn't thought about them in a few days, his brain filled with contract negotiations.

What were they?

He'd been snooping in company records for decades. In the old days it was a peek here and there into paper files. Then copy machines made it possible for spies to bring the information to him. Computers made things both easier and more difficult, with their passwords and firewalls. But little within the company network was beyond his scrutiny.

Except these numbers.

The desktop computer dinged for a new email.

He was moderately computer-literate. Ashley had taught him a lot. He appreciated technology, seeing the wisdom in its many uses. He sat before the monitor and saw that the email came from the union member he'd assigned to deal with Paul Zimmerman's family. When a member died the membership did everything they could to ease the family's pain and burden. This death was particularly heartbreaking, considering its suddenness and the children. The widow was terrified how she was going to pay the bills and feed her kids. He'd told his man to assure her there would be no problems with either.

The email was an update on what was happening.

He read it with keen interest. He cared for every one of his members, good and bad alike. He was their leader and a leader led.

His man noted in his report that the death benefit form had been completed and he urged it to be quickly processed. He clicked on the attachment and opened it, making sure everything was in order. And it appeared to be so. He would process the form tomorrow through industrial relations and make sure the $50,000 death benefit was promptly paid. That should help alleviate some of the widow's fears.

Then he noticed something.

Paul Zimmerman's Social Security number.

Handwritten into the space reserved for that information. Since it was the only Social Security number he possessed on his members, he decided to take a quick look. He grabbed the clipboard with the list still attached.

034156901
456913276
343016692
295617833
178932515
236987521
492016755
516332578

And found a match on the seventh line. 492-01-6755. Paul Zimmerman's Social Security number.

There.

Part of the list.

Coincidence? No friggin' way.

He sat back in the chair, which squeaked from the strain, and stared at the clipboard.

Now more intrigued than ever.

DAY FIFTEEN
TUESDAY, JUNE 20

9:34 A.M.

HAMILTON LEE FIDGETED BEHIND HIS DESK IN THE BLUE TOWER and watched De Florio, who sat calmly on the other side. He sensed his subordinate was deriving a certain twinge of pleasure at seeing him squirm.

"What happened after your man was almost caught in Reed's house Saturday?" he asked.

"I had him reenter this morning."

"Why not wait till dark?"

"Reed was at work. His cleaning lady doesn't come until tomorrow. Daylight presents an opportunity without unnecessary risks."

"What happened Saturday?"

"The daughter was at Reed's house, but there was no vehicle outside. Luckily, things worked out and my man was in and out without detection."

"What did he find today?"

"The list was in Reed's office. But nothing indicated he was aware of its significance. The telephone and office were bugged for later monitoring."

He couldn't believe this. In the twenty-plus years since the start of the Priority program this was their first security breach. They were always so careful. So precise. Hired only the best and demanded

210

absolute perfection. Anything less was dealt with severely. Now a damn lightning bolt might crash it all?

"There's more," De Florio said. "Last Thursday, Mr. Bozin conducted a private meeting with Brent Walker. It lasted about fifteen minutes in the main conference room, after a staff meeting Bozin specifically included Walker on. Yesterday, Bozin ate lunch with Walker and other company people during a break in the negotiations. I place no special significance on that. However, afterward, the two of them were alone for a few minutes in the restroom. The man I have stationed at the negotiations was unable to find out if they actually spoke or not."

"But they were alone in the restroom?"

De Florio nodded. "My man went in right after to be sure."

He instantly recalled how Bozin had made a point last week to ask that Brent Walker be included in the negotiations. At the time he'd understood the wisdom of the move. After all, that was the main reason they'd hired Walker in the first place. But why would they now be having private conversations? Talks that Bozin had made no mention of.

"Why do you find it necessary to so closely monitor your partner?" De Florio asked.

"Mr. Bozin has exhibited what Mr. Hughes and I consider unusual behavior of late."

"You doubt his commitment to the company?"

"I'm not sure. As you know, Chris is a man of few words, making it difficult ever to know exactly what he thinks."

"Mr. Bozin has always shown a strong dedication."

"But he's getting old and hasn't been looking well of late."

"I've noticed some deterioration myself. Is there some concern about Brent Walker and Mr. Bozin?"

"I'm not sure. I just find it significant that Chris wants to talk with Walker."

"It could simply concern the negotiations or perhaps Walker's association with Reed."

"Brent Walker is green to this industry. Outside of helping with Reed, there's little he could offer Chris. But it's Walker's association with Reed that worries me. Reed could discuss the list with him. They were quite close once. Probably still are."

"That would certainly broaden our already difficult containment problem."

"Hell, Jon, we can't go around killing everybody. The idea was to save money, not help with overpopulation."

"Now it may simply be a matter of survival."

He glared at De Florio. "And not just ours, huh?"

"I have a definite stake in this."

"Really, now? I assume you're mobile as a bird. All the money we've paid you is probably in Europe or the Caribbean, safely hidden behind myriad protective laws. You're not married. No family. We provide everything you need. You could disappear in a blink of an eye."

"Perhaps. But I do not desire to spend my life in jail, or on the run from the law."

"Neither do I. But, unlike you, I have no place to run. My roots are all here."

"I understand," was all De Florio seemed willing to concede.

He returned to business. "What do you recommend?"

"We need to continue monitoring Reed and learn what he does as soon as it happens. And we certainly don't want to overreact. He may not be interested in that list at all."

"I agree. We still need to get it back."

"That would draw attention. But I have erased all vestiges of it from our system. It doesn't exist here anymore."

"Good to hear."

"Brent Walker's house phones should be bugged," De Florio said.

"Do it."

"I recommend that the phone where Reed stays at the mill be tapped. I believe he calls the place the Boar's Nest."

"Do it."

"Depending on how extensive this gets, I may need some freelance help for a limited time."

"Hire it."

"I would also recommend keeping a constant eye on Mr. Bozin and Brent Walker. That should be easy since they'll both be at the negotiations. I already have a man there."

"What about evenings?"

"I have a person I can depend on inside Bozin's house at the Row."

He was intrigued. "I wasn't aware you had people inside our private homes."

"I don't. I cultivated this source last week when you instructed me to monitor Mr. Bozin."

But he wasn't so sure. That concern, though, would have to wait until another time.

"Do we need electronic monitoring at Bozin's house?" he asked.

"I don't think so. My source should keep me adequately informed."

"To keep up appearances, I want you to report to Bozin everything learned so far. He asked for that. Leave off the fact you and I have talked."

De Florio nodded.

"I still want to be kept instantly informed, though. If necessary, we'll move to Priority orders on a moment's notice. You need to be prepared."

"I already have some information gathered on Reed and Walker."

"Good. The way things are headed, you're probably going to need it."

3:20 P.M.

BRENT HAD BEEN CORRALLED AT THE COMFORT INN ALL DAY. HANK found him right as the lunch break ended and asked him again about the list of numbers. *I really need you to do this.* But nothing more had been offered. He'd probably kicked that can as far down the street as he could. So when the day's session ended early, he headed straight back to the office. The list and his notes were still tucked inside his desk drawer. He retrieved them, started his search again with the third set of numbers, and found a new name. The fourth match rang bells. Brandon Pabon. The workers' comp case that died of a drug overdose.

He kept going until he found a name for each set of numbers.

034156901 William Mesnan, May 23, Heart attack
456913276 Patrick Brown, May 21, Kidney failure
343016692 J. J. Jordon
295617833 Brandon Pabon, June 6, Drug overdose
178932515 Tim Featherston
236987521 Melvin Bennett
492016755 Paul Zimmerman, June 13, Hunting accident
516332578 Michael Ottman

So what was this? A list of recently deceased employees?

That couldn't be.

Hank gave him the list last Saturday, June 10. Maybe the fact that each person was dead didn't matter? Just a coincidence that Zimmerman was included. Or maybe not.

He had to know more.

So he selected one name from the list, Tim Featherston, and found the man's employment records, learning he was a former electrician who retired six years ago. His current address was in Reeling, Georgia. The 912 area code meant the town was somewhere in middle or south Georgia.

He grabbed the phone and dialed. Two rings later the familiar tone came through with the irritating announcement, *"The number you have dialed is not in service."* He dialed again, just to make sure he'd dialed right, but got the same response. He checked the records again and saw that Featherston's beneficiary, in case of death, was a daughter. She lived at the north end of Woods

County. Her contact information was there. He dialed. A woman answered and he introduced himself.

"I work in the general counsel's office at the mill. I was trying to get in touch with your father, but the number we have on file no longer works."

"I'm sorry, but my father died the week before last."

He was surprised. "You have my deepest condolences." But he had to know, "How did it happen?"

"A silly bee sting. He had a bad allergy to them, and some got into his trailer during the night."

The question formed immediately. "Could I ask what day he died?"

"Sometime early on the seventh."

"I'm so sorry for troubling you. Again, my condolences."

He told her goodbye and hung up. Five out of eight were dead. That was no coincidence. That was a pattern. But he needed to know one other critical piece of information. Unimportant.

Until now.

When exactly had Hank obtained the list?

5:40 P.M.

BRENT WAS IMPRESSED WITH HICKORY ROW. WHITE-FENCED emerald pastures held grazing sable thoroughbreds. Does and bucks wandered openly, unconcerned about harm. Wild turkeys, colorful ducks, and geese milled about under a thick canopy of enveloping trees.

Originally, he and Ashley had planned to go out for a pizza. But she'd understood the importance of Bozin's invitation, and they decided to do something else over the weekend. He'd noticed Ashley's edginess over the past couple of days. Last night he thought she'd wanted to talk to him about something, but the subject got changed and she never steered it back. She was like that sometimes. Secretive, quiet, withdrawn. Odd for a person with such an outgoing personality. He'd tried several times to find Hank, but his calls had gone unanswered, his messages unreturned.

The security guard at the main gate provided a printed map with directions to Bozin's cottage, informing him that it sat at the end of a paved lane bearing the owner's name. Before heading that way he took advantage of the opportunity and drove around the entire complex, admiring the rustic opulence. Finally, just before seven, he found the house.

Long shadows from the surrounding trees stretched across a cut lawn littered with straw. Two peacocks with full plumage meandered about. The exterior was a mixture of brick, limestone, and mortar. On one end a stone chimney arched high, thick with ivy. Like a French manor house had been transported across the Atlantic and deposited in the Georgia woods. He parked in the drive beside a familiar crimson pickup. The same sticker that had been attached to the bumper for years was still there. AIN'T MAD AT NOBODY. Hank Reed's truck. Now he realized why he'd been ignored. His old friend was trolling for bigger fish.

The front bell announced his presence in the soft chime of church bells. A moment later the door opened.

"Please, come in," Bozin said. "Did you find your way all right?"

"Nothing to it."

He entered the elegant foyer, the room ringed with lovely walnut furniture. "Hank's here?"

"He's waiting in the living room."

Bozin gestured toward a short hall that led to a spacious den with a high, arched cathedral ceiling. His eyes were drawn to the rear wall, which rose nearly all in plate glass. Outside, a patio was rimmed with bright marigolds. Beyond rose tall pines, then a shimmer of a lake. It felt like they were outside.

"I didn't know you were on the guest list for tonight," Hank said, standing by a wall bar.

Bozin moved toward the sofa. "I have to confess, I arranged this dinner and didn't tell either of you about inviting the other. I hope you don't mind."

Neither he nor Hank said anything. What could they say? Bozin was the boss. But he wondered what the old man was up to.

"Have a seat. Dinner will be served shortly. Can I get either of you anything to drink?"

He and Hank declined, saying they would wait until dinner.

"It's a lovely house," he said.

"My home in Atlanta is mostly Italian. My office English. So I decided to make this place decidedly French."

They chitchatted for a few minutes about nonsense. Finally, Bozin asked Hank, "How do you think the negotiations are going?"

"So far, so good."

"What about after tomorrow? We're going to change our offer from three to five years in the morning. The unions ready?"

"They don't like it, but they're expecting the shift. I already have my counteroffer ready. So do the other locals. It wasn't easy. Everyone is greedy as hell, but everything so far is within the arranged deal."

Bozin smiled. "Efficient as always, Hank. I knew you could pull it off. But it's a good deal for the employees. Three percent on wages is generous, considering all the extras we provide. Our people have the best health care and retirement program around. Name one mill with anything better."

"You're preachin' to the choir on that one," Hank said. "I have no complaints."

"We did the right thing, years ago, going self-insured. It's allowed great flexibility in dealing with a changing marketplace. I don't mind telling you it scared the hell out of me at first, but internalizing health care and retirement has proven a sound move. Which really paid off when the Affordable Care Act was passed. It didn't take much to match our plan to its mandates. We are one of the few companies to do that successfully," Bozin continued, pointing a finger, "without breaking the bank. I hope we can keep that up. Times are getting rough."

The comment was strange, so Brent asked, "How so?"

"The domestic paper industry is not in one of its strongest

cycles. Foreign competition is driving our prices below production costs. Most companies are expanding overseas, taking advantage of cheap labor, but we haven't. Southern Republic has committed itself to being one hundred percent American. Perhaps a foolish decision, but our employees should certainly appreciate it."

Brent couldn't help but wonder if the information was true or just another ploy used in bargaining, perhaps like the dinner invitation itself.

"Thankfully, we're sufficiently diversified into lumber and building products. As the price of paper plummets, selling building products can buoy our bottom line, and has for years now."

The older man seemed genuinely pleased.

"Caution is the word," Bozin said. "Hank, the deal you and Hamilton hammered out is a good one. It'll allow us to keep moving forward. We're talking about building a massive new plant to handle recycled paper, a $100 million investment, which will probably be located here in Woods County, or nearby. Think of the jobs."

A steward appeared in the doorway and informed them dinner was ready.

"Shall we, gentlemen," Bozin said, gesturing.

6:00 P.M.

BRENT SAT AT THE TABLE.

Dinner was served in a formal dining room, opulent with a polished black marble floor and oversized gateleg table lined with eight high-backed upholstered chairs. A carved chest acted as a server, a seventeenth-century oil painting Bozin called *Portrait of a Young Girl* hung above it. The main course was a bass fillet that their host explained came from the lake behind the house. A baked potato, corn soufflé, and citrus salad rounded out the meal. Everything was served on bone china that bore the gold-embossed Hickory Row emblem. Wine was offered but he and Hank both declined, having iced tea instead.

"Hank, exactly how long have you worked at the mill?" Bozin asked, while they ate.

"Thirty-seven years this October."

"Have you liked it?"

"Southern Republic provides an excellent living."

"Brent, your father worked at the mill, didn't he?"

"Over forty years. Started with Republic Board. He helped build the plant, then was hired on as a machinist."

"I never knew him, but there've been a lot of men like your father through our years in business. They've been good to us."

They certainly have, Brent thought, looking around the room again.

"Concord survived thanks to Southern Republic," Hank said.

"For the better?" Bozin asked.

"I'd say so. Paved roads. New schools. Water and sewer system. The hospital. Convalescent center. We couldn't have afforded any of those improvements if not for Southern Republic. Republic Board changed us some, but that company didn't invest in the area like you have."

Brent thought back to when Southern Republic arrived. He was still in Cub Scouts but Hank was right, the changes even during his lifetime were profound. Car dealerships opened, banks sprouted, businesses flourished, two shopping centers were constructed. Franchise food places arrived. Cable television became available. Natural gas lines came their way. And with one small but convenient substitution, rural routes were abolished and addresses assigned that allowed home delivery of mail. In the span of a few decades, things were altered forever. A lot like his own life, which during the past few weeks had irrevocably changed too.

"I remember coming here just before we bought the company," Bozin said. "The mill was in bad shape, ready to close. Republic Board was on the verge of bankruptcy. Concord was just a small agricultural community, a world unto itself. I knew it was going to take a lot of work and a lot of money to make things go. And it did. But I think we now have a town and county that's a good place to live. In our favor, I'd say we've been a good corporate citizen. Always paying our taxes, as assessed, on time."

But Brent knew how things worked. Company employees perennially filled seats on the board of tax assessors, city council, and county commission. Not to mention Hank's long tenure as mayor. Friends in high places never hurt when it came to decision time.

Bozin looked at Hank. "Would you say Concord is a company town?"

"I used to hear that all the time. Out-of-town reporters wanted to know if Southern Republic controlled everything. I told folks, to my knowledge, there's no company store where employees spend their whole paycheck trying to keep accounts current. The company doesn't dictate city or county policy. We have franchise operations and small businesses owned and operated by a bunch of folks that don't have anything to do with Southern Republic."

Listening to Hank's description brought to mind what Brent always equated with *a company town*. Were they still around? Barely. Look at the decline of the American steel industry, the problems with U.S. automobile manufacturers, and, just like Bozin said earlier, don't forget about overseas competition, which was driving the price of everything to rock-bottom lows. It was hard enough to just survive. But survive and control everything?

Nearly impossible.

"It really insulted me when people thought the company ran everything here," Hank said. "I always thought I did."

Brent smiled. "You didn't?"

The sarcasm in his voice was clear.

"Believe it or not, it was a democracy."

"Until the council, or anyone else, disagreed with you."

Bozin chuckled. "He's got you there, Hank."

Dessert was served in the living room, a delicious key lime pie topped with real whipped cream. Brent could have actually eaten another piece, but wasn't offered seconds.

"How long do you think it'll take to finish the negotiations?" Bozin asked Hank.

"Probably by Monday or Tuesday of next week."

"No chance of anything sooner?"

"I doubt it. The members are going to have to digest the changes and get used to the idea of five years again. That takes a little time to get right."

"This is the tricky point," Bozin said. "I always worry about the other unions. Whether we can bring them in line. Have you ever had any reservations, Hank, about the way we do this?"

"Not a one. It's the only way to bargain. The privacy allows a reasonable deal among reasonable men."

The older man sighed. "I remember in the beginning when we negotiated everything in the open. Long, hard bargaining sessions. Robbie Shuman made things tough, didn't he?"

"You got that right."

"Brent, did you ever meet Shuman?" Bozin asked.

"No, sir. But I went to high school with his son. He was shot to death, as I remember. What a terrible thing."

"Robbie was tough as nails," Hank said. "But he was also pigheaded."

"I'm curious, Hank, when did Hamilton first suggest the more private bargaining sessions?"

"A long time ago. He called me to the front office one day and we had a talk. That was the first time we ever sat down with the door closed."

"You may not know this, but Robbie was offered that chance too. He refused. He was, indeed, difficult to work with."

"It doesn't surprise me. Robbie was a good union president, he looked after his people, but there are many ways to get the job done. You gotta be tough. That's true. But you don't have to be an asshole."

"You must have been thrilled at the time, though. An offer to act as the ultimate deal maker between the unions and management."

"Every negotiation since has run a thousand percent smoother."

Bozin nodded. "How do you get the other two unions to go along? That has to be difficult."

"I've been lucky there. The presidents of IAM and UPIU have always been friends. They listen to me."

"The deals you helped forge have been good for everybody. You understand things, Hank. And you never lose sight of the ultimate goal. Keep the mill operating. Keep people working. That's what's important."

"I say a steady paycheck is far better than some onetime fat raise, or overly generous benefit, that will ultimately have to be paid for in lost jobs."

They talked for another half hour.

More about the negotiations, the company, and Concord.

Bozin seemed to genuinely enjoy bantering with Hank, and Brent enjoyed watching the two older warriors. It was 8:30 when they were standing back in the foyer saying goodbye.

The front doorbell rang.

Bozin opened the carved-paneled door.

A man stood outside.

He was tall, with a sinewy, hard, athletic physique. Early forties, brown hair faded to a dull sheen by gray streaks. A gravitas look dominated the chiseled face, which cast a nothing stare reminiscent of a funeral director. Brent vaguely recalled seeing the face once before, at the opening of the negotiations yesterday. The man had talked briefly with Bozin.

"Jon, I don't know if you know these gentlemen or not."

"No, sir. I don't believe I do."

The voice was soft and low, no syllable given any overt inflection.

He was introduced as Jon De Florio, chief of company security.

"I've heard your name, but this is the first time I think I've ever actually met you," Hank said.

"I believe it is," De Florio said. "I can come back later."

Bozin waved him off. "There's no need. Brent and Hank were on their way home."

Bozin escorted them onto the front porch. "It was good of you to come. I enjoyed our talk. I hope it was enlightening. Maybe we can get together again before I go back to Atlanta."

Brent and Hank headed for their vehicles.

"We need to talk," Brent whispered to Hank, keeping his gaze straight ahead.

"I saw you called a few times. About what?"

"Those numbers. I found something."

"Since you're telling me this, does that mean the list is not nothing?"

"What day did you get it?"

"The night you got back to town."

June 6.

He connected the dots. "It's definitely not nothing."

Then he glanced back.

Bozin waved goodbye and he returned the gesture with a smile. He then climbed into his car and started the engine but took a moment and looked beyond Bozin at Jon De Florio.

Who, through the open front door, watched everything.

8:45 P.M.

CHRIS SAT IN THE DEN AND LISTENED AS DE FLORIO REPORTED WHAT he'd learned so far about Reed and the list. He absorbed the necessary details for what he had in mind, his face betraying nothing, his words a lie.

"When I hadn't heard anything from you," he said, "I decided to ask Reed here to see what I could personally find out. Hank and I have always been able to talk in the past."

"Did you learn anything?"

He shook his head. "He never mentioned anything remotely connected with the list." Then he feigned disappointment but was actually pleased. Questions had to be swirling in De Florio's inquisitive mind. Especially one. Why was the new kid on the block also here? Intentionally, he'd offered nothing on that subject. Instead, he asked, "What are you going to do now?"

"Maintain surveillance. Perhaps even step it up some. Until we know the extent of this, we have to keep a close eye on Reed."

"I agree." He hoped De Florio would expend all his resources there. He needed some freedom to finish what he'd started. "Have Hamilton and Larry been informed?"

"I'll leave that to you."

He was not naïve enough to think that De Florio had not already talked with Lee, but he played along. "I'll take care of that in the morning."

De Florio rose from the chair. "Is there anything else you need from me tonight?"

He stood too. But immediately winced in pain, grabbing his abdomen, catching his breath.

De Florio reached out to help. "Are you all right?"

A couple of deep breaths and he gathered himself. "I'm fine. Really." He steadied himself, then stood straight. "It's nothing. Just a small medical problem I've had to deal with lately. Nothing serious. That'll be all. Thank you."

"You want me to call a doctor?"

"That won't be necessary." He sucked a few more deep breaths. "Are you staying at the lodge or in one of the guesthouses?"

"I have one of the guesthouses."

"I know where to reach you then."

De Florio excused himself and left through the front door.

He'd actually been having a fairly good day with the pain. Only during the last hour or so had that changed. He still could have easily kept the discomfort to himself, God knows he'd suffered through enough practice, but he'd intentionally not. Hopefully, the message did not go unnoticed by the messenger.

He crept up the stairs one step at a time. The chime from the grandfather clock in the foyer announced 9:00 P.M. He could hear the staff tidying the kitchen and the dining room and knew they would switch off the remaining lights and lock up when finished.

Upstairs, he carefully undressed and slipped on his pajamas and robe. He brushed his teeth and, not yet ready for sleep, strolled out onto the balcony into the warm night, the cedar deck damp from an earlier shower.

Crickets and frogs serenaded one another through the blackness. His house was in the extreme west corner of the property, away from the river and most of the other facilities. He liked the solitude. He also liked that his fellow shareholders were nowhere nearby.

De Florio's appearance had been fortuitous. He assumed Lee was having him watched. He also assumed De Florio had recruited one of his house stewards as an accomplice, exactly why he'd arranged for the dinner here. But De Florio showing up and witnessing things firsthand seemed perfect. Lee and Hughes had obviously yet to find what he'd left. Before tonight, though, there really was no need to look. Once they did, he knew the situation would gestate rapidly. From that point on time would be short. He needed to be ready to move on a moment's notice and finish what he started.

He angled his head toward the sky. A first quarter moon hung to the north, thin clouds swirling in slender fingers, veiling and unveiling the stars.

How much longer until relief?

The weekend?

Next week?

Hopefully, sooner than that.

9:40 P.M.

BRENT SHOWED HANK WHAT HE'D DECIPHERED SO FAR.

034156901 William Mesnan, May 23, Heart attack
456913276 Patrick Brown, May 21, Kidney failure
343016692 J. J. Jordon
295617833 Brandon Pabon, June 6, Drug overdose
178932515 Tim Featherston June 7, Anaphylactic shock
236987521 Melvin Bennett
492016755 Paul Zimmerman, June 13, Hunting accident
516332578 Michael Ottman

"You got this on June 6," he said to Hank. "Pabon died that same day. Featherston dies on the seventh. Zimmerman a week later. Something's wrong here. If this is a list of deceased employees, how did Featherston and Zimmerman get on it?"

"That's a really good question."

Yes, it was.

"Jordon, Bennett, and Ottman have been retired a long time," Hank said. "Let's see what I can find out about them."

They were parked in the grassy lot for the county's main recreation center, where the two baseball diamonds and football field were located, not far outside Concord. Nobody else was around. That, and the darkness, offered a great measure of privacy. They'd driven straight here from Hickory Row. Hank worked the cell phone for twenty minutes, making calls until he learned that all three men were also dead, along with the dates that it happened.

034156901 William Mesnan, May 23, Heart attack
456913276 Patrick Brown, May 21, Kidney failure
343016692 J. J. Jordon, June 6, Heart failure
295617833 Brandon Pabon, June 6, Drug overdose
178932515 Tim Featherston, June 7, Bee sting
236987521 Melvin Bennett, June 8, Anaphylactic shock
492016755 Paul Zimmerman, June 13, Hunting accident
516332578 Michael Ottman, June 9, Heart attack

"All total," Brent said, "two died on the sixth, the same day you got this list. Four died after."

"What about Mesnan and Brown? They were before that."

"We have no idea how long that list was in the company computers. It could have been created even before those two died, meaning this is a list of people who are *going* to be dead."

He could see that Hank agreed.

"I don't know a lot about these other people," Brent said. "But I do know Brandon Pabon had a workers' comp claim that was going to cost the company several hundred thousand dollars to resolve. And his drug overdose ended that."

"Okay, Pabon was an injured worker, but most of the rest were retirees. Some gone from the mill for years. Only Zimmerman was still on the payroll."

"Retirees draw a pension," he said. "They also have lots of medical claims. I did see in our records that Melvin Bennett had terminal cancer. Ottman, heart problems."

"What about Zimmerman?"

"Not a thing. But his kids had some expensive medical problems."

"That's right. I was over there last weekend before the funeral. His wife was hysterical wondering how she was going to pay all the medical bills without the company health insurance."

"Everybody on this list was costing the company money. Seems like a pretty good reason for a self-insurer, like Southern Republic, to get rid of somebody, wouldn't you say?"

Hank shook his head. "You've been a prosecutor too long. Southern Republic handles hundreds of comp claims every year. They've funded that system with millions of reserve dollars. It's rock-solid and solvent. The health insurance is the same way. The employees pump millions into it every year. There's no need to kill people. You just litigate the hell out of things until they go away."

"Ever heard of greed?"

Hank was silent.

"I was reading something a few days ago in a workers' compensation journal that chronicles cases from around the country," Brent said. "A logging company in Washington State got sued by the widow of an employee. She claimed the company intentionally withheld comp benefits and stonewalled her husband's medical treatment, all of which she said led to his premature death. The state's workers' compensation statute provided for a onetime $50,000 payment on the death of an employee, but if he'd lived the settlement would have been in the $500,000 range. So the company had an incentive to hasten her husband's death."

"Did she win?"

"The jury gave her the $500,000 and stacked another $2.5 million in punitive damages."

"Is that rule the same in Georgia?"

"Oh, yeah. Far cheaper on an insurer, or an employer like Southern Republic who's self-insured, if the injured worker dies than just gets hurt. Corpses don't go to the doctor."

He knew the drill. Workers' compensation had nothing to do with fault. Instead, that concept had been replaced with certainty. Every worker injured on the job was compensated. Period. The only issues were how much and for how long.

"Things like pain and suffering, punitive damages, and general damages don't apply," he said. "The idea is to get the worker paid, healed, retrained if needed, and back on the job."

"You think Southern Republic had something to do with Brandon Pabon's death?"

He shrugged. "That's impossible to say. I read his file. He was a long-standing druggie. The coroner's report indicated he was loaded up on heroin. Pabon could have just overdosed. A lucky occurrence for the company. And the others on this list could have just happened to die, too. But think of the money to be realized by the company from those deaths."

"I think you're reading far more into this than there is. Killing people isn't that easy. You always get caught. And retirees die every day."

"But not before drawing a pension that costs the company money."

"Our pensions are financed over long periods of time with funds invested and set aside especially for that. We fight over that amount every time we negotiate a new contract."

"Doesn't the company make parallel contributions for employees?"

"That's what we fight over. It seems to get smaller and smaller with each new contract."

"So if the company can eliminate costs on the back side from what it has to pay out, it'll have more on the front side to bargain with. Right? Why use company money when you can use the employees'. Also, while you're at it, eliminate some costly retirement and medical payments and some especially expensive workers' comp claims. All that generates cash savings that can be used for other things like raw materials, cost overruns, price increases, things like that."

Brent had thought about this all afternoon, even asking his boss a few casual questions about the paper business. The costs of timber, water, electricity, coal, oil, chemicals, all the other things needed to make paper were pretty much the same for every mill. The real variable among companies was the big-ticket item. Labor. Which was the number one cost of any manufacturing plant. Each mill had its own local unions that made their own local deals. No two were alike. But it stood to reason that any company that could control its labor costs, even predict them with some certainty, would definitely have an edge.

He motioned at the list. "Again, Hank. If this is something innocent, how did the last four names get on there?"

"I have no idea."

"We need to find out."

DAY SIXTEEN
WEDNESDAY, JUNE 21

9:03 A.M.

LEE AND HUGHES MET IN THE BOARDROOM. LEE HAD DECIDED ON its assured privacy after De Florio telephoned last night and expressed an urgent need to talk. A speakerphone sat on the conference table.

"Jon, you there?" Lee asked the beige box. "Where are you?"

"Inside a guesthouse at Hickory Row."

"Tell Larry what you told me last night."

De Florio went over what he'd witnessed at Bozin's house and his conversation afterward.

"And your assessment?" Lee asked.

"Mr. Bozin definitely needs watching."

"Quite a change in attitude from the other day."

"I see no reason why Reed and Walker would be at Mr. Bozin's house."

"Maybe it's just like Chris explained," Hughes said. "He was trying to find something out."

Lee was not persuaded. "And what could he find out? Chris knew the deal was done. There was no need to have any conversations with Reed or Walker. And I doubt seriously if Reed was going to ask Chris' opinion on what the list is."

"I agree," De Florio said. "There is also one other observation. Mr. Bozin did not feel well. He was in obvious discomfort."

"Anything particular?" Lee asked.

"When he rose from the chair he experienced a sharp pain in his abdomen and almost lost his balance."

"I've noticed that Chris seems to have thinned lately," Hughes said. "I just attributed it to exercising or dieting. He's always been a nut about that."

"Mr. Bozin indicated the situation was a minor medical problem. Nothing serious."

"Maybe we should check a little further," Lee said. "We'll get back to you, Jon. Keep us informed of any further developments." He clicked off the speakerphone. "Can you access the medical insurance records from here?"

"What are we looking for?"

"Any claims by Christopher Bozin."

Hughes turned to the computer and punched the keyboard. A minute later, he announced, "On Bozin's policy a claim was filed two days ago by a Dr. Darrin Edwards for diagnostic tests and an office visit."

"How much?"

"One thousand eight hundred and forty-two dollars, which includes lab work done in-house."

"How do we find out more?"

"I can request our claims handler verify the treatment."

Even though the company was self-insured, it had proven too expensive to process claims in-house. Instead, the task was subcontracted to an outside firm. Still, all payments had to be approved by the accounting department before being forwarded.

"How long will it take to check this out further?" he asked.

"Beats the hell out of me. I've never done it before."

12:00 P.M.

HANK PASSED ON LUNCH AT THE COMFORT INN AND LEFT OUT A side door, quickly driving two miles east into Concord. He arrived

231

at S. Lou Greene's office just as the lawyer was bounding out the back door toward his red Jaguar.

"I was on my way to eat. Why don't you come with me?" Greene said.

He'd never been seen in public with Greene and wasn't about to start now. "I don't think so, Lou. Order in? We need to talk."

"I was looking forward to Chinese."

"Domino's delivers."

They went back inside and upstairs to Greene's office and took a seat.

"Take a look," he said, unfolding the piece of paper and handing it over.

```
034156901 William Mesnan, May 23, Heart attack
456913276 Patrick Brown, May 21, Kidney failure
343016692 J. J. Jordon, June 6, Heart failure
295617833 Brandon Pabon, June 6, Drug overdose
178932515 Tim Featherston, June 7, Bee sting
236987521 Melvin Bennett, June 8, Anaphylactic shock
492016755 Paul Zimmerman, June 13, Hunting accident
516332578 Michael Ottman, June 9, Heart attack
```

"When I got my hands on Lee's contract memo, I found this list. It was stored in a secured file that the main office maintains in the system. Blocked by a fancy firewall and password."

"How in the world did you get past those?"

"Just a fluke. Lightning damaged the system. I don't really know how it happened, all I know is it did."

"Did it come like this?"

He shook his head. "Brent figured out they were Social Security numbers. He matched names to numbers, then noticed something funny and brought it to me. The two of us worked last night and filled in the gaps."

Greene studied the list. "This guy here, Brandon Pabon, was

a client. He died a couple of weeks ago. Broke my heart. I had a damn good case."

"That's what Brent said too."

"He worked at the bag plant and got hurt on the job. Southern Republic tried to settle quick, but this guy had been around. He came to me, went to all the right doctors, said all the right things. I had the case ready to milk for two-hundred-thousand-plus when he popped one too many Valiums. Heroin too, I think."

He wanted to know, "Was the company fighting the claim hard?"

"The usual. But Pabon understood how to play the game. He did what I told him." Greene shook his head. "I lost some good fees on that one."

He told Greene what he and Brent thought about the list.

"Brent is right about comp claims," Greene said. "It's far cheaper on the company for a worker to die than be injured. Your man Walker had a good eye on this one."

"I told you he was smart."

"What's he going to do about it?"

"Nothing. Until he hears from me. I told him I wanted to look into it further and run it by you. Can you offer any wisdom?"

Greene studied the list. "I have to say, it's damn suspicious. There are a whole lot of unanswered questions here. Ones only Southern Republic can offer. They may need to be confronted. Head-on."

"Not until the contracts are done and final. I told Brent the same thing. I have to get those deals sealed first. The people on this list are dead. Waiting a few days to get to the bottom of this isn't going to make a difference to them."

"That's a bit cold, isn't it?"

"Yep. But at the moment I have to deal with the living who need their paychecks and benefits."

He checked his watch.

"Speaking of which, I have to get back to the negotiations. All hell's about to break loose. We're going to get the company's new offer changing the proposed contract length from three to five years. The other unions are not going to like that. It will be a long afternoon."

Greene seemed in thought. "Before you go, let me make a copy of this. I want to think on it some more, too."

12:45 P.M.

"I DON'T LOVE YOU," BRENT SAID TO PAULA. *"IT'S THAT SIMPLE."*

"It's her again, isn't it?"

"No. It's you and has been you for a long time."

"Brent, we've been through this before."

Little concern filled her voice. It was like they were having a disagreement over whether to eat in or go out. Not that her husband wanted a divorce.

"Again, Paula, we haven't been through it. That's the whole point."

"You seriously plan to divorce me? What about our parents?"

"Not that they have anything to do with this, but they'll understand."

"And if they don't?"

She always used others as her weapon of last resort. "Millions of people divorce and get along fine. There's no reason why we can't be one of those couples."

"You plan to stay here in Concord?"

"Of course. This is my home. I practice law here."

"You couldn't seriously be considering marrying that ragamuffin?"

He could almost hear the thoughts swirling through her convoluted mind. What would the bridge group think? How would she explain things to her Thursday women's club meeting? And the book club?

What others thought had always been important to her.

"Could you imagine Ashley Reed at a State Bar of Georgia function?"

In fact, Ashley would be far better there than the Academy Award performances he'd many times been forced to endure. Paula small-talking her way through the evening only to tell him on the way home how she despised nearly everyone there, repeating gossip he really didn't want to know.

"Can we do this friendly, or will there be war?" he asked.

"What do you propose?"

"You keep this house and your car. I'll help for a while with the mortgage and car payment. But you'll need to go to work. I'm sure the board of education would love to have you back. We don't have much debt, but what little we have I'll take care of. The cash we have in the bank, we'll split."

"And what about your law practice?"

"That's not on the table."

"What if I want to make it an issue?"

"You don't," he said, and she seemed to understand that the battle lines would then be drawn, his eyes asking, Do you really want that fight?

"It's over, Paula. It's been over for some time. Let this end quietly."

"I'm no fool, Brent. I know she's a part of this."

"Then you are a fool, because she's not a part of anything. Yes, Ashley is someone I care about—you knew that going in—but I've never been unfaithful to you. I'll admit. In my mind. In my heart. I wanted another woman. But I never did anything about that. I've tried for three years to make this work—"

"I don't understand you, Brent."

"That's your whole problem. You never have understood me."

"I understand that she's the problem and has been since day one."

"If you recall, I came and told you I didn't want to get married."

"But there was the matter of our child."

235

"There was always something that seemed to make it easy for us to put off the inevitable. This time there's nothing."

"I could hire the meanest divorce lawyer in town and fight you every step of the way."

"You could. But you won't."

Containment was surely her major worry. And she needed time to generate an appropriate cover story to adequately explain the breakup. Pressures from the job. He was always working. No time for her. Maybe, if necessary to extract maximum sympathy, drop the rumor of another woman. But careful there. That might mean she'd been inadequate in some way.

He watched her as the seriousness of the situation seemed to be settling in. For the first time in a long while she actually appeared concerned, perhaps thinking this was real.

"You love her? Don't you?" Paula asked.

It had been the question he most dreaded, but he decided to be honest.

"I do."

"You sorry bastard."

"Ten minutes later she stormed out of the house. An hour later she was dead," Brent told his mother.

"You didn't kill her," his mother said.

"I might as well have."

"You can't keep doing this to yourself."

They were sitting at the kitchen table. He'd come home for lunch, finally deciding it was time his mother knew the truth. Outside, he could hear Grant and James from next door playing. It was only the second time he'd ever told anyone what happened that last day.

"Son, I realize Paula wasn't the easiest person in the world."

"I learned to deal with it."

"What do you mean?"

"There were times when I genuinely cared for her, especially in the beginning. But other times I had to fight hard not to hate her. It seemed the older we got, the worse she became."

"Paula just wanted to be something she wasn't."

"I was never unfaithful to her." He felt a need to say it again.

"I know that. It wouldn't be your nature to do otherwise."

"But I couldn't deny to her that I cared for Ashley."

"Does Ashley love you?"

He nodded.

"She's a fine woman. A little flirty, but the last time I looked that wasn't a crime."

He smiled. "No, thank God for that."

"Everyone in this town would tell you she's an excellent mother. She works hard, pays her bills. I've never heard anyone speak ill of her."

"I made a mistake years ago. I should have never let things go as far as they did. Paula and I dated two years before we married. But I didn't think a life with Ashley was possible. She was hard to pin down. So I settled for the next best thing. That was wrong."

"But Paula made her own choice when she got into that car. You had no idea what she was going to do."

No, he hadn't. "She'd been depressed for a while, but that was nothing unusual for her. She had her moods. I guess she thought dying was better than divorcing. Who knows?"

"You have to let the past go. You can't feel guilty all your life."

"I keep thinking about that day and how upset she must have been when she died. I've tried to convince myself that she wouldn't have been single long. A lot of men would want a woman like her."

Similar, he thought, to the preference between solid wood furniture and wood veneer.

"You told Paula that day that you thought you loved Ashley. What about now, all these years later?"

He did not hesitate. "I still love her."

"Then, son, it's about time the both of you do something about it."

6:05 P.M.

LEE GLANCED UP AS HUGHES BURST INTO THE OFFICE AND CLOSED the door. "Darrin Edwards is an oncologist. Chris's been a patient for some time. He's dying, Hamilton. Prostate cancer. It's spread all over. There's nothing they can do."

"I knew it," he said. "I've had that feeling all day. It's starting to finally make sense. That old man is up to something."

"But why? He'd only implicate himself."

"He figures he'll be dead by the time that happens."

"Even so, his estate would be at risk."

Lee rose and walked to the outer glass wall, downtown Atlanta framed before him. "Chris has no immediate family, and he doesn't give a damn about money anymore. What he wants is our asses. He knows we've long shut him out of any real say in the company. He's always on my butt about not working. You heard him at the board meeting. He doesn't think I do a damn thing."

He turned and marched for the office door.

"Where are you going?"

"To find out what that bastard's up to."

It was nearly an hour past quitting time and the twenty-ninth floor loomed quiet. Just the soft rush of the air-conditioning and the occasional pop of the outer walls as the tinted glass expanded and contracted from the late-afternoon sun. They entered Bozin's space through tall glass doors. A stained mahogany door led from the secretarial station into the private office.

The knob was unlocked.

"Seems Chris is expecting us," Lee said, as they walked inside.

"I've never known him to leave it unlocked," Hughes said. "Maybe Nancy just forgot."

"You and I both know that woman doesn't do a thing without checking with him, and she doesn't forget anything either. It's unlocked because Chris told her to leave it that way."

The building's angular shape provided a multitude of corner spaces and each owner possessed a pentagon-shaped office large enough to include two exterior walls. Bozin's carpeted space reflected his noted dislike of a mess. The desk sat devoid of paper, its top shiny and dust-free. A few files were stacked in a blue leather basket on one side, telephone messages and mail neatly piled atop a blotter awaiting review. A leather cup contained pens and sharpened pencils. A brass banker's lamp sat in the center. The draperies for the two outer walls were open, the evening sun pouring in.

"Doesn't look like anyone even works here," Lee said.

Hughes gestured to the computer. "Chris does almost all his work electronically."

"Check the desk?"

Hughes walked behind and tried the drawers, which opened. No surprise.

He watched while Hughes searched. There was some stationery, a telephone book, pens, paper clips, stapler, and calculator. Everything neatly in place. Two file racks rested on a credenza behind the desk. He scanned them. Nothing of interest.

"What exactly are we looking for?" Hughes asked.

He motioned to the monitor. "Fire that thing up."

Hughes rolled the chair closer and booted the terminal to the main menu.

"Any personal files?"

"I doubt if we could access them without knowing Chris' password."

"I don't think that's going to be a problem."

Hughes opened the directory, which was unprotected. "How did you know we could get in?"

"Because we're supposed to look."

They scanned the index. Mainly company financials. Most he recognized. Occasionally a personal file appeared that might bear investigating.

Toward the bottom his eyes locked on

FOR HAMILTON AND LARRY

"What is that?" Hughes asked, staring at the screen.

"It's what we're supposed to find. Call it up."

Hughes did and they read the file in its entirety. Twice.

"We have a big problem," Hughes said. "What's gotten into Chris?"

"Revenge," he muttered. "Is that file in the main system?"

Hughes shook his head. "It's only stored here on this computer."

"Erase it. Though I'm sure there's more than one copy."

Hughes pounded the keyboard. "What are we going to do, Hamilton?"

He studied his watch. 6:23 P.M.

"Nothing tonight. But first thing in the morning we're going to get our tails to Concord."

DAY SEVENTEEN
THURSDAY, JUNE 22

11:16 A.M.

CHRIS FINALLY PUT IN AN APPEARANCE AT THE MORNING SESSION of the contract negotiations. He'd been delayed at the mill, where he spent nearly an hour giving the flash drive a final revision. His arrival at the Comfort Inn came just as UPIU concluded its contract negotiations. Amazingly, a consensus on all points had been reached with the paperworkers, the head of the company's delegation proudly informing him that a preliminary agreement had been initialed. The quickness surprised him, particularly after Reed's prediction from the other night, but a wink from Reed during a break signaled that he'd been more successful than anticipated.

"One down, two to go," Chris told the CEO from his cell phone in the hall. They were both glad a third of the work was done.

He hung up and was starting back to the meeting room when the security guard stationed outside all week approached. He had his doubts about the man and wondered if he worked for De Florio. Certainly, at a minimum, he was reporting to him.

"Mr. De Florio dropped by earlier," the guard said. "You weren't here so he left this note for you."

The man handed him a piece of paper. As the guard walked off he unfolded and read

WE'RE WAITING
YOU KNOW WHERE

He smiled.

That he did. Apparently, his partners finally got the message.

He deliberately loitered another half hour before leaving the Comfort Inn. Then, in one of the white Hickory Row cars, he drove himself directly to Dracula's Place. His staff had told him the cottage's nickname and he thought it more than appropriate. Not only as a reference to the unique architecture, but as a fitting description for its occupant. A steward opened the front door and escorted him to Lee's private study.

He entered and the door was closed behind him.

Lee sat at a small writing desk. Hughes in front. Their faces conveyed that neither was in a good mood.

"And what brings you two down to the woods of middle Georgia?"

"You know damn well why we're here," Lee said.

He eased himself into a chair and decided to be coy. "Please, enlighten me?"

"We know about your health problems," Hughes said. "And we read that confession in your computer. What are you trying to prove, Chris?"

He glared at Hughes. "I'm not trying to prove anything. On the contrary, I'm trying to disprove things."

"What does that mean?"

"Thirty years ago, what were you, Larry? A half-assed salesman hocking brown paper bags to grocery store chains worrying about your next commission check. You lived in a three-bedroom cracker box and probably agonized every summer if you had enough saved to take a lousy two weeks off. What did you drive? A clunker with a hundred thousand miles on it? Look at you today. That suit must have cost $1,000. Those cuff links, that much and more. That diamond watch has to be worth at least twenty grand.

What do you have, two mistresses? And how did you get down here today? The jet? You've come a long way."

"You're damn right I have."

He turned to Lee. "And what were you, Hamilton? An assistant production manager at a paper mill. Salaried man, paid for forty hours and working sixty. Subject to being fired at the whim of management over nothing at all. Not unlike the hundreds who now work for you. All the country-club memberships, dinners at the governor's mansion, and lunches with the mayor you now enjoy don't go with that kind of job, do they?"

"What's your point, Chris?"

"You know. You've both known for years. Ever since you decided to freeze me out. I guess you forgot who found the money that made this possible, and who managed it. If it'd been up to you two, we'd have been bankrupt twenty years ago. Through careful management we prospered, not from hobnobbing with bureaucrats and fattening the pockets of politicians."

Lee said, "No one said your contribution wasn't appreciated."

"And no one said thank you either."

"That what this is about? Pissed we outvote you?"

"You know what has to stop."

Lee sat back and seemed to consider the words. "As I recall the whole Priority idea was yours in the first place."

"I don't deny that. I was young and greedy. But we don't need Priority anymore."

"A little late for repentance, isn't it?"

"It doesn't bother you, Hamilton? Don't you ever think of the families left behind?"

Lee shrugged. "Thanks to that program we've been able to provide a solid living, for a lot of people, for a long time."

"Let's face it, Chris," Hughes said. "Without Priority we'd have gone under, or certainly scaled back. It's proven a great way to keep costs under control."

He said again, "We don't need it anymore."

"Get real," Lee said. "How many paper companies have folded in the last ten years? We've got competition from the Japanese, Canadians, Mexicans, and Brazilians—places we never dreamed about thirty years ago. I can name a dozen other companies in the Southeast alone that never made it. Think of all the jobs lost for those communities. Concord didn't suffer anything like that. In fact, while all that misery was going on, we expanded and hired more people."

"A prosperity built with blood."

"So?" Lee said. "Who knows that? And no one would have any way of ever knowing it. All our employees know is that there's a paycheck every first and third Thursday. When they go to the doctor the bill gets paid. And when they retire there'll be a pension check every month to supplement Social Security. They have a great life. Stable and secure."

"Until we send De Florio, or one of his associates, for a visit."

Lee was nonchalant. "Why are you so philosophical? Is it because you're dying?"

"It's the thought that you two will keep going—once I'm gone."

"We erased what was on your machine," Hughes said.

"I have plenty of copies."

"What do you plan to do with them?" Lee asked.

"I haven't decided."

Lee sighed. "You realize you're leaving us no choice."

"There are always choices, Hamilton."

"Why have you been talking to Brent Walker and Hank Reed?" Lee asked. "Why did you have them to your house? Why involve others, Chris? You know what we'll have to do. Doesn't Walker have a mother? Reed a daughter and granddaughter? Whatever it takes, it will be done. I'm not going to jeopardize the future of this company or the future of the people who depend on us. Why not save them all the pain?"

"It'll certainly be interesting, Hamilton. That much I can promise."

Lee shrugged. "Have it your way."

He rose. "I assume this will be our last meeting. I'd wish you luck, but it would just be a lie. Instead, I'll see you both in hell."

Not giving either one of them time to reply, he left.

Outside, he climbed into the car and drove straight toward the other side of Hickory Row. As he turned out of Lee's driveway he reached inside his jacket and removed the microcassette recorder.

A bit old-school, but effective.

He slid the PLAY/RECORD button to OFF and smiled, staring at the last piece of evidence he'd need.

1:20 P.M.

LEE SAT SILENT.

"That old fart is going to sink us," Hughes said.

"Not if I can help it."

"We have no idea what he intends to do."

"Whatever Chris's planned has been done carefully. And right now, he has the jump on us."

"De Florio needs to handle this."

He agreed. "But it has to be done right."

A knock came at the study door. A steward entered and said, "Lunch is ready."

"We'll be there in a few minutes."

The steward left.

"Keep your voice down," he said, "we're not in the boardroom." He thought for a second. "Chris is already dying of cancer, it shouldn't be too hard to induce death consistent with that."

"What about an autopsy?"

He gave a knowing grin. "As his close partners, Chris left specific instructions to be cremated. We, of course, honored that request and immediately disposed of the body. There's no family to question anything and, by the time anyone notices, he'll be ashes. Besides, once everybody knows he was dying of cancer there'll be no questions."

"I guess we're going to make sure that information gets out."

"We'll issue a press release. Chris was widely known and liked. It'd be expected that the company would make a public statement."

"What about Walker and Reed?"

"We know Reed has the list. Brent Walker's involvement could be just a wild goose chase Chris is leading us on. But, for safety's sake, I'll have De Florio watch them both carefully."

"Chris' fate could send them a message."

"Let's hope," he said.

1:40 P.M.

IT TOOK CHRIS ONLY A FEW MINUTES TO DRIVE ACROSS THE PROPERTY to his house and make it upstairs. With the bedroom door closed and locked he listened to the entire recorded conversation. The device had functioned perfectly, everything memorialized. At the end he activated the RECORD button and added, "Conversation among myself, Larry Hughes, and Hamilton Lee dated June 22. Occurred in the study of Hamilton Lee's house at Hickory Row at approximately noon."

He rewound the tape, then retrieved an oversized brown envelope from one of the desk drawers. He favored that particular brand because the manufacturer used brown paper produced by Southern Republic. From his jacket he removed the flash drive and dropped it inside. On a couple of pieces of personal stationery he penned two notes, taped both shut, and stuffed them in the envelope. He then slid the microcassette recorder with its tape loaded inside, licked the flap shut, and added a layer of tape to the outside for added security.

He was now living on borrowed time.

Little doubt remained as to what Lee and Hughes would do. He probably had until dark.

But no longer.

He crept into the bathroom, splashed water on his face, and tried to compose himself. The pain in his abdomen was steadily increasing. He needed to get back to the negotiations and it was important he appear calm.

Later, he'd complete the final step in his plan.

1:50 P.M.

LEE CLIMBED INTO A GOLF CART AND DROVE TOWARD THE NORTHEAST corner of Hickory Row. The county line divided the property nearly in half, a series of guesthouses lying within walking distance of the Savannah River and the largest of the three quail hunting fields.

A paved road appropriately dubbed Shade Tree Lane wound north through the hickory trees. The sweltering afternoon air draped things like warm syrup. A mixture of grass and matted straw littered with oversized pinecones formed a front yard for one of the smaller guesthouses. Squirrels scurried for cover as the cart's electric whine announced his presence. He parked behind the white pickup truck already there and knocked on the front door.

De Florio answered.

He stepped inside to the air-conditioned interior and they sat.

"Mr. Hughes and I have decided Bozin must be processed immediately. He apparently intends to see all of us, including you, in jail."

"Are there any conditions?"

"Chris has terminal prostate cancer. Make it consistent with that."

De Florio nodded.

"Bozin will most likely be expecting you. Let's not disappoint him. Proceed immediately. But not until tonight. That'll give Mr. Hughes and myself time to get back to Atlanta. And after the discovery of his death, I want the body immediately cremated. It was his wish. Chris told me so many times."

"I'll take care of it."

He loved how De Florio questioned little and merely performed.

"I knew you would."

4:40 P.M.

"I WANT TO KNOW," BRENT ASKED AGAIN. "IS LORI ANNE MY DAUGHTER?"
His voice had risen with each of Ashley's denials.
"No. And don't flatter yourself."
"I'm not. But I want to know the truth."
"When she was conceived I had a husband."
"She was born eight months after the two of you married."
"I know you're familiar with premarital sex."
"Which you and I engaged in, about the same time."
"Brent, Lori Anne is Manley's daughter."

"I believed you," Brent said, recalling the conversation of ten years earlier.

"It's the only time I ever lied to you," Ashley said.

Her face was wound tight, eyes watery.

"I planned to tell you, but when you told me you were going to marry Paula, I thought it better to let it go. There seemed no need for you to ever know."

"You should have told me."

"And what would you have done? Dumped her and married me? She told you she was pregnant. Remember? It's why you married her."

"I would have married you."

"So you would have chosen the daughter already born, over the child on the way? Get real, Brent. You don't have a clue what you would have done."

"How did it even happen? I thought you were careful."

"The pill's not one hundred percent."

"Was there ever any question who was the father?"

She shook her head. "When Lori Anne was conceived, you were the only man I was with. Sure, Manley and I slept together. But not during the time she was conceived. And I want you to know, I didn't then and haven't since jumped from bed to bed. There have only been four men in my life. Three husbands, but God knows I wasn't much of a wife in that department, and you. Nobody else."

"Does Manley know?"

"Not for a fact. But he suspects. To his credit he's never said one word and has been good to Lori Anne. He's the only father she's ever known."

"How will she react to this?"

"That's a good question. And another reason why I kept it to myself."

"So why the truth now?"

"We can't build something on lies. And your mother came to see me."

That shocked him.

"She told me about her illness. She deserves quality time with her granddaughter. We can't keep making the same mistakes over and over. People are being hurt by our foolishness."

She was right. Together, they'd really screwed things up.

"I'm so sorry, Brent. For everything."

"I think I should be the one apologizing. We both wasted a lot of years."

"I wouldn't say that."

He knew what she meant.

"We have Lori Anne."

He left half an hour later and drove home. He should be mad over the years he'd been deprived of a daughter. But he'd been angry long enough. And he was a father. Incredible. Maybe he and Ashley could finally start building something good. He'd been apprehensive about coming back to Concord, thinking the physical distance enough to keep the past at bay. Now he was glad he'd made the move. He'd never wanted Paula to die. She made that choice. And perhaps that had been her intent. To wreak guilt upon him so deep that he could never be happy. Hard to say. But there was no denying that had been his life these past years.

No more.

Time to start over.

He turned onto Live Oak and slowed at his parents' drive.

Nestled next to the curb was a white Hickory Row vehicle. He parked and quickly headed inside. His mother met him at the front door.

"There's someone here to see you."

He glanced to his right and saw Christopher Bozin sitting comfortably in the front parlor.

His boss stood. "I should have called first, but I really needed to see you before I went back to my house for the night."

"I'm sorry you had to wait."

Bozin waived off his apology. "Your mother and I have had a wonderful chat."

"I'll leave you two to talk," his mother said. "It was so nice to finally meet you."

Bozin acknowledged her with a nod and a smile.

They sat. He noticed that Bozin wore the same suit and tie from earlier at the negotiations.

"This is a lovely home."

"My parents bought it when I was a little boy and fixed it up through the years."

Bozin gestured to one of the pictures angling from atop the table next to him. "Is that your father?" A tarnished Victorian frame surrounded a man and woman, both middle-aged.

He nodded.

"Were you and he close?"

"I was an only child, so there was no way we wouldn't be."

"He seems to have provided for you and your mother."

"He did. But some of that credit goes to Southern Republic. The mill made sure we had the benefits needed, not to mention a good wage."

Bozin nodded. "We talked about that the other night. You really think we did some good here in Concord?"

"Without a doubt."

Bozin paused for a moment, seemingly catching his breath. Then said, "I'm sure you're wondering why one of the owners of the company stopped by unannounced?"

"That thought has crossed my mind."

"First, tell me what happened at the negotiations. I wasn't able to get back that way."

"IAM and IBEW argued all afternoon. One of the members on Reed's negotiations committee turned on him, in open revolt, on any five-year deal. There were some harsh words said at the table."

Bozin chuckled. "I bet Hank was beside himself. That is the one thing he tries to avoid. Never let the other side see conflict. Too good an opportunity for us to divide and conquer."

"He's called an IBEW membership meeting for tonight. He assured me that by morning all opposition would be quashed."

The older man smiled. "And I have no doubt that it will be."

He wanted to know, "What is it I can do for you?"

"I have something I want you to keep for me." Bozin reached beside him for a brown envelope. "It's important that I know someone from the company has this information. I'd like for you to store it somewhere safe. If I become incapacitated, or die, please do exactly as it asks."

What was going on? At the DA's office months went by before he even spoke with his boss. Here, already there'd been private talks, a dinner at Hickory Row, and now one of the owners was sitting in his living room asking a personal favor. He was green to the paper industry, little more than a stranger to Bozin. Yet the man wanted to connect.

Why?

And he was still disturbed by the list of Social Security numbers and the deaths associated with each one. He wanted to make some official inquiries with management. But Hank had asked him to keep it to himself until the negotiations ended. There'd be serious questions raised as to how it was obtained, ones Hank did not want to deal with until the contracts were signed and sealed. He suspected Hank was also looking out for the source who'd done the actual snooping in the system. There would surely be repercussions. He debated bringing up the subject here and now, but decided to respect Hank's wishes and simply asked, "Don't you have a personal lawyer who should handle this?"

"Several, in fact. But they're in Atlanta and you're here in Concord. Besides, this is company-related."

"What about the general counsel? Shouldn't he be the one to hold on to this?"

"I prefer you do it. Consider it a specific request employer-to-employee, if you will."

Now he was pulling rank. "Mr. Bozin, I have reservations. I mean my boss could take this the wrong way. Concord's a small town. News travels fast. Hell, there's a company car sitting in front of my house. I certainly don't want anyone thinking I'm less than a month on the job and already after my boss' position."

"I assure you, no one will have knowledge of what we're doing. This is solely between you and me."

He was still hesitant and Bozin appeared to sense his reservations.

"I realize I could have asked the general counsel to handle this. But the fact that you are less than a month on the job is why I'm asking you. I understand you're new to the company and the industry. I, on the other hand, am not. So I ask you to trust me, as employer to employee, and do this favor for me."

"You're not going to take no for an answer, are you?"

"What do you think?"

Bozin handed him the envelope and smiled.

"I appreciate this, Brent. I'll rest easier tonight knowing this matter has been taken care of."

OUTSIDE CHRIS STOOD FOR A FEW MINUTES AND ADMIRED THE flower beds full of white impatiens and bushy green shrubs, happily saying goodbye to Catherine and Brent Walker. Finally, he climbed into the white Ford and headed off. Several cars lined the street. One was a dark-blue Buick, parked and apparently empty.

But as soon as he passed and began to turn the corner, he caught a glimpse in his rearview mirror—

Of it following.

6:30 P.M.

THE GRANDFATHER CLOCK CHIMED ONCE FOR THE HALF HOUR WHEN Chris opened the front door and entered his house inside Hickory Row. He declined dinner and marched straight upstairs. A hot shower relaxed him. With pajamas and robe on he settled into an upholstered French chaise that angled from one corner of the bedroom.

Once he was gone, little doubt remained that Lee and Hughes would drastically escalate the Priority program. Proof of that had been building for some time. Three months back Lee had attempted to use the program to narrow the company's competition on a government bid submission. But he'd blocked that effort thanks to a nervous Larry Hughes who got cold feet and, for once, sided with him. There'd been repeated talk about eliminating some of the more aggressive and successful salesmen at their competitors. And there was the totally unauthorized use last summer when, to close a deal, Hughes had ordered De Florio to blackmail a grocery store chain's purchasing agent with the misfortune of having not one, but two, girlfriends and a wife. None of that had been contemplated when the program began. Which was one reason why he'd done what he had. The other, perhaps the more important reason, was his hatred for the two men who'd soon inherit total control of what he'd built.

Yet he wasn't naïve.

Lee and Hughes would stop at nothing to plug the gushing leak he'd left behind. He'd been followed from Concord, so they probably already knew of his visit to the Walker home. He'd also openly carried the brown envelope inside, then left without it. Lee earlier made a point of mentioning Brent's mother. Was it right to involve the younger lawyer? To put him, and his family, in obvious danger? And what about Hank Reed's daughter and granddaughter? They were now in the crosshairs too. No doubt existed that De Florio would be dispatched, following his files, instructing his associates on precisely what to do. He'd be efficient and merciless. *Purely business.* As he himself had voiced on more than one occasion. Maybe what he'd prepared would provide Reed and Walker with at least a chance at success.

That was the hope.

One thing was certain, though.

Brent Walker and Hank Reed would have more of a tactical advantage than any previous Priority—excluding, of course, himself.

11:59 P.M.

JON TURNED THE BRASS HANDLE TO THE PATIO DOOR.

Unlocked.

He smiled.

Then pushed the door inward, stepping inside without a sound.

The foyer clock chimed loud for midnight. He slowly climbed the stairs, one at a time, a carpet runner cushioning his feet, the upstairs hall likewise carpeted, masking all sound.

At the bedroom, he swung the door inward.

"GOOD EVENING," CHRIS SAID THROUGH THE DARK.

He was still reclined in the chaise, drifting in and out of a light sleep over the past few hours, patiently waiting.

De Florio closed the door. "Good evening, Mr. Bozin. Mr. Lee said you'd most likely be expecting me."

"I assume I've been Prioritized?"

"Unfortunately."

"Ironic, isn't it? A program I conceived now being used to eliminate its creator."

De Florio said nothing.

"Is this how's it's done?" he asked. "You just appear?"

"Surprise is an element we use to our advantage. Of course, here, there was no surprise."

"How many have there been, Jon? How many visits in the night?"

"I don't keep a tally. I just do my job. As ordered by you and your fellow shareholders."

He stood, walked to the bed, and sat on the edge.

De Florio approached in front of him.

"Is there a file on me, Jon?"

"No, sir. Neither the time nor the need. You left a clear trail to your doctor, which answered all questions."

"How am I to be processed?"

"Actually, I thought I'd give you a choice. I brought chemicals for heart or lung failure."

"How thoughtful. All consistent with my cancer, I assume?"

"Of course."

"What about an autopsy? Is it not a possibility? After all, my illness is not exactly life threatening at this point. I have some time left."

"Mr. Lee left instructions for you to be cremated in the morning."

He nodded. "Once everyone is told I was dying anyway, nobody will question a thing. My doctor will confirm the cancer, all will be right."

"It also helps that the local coroner works at the paper mill. He'll be most cooperative, I'm sure."

"That he will. Will you mourn me, Jon?"

"You were an excellent employer. I will miss you, as will a great deal of other people."

"I'm not so sure. Once the world discovers what we did, I doubt I'll be missed at all."

"And how will they find out?"

A light chuckle. Brevity in the face of death. "Clever, Jon. I'm sure Hamilton wants you to learn all you can."

"Only doing my job, sir."

"And you do it so well." His sarcasm was clear. "Will the choices you've been so kind to provide cause instant death?"

"They will. That's all we deal with."

"Any associated pain?"

"None. I was careful to choose chemicals that were painless."

"That was, again, most thoughtful."

"As I said, it was a pleasure to work for you." De Florio stepped closer. "Mr. Bozin, may I ask, on a personal level, why you're doing this?"

He stared through the darkness at the shadow of death. It had come just as certainly as if he was taking his own life, which in a loose sort of way he was. "Cancer is a slow, painful way to die. Believe me, what you're about to do is nothing but relief."

"But why destroy the company, your reputation, your partners?"

"*What good is it for a man to gain the whole world, yet forfeit his soul?* Mark 8:36. I lost mine a long time ago."

He stood and, like every night, slipped off his silk robe and carefully draped it across the foot of the bed. He lay down on the sheets and jerked up the left pajama sleeve, exposing his arm. "I assume, since there'll be no body to examine, there's no point in disguising the injection point."

"It does seem unnecessary."

"Heart failure. Let's go with that."

De Florio reached into his right coat pocket and removed a syringe.

"How do you know which one?"

"I wrap rubber bands around the outside. One or two. Touch is an important sense a lot of people tend to ignore."

He smiled.

De Florio found a penlight in his trouser pocket, switched it on, and stuck it in his mouth.

"Would you like me to hold that?" he asked.

De Florio removed the light. "If you like."

He held the light above his left arm. De Florio carefully inserted the needle and emptied the barrel. He handed the light back, then settled into the pillow.

"Good luck, Jon."

"Same to you, Mr. Bozin."

His heart stopped.

That was fast.

Strange, not to feel it beat.

He stared ahead, into blackness, and as his brain consumed the final few molecules of oxygen available, his last conscious thought was of Brent Walker and Hank Reed.

Wishing them good luck also.

DAY EIGHTEEN
FRIDAY, JUNE 23

11:50 A.M.

BRENT SHUFFLED ALL MORNING BETWEEN THE IAM AND IBEW negotiating sessions, helping the company representatives with details of a final deal. At midmorning IAM suddenly came to a tentative agreement, their negotiations committee tired of the bickering and satisfied with the wage increases and extras the company finally offered. The five years seemed a bitter pill, but the machinists wisely recognized they possessed little to negotiate with other than the two additional years.

"How'd it go last night at the union meeting?" he asked Hank during the break.

"I don't think there'll be any more lip from my committee."

"You handled things?"

"Totally. Damn idiots. Haven't got the sense God gave a billy goat. They think all you have to do is snap your fingers and the company'll jump. Finally, I told 'em all to strike. That's what they need to do. Walk out until the company says three years is okay. Go for it."

"I'm sure that hit home."

"We found out they all have bananas for backbone. They'll do what I say from now on."

"IAM coming to agreement seemed sudden."

"I worked hard with their committee last night after the IBEW meeting."

"Looks like your guys are last to the table again."

Hank smiled. "That's one tradition I like."

"We're going to have to deal with that list of numbers on Monday," he said. "We have to find out what they are."

"I know. I appreciate you workin' with me and holdin' off until the deals are done. I can't jeopardize this."

"I get it," he said. "But Monday we're on it. I wonder where Bozin is this morning?"

"We can't formalize the deal with IAM until he's here," Hank said. "I'd like to seal that thing before the machinists change their minds."

He glanced at his watch. "Looks like that'll be after lunch, so I'm going home."

Hank grinned. "Can't take that fatty barbecue and fried chicken on the buffet anymore?"

"Mom's vegetable soup from last night will be a lot better on my stomach and waistline. You want to come?"

Hank shook his head. "I need to hang around here. With these numbnuts, you never know what could happen."

Brent felt good driving home.

Only his concerns about that list of numbers marred his good humor.

Last night, after Bozin left, he and his mother had talked for nearly two hours. For once everybody seemed to be on the same page, and he was pleased the two women in his life apparently were going to get along. She apologized for going to Ashley behind his back, but he was actually grateful that she had. He was concerned, though, about Lori Anne. But Ashley assured him that she'd talk to their daughter and explain everything. To make a start they decided to do something together over the weekend, something fun all three of them would enjoy.

He arrived home and found his mother in the kitchen preparing ham sandwiches for the boys next door. Grace Tanner had gone to the store and his mother was babysitting.

"They're not having soup?" he asked.

"They placed an order for sandwiches and Doritos."

"Where are they?"

"Last I saw they were headed down the street with a pack of the kids from the next block. I told 'em to be back here by 12:30."

He grabbed a piece of wheat bread. "We're down to one. IAM settled this morning."

"Hank waiting to be the grand finale?"

"As always. He seems to come alive during these things."

The house phone rang. He walked over and answered.

It was Hank. "Chris Bozin is dead."

"Dead? The man was in my living room last night."

Delivering an envelope.

"He's dead now. Prostate cancer."

He told himself to keep his voice calm. "You'd have never known. He did a good job concealing it."

"He apparently kept it a secret from everyone."

"That's a shame. He seemed like a fine man. What about the negotiations?"

"Suspended for the afternoon out of respect. Brent, what was Bozin doing at your house last night?"

"That's a good question. When I find out, I'll let you know."

He hung up and told his mother what happened.

"That poor man," she said.

"I'll pass on lunch. I need to get back to the mill."

But before he did he left the kitchen and walked straight upstairs, Bozin's words from last night ringing in his ears. *"It's important for me to know someone from the company has the information contained in there. If I become incapacitated or die, please open it and do exactly as it asks."* He'd respected that request and told no one about the envelope, not even his mother. The whole thing was strange, though a bit clearer now with Bozin's secret illness and sudden demise. He retrieved the envelope from the top of his closet, broke the seal, and spilled out the contents on the bed.

Four items.

Two sheets of paper tri-folded and taped closed. A flash drive. And a microcassette recorder with a tape inserted. Written on the outside of one of the tri-folded single sheets was

READ THIS FIRST

On the outside of the other

READ THIS LAST

He did as Bozin instructed, breaking the tape holding the first sheet together. Inside was a handwritten note.

I appreciate you following my instructions. It's important you do. I've prepared a narrative on the enclosed drive. Please read it in private, then open the sheet that says to be read last. Everything will be made clear once you've viewed the drive and listened to the recording. I thank you for your service and patience.

Christopher Bozin

His first thought was to ignore the instructions and read the other note now. But the lawyer inside him advised otherwise. Bozin had trusted him with something of importance and obviously went to a lot of trouble to organize things. The least he could do was follow his wishes exactly.

And not here.

Go to the office. This was business.

So he stuffed everything back into the envelope, hustled downstairs, and told his mother goodbye. Outside, he climbed into the Jeep and headed off. About a quarter mile away he passed James and Grant on their bicycles as they pedaled back to his parents' house.

He honked. They waved back.

Passing the kids, he glanced in his rearview mirror to check on them, seeing only a dark-blue Buick that had just turned onto the street behind him.

1:00 P.M.

LEE PATIENTLY WAITED ALL MORNING.

The first call came into the Blue Tower around noon. One-third of Southern Republic Pulp and Paper Company was dead. The twenty-ninth floor went into mourning. Nancy Fringe lapsed into shock and had to be taken to the emergency room. He and Hughes showed their dismay over the untimely death of their partner by retiring to their respective offices on the pretext of being alone. Neither did much grieving.

Instead, they both waited for the next call.

"He was ready for me," De Florio said. "He cooperated fully. The body was found about ten this morning. The coroner and a doctor came. Death was verified, consistent with the processing. The body was immediately taken to Savannah, cremation is occurring now."

"Did he say anything?"

"He wished me luck."

"For what?"

"He wouldn't say."

"Did he mention anything else?"

"Nothing of value."

"Okay, that problem's history. What about Reed and Walker?"

"Prior to returning home last evening, Bozin visited the Walkers' residence. He carried a brown envelope inside and was there about thirty minutes. He carried nothing out."

Not good. "What about Walker?"

"He stayed at the negotiations all morning, then went home for lunch. After a few minutes, he returned to the mill. Carrying a brown envelope."

Double not good. "And Reed?"

"He was present at the negotiations all morning. An announcement about Bozin's death was made and he immediately went outside and made a call. The last I was informed Reed was still at the Comfort Inn."

"We have a press release ready to go on this end. I believe it's time to issue it."

"What do you want me to do?"

"We don't know exactly what Bozin has done, so we can't act till things are clearer. That brown envelope is a concern. There's no indication at this point that either Reed or Walker can, or will, hurt us. Bozin could be bluffing, hoping we'll make a mistake and expose ourselves. That old man was clever and jumping in blind could create even more problems. For now, just watch those two. Carefully."

1:25 P.M.

BRENT ARRIVED BACK AT BUILDING B AND LEARNED THAT HIS BOSS had been called to Hickory Row. The information trickling in was that Bozin had been discovered midmorning when the house staff became worried. They found him snuggled under the covers apparently sleeping, death coming sometime during the night. The coroner was called, but since he wasn't a physician, merely an assembly-line supervisor at the mill elected to his position, a medical doctor was also summoned. Heart failure brought on by the stress from prostate cancer was the official cause of death. A prescription medicine bottle found in the house provided the name of Bozin's Atlanta doctor, who verified the cancer and its extent. The whole thing was awful, and a solemn sense pervaded the building.

Obviously, Bozin would be missed.

He lingered a little with the secretaries before going into his office. He hadn't been around much during the past week and noticed a few new files stacked to one side. They needed attention.

Hopefully, negotiations would be over by Monday or Tuesday and he could get back to work.

He removed the flash drive from the envelope and inserted it into his desktop. Remembering Bozin's instruction that he view the material in private, he closed and locked the office door. He punched the keyboard and called up the drive's index. There was only one file, titled REVELATION.

He brought it to the screen.

It was a narrative addressed specifically to him, dated yesterday. He resisted the temptation to scroll through its entire contents.

Instead, he began to read.

I have always been a history buff. Years ago, I read the story of Qin Shi, a second century b.c. ruler who consolidated what would eventually be called China into a single political entity. Qin Shi had enemies, though. Lots of them. Scattered everywhere, protected by mountains, rivers, forests, walls, or sometimes mere anonymity. In order to maintain his empire a way of controlling those enemies had to be found. But how? That was a problem which plagued his advisors for years. They thought of force, execution, imprisonment, and banishment. But each carried a price in terms of time, energy, and retaliation. They thought of doing nothing. But the message sent by indifference cautioned otherwise. Finally, the emperor himself came upon the method that proved most effective.

He ordered the construction of a city littered with magnificent palaces and splendid manor houses, each richly suited for the aristocracy who would soon occupy them. He staffed the city with hundreds of servants charged with providing all of the labor the inhabitants would ever need. He made the city an opulent place. A place of envy. A place where people wanted to live. Then he commanded all of his enemies to live there.

Many grumbled at first. But once there, accustomed to the luxuries freely provided, it became hard for any of them to leave, and none ever did. But that was the whole idea. For the residents it was a good life. For Qin Shi even better since his enemies were all contained in one place. Rebellion became next to impossible. Sedition disappeared. Qin Shi rested easier each night knowing his enemies were monitored around-the-clock by servants absolutely loyal to him, and his descendants ruled China, unchallenged, for another two hundred years.

Southern Republic Pulp & Paper's methodology is a step back to Qin Shi's time. We too built a town and within the limits of Concord we dominated. But just like with the enemies of Qin Shi, who over 2000 years ago basked in ignorance amongst the luxury of their surroundings, no resident of Woods County ever realized the full extent of our presence.

For the first few years of our existence, we obtained our operating capital through borrowing and remained heavily in debt. We based the company out of Atlanta, renting space in a variety of downtown office buildings. Not until twenty years into the venture did we build the Blue Tower.

Keeping trained and stable employees is critical to any business' long-term success. So we immediately implemented a development program to upgrade Concord and Woods County. Our first venture was the Woods County State Bank, which offered a variety of services not then available locally. The institution immediately prospered and complemented the Southern Republic Credit Union, which was also company-controlled.

Eventually, we diversified into more covert investments, ones that didn't leave an obvious link back to the company

or any one person. The decision to conceal our ownership was designed more as a public relations move than
anything else (negating any charge of a company town)
and a lot of money was spent purchasing these varied
businesses.

Here are some examples. Hamilton Lee owns the Hard-
ee's, Burger King, Ace Hardware, the building supply
center, Ford dealership, NAPA store, and, with some other
partners, the Oak Trail shopping center.

Larry Hughes invested in convenience stores, buying commercial tracts all over the county. Hughes also has exclu-
sive gasoline supply contracts through several wholesale
suppliers. Home construction was another area Hughes
concentrated on. Over fifty percent of the houses built
in Concord during the last thirty years were by his companies. Hughes also owns the GM dealership, produce
market, funeral home, flea market in the north end of the
county, a variety of commercial office space, and the Bull
Creek shopping center.

I stayed in banking, opening the competing South Central
Georgia Savings. We assumed enough business existed
for at least one other financial institution, so before someone else moved in we agreed I should open it. I also hold a
controlling interest in the Toyota dealership, Econo Lodge,
Eagle Lake Lodge, McDonald's, the truck stop on Highway
16A, the cable television company, and, like Hughes, various commercial buildings all over the county.

All of these holdings are noted at the end of this narrative
in Appendix A. Appendix B is a listing of undeveloped real
estate we still own. Our landholdings are extensive. Early
on we recognized what could happen if we were successful

with our investment, so a point was made to buy as many parcels as possible.

You should know that these businesses and land tracts are controlled through management companies, themselves owned by holding companies, which are in turn run by corporations controlled by one, two, or all three of us. The names of all these various LLCs and partnerships are provided in Appendix C.

None of these ventures were overly profitable and some even lost money. And, unlike Qin Shi, we do not own or control everything in town. But we have enough to provide the means by which a substantial amount of company wages could be recycled back into our pockets. Someone, or some entity, was going to secondarily profit from our investment. It might as well have been us who derived the bulk of any money to be made. We even coined a name, "recycled payroll," for the dollars realized from these secondary businesses.

This diversification ultimately provided another benefit, one we initially did not realize, but one we now regard as priceless. Access to an enormous amount of personal information. Banking records, tax records, credit information, sales histories, new and used car purchases, and the like.

Our original plan called for ten years of investment then several decades of profit. However, unexpected dips in the economy, two recessions (one quite deep), and foreign competition plummeted the price of paper. At the same time our three labor unions relentlessly demanded more in the way of wages and benefits. A dangerous spiral evolved, one that easily could have forced either reductions in our work force or the shutting of our doors. But that didn't happen, and to fully understand why a few other points about Southern Republic need explaining.

Initially, like most companies, we maintained employee health insurance through a variety of outside insurers. The same was true for our workers' compensation coverage and retirement programs. Over the years the costs associated with these third-party providers skyrocketed and the continuous demands from the unions for more benefits compounded an already difficult situation. Then, with the enactment of the Affordable Care Act, new financial pressures were placed on our coverages. So imagine if a way could be found to control those costs. Perhaps even predict them with reasonable certainty. A company with that capability would certainly have an advantage.

We found such a way.

Murder.

Robbie Shuman was first. We discussed him the other evening at my house. Suffice it to say Shuman was not the victim of a random act of violence, as the police and everyone else so easily assumed. He was slain by a hired killer, then posthumously revealed to be a thief to destroy his credibility.

The second time was a fortunate accident. Corey Horne was a retired paperworker who unfortunately needed a heart transplant. Our health insurer at the time shuddered at the projected costs involved. Luckily for the insurer, and us, Horne died naturally before any expenses were incurred. Horne's death, combined with how easily the problem of Robbie Shuman was eliminated, stimulated my thinking. Eventually, I was the one who conceived the entire scheme.

Seven years after we bought the company we canceled our health insurance and workers' compensation coverage with the respective third-party providers. We then borrowed enough money to become self-insured, creating a fund to finance medical coverage along with a reserve to provide retirement and pension benefits (which were also simul- taneously internalized). Employee contributions multiplied this fund and allowed for lucrative stock investments, which eventually paid off handsomely. Overall, our self-insured fund is now solvent to hundreds of millions. But to assure continued vitality we knew that costs had to be controlled on the back side.

So the Priority program was created.

The first hired killer (who we then referred to as an "employee" but now as an "Associate") was found through the same people who connected me with Robbie Shu- man's killer. Initially, we concentrated exclusively on retir- ees, eliminating people with expensive vested benefits. Almost immediately large sums of capital were realized that could be recycled back to finance front-end exten- sions of health insurance benefits demanded by the unions.

As we became more proficient, we expanded the program to encompass not only vested retirement benefits but the ridding of excessive health risks, what we considered to be unreasonable workers' compensation claims, and the elim- ination of some particularly disastrous third-party claims against the company.

Through a series of collective bargaining sessions (and with the unwitting help of Hank Reed who repeatedly sealed the deals), we were able to fine-tune our coverage. Eventually, the Priority program not only financed itself, it paid back the original loan that led us to be self-insured and generated enormous surplus capital. Some of this surplus capital was invested back into the fund, the rest was used for expansion of our physical plants and general operating expenses.

How is it done? At first, informally. We would scrounge through our personnel records and identify potential can-didates. A list would be made and placed in a precise order, hence the term "Priority." One by one Priorities would then be eliminated. Later, as our records became computerized, so was the list. And it was here the con-stant flow of information we already possessed from our secondary businesses began to become important. By being self-insured we had direct access to all of our employees' (both past and present) medical histories. The Woods County Regional Medical Center was built (and partly funded by us) on the public pretense of providing quality and convenient medical care. More importantly, the facility allowed direct access to vital medical informa-tion (and to the patients themselves), which aided tremen-dously in the subsequent implementation of the Priority program. The same is true of the local convalescent center.

Computerization eventually made it easier to Prioritize, especially once we developed a program that could quickly scan our payees and identify candidates based on such factors as age, health, medical history, claims history (both medical and workers' comp), number of dependents, dependents' medical history, and the like.

All processings of Priorities are governed by a precise set of Rules designed to lessen the possibility of exposure. Associates are required to follow Rule exactly. Mistakes are never tolerated.

How could we do this? That's certainly a question I've asked myself many times over the last few years. The first time was easy. Robbie Shuman was an obnoxious braggart who caused both us and our employees nothing but trouble. I had no reservations in having him killed, and the company ran one hundred percent smoother after his death. Perhaps the lack of remorse associated with Shuman made the rest possible. It certainly didn't hurt. Recently, Larry Hughes calculated a rough approximation and estimated that the average Priority saved the company around $260,000. Using a median of 1700 deaths (which is conservative), that would mean in excess of $440,000,000 has been generated. The actual figure is most likely even higher.

The Priority program provided an edge over the competition. Enough to allow, if needed, a five percent drop in the price of our paper (which sometimes could be enough to make a sale), or the granting of a half percent wage increase at negotiation time, or the financing of additional benefits that helped keep our work force satisfied and productive. It was a tool that, combined with careful management, eventually helped make the three shareholders multimillionaires.

But we weren't the only ones who benefited. Jobs were generated. Billions in payroll paid. Woods County prospered. Life changed for the better. You told me that yourself. Concord suffered none of the layoffs and shutdowns all too common in the paper industry over the last twenty years. In fact, while others closed or scaled down, we expanded.

Is it still going on? Definitely. Jon De Florio oversees the program. There are two associates who work under him, however no one, other than De Florio, knows anything about them. Also, absolutely no one within the company, other than the three owners, De Florio, and his two associates, has any knowledge of the program. To them, this is a paper company run just like any other.

Brent, the killing must stop. So I am providing you with the information and resources needed to do that. Expose the program. Stop the madness. Cowardice kept me from doing that myself. I've spent years forging a reputation, trying to gain a measure of respectability. I prefer to go to my grave, perhaps foolishly, thinking my life a success. But, if it's any consolation, know that the creator fell victim to his own evil. My death was not the result of terminal cancer. I was Prioritized and processed. I assume De Florio himself handled the task. Perhaps with your help I can be the last Priority.

You will need to corroborate what I am telling you. What you may or may not know is that Hank Reed has one of our Priority lists. He obtained it by accident when he had one of our employees search our e-files. That searching was expected. In fact, Hamilton Lee intentionally planted a memo containing false information designed to misdirect Hank during the negotiations. But through a stroke of luck Reed obtained the Priority list the board approved for processing at its May and June meetings.

Be aware Lee and Hughes know of my contacts with you and Hank. They also know I am attempting to stop them.

They have even read an early version of this narrative. De Florio will surely be sent after you both. Precisely when is hard to predict, but he will come. De Florio has the capability to maintain constant physical and electronic surveillance of your activities (phones, offices, and homes). He is good at what he does, but you have an edge he has never contended with before.

You know he's coming.

I recently executed a codicil to my will that leaves everything I have to a trust. I have placed you in sole control of that trust. My estate is worth between $240 and $300 million and includes cash, stocks, bonds, businesses, and real estate. What it does not include is my interest in Southern Republic. Per our shareholders agreement, at death, my one third interest immediately passed to Lee and Hughes.

My instructions (as detailed in the will) are to liquidate everything I have and distribute the money to as many families of past Priorities as can be located. In order to do that you need to know their identities. Certainly, not every past employee who pressed a claim against the company, or reached retirement age, or incurred a medical bill was killed. In fact, only a small percentage of the tens of thousands who've worked for the company were ever Prioritized. Who are all these people? It's impossible now to say. No records were kept. Only in the last few years did I start keeping an informal tally, but even that is incomplete. Appendix D is a partial list of names which can serve as a good starting point.

One final thing. If you manage to get Lee and Hughes prosecuted please do not let the government seize the company or shut it down. They will surely try. Fight for control. Fight for employee ownership and a share for the families of those Prioritized. Keep the company going so Concord can survive. Maybe then some good can come from this monstrous evil. I have made a special provision in the will that gives you the express power to use my wealth to achieve that purpose.

It's okay to hate me. Who could blame you? If it's any comfort (and if you believe) I'm surely burning in hell, the devil my eternal companion. I deserve nothing less. I've spent a lifetime using people for profit. Your own hiring was another selfish act, designed to provide us a direct line into Reed's innermost thoughts, one we could make use of, if need be. I'm ashamed again to say that was my idea, too. Yet, after I came to meet you, I realized you were a man who could be trusted with what I have left. You have a chance to right the wrong. To turn something evil into something good. Perhaps God truly does work in mysterious ways.

Survive, and tell the tale.

Brent closed his eyes and sucked in a few deep breaths.

Then he scanned the narrative again.

His stomach started to churn, a wave of nausea rising in his throat. He now knew what the list Hank had found meant. Southern Republic had engaged in organized murder simply to keep the company competitive and the bottom line in the black. It was too incredible even to fathom. Yet here it was, in the deathbed confession of one of the company's founders, the man who supposedly conceived the whole idea.

The sickening feeling that swept through him was rapidly tempered by anger. He'd obviously been used. Hired for no other purpose than a means to keep an eye on Hank. A conduit for information. But there was something else. Something even more horrible. He almost didn't want to look. Yet he had to. He scrolled

274

back up and read the words again. Only in the last few years did I start keeping an informal tally, but even that is incomplete. Appendix D is a partial list of names which can serve as a good starting point.

Something about what happened two years ago had always bothered him. His father had been in and out of Brooks Creek hundreds of times. How could he have *misjudged the clearance of low overhanging branches,* as the police so easily concluded? Lingering doubts had never allowed him to fully believe the death as accidental. But he'd dismissed those doubts and finally accepted the sad reality. After all, tragic, inexplicable things sometimes rob the living of loved ones. Like car wrecks, plane crashes, or being struck by lightning, boating accidents do happen.

Or do they?

He scrolled to where the narrative stopped, bypassing Appendixes A, B, and C, each long lists of land and businesses broken down in three subparts titled LEE, HUGHES, and BOZIN. Appendix D was ominously titled PARTIAL LIST OF PRIORITIES FOR PAST FIVE YEARS. He glided through the names, listed chronologically by the approximate date of death and manner. He knew many of them. Fathers of childhood friends. Neighbors. Acquaintances. Clients. He didn't want to look. But as the names moved up the screen there appeared, with a date for August, two years ago—

WALKER, BRIAN — DROWNING.

Dear God.
No.

1:30 P.M.

BRENT STARED DOWN AT HIS DESK.

He'd sat quietly for a few minutes, his stomach still flip-flopping, like he'd just taken three trips on a roller coaster. He thought back to that summer day, almost two years ago, when the call came from

275

his mother to Atlanta, telling him that his father had drowned in Brooks Creek.

He hit his head and went into the water early this morning.

He'd just talked to his father the day before. He was planning a trip to Concord in a couple of weekends and they'd agreed to a Saturday of fishing. But dead? He remembered wondering how that was possible. Now he knew. His father had been murdered. A victim of a systematic, methodical elimination of select people simply for the realization of profit.

A Priority. In a Priority program. A name on a list.

He glared back at the computer screen, his father's entry bleakly staring back. He grabbed hold of himself and reached for the envelope, finding the sheet that indicated it should be read last.

He popped the tape holding the folds shut.

You're most likely filled with emotions that range from shock to hatred. Who could blame you? As you now most likely know, your father was murdered. I thought you had a right to that information. I also thought it might motivate you. To help in that fight, the microcassette is of a recent conversation among Lee, Hughes, and myself. The discussion is extremely incriminating and should be of value to the authorities. With regard to my will, the lawyer who drew the document is Mark Durham. His office is in Atlanta. Durham knows nothing of any of this. He simply knows that I changed certain provisions of my will and he's expecting your call. He can help in setting the trust into motion, but remember only you know its actual purpose. One final thing. What I have set in motion is unfair to you. I know that. But it is necessary. Lee, Hughes, and De Florio will act. They will have no choice. When they do, catch them. You have a distinct advantage, as I noted in the narrative. You know they are coming. Use that wisely.

Christopher Bozin

Stay in control. Get hold of yourself.

He kept repeating those words over and over.

This couldn't be happening. Could he really now be the target of Jon De Florio and two hired killers? Should he go to the police? No. Obviously what happened through the years had left no evidence to track. But he had the narrative. That offered some corroboration. Surely, though, any trace of it was now long gone from the company servers. Which meant Lee and Hughes could simply brand the whole thing a figment of an old man's imagination, lay low for a while, then start again, with him, or worse, his family, their next Priority.

That wasn't the smart move.

Could he go to the press? They might run the story, but then again they might not. He was seasoned enough to know the *Concord Record* and the other community newspapers in the area wouldn't touch it, aware Southern Republic kept a standing account for constant advertising, tacitly ensuring favorable treatment on any story related to the company. The Atlanta and Savannah papers, though, might be a different story. They were big enough not to be susceptible to financial pressure, but they'd want verification to protect from a charge of libel.

And right now, he did not possess enough of that commodity.

He needed a hard copy of the narrative, so he punched the appropriate buttons and instructed the laser printer in the outer office to work. He then closed the file and stuffed everything back in the envelope. He hustled out and retrieved the pages from the printer before anyone paid them any attention. Luckily, because of Bozin's death, only one woman sat at her desk and she was preoccupied. With the hard copies in hand he retreated into his office, closed the door, and reached for the phone.

He'd dialed three of the seven digits when it hit him what Bozin had warned about. De Florio has the capability to maintain constant physical and electronic surveillance of your activities (phones, offices, and homes). He's probably already doing just that. Deliberately, he misdialed the remaining numbers and the recording, which any other time would have been annoying, announced, *"We're sorry, your call cannot be completed as dialed."*

He hung up and calmly left his office, walking down the hall to the plant's safety office. If De Florio was monitoring phones, that was most likely confined to the general counsel's area. From his days as a DA he knew that electronic surveillance was actually cumbersome and time consuming. There were literally hundreds of phones in the mill and, according to what Bozin had said, De Florio employed only himself and two helpers. Out of necessity they'd have to limit the number of extensions they could reasonably watch. So he hoped the phones in the safety office were untapped. He borrowed one and called Hank's house, but no one answered. He walked back to his office, mind still reeling.

He recalled the microcassette.

So he closed the door and listened to the entire conversation three times. He then switched the recorder off and dropped everything back inside the envelope.

Where was Hank?

He decided to take a gamble and see if he was possibly at S. Lou Greene's office. If their relationship was anything like his and Hank's used to be, Hank should hang out there a lot, particularly during negotiation time.

He stuffed the folded envelope in his inside jacket pocket. Then he grabbed a couple of expanded folders and headed out of the building, informing the sole assistant he was going to meet with Greene in an attempt to settle a couple of pending workers' comp files. He didn't know if or when he would be back. He walked slowly and deliberately, cautioning himself to stay in control, maintain the pretense of his position, do nothing that, if noticed, would arouse suspicions. But keeping up that appearance was hard, his guts a volatile combination of rage, anger, sorrow, and fear.

He left Building B and nonchalantly strolled to the parking lot. Along the way he waved at a couple of friends and even stopped a moment to chat with a few people about Bozin's death. He finally climbed into the Jeep and drove from the mill toward town. He kept a leisurely pace, but checked his rearview mirrors more often than usual. Southern Republic Boulevard was filled with cars, several that stayed behind him, difficult to tell if any were actually following.

He crossed the railroad tracks of the Southern Republic Line and entered downtown. He parked on the street east of Greene's granite-faced office. Hank had told him the story of the flag and, climbing out of the Jeep, he glanced up and saw the yellow banner swaying in the light afternoon breeze. He carried his files down the sidewalk, passing a couple of people he knew. Finally, he excused himself and leisurely entered the office through a glass door. A bronze plaque affixed to the granite announced LAW OFFICE OF S. LOU GREENE. Inside, he resisted the temptation to look back and kept going into the lobby where a woman sat pounding a word processor.

"Brent Walker to see Mr. Greene."

"He has someone with him right now."

He took a chance. "I know. It's Hank Reed. They're expecting me."

The look on her face confirmed that he'd guessed right.

"Let me call up."

She reached for the phone and announced his presence. Apparently permission was granted as she motioned toward the top of the stairs. He loped up two at a time and rushed across the second-floor foyer. At the closed door marked PRIVATE he entered.

"What brings you here?" Hank asked, standing and coming toward him. Hank still wore his dress shirt, cuff links, and tie from the morning negotiation session. Greene's ensemble of a wrinkled pale-blue shirt, dark pants, and yellow tie looked like he'd slept in it the night before.

"We need to talk, Hank. It's about the list of names you showed me."

He knew Hank had brought Greene into the loop.

"What's happened?" Hank asked. "Have you found out more?"

"You could say that."

He tossed the files he was carrying to the floor. Now that he was away from the mill, inside a closed room, not susceptible to observation, the composure he'd used to successfully get him here dissolved. All he could see was the sight of his father's body, laid out in a coffin. He'd sat with him for hours before the funeral.

Hank stepped over and gripped his shoulder, seeing he was upset.

"How bad is this?" his old friend asked.

He grabbed hold of his emotions. "Really bad."

"Tell me what you know," Hank said.

"Hank, you have no idea what you're into. These bastards are deadly serious."

"You need to get ahold of yourself. Relax. Sit down. Tell me what this is all about."

"They're killing people, Hank. One by one. Systematically, they're killing people for profit."

His voice had risen. Hank looked at Greene, who sat up in his chair. He reached into his jacket, found the envelope, and handed Bozin's narrative to Hank. "Read it."

Greene stepped over and read over Hank's shoulder.

"My God," Hank said, when he finished the last appendix. "I know just about every name here." Hank looked at him. "And your father was one of them."

"We're next."

Hank said nothing, but the look on his face said he agreed.

"Not necessarily," Greene said, wedging himself back down in the chair behind his desk. "They've got to be unsure what you know and what you have. They can't take a chance on the unknown. They'll be sure before they act."

"I don't think these guys really give a damn," Brent said.

"Sure they do. If they've really done this, which apparently they have, they certainly don't want to get caught."

"If we're dead, they won't have to worry about that."

"Not necessarily. Bozin went to a lot of trouble latching on to you. They've got to be wondering about that, just like you are."

"They're following us."

"If they are, then they know both of you are here right now," Greene said.

He pointed to the files lying on the floor. "That's what those were for. You've got several cases against us. I told my office I was coming over to discuss settlement. I didn't hurry or do anything suspicious. So if somebody was following me they didn't see anything unusual."

"And I come here all the time," Hank said.

"Let's hope they're sufficiently confused to still not know what to do."

Brent reached into the envelope and removed the recorder. "You ought to listen to this."

Greene and Hank listened. Afterward, they read the two remaining sheets.

"These guys are amazing," Greene said. "They've taken the concept of a company town to its most logical extreme. They own or control most of the really profitable local businesses, along with banks and the credit union. And they've always had a hand in the hospital and convalescent center. It'd be easy for them to know everything there is to know about somebody."

"You almost sound like you admire what they've done," Brent said.

"Not at all. But you have to marvel at the ingenuity."

"They killed my father."

Greene held up his hands. "I know. I get it. I'm sorry as hell about that. But to stop this, we have to understand it. They've become the ultimate self-insurer. A guy works thirty years, retires, and expects a pension and his medical bills paid. Instead, he gets knocked off by some goon in the night and everybody just thinks he worked too hard. Bad heart. Weak kidneys. Tragic accident."

"Was your father ill?" Hank asked.

"Not that I knew of. But he liked to keep things to himself."

"I used to wonder about people," Hank said. "Men I worked with for a long time retiring, then dead within a year or two. But you're right, Lou, I just thought it went with the territory. The mill's a tough place to work. It's hard on the body."

"The vast majority died on their own, Hank," Brent said. "According to Bozin only about two thousand were killed. There must have been tens of thousands of people who've worked for Southern Republic. They can't kill 'em all."

Hank shook his head. "Bastards. When I was mayor the company always insisted that some of their people serve on the council. Same was true at the county, especially on the board of tax assessors. Lee would push me hard to make sure there was some element of political control always there. But these guys didn't need looking after."

"I'd imagine that was all for show," Greene said. "A certain pretense would have to be maintained. But a few tax breaks and some undervaluation of property wouldn't hurt the bottom line either. Those were little favors you could easily deliver. If they hadn't asked, you'd become suspicious."

"These three SOBs are mass murderers," Brent said, talking like the prosecutor he used to be. "We need to do something. Now."

"Bozin is right," Greene said. "Drawing attention to them is the key. But I'd stay away from the local press and local law enforcement. We don't know how far Southern Republic's reach is. It would be logical to assume they'd have friends there. Atlanta is the place to spring this."

"You got somethin' in mind, Lou?" Hank asked.

"This room could be bugged," Brent said.

Greene shook his head. "There'd be no reason to bug this office—until now. And yes, Hank, I do have something in mind. I have a friend from law school who works in the U.S. Attorney's Office in Atlanta. I also know a couple of reporters with the *Constitution*. I have to be in Atlanta Monday and Tuesday for workers' compensation hearings at the state board. The trip's been planned for some time, so it won't raise any eyebrows. While I'm there I can get this stuff to the right people."

Brent immediately didn't like the idea. "That's putting you in the line of fire with the rest of us. I can go straight to the Fulton County DA."

"I'm already in the line of fire thanks to you two coming here today."

"They'll probably put a tail on you now," Brent said.

"Maybe. But I'll be careful. I always drive, that'll give me time to see if I have an escort. And I'll go straight to see my friend tomorrow."

Brent shook his head. "I don't want to involve you."

"I'm already involved. Besides, it's the only practical solution. There's no way you two would ever make it to the police or the press. This De Florio would be all over you. And don't forget about your families. You can't risk them. You need to keep the other side in a state of confusion. Go about your business. If they're watching, there won't be anything to arouse suspicion. Sure, they kill. But they kill carefully. It's planned. Not spontaneous. By tomorrow, I'll have this stuff to the right people. After that, they wouldn't touch either of you."

"I think that's a good idea," Hank said.

He didn't like it. Not at all. But the reference to his mother struck home. Not to mention Ashley and Lori Anne. "Okay. But let us know the minute you make contact."

"I'll call Hank," Greene said.

"No," he quickly said. "Remember the phones. Call your wife and leave a message for Hank. Make it cryptic enough so we'll understand, but she won't. We'll check with her somehow."

"Good idea. I should have something by tomorrow afternoon. Right now, I'd better copy all of this. They'll want to see everything. Can I take the recording?"

Brent shrugged. "Sure. You'll need it."

3:14 P.M.

HAMILTON LEE STRUTTED ACROSS THE TWENTY-NINTH FLOOR toward Larry Hughes' suite of offices. He entered and noticed that Hughes' assistant was still crying.

"How's Nancy?" he asked, feigning concern for Bozin's employee.

"She's home, under a doctor's care."

"This is all so terrible. So tragic."

"Yes, it is," she said through the tears. "Mr. Bozin was a wonderful man."

He agreed, then excused himself and slipped into Hughes' office. Closing the door, he instantly dropped the pretense. "There's something we need to do. Chris' will. We need to get it."

"And how are we going to do that?"

"He had no family. Wouldn't it be logical for his business partners to handle his affairs?" He plopped down on the camelback sofa. An oval mahogany table with an exquisite Tiffany lamp sat next to it, a phone beneath. He grabbed the handset. "Chris' lawyer was Mark Durham. He told me about him back in friendlier times."

He'd already located the phone number, writing it down, so he dialed and was ultimately connected with Durham, after explaining who he was and the nature of the emergency.

"I don't think we've ever met, but Chris Bozin spoke highly of you all the time," he told Durham. "I wanted you to know. Chris died this morning."

Durham sighed. "That's awful. Terrible. I knew time was short, but I never suspected the illness was so far along."

"Terminal cancer. We've all been upset about this for some time. The reason I'm calling is that Chris' estate is going to need handling, and he specifically asked us to look after things."

"Not a problem, Mr. Lee. Mr. Bozin left an envelope for you here last week. He told me about his medical condition then and said for me to expect your call in the event of his death. I just didn't realize it would be so soon. He instructed me to promptly deliver the envelope. I'll have it sent over by messenger right away."

An hour later, the envelope arrived.

Lee read the handwritten note alone in his office.

By now I have been Prioritized, processed, and you've attempted to get a copy of my will. You're so predictable, Hamilton. Last week, I rewrote my will. All of my estate, including the payment owed to it by the company (and payable within the next 90 days per our shareholder's agreement), is now in a trust. My lawyer has been instructed on what to do and the named Trustee, Brent Walker, has been provided some specific written instructions. I think you'll find the whole thing exciting. I know I do.

He smiled.

The old man had style, he'd give him that. Whatever Bozin conceived had obviously been carefully planned.

Everything apparently thought through and anticipated.

Or was it?

DAY NINETEEN
SATURDAY, JUNE 24

S. LOU GREENE NAVIGATED HIS CHERRY-RED JAGUAR THROUGH THE weekend traffic. He flashed a left blinker, then turned off the busy boulevard into the subdivision. His car was not out of place—Cadillacs, Lincolns, Mercedes, BMWs, and at least one Rolls-Royce adorned the drives in front of the mansions lining the curbed street.

The development carried the prestigious name of Peachtree Estates. He assumed the applicable restrictive covenants mandated at least a two-acre-minimum lot size and ten thousand square feet under roof. No guard gate protected the entrance, probably because the residents deemed it more economical to dedicate the streets to the city and let the taxpayers pay for upkeep, reserving their money for decorative fences, private security services, and guard dogs, as much status symbols as practical.

The houses varied from one to four stories in height. Most were brick and stucco with columned façades and steep gabled roofs, yards meticulously planted with an assortment of trees, shrubs, ferns, and summer flowers. Not a bare spot or weed in sight. He was accustomed to such luxury. His own house was every bit as nice, the only difference being that his four thousand square feet with a pool did not sit on astronomically high-priced real estate in the hills of north Atlanta.

286

Surprisingly, he'd learned the address from the internet, which contained a listing for Lee, Hamilton J. He found Peachtree Estates from Google maps. The house he thought belonged to Lee dominated the far end of a cul-de-sac. A rough granite wall surrounded it, broken only by two iron gates accommodating a semi-circular drive. The architecture leaned toward Greek Revival—a full two stories with matching symmetrical wings, white brick, its front graced with a pedimented gable portico supported by fluted columns.

The gate was open so he drove in and parked next to a late-model silver Mercedes coupe. He climbed out of the Jaguar and took a moment to admire the scene. The drive was lined with trimmed shrubs and colorful flowers, the front yard a carpet of close-cut Bermuda grass. He half expected to see flagsticks periodically since it reminded him of a practice putting green. He shook his head and smiled. Hamilton Lee certainly knew how to live.

He'd dressed casually. Khaki shorts, a pullover polo shirt, and Top-Siders, no socks. Under the circumstances, he didn't deem formalities necessary.

He climbed the portico and rang the bell.

A solemn-faced butler answered.

"Is this the residence of Hamilton Lee of Southern Republic Pulp and Paper?"

"It is."

"My name is S. Lou Greene. I'm here to see Mr. Lee."

"Is he expecting you?"

"No."

"Then it would be out the question to disturb Mr. Lee on Saturday."

He nonchalantly reached into his shorts pocket and removed the folded copy of the list. "Show him this. I believe he'll see me."

He tried not to smile.

The butler took the offering, but did not unfold the paper.

"I'll be a moment."

The door closed. Three minutes later it reopened.

"Mr. Lee will see you."

"Surprise, surprise," Greene muttered.

"Follow me, please."

He was led through a marble foyer that carried the look and feel of a Roman temple. A wide carpeted hall stretched to the rear of the house, ending at a set of stained double doors. The butler opened them and invited him inside.

"Wait here, please."

He stood alone in a library. Bookshelves lined two walls, mostly novels and nonfiction, though two shelves displayed an impressive collection of *National Geographic*s in leather binders. Oil paintings in gilded frames dotted another wall, each tastefully illuminated by a tiny brass fixture. In the center sat an ensemble of a leather sofa and three upholstered wingback chairs. Sunlight poured through towering leaded-glass windows. Framed photographs angled off a side table. Lee obviously had two daughters, most of the pictures were of them and his grandchildren. He was intently studying the faces when the doors suddenly opened.

The man who entered was in his fifties with brownish-gray hair, a matching mustache, and a rich tan. He too was dressed casually, in a pair of dark-blue trousers and a cream-colored Robert Graham shirt. He carried the copy of the list, unfolded, in his left hand.

"I received your message," Lee said, closing the doors behind him.

"Lou Greene. I'm a lawyer from Savannah."

He extended his hand to shake.

Lee did not return the gesture. "As I understand it, Mr. Greene, you derive the vast majority of your income from Concord, Springfield, Sylvania, and a number of other small towns. Not Savannah."

"It's just easier to say Savannah."

"And perhaps more prestigious than, say, Rincon?"

"Perhaps."

Lee held up the list. "Where did you get this?"

"Could we sit down?"

"If you like."

He took a seat on the sofa, Lee across from him in one of the chairs.

"I'll ask again. Where did you get this list?"

"A mutual friend gave it to me."

"Who might that be?"

"Hank Reed."

"And its significance?"

He chuckled. "You're good."

"What do you mean?"

"Look, I understand you're being cautious. Who could blame you? You don't know me at all. You're probably wondering if I'm wired or something." He stood and rolled up his shirt. "See, no wires. If you want, I'll be glad to drop my pants or you can just pat me down, whichever'll make you happy."

"That won't be necessary. I get the point."

He replaced his shirt and sat.

"Why are you here?" Lee asked.

"You have a serious problem that I can help with."

"And what might that be?"

His tone hardened. Time to play the hole card. "The problem your dear departed ex-partner created with Brent Walker. So let's cut through the crap, Hamilton. You don't mind me calling you that, do you?"

Lee said nothing.

"Frankly, I don't care whether you mind or not. I read that confession Bozin left Walker. Pretty revealing. You're not a nice man. And by the way, it explains things clearly, including that list in your hand."

"And how can you help?"

He got comfortable, spreading his arms across the back of the sofa. Now he was getting somewhere. "It's lucky for you they came to me. So far, nobody knows anything but me, Reed, and Walker."

"And you have what Bozin gave Walker?"

"Yep," he lied.

"What is that?"

"A couple of handwritten notes, a flash drive, and a tape recording."

"Tape recording?"

"You didn't know about that? Seems Bozin taped a conversation among the three of you. Happened Thursday, I believe, in your house at Hickory Row." He shook his head in mock disgust, then reached back and removed the recorder Brent Walker had surrendered to him from his pocket. He pushed PLAY and allowed it to run a couple of minutes. He'd already selected one of the more salacious points of the conversation. He stopped it. "Really incriminating stuff. You should watch what you say."

"What are you proposing?"

"A partnership."

"Involving what?"

"Bozin left a list of some of your more recent Priorities. It really irritated the hell out of me that one of the guys you whacked was a client. That untimely death cost me $100,000 in hard-earned fees."

"And what do you want? Payment?"

"I'm a reasonable guy, Hamilton. The way I look at it, the past is the past. What I care about is the future. Seems to me the two of us could work well together."

"Why would I want to do that?"

"To keep me from doing what I told Reed and Walker I would do."

"Which is?"

"Go to the press and the appropriate prosecuting authorities with what I have."

"And what's to stop me from simply—" Lee paused. "Eliminating the problem?"

He smiled. "You don't know what I've done or where I've put everything. And even if you did Prioritize me, you'd still have the problem of Reed and Walker. Dealing with me comes with the benefit that I'll handle them for you."

"And how will you do that?"

"Don't worry. I'll deal with them. And without all the risky killing you like to use. They won't be a problem."

"What if I don't need your help?"

"I'm betting you can use all you can get."

"Assuming for the sake of discussion that I may be interested in such an arrangement, what do you want in return?"

He grinned, pleased with the progress. "All I want are some generous settlements on the workers' comp claims I'll have against the company. Your people have an irritating habit of fighting hard. That's fine as long as I'm assured you'll settle in the end... on my terms. And don't worry, I'll be fair with you. I won't take advantage. Just some reasonable dollars that not only fatten my pockets—"

"But help establish a reputation for you at the same time."

"Exactly. While you continue with your Prioritizing. Which, by the way, will not include any of my claimants. Kill off the other comp lawyers' cases, but leave my guys alone. Also, you're right, I want the money Pabon's death cost me... in cash."

"You've obviously given things a great deal of thought."

"I try to be thorough, Hamilton. Especially when it comes to my law practice."

"I have to think about all this."

"I understand. Really, I do." He rose. "I'll be in Atlanta till Tuesday. I'm staying at the Regency Arms, downtown. Take your time. But if I don't hear from you by Tuesday noon, I'll assume you're ready to read all about yourself in the *Atlanta Constitution* on Wednesday."

Lee stood. "I assure you, Mr. Greene, you'll be hearing from me long before then."

1:20 P.M.

LEE WAITED FORTY-FIVE MINUTES FOR DE FLORIO TO RETURN HIS call. He picked up the receiver in the library. "Jon, I want you and your associates back in Atlanta immediately."

"Is there a problem?"

"We have a matter that needs immediate attention."

"What about Reed and Walker?"

"Forget them, for now. The problem's here, not there."

"How will I receive instructions?"

"Meet me at the office at four o'clock. The company jet is already en route to bring you back. Get your associates here however you need to. But not on the plane."

"May I ask the nature of the matter?"

"Retribution."

4:46 P.M.

JON LISTENED INTENTLY AS LEE EXPLAINED WHAT HAPPENED WITH the lawyer, S. Lou Greene. They were sitting in the boardroom on the thirtieth floor of the Blue Tower. He'd been driven straight here from the airport after landing in Atlanta.

"That pompous bastard actually thinks he can blackmail me," Lee said. "What do you know about him?"

He shrugged. "Greedy. Arrogant. Cocky. But successful. He's been doing workers' comp claims for years. Has a reputation as one of the best in the state. He came to Concord nine years ago. He's the most difficult of all the workers' compensation lawyers that industrial relations deals with. Steadfastly refuses to compromise for anything less than what he demands. He backs that up by a close relationship with the local administrative law judge. They play golf and tennis together. We learned that Greene's paid for several stays at a Jamaican resort for the old man. That's certainly an ethical violation and would make for excellent extortion. I've kept a file updated in case the board's patience ran out."

"What about personal stuff?"

"He's nicknamed Cue Stick by the lawyers in the area. For obvious reasons. Drinks a six-pack a day of imported beer. Thinks of himself as a gourmet. Doesn't bat an eye at spending $500 on dinner. He's forty-one. Married. But that doesn't stop him from keeping a girlfriend on the side. There are three little Greenes. A boy and two girls. They live on twenty acres in northwest Chatham

County. His wife's a registered nurse, but doesn't work much anymore. She mainly oversees the maid and gardener and keeps Greene happy."

"How do you remember all that?"

"I prepared the file myself."

Lee shook his head. "Bozin has placed us in a totally untenable position."

"But I'd bet Mr. Bozin didn't figure on Greene's involvement."

"I agree. This is, what did you say? Cue Stick's doing. Unknown to Reed or Walker too. Has there been any contact between Greene and Walker?"

"Yesterday, Walker went to Greene's office. My man reported that Walker left the mill around 1:30 and casually made his way there. He carried files and left word that he was going to try and settle some claims."

"That's obviously where Greene found out what he did. Otherwise, we'd have heard from him earlier. What about Reed?"

"I had to pull my man off Reed to stay with Bozin's body. As you recall, I'm shorthanded with only two associates. I tracked Reed myself till noon. My associate was not able to return and pick him back up till late afternoon. By then he was home. There was a three-hour stretch I couldn't monitor."

"So he could have been at Greene's office too?"

"Possible. He hangs out there quite a bit."

"Obviously there's been communication among all three. Greene knew all about Bozin. He even played a damn recording, which was news to me."

"Greene's most likely acting alone. He sees an opportunity and is trying to make the best of it apart from Walker and Reed."

"How fortunate for us," Lee said. "We need to take advantage of this opportunity, Jon. I want Greene dead. Tonight. Something out of the ordinary. More public. I want to send a message that our two friends in Concord will understand. Can you do that?"

"Greene said he was staying at the Regency Arms?"

Lee nodded.

"Afterward, what are my instructions?"

"Return to Concord and get ready for Reed and Walker. I'm not sure exactly what our course of action will be as yet. Needless to say, we certainly need to retrieve Bozin's confession and that tape before we tie up the loose ends. A memorial service is planned for Bozin in Concord on Monday. Mr. Hughes and I have to attend. If we don't have all the originals by then, I'm going to talk with Walker myself and up the ante."

He checked his watch. 4:57 P.M. "My associates are due here by 6:00. Greene will be processed by 8:00 and we'll be back in Concord by midnight."

"Excellent," Lee said.

7:03 P.M.

JON STARED OUT THE WINDSHIELD AND THOUGHT ABOUT BURT Wyler. The man owned three auto transmission stores spaced triangularly around I-285, the eight-laned perimeter interstate encircling metropolitan Atlanta. In the beginning, when there was only one store, Wyler had managed it himself, spending most of each day working under cars. But now he employed a manager at each location and spent the majority of his time commuting among the three stores. It was a prosperous business, one that made him a solid six-figure income, and he was already telling people store number four was in the works.

Wyler was a burly, slightly overweight, likable man with bushy brown hair. He shaved only twice a week, which kept his fleshy neck and puffy cheeks dusted with a perpetual stubble. He owned a house on the north side of Atlanta, not a mansion or anything pretentious, just a respectable two-story in an upper-middle-class neighborhood. He wasn't a big spender. His only real luxuries were the red Corvette convertible he bought a few years back and the eighteen-foot fiberglass speedboat kept at Lake Lanier for weekend waterskiing. His only problem was his wife, who'd moved out three months ago but had yet to file for divorce.

He'd tried everything to win her back. Gifts. Expensive nights out on the town. Promises of change. Agreements to seek counseling. Whatever it took. Yet nothing seemed to work.

Burt Wyler was forty-eight. Vikki Wyler, thirty-eight. She was his first wife, he her second husband. She was a career woman, trained as a vocational rehabilitation specialist, initially working for a group of rehab providers whose services were heavily depended upon by workers' compensation lawyers, insurance companies, doctors, and employers. After their marriage Wyler staked the money that allowed her to start her own practice and soon she developed an extensive clientele, rapidly expanding her presence statewide, and realizing a high-five-figure income.

They'd been married twelve years, trying the whole time to have children. Wyler wanted a son or a daughter, it really didn't matter which. But nothing had happened. They'd consulted specialists and both were tested. The lack of success bothered Burt a lot more than it did Vikki, which in itself bothered Wyler since he'd come to believe that his wife had no real interest in having children. Three months back, things came to a head and Vikki left, moving in with a girlfriend. Their contact since had been only sporadic. Wyler openly had told friends he thought Vikki was seeing someone else. All the signs pointed in that direction. But she repeatedly denied the allegation and skillfully turned the accusations around, arguing that Wyler's jealousy was the main problem in their marriage.

And perhaps it was.

Wyler had admitted to others that he was possessive. But Vikki did nothing to alleviate his fears. She liked clingy silk blouses and tight-fitting dresses. Her hemlines stayed short, exhibiting her thin thighs and long shapely legs. She sported a thick head of brunette hair she liked to curl and tease. And she owned an assortment of cosmetic lenses that tinted her eyes a variety of colors, a bright azure her favorite. She wasn't beautiful, just rawly attractive, and she liked to flaunt her appearance with a deliberate air of promiscuity.

They were a strange couple. A study in contrast. Wyler's friends told him he was better off without her. Unfortunately, Burt Wyler adored Vikki and wanted nothing more than for them to be together.

Jon smiled.

Burt Wyler was about to get his wish.

He glanced next to him. Frank Barnard sat behind the wheel. He checked his watch. 7:12 P.M.

Just about time.

Burt Wyler's third store sat on a corner lot in southeast Atlanta, a mile off the I-285 perimeter. It wasn't his busiest, or his slowest, but it was the closest to the apartment complex where Vikki now lived. Wyler had spent the entire Saturday at the store, a call earlier revealing its manager was on vacation. Jon assumed that afterward Wyler intended to go see his wife to try again to convince her to come back home. The red Corvette was parked catty-cornered to the east end of the brightly painted block building. At 7:15 Wyler locked the front door and headed straight for the car.

"Now," Jon said.

Barnard cranked the Buick and sped across the busy boulevard into the parking lot. Wyler was only a few feet from the Corvette, about to unlock the driver's-side door, when Barnard wheeled up.

"Burt Wyler?" Jon said, climbing out the passenger-side door. "I'm Walter Mason, a private investigator." He flashed a brown leather case containing a fake investigator's ID, identical to the actual ones issued by the state of Georgia.

"Am I supposed to be impressed? What do you want with me?"

"I think I could be of some assistance to you."

"Look, buddy, I'm in a hurry."

"It's about your wife."

He knew that would get Wyler's attention. "What the hell do you know about her?"

"Could we go inside and talk?"

Wyler hesitated, sizing him up, then said, "Follow me."

Jon signaled for Barnard to wait and keep his eyes open.

Back inside, Wyler asked, "Okay, Mr. Mason, what's this all about?"

"I've been hired by a woman in Savannah who believes her husband is having an affair with your wife."

"Who's the bastard?"

"A lawyer named S. Lou Greene. Your wife handles rehab services for a lot of his clients. They met about a year ago. He regularly comes to Atlanta and they spend quite a bit of time together. The Greenes are in the middle of a divorce and my agency has been hired to gather evidence for Mrs. Greene's side of the case."

"Why are you tellin' me this?"

"Mrs. Greene thought you could use the information. We've been doing some electronic monitoring. It seems your wife is getting ready to file for divorce. Greene has been giving her advice and they are intent on trying to get a piece of your business."

"No-good bitch," Wyler spat out. "A month ago I talked to a lawyer myself. She told me that twelve years of marriage was certainly enough to give her a claim. But I convinced myself she'd never do that. Hell, I bankrolled her career."

"I'd caution you against trusting too much or assuming the other side will be fair."

"Exactly what my lawyer said."

"Sound advice. Your wife not only has a lawyer for a boyfriend, but seems intent on taking you for whatever she can get. I've heard the tapes myself. Your wife right now is downtown in a hotel suite with Greene. We'd like to take you there."

"The crap for?"

"You need to see it for yourself. We also have electronic monitoring set up. Their conversations may be helpful in defending her claim against you. I don't mean to be insensitive, but they like to pillow-talk and we've learned a lot from those conversations."

"I didn't hire you. Why go to all the trouble?"

"Mrs. Greene wants to help. Thank her."

"Yeah, right. This was the last thing I wanted to hear. What I want is my wife back. I'd do about anything to make that happen. I was just on my way to see her."

He twisted the knife. "She's not home."

Wyler paused, seeming to consider what he'd said. "No, she's downtown in a motel room with some shyster lawyer screwin' his brains out. Maybe you're right? I do need to see it for myself."

"We need to coordinate how this is going to happen. I have a man stationed near the room where your wife and Greene are now. I don't want to raise any suspicions on anybody's part, so please follow us downtown in your car. The hotel is the Regency Arms. Park in the underground garage and head up to the lobby. There's a sitting area near the elevators. Wait there. When my associate and I arrive, follow us into the elevator. Don't act like you know us. We're uncertain of who Greene knows at the hotel. Since he's a regular, the staff is familiar with him. When we get up to the floor stay quiet, just follow us into our room. We'll talk there. Understand?"

Wyler nodded. "I got it."

"You know where the Regency Arms is?"

"Yeah," Wyler said, voice breaking. "Vikki and I spent a weekend there once."

7:50 P.M.

JON SMILED.

Burt Wyler followed instructions to the letter and stayed behind their maroon LeSabre all the way downtown.

This should be easy.

Thankfully, S. Lou Greene was a creature of habit. When in Atlanta the lawyer stayed in Room 478 at the Regency Arms, a two-room suite with a whirlpool tub that faced the front of the hotel. Greene's affair with Vikki Wyler had been easy to document. As was Burt Wyler's weakness for his wife. Greene had been seeing Vikki nearly a year, and ever since she'd moved out they'd regularly spent the weekend together whenever Greene was in Atlanta.

He thought it strange somebody like Greene would even have

a mistress. After all, the lawyer wasn't all that visually appealing. But the money liberally spent on meals, gifts, liquor, and hotel rooms apparently more than made up for any lack of physical presence.

And Vikki was an easy mark.

An ambitious woman who openly used Greene to ingratiate herself into the workers' compensation bar. In fact, it was thanks to Greene that a lot of claimants' lawyers from around the state now routinely used her professional services.

Arriving at the Regency Arms, Burt Wyler continued to follow instructions, dutifully turning into the underground garage and stopping at the automatic gate. The dispensed receipt would later provide excellent corroboration on the precise time of arrival.

Jon did not have Frank Barnard follow Wyler into the garage. He assumed each level was closed-circuit-monitored by hotel security and the last thing he wanted was a videotaped record of his arrival and departure. That privilege was reserved solely for the red Corvette, the videotape providing more than enough corroboration to the tragedy he was about to stage.

Barnard parked on the street, a couple of blocks west of the hotel's main entrance. Jon filled the meter with quarters so there'd be no danger of receiving a citation. He and Barnard then strode back to the Regency Arms and entered the plush main lobby. The hotel was one of Atlanta's oldest, lovingly remodeled into a four-star jewel with elegantly decorated suites and first-class service to guests who could afford the luxury. It was a favorite of businessmen during the week and couples on the weekend looking for two days of peace and quiet. He and Barnard strolled through the lobby, appearing like two businessmen in town for the weekend returning from an important Saturday meeting. Barnard toted a burgundy leather briefcase.

They headed straight for the elevators but kept their faces turned from the lobby cameras. To his left, he caught a glimpse of Burt Wyler sitting exactly where instructed. Wyler saw him too and dutifully rose, following them onto the elevators. He pushed the button for the fourth floor and was pleased Wyler continued to say nothing. When the doors parted, he, Barnard, and Wyler stepped off.

He pointed right.

They headed down the hall.

At Room 479 he inserted the plastic card and tripped the lock. He pushed against the spring-loaded hinges and inched the door inward, inviting Wyler in first. At the end of a short entrance hall was a double bed, desk, chair, and luggage rack.

Wyler calmly stepped forward into the room.

Once past the short entrance way Victor Jacks pounced, wrapping an arm around the man's neck and clamping a cloth soaked in anesthetic across the face. Wyler resisted, but the compound worked fast and the big man's body went limp. Jacks allowed it to ease down to the carpet and released his hold.

No one spoke. No one had to.

Each knew exactly what to do.

JACKS WAS ALREADY WEARING A WHITE SHIRT WITH DARK PANTS AND black bow tie to look like a room steward. Skintight latex gloves were quickly camouflaged beneath a white-cloth pair that Jacks yanked from his pocket. A bottle of champagne was chilling in a silver bucket, two crystal glasses and a red rose beside on a tray. Jacks carefully balanced the tray on his fingertips. He held the gun in his right hand, finger on the trigger, concealed behind his back and headed for the door, stepping over Wyler's body.

Barnard opened it.

He approached, looked both ways, then stepped out.

Room 478 was across the hall, a few feet down to the right. Quickly, he exited and was able to tap on the door with the sound suppressor at the end of the gun barrel without being seen. The first knock went unanswered. The room was a suite, Greene most likely in the outer bedroom.

He knocked again.

A door opened, then closed on the other side. A peephole provided only the appearance of a bow-tie-wearing steward balancing a tray of champagne.

"What do you want?" Greene asked from behind the door.

"Champagne, Mr. Greene. Compliments of the hotel. Our thanks for your patronage."

He understood the plan. Greene's vanity should allow a momentary drop in guard. After all, Greene had been staying at the Regency Arms for years, feeling right at home. A complimentary bottle of champagne would be expected, not suspected.

The door's lock released, then opened.

Jacks moved forward, turning slightly to the right and shielding the gun. "Where would you like this, sir?"

"Over there on the table is fine."

The lawyer was dressed in one of the hotel's terry-cloth bathrobes, loosely tied at the waist, the distinctive gold crescent logo embroidered on the pocket. Thin hairy legs and bare feet stuck out the bottom. Jacks deftly set the tray down on the table. Greene closed the door and momentarily turned his back on what he thought was a room steward.

Jacks used the moment to level his gun.

"Mr. Greene, keep your mouth shut and do exactly what I tell you."

To the right was the closed door leading to the bedroom. He knew Vikki Wyler was waiting for Greene to return and he didn't want her to hear him, so he kept his voice low.

"Move away from the door."

He waved the sound-suppressed barrel of the gun.

Fear filled Greene's square face. The lawyer backed away.

Jacks approached the hallway door and cracked it open.

JON SAW THE DOOR MOVE.

Immediately, he and Barnard popped out of Room 479 and entered 478.

"Good evening, Mr. Greene."

He closed the door and signaled Barnard, who whipped out a sound-suppressed pistol and leveled the barrel at Greene, taking over the watch. Jacks grabbed a pillow from the sofa, approached the bedroom, turned the knob, and swung the heavy door inward. The outside wall was lined with tall windows, their sheers and tapestry draperies drawn, casting the furniture in dim shadows.

Vikki Wyler lay naked on the covers.

She rolled over as the door opened. "Who was that, Lou?"

She stopped in mid-sentence, realizing the man in the doorway was not Greene and he had a gun. She was just about to scream when Jacks positioned the pillow over the gun and pumped two shots into her chest, then another in her head. All three came out as soft pops from both the pillow and the sound suppressor. The slug in her head never exited, but the two in the chest went right through, blood and sinew splattering the mahogany headboard and papered wall.

She never uttered a sound.

Jacks lowered the gun. "Nice breasts."

"Yes, they were," Jon said, standing behind him.

Greene was forced into the bedroom. One look at Vikki's bloody body contorted across the bed and he started to panic.

"Why are you doing this? All I wanted was a simple deal. I want to play ball with you guys."

Jacks and Barnard held the lawyer tight.

"We don't need partners or assistance," De Florio calmly said. Greene was thrust onto the bed and Victor Jacks fired three more suppressed shots through the pillow. The white robe splotched with a blood rose at each impact, Greene's body contorting then draping across Vikki Wyler's.

Jon checked both pulses.

Dead. Confirmation.

He then signaled Barnard and Jacks. Both headed back to Room 479.

He stood at the hall door and kept watch. A moment later they appeared with Burt Wyler, his outstretched arms across their shoulders, raising him high enough so the feet would not drag on the carpet.

No one in sight.

He signaled.

They crossed into Greene's suite where Wyler was laid on the bedroom floor. Jacks then placed the gun used to kill the two on the bed into Wyler's hand, which would assure that enough residual prints were left to suggest the obvious. Jacks and Barnard brought Wyler's body up to its knees and helped the hand raise the gun to Wyler's temple. Jacks adjusted the angle for the expected upward trajectory, then helped Wyler's finger pull the trigger. The round entered the head and quickly exited, splattering more blood onto the wall. Jacks released his grip and allowed Wyler's lifeless body to slump into the carpet. He released the gun, which settled on the carpet too. Carefully, Jacks bent down and unscrewed the sound suppressor, pocketing it. The pillow lay off to the side. They then stood back and surveyed the scene.

So did Jon.

A double murder then a suicide would be easily presumed, and everything would point to Burt Wyler.

Or would it?

"Mr. Jacks, there's an error," Jon said from the bedroom doorway.

Jacks looked around.

"You shot the man in the right temple. There's an entrance wound and powder burns. The gun, though, is at an odd angle to the body, suggesting something different."

Jacks looked down. "You're absolutely right. A stupid mistake."

"The kind that could raise questions. But it's okay, this one time. That's why I'm here. This was a rush job and complicated. Mistakes will happen under such circumstances. Use it as a learning experience. Now please, adjust the gun's location. That way the evidence will not be ambiguous."

Jacks did exactly as instructed.

He re-surveyed the scene. Perfect.

"Start searching," he said.

They knew what to look for and Barnard quickly found the copies of the two handwritten notes to Brent Walker, the list Hank Reed had provided, and the tape recorder with tape. No originals were there beyond the tape recording. But De Florio had already concluded that Greene didn't have the originals.

All part of the bluff.

He was confident Brent Walker had retained those.

"The champagne bucket," he said to Barnard, who retrieved the tray from the table in the other room. Jacks grabbed the pillow.

They left.

He closed the door for Room 478 and hung a DO NOT DISTURB sign on the outer knob. Checkout time on the weekends was not until two o'clock so the bodies would not be found until tomorrow afternoon at the earliest. Jacks had checked earlier and determined that this section of hallway was not subject to any video surveillance. Conveniently, older hotels routinely contained gaps in coverage.

They returned to Room 479.

Barnard opened the champagne and poured three-quarters of the bottle down the bathroom drain, rinsing the sink clean. Jacks unmade the bed and rumpled the sheets and pillows. Barnard then wedged the nearly empty champagne bottle back into the ice but, before he did, rinsed the stemmed glasses with a little of the alcohol, leaving a swig of residue. Barnard then placed the tray with bucket on the nightstand beside the bed, one glass there, the remaining on the nightstand on the other side. The room was paid for in advance using fake identification. Easy to assume it had been used for a weekend rendezvous the occupants wanted secret. Barnard and Jacks removed their gloves and tossed them into the empty briefcase.

He did the same.

The cloth with antiseptic was already there.
All, including the pillow, would be disposed of later.
"Let's go," De Florio said.
"Where to?" Jacks asked.
"Back to Concord to finish this."

THE FINAL DAY
MONDAY, JUNE 26

7:10 A.M.

BRENT STOOD IN THE SHOWER AND DOUSED HIS BODY WITH HOT water. He was glad the weekend was over. The two days had been the longest of his life. He'd worked in the yard most of Saturday. To keep some semblance of a regular routine he and Ashley went out Saturday night, then took Lori Anne to an air show yesterday at the Screven County airport. They hadn't, as yet, talked with Lori Anne about him being her father. But they would soon. After they became a little bit better acquainted. On the way home they'd stopped by Hank's house, where he learned nothing had been heard from Greene.

His mother sensed something was bothering him and tried last night to get him to talk. But he knew, at least for now, it was better to keep things to himself. Ashley had probed too. But it was bad enough that he might be in danger, he wasn't about to involve her. He thought about staying away from Ashley and Lori Anne altogether, but decided that if De Florio was watching he would already know all about his contact with her, and he didn't want to do anything that would raise suspicions. He hoped Greene was successful. Once public attention was focused on Lee and Hughes, neither would be foolish enough to harm anybody. Or at least that's what he'd tried to convince himself of all weekend.

He finished showering, stepped from the tub, and towel-dried his hair. He walked out into the bedroom and switched on the radio set to WODS, the local FM station that had serviced Concord and Woods County for decades. He'd always liked listening to the country-western format. But his enthusiasm for the station had forever dampened Friday when he noticed on Bozin's itemization that Lawrence Hughes owned a controlling interest.

"Good morning, Woods County. Here are the morning's top stories. Tragedy struck Saturday as police report that local attorney S. Lou Greene was killed in a downtown Atlanta hotel."

A chill shot down his spine.

"Greene's body was found along with the bodies of Victoria Wyler, a thirty-eight-year-old vocational rehabilitation specialist, and her forty-eight-year-old husband, Burt Wyler, an Atlanta businessman. Police theorize that Burt Wyler shot both, then killed himself. Neighbors of the Wylers verified that the couple was having marital problems and had been separated for some time. Greene and Vikki Wyler were shot with the gun found next to Burt Wyler's body. Wyler died from an apparently self-inflicted gunshot wound to the head. Police estimate the tragedy occurred sometime Saturday afternoon or evening and the investigation is ongoing. No funeral arrangements have been announced. Greene is survived by a wife and three children."

He never heard what the announcer said next. His mind reeled. He barely heard his cell phone ring on the nightstand. Coming back to reality, he reached down and grabbed it.

"Brent."

It was Hank. And he'd used his first name.

Surely playing to anybody listening.

"I couldn't talk with you about it yesterday, but you didn't tell me you and Ashley were seeing each other."

"I just didn't think about it," he said, trying to figure out where the conversation was going.

Hank laughed. "She's a tough one. Better watch yourself."

He faked a laugh too. "Don't I know."

"Look, why don't we have breakfast in the mill cafeteria. I'd like to know more about you and Ashley."

Hank knew all about him and Ashley and never ate breakfast at the mill cafeteria. In fact, he knew Hank religiously avoided the place. Obviously, he wanted to talk and thought a public spot the best location. "Sure, that'd be fine. I'll be there in about forty-five minutes."

Hank was right.

They needed to talk.

8:03 A.M.

BRENT WHEELED INTO THE MILL PARKING LOT AND HEADED STRAIGHT for the cafeteria. He wasn't sure, but he thought a car followed him from town. The mill's eatery filled an appendage of Building C directly adjacent to the main gate leading back into the central production areas. It was used by almost all the employees, both hourly and salaried, and represented one of the few services the company contracted to an outside firm. The daily breakfast included a small buffet, nothing like the extravaganza at the Comfort Inn, but a bargain at under $5.

Out of respect for Bozin, contract negotiations had been suspended for Monday and Tuesday. So the IBEW committee, the only one yet to come to an agreement, had returned to the mill until Wednesday. A memorial service was scheduled at St. Nicholas Catholic Church later in the afternoon and all company employees had been invited. Until hearing the news about Greene, Brent had planned to attend. Hank was ensconced in one of the red-and-white laminated booths, a cup of steaming coffee and a newspaper before him.

"Good to see you," Hank said in a raised voice, obviously playing to the audience. "Get yourself something to drink or some food."

Hank's eyes said he should play along. So he filled a plate with eggs, grits, and toast. He wasn't the least bit hungry but understood the importance of appearances. He grabbed a glass of orange juice and sat. Hank started to talk. Animated. His expressions not matching the words.

"Obviously, you heard about Greene." Hank smiled for whomever may be watching.

He got the idea and faked laughter. "Sure did."

Hank gazed down, turning his attention back to the newspaper. Today's *Savannah Morning News.* "You better eat some of that food. A couple of security guards just moseyed in for coffee." Hank glanced up and continued to act like they were having an amicable morning conversation.

He forced himself to take a few bites of egg. "We've got trouble, Hank."

"No shit, Sherlock." Hank slid him the folded newspaper. "There's a front-page article on Greene. If you believe what's there, seems Cue Stick got caught in the sack by a jealous husband. He and the woman were found naked."

"That's crap, Hank, and you know it."

"So what happened?"

"Hell if I know. But if Greene was whacked because he knew too much, guess who's next?"

"Good point."

"We blew our one chance by trusting him."

"They're not going to get us if I can help it."

"You have something in mind?"

"We're going to get the hell out of this mill."

"We shouldn't have come in the first place."

Hank shook his head. "That would have sent red flags everywhere. No. They're still unsure about us. They have to be or else they would have already moved. The better tactic is for us to show up, then slip out quietly and find the cavalry."

"That may not be so easy."

"Now who's underestimating who?"

"I have a huge measure of respect for the people we're dealing with," he said.

"Sit tight and keep your cell phone close."

"What are you up to?"

"You'll see."

9:04 A.M.

BRENT GLANCED UP AS ONE OF THE ADMINISTRATIVE ASSISTANTS appeared in his doorway. "They want you over at the front office."

"You know why?"

"They just said your help was needed on something right now."

He thought about checking in with Hank but decided against it. Like Hank had said earlier, appearances needed to be maintained, so he grabbed his jacket and cell phone and left his office, walking straight to Building A.

The day seemed another summer scorcher. Both yesterday and Saturday had been marred by afternoon storms, a few turning violent with thunder and lightning. Today's stifling humidity signaled a repeat in the making. The envelope with the originals from Bozin was safely hidden away in his parents' garage, which seemed like the best place for it. The tape recording was gone, surely now in the hands of Hamilton Lee and Larry Hughes.

Inside Building A he zigzagged the carpeted halls directly to the CEO's office and announced his presence to the assistant. The wooden door leading into the CEO's private office was closed, but a man informed him they were waiting in the main conference room, the same room where, eleven days ago, he'd first talked to Christopher Bozin. He crossed the hall and opened the door. Two men sat at the long table.

"Come in, Brent," one man said, rising and extending a hand to shake. "I'm Hamilton Lee."

He kept his hands glued to his side.

Lee seemed to understand. "That any way to treat your employer?

He said nothing.

Lee withdrew his hand and motioned to the other man. "You remember Mr. De Florio, don't you?"

He shot a stare at De Florio. Did he kill his father? Or was it one of his associates? No matter. Even if he didn't personally perform the act, according to Bozin, De Florio definitely oversaw it all. He resisted the temptation to leap across the table and strangle the son of a bitch.

He had to be smart here. Real smart.

"Why don't you sit down?" Lee said. "Jon, please close the door."

With little choice he took a seat along with Lee. De Florio sat after closing the door, which Brent noticed De Florio locked.

Lee said, "I understand you have some writings of Chris Bozin."

"I understand you have a tape recording."

Lee grinned. "I see why Hank Reed relied on you. You're quick. Let's just say the company decided not to associate itself with Mr. Greene."

So the fool had tried blackmail. What an idiot. Did Greene think Southern Republic was just playing around? How did he think he could successfully pull that off? He congratulated himself on not succumbing to Greene's offer of holding on to all the originals. Greene had been persistent, but something told him not to do it. Though now dead, he felt little sympathy for the bastard. Greene's recklessness had placed them all in jeopardy.

"Now you're dealing directly, without the middleman?" Brent asked.

Lee smiled. A thin irritating gesture he instantly disliked. "In a manner of speaking. So let's be realistic. All I want are the things you have. As I'm sure you've surmised Bozin and I didn't get along. His fanciful fiction about what this company has supposedly been doing doesn't need to be aired publicly. It's all lies. He just wants to harm me and this company. To do that he concocted some incredible malarkey."

He noticed the two file folders lying on the table in front of Lee. "You have the copies of what Bozin gave me?"

Lee pointed to the top file. "Mr. Greene provided those. I've read the narrative and the two notes, and I listened to the tape. Like I've already told you, this is nothing but lies designed to hurt me, Mr. Hughes, and this company."

"Those lies include what happened to my father?"

"That's an excellent example of what I mean. Your father was

311

the victim of a tragic boating accident. A terrible thing. Bozin, quite insensitively I might add, tried to fabricate murder. Don't you think the police would have long ago come up with evidence to support that, if true?"

"Not necessarily." He looked at De Florio. "From what I've been told your associates are good."

De Florio's face stayed like granite.

"Brent, we need to be reasonable," Lee said. "I'm trying to make this as painless as possible. I see no reason for you to be involved in a personal feud between Mr. Bozin and myself. It was wrong of Chris to include you in the first place."

"That's the first thing you've said I agree with. Unfortunately, it's far too late to turn back now."

"All I want are the original writings you have. After that, we can consider the matter dropped with your assurance there are no copies and you won't be talking to the press or some prosecutor. You have my word nothing more will come from any of this."

"You've got to be joking. I'm supposed to trust your word?"

"It appears you have little option. Greene said he had all of what Bozin left. I didn't believe him." Lee pointed. "Because you have it."

"I have the originals. Greene had copies, except for a tape recording."

"I want your originals, including the list Hank Reed obtained."

He realized the only reason Lee was even talking to him was he first needed to retrieve all those items. So he bought more time. "I can go get them."

"Mr. De Florio will accompany you."

"Not a chance."

Lee looked at his watch. "All right. It's 9:15. I want you back here by 10:00. With everything."

"I'm not Greene," he made clear.

"No, apparently you're not. But I'm no fool either." Lee passed the second folder to De Florio. "Jon."

De Florio opened the file. "You live at 328 Live Oak Lane. Your mother is Catherine, age sixty-six. She likes gardening, does it most mornings for a couple of hours, plays bridge on Thursdays. Sadly, she's been diagnosed with dementia—"

"Enough." He shoved back the chair, stood, and moved toward the door. "I get the picture."

Lee stayed seated. "I hope you do. I expect to hear from you within the next forty-five minutes."

He left.

LEE STARED AT THE CLOSED DOOR.

"Jon, I don't think Mr. Walker is going to be as cooperative as he'd like for us to think."

"There's no reason for him to trust us, or for him to think you will keep your word."

"Understandable, considering I won't." He paused. "What did he do over the weekend?"

"Yard work on Saturday. Went to an air show with Reed's daughter and granddaughter on Sunday. He's been seeing the daughter socially. On the way back they stopped by Reed's for a few minutes."

"Were you able to listen in on the conversation?"

"They didn't talk in the outer office, that's the only room we have bugged. But they made a call to Greene's house, looking for him."

"I bet they were. Any more contact between Reed and Walker?"

"A call this morning. Then they met together in the cafeteria before work. The conversation appeared pleasant and friendly."

"I can't help but feel we're being rocked to sleep." He thought for a moment. "Mr. Walker is not going to bring us what we want. So there will almost certainly have to be retribution. You said his mother was how old?"

"Sixty-six."

"And Reed has a daughter and granddaughter?"

313

De Florio nodded.

He considered the options.

"Let's be in position to move on Walker's mother at 10:01. But not a moment before. And make it awful. Crime is running rampant these days. Burglaries and robberies occur all the time. The drug traffic causes such mayhem. That should send an appropriate message to all involved."

9:20 A.M.

BRENT HEADED BACK TOWARD HIS OFFICE. HE ENTERED BUILDING B, but instead of climbing the stairs to the general counsel's office he stayed on the ground floor and slipped into receiving. He desperately needed a phone. De Florio had unnerved him, the message clear. *Play ball or we know all about your family.* He needed to get in touch with his mother, and fast.

He found a phone in an empty office and dialed his home number, but all he got was the answering machine. Where was she? Even when she was working out in the yard she always toted the cordless with her. He thought hard, then it hit him. She'd mentioned yesterday a dentist appointment to get her teeth cleaned. What he couldn't recall was the name of her dentist.

Maybe if he saw it he'd recognize it.

He rambled through the desk drawers. In the second one he found a Woods County telephone directory. He opened to the yellow pages and scanned the section for dentists. Three names. Spencer, Molis, and Young.

Molis. The recall triggered what else his mother said. New to the area, came about five years ago, young, reasonable about appointments.

He quickly dialed the number.

"This is Brent Walker. My mother Catherine is there having her teeth cleaned. Is she still there?"

"No, sir, we finished with her a few minutes ago. She's already gone."

He hung up.

Damn. Any other time she'd have to sit an hour in the waiting room. He dialed home again but still got only the answering machine. Unfortunately, she did not own a cell phone. No need, she always said.

His panic cemented.

Hamilton Lee would do whatever was necessary to get what he wanted. Of that he was sure. If that meant harming his mother, or maybe Ashley and Lori Anne, that's exactly what he would do. Greene pushed his luck. He was not going to make the same mistake. He had to get everyone close to him out of Concord. But he knew he couldn't leave the mill. That would only point De Florio directly toward them. What he needed was to keep them out in the open, around people, away from the privacy De Florio and his associates liked to use. *What to do? Think.*

Yes. That's it.

He reached for the phone and dialed again.

9:35 A.M.

FRANK BARNARD'S CELL PHONE SPRANG TO LIFE.

De Florio was calling.

"That older woman you've been monitoring along with your main interest, please be ready to process her after 10:01. A criminal implication is preferred. I will text when to move."

"Understood."

He hung up.

Barnard had been stationed outside the mill at a convenience store, ready to pick up Reed or Walker if either left the plant. He knew Victor Jacks was inside the mill, still dressed as a security guard, there to directly deal with Reed if necessary. He cranked the car engine and drove west toward Concord. Ten minutes later he cruised down Live Oak Lane, making a cursory pass in front of the Walker house, noticing no Prius in the drive. He rounded the corner and parked the next block over. He then made his way back on foot and approached the house from the rear. The dead bolt on the rear French door took twenty-eight seconds to trip.

He stepped cautiously inside.

The house seemed quiet, apparently empty, but he decided to be sure. Confirmation came on the refrigerator door where a printed card from the office of Dr. Ryan Molis showed that Catherine Walker had an 8:30 dental appointment today. He searched the kitchen drawers and found a sharp boning knife. The meaning from De Florio's instruction of "criminal implication" was clear. After he slit Catherine Walker's throat, he would ransack things, stealing just enough to imply a drug-related burglary.

He crept to the front of the house and studied his watch.

9:52 A.M.

Catherine Walker should return shortly.

He stationed himself in the front parlor, with a clear view of the driveway out the windows.

And awaited further orders.

9:54 A.M.

BRENT DIALED THE NUMBER FOR GRACE TANNER. SEVENTY-THREE years old, a widow, she'd lived next door all his life. She was a lot like his mother. Fiercely independent, did all her own yard work, and possessed the kind of personality people instantly liked. Two rings and the irritating recording announced, *"We're sorry, your call cannot be completed as dialed."* He'd apparently pushed the buttons too fast, so he cleared the line, calmed down, and dialed again, this time slower, making sure he hit the right keys.

Three rings.

Four.

Five.

He was just about to hang up when the phone was answered.

"Grace, it's Brent Walker."

Since moving back to Concord he'd talked with her several times, along with getting to know her two grandsons.

"Is my mother at home?"

"I haven't seen her this morning. Let me look." The echo of steps across a hardwood floor came through the earpiece.

"Brent, her car is not in the driveway."

"Mrs. Tanner, this is important. Mom went to the dentist. She should be on her way home. Please watch and have her come into your house and call me the second she gets there. Tell her not to go into our house." He wasn't sure what De Florio would do, but his main concern was the house phone. If it was being monitored he sure as hell didn't want the son of a bitch hearing what he told her. "Will you do that?"

"Of course, Brent. I was outside doing some weeding when you called. I'll keep a lookout."

"Please watch carefully. She should be there shortly. Remember, have her use your phone. Let me give you the extension here in the mill."

BARNARD KEPT WATCH THROUGH A BREAK IN THE LIVING ROOM sheers and saw when Catherine Walker turned the corner onto Live Oak Lane and headed for her driveway. Next door an elderly woman was out in the sultry morning weeding her front flower beds. Mrs. Walker pulled into the driveway and parked. Two young boys ran over from next door and started talking to her. The neighbor followed, walking through a narrow opening in the waist-high row of red tips and azaleas that formed a hedge between the properties.

The two older women talked.

The kids ran up on the porch and impatiently turned the locked front doorknob, apparently wanting to go inside the Walker house.

"I'll be there in a minute," Catherine Walker called out.

He kept watching.

The two older women were engaged in a discussion, but he could not hear what they were saying thanks to the incessant chatter of the boys and their stomping on the front porch.

317

"Come with me," the other older woman called out.

The children fled the porch and, along with the two women, walked next door.

THE PHONE RANG, ENDING THE LONGEST TEN MINUTES BRENT COULD ever remember. He jerked up the receiver.

"Brent?" It was his mother.

"Where are you?"

"At Grace's."

"Mom, you must listen to exactly what I'm about to tell you and follow my instructions precisely."

"What's wrong, son?"

"Mom. Please. Not now. Go outside, get in your car, and leave. Go find Ashley, she's on her morning route, probably near Registry Boulevard by now. Get her. Then go get Lori Anne. All of you drive straight to Uncle Erik's. Don't stop anywhere along the way. Go straight there and stay until you hear from me. Understand?"

Erik Walker was his father's younger brother who lived seventy miles to the west in northeast Bulloch County on a large farm, with employees, family, and neighbors, plenty of people to discourage De Florio and associates, even if they knew where to look, which he was betting they didn't.

"If you think you're being followed, go to the sheriff's department."

"Son, you're frightening me."

"I don't mean to. Just please do as I ask. Tell Ashley to park that damn van and go. Don't worry about her job. She's got to trust me on this. Believe me, this is far more important than delivering the mail. And none of you tell anyone where you're going. No one. Including Grace. I'll call you later in the day, but under no circumstances are you to leave Uncle Erik's until I call."

"Can I go in the house and get a few things?"

"No. If you need anything, buy it there or borrow it. Don't worry about the money. Just go. Now."

"Calm down, son. I'll do it."

BARNARD WATCHED FROM THE PARLOR WINDOW AS CATHERINE Walker climbed into the Prius and drove away.

Strange.

On a hunch he yanked off his rubber gloves, left the house, and retraced his steps to the car. He fired up the engine, rounded the block, and parked in front of the Walker house. He approached the front door and rang the bell, using the end of a ballpoint pen to push the button. When no one answered he descended the porch and walked next door, where the older woman was tending her garden.

"I was looking for Mrs. Walker," he said in a pleasant voice, adding an equally pleasant smile.

"You just missed her."

"Darn," he feigned. "You know when she'll be back?"

"She didn't say. She called her son, then left. Maybe she went to see him."

"You know where he is?"

"He works at the paper mill. His name is Brent Walker."

"Thank you, ma'am. I'll try there."

He walked back to his car, reached for his phone, and dialed. An open channel cautioned a choice of words. "The processing is impossible. A call came from the mill and the next thing I saw was a car leaving with one person inside. Destination unknown."

"Anything else?"

"The next-door neighbor may have been on the lookout. She verified that the son talked to the mother by phone."

"Return to your original station. I'll be in touch."

JON ENDED THE CALL AND LOOKED AT HAMILTON LEE. "THE MOTHER left before going into the house. She received a call from Walker."

Lee was surprised. "He had no idea your man was in the house."

"But, like Walker said earlier, he's not Greene. He's a step ahead of us thanks to Mr. Bozin. He probably assumed we were monitoring the house phones."

Lee looked at his watch.

"It seems Brent Walker has left me no choice. Bring him and Reed in now. Take them to a secure location and let me know when you have them."

10:06 A.M.

BRENT HUNG UP FROM TALKING TO HIS MOTHER AND CALLED HANK on his cell phone. He quickly summarized the meeting with Lee and what he'd done with his mother and Ashley. He figured with everything happening so fast, Hank's cell phone would still be safe. "We have to get out of here."

"I'm already working on it. Meet me at the barge dock in ten minutes. You know how to get there?"

The past couple of weeks he'd made a point of learning his way around the mill. "I know where it is."

"Head there now," Hank said.

JON REACHED FOR HIS LINK TO VICTOR JACKS. HE PUSHED SEND ON the portable radio. "Bluebird. Robin." The walkie-talkies were used all over the mill by a variety of personnel, though he utilized a different frequency. They were fast and efficient, but careful with their words. "Your location?"

"Outside paper machine number three."

The mill's electric shop was inside that building, the Boar's Nest part. "Find and retrieve. Once in the cage, advise."

"Roger."

He decided to corral Brent Walker himself. Much wiser to keep Frank Barnard outside on the highway, just in case.

He exited the main conference room and headed for Building B.

BRENT LEFT RECEIVING.

Like every morning, ninety minutes ago he'd tossed his car keys into his top right desk drawer. But if they were leaving the mill he assumed he'd need the Jeep, so he scampered up the stone stairs two at a time and headed for his office. He pocketed the keys and left, telling his assistants that he needed to go into the mill and would be back shortly. His boss stopped him at the door, curious about what the front office wanted. He begged off, saying he had to tend to something immediately and would give him a full report when he got back.

He fled the general counsel's office and loped down the hall toward the stairs. At the first step leading down from the second floor, he glanced down.

Jon De Florio opened the glass front door and entered the building.

He froze.

De Florio started up the stairs.

The first available door was to his left. He ducked inside just as De Florio turned at the landing and started up the last flight. The woman inside gave him a quizzical look but he headed straight for an open office, not caring who might be inside. Thankfully, the space was unoccupied and he slipped in just as De Florio passed in the hall.

He returned to the doorway and peered right.

De Florio opened the pebbled-glass door marked GENERAL COUN-SEL and stepped in. Brent turned left and darted down to the first floor. He avoided the front door and dashed out the rear exit. A concrete walk led directly back to the production area, a guard gate in between. Procedure required signing in and out, noting the time and destination. He stopped long enough to write his name, adding *General* for his destination and recording the time.

10:12 A.M.

JON ASKED THE WOMAN, "IS MR. WALKER IN?"

"You just missed him."

This was becoming a habit with the Walkers. "Do you know where he went?"

"He said he was going into the mill and would be back shortly."

He retraced his steps downstairs and headed for the rear door. Outside, he fished the radio from his pocket and called Frank Barnard.

"Redbird. Robin. Has either left?"

"No."

"Advise immediately if so."

"Roger."

He walked directly to management's gate. If Walker went into the mill, he would have passed through there since the main gate was a hundred yards on the other side of the building and, on his way over, he would have seen him.

At the gate, per procedure, he stopped and signed the sheet. Instantly, he noticed the entry above his.

Made three minutes earlier.

B. Walker.

HANK HAD ARRANGED EVERYTHING BY 9:30, ALL HE'D BEEN WAITING for was word from Brent. Once that happened, the final arrangements were put into motion.

He left the Boar's Nest and headed down the steep metal stairs into the turmoil of paper machine number three. He took up a position across the building, concealed by the heavy equipment.

The idea was to get out unnoticed.

So he'd arranged for a distraction to occur in exactly four minutes.

AFTER RECEIVING DE FLORIO'S INSTRUCTIONS, VICTOR JACKS ENTERED the building that housed paper machine number three. It was nearly a hundred degrees outside under a blazing summer sun. Yet that seemed cool compared with the stifling humidity inside the gargantuan brick structure. Hundreds of workers hustled about tending to the seemingly insatiable needs of the roaring equipment. The paper machine spanned the length of a football field, an alternating series of wires, felt, and dryers that collectively sped wet pulp from one end to the other, eventually converting brown mushy goo into dry solid paper. Water was a huge component of the process, steam the number one by-product, and everyone wore either earplugs or a headset to shield from the deafening roar. Communication was through hand gestures and sign language. Not a whole lot different from his own line of work, Jacks thought.

He was dressed as a security guard. His presence virtually unnoticed. The guards constantly wandered through the mill. He knew exactly where break room number five, or the Boar's Nest, was located, so he threaded his way between the machinery toward the metal stairway.

Before starting his climb, he casually glanced around to see if anyone was paying him the slightest attention.

HANK WATCHED THE GUARD AND SILENTLY CONGRATULATED HIMSELF on the hasty evacuation. His main objective was simply to get out of the building unnoticed, the appearance of the uniformed man suddenly adding a complication.

He studied the guard's face.

The same man who'd been stationed at the contract negotiations all last week and one of the guards who'd come into the cafeteria earlier. That was way too many coincidences. Probably one of De Florio's associates.

The guard climbed the metal stairs toward the Boar's Nest.

Hank glanced at his watch.

10:19 A.M.

He knew what was happening one floor below, in what was referred to as the basement. Tony Wright, one of his electrician helpers, had surely started his approach to the lowermost rollers of paper machine number three. Twenty-two and a troublemaker, Wright was eternally grateful to Hank, who both got him his job and made sure the company kept him on the payroll. Thirty minutes ago he'd told Wright to toss a screwdriver into the felt rollers at precisely 10:20.

Paper breaks were common, with a set procedure that engulfed everyone associated with the machine until the broken sheet could be fed back across the rollers and production restored. Breaks happened mostly when small debris or parts of machinery fell into the run. But they could be induced. A screwdriver would not only tear the paper but also destroy the felt on which the pressed pulp rode. The resulting damage would take time to repair.

Hank checked his watch.

10:20.

He hoped Wright was punctual. No one else would be in the basement. It was the hottest place in the building, notoriously avoided unless absolutely necessary. Scalding steam misted. Machinery screamed.

Then he heard it.

The unmistakable sound of a tear reverberating throughout the building.

An alarm sounded.

Amber lights twirled.

Workers raced to their assigned stations, the idea being to get the machine back online as quickly as possible.

Distraction accomplished.

Hank glanced at the guard standing at the top of the stairs. He'd locked the Boar's Nest, so the man was gazing inside through a side window. He took advantage of that opportunity and darted for the door.

It took only a few seconds for him to cross the open area at the north end of the building and step outside.

VICTOR JACKS TURNED TO SEE WHAT HAD SPURRED ALL THE COMMOTION.

Workers scurried everywhere.

Then, across the building, he caught a glimpse of Hank Reed.

Slipping out a door.

HANK CASUALLY STROLLED ACROSS THE HOT SAND AND GRAVEL OF the open yard that surrounded the massive brick building. The midmorning sun burned bright, made even more brilliant by a sharp reflection off the white chalky ground. He yanked sunglasses from his shirt pocket and shoved them on, which helped with the glare. Fifty yards away he passed the lime kiln, its metal grotesquely encrusted with thick layers of white paste. A hundred yards from paper machine number three he glanced back and saw the security guard bolt out the door and head toward him.

That wasn't good.

Change of plan.

He picked up his pace and nearly jogged toward the door that led into paper machine number two. Though he'd gained a slight lead, extra time would be needed at the barge dock. He shot through the door, jerked off his sunglasses, and headed straight for the storeroom, one of the few secure places within the plant. Though several alarmed doors led out, only one provided access in. In years past the entrance had been secured by a simple lock, a shift supervisor the only person with a key and charged with the responsibility of admitting people and accounting exactly for what was taken out. Now the door was electronically controlled, activated from within a small glass cubicle where access could be videorecorded. The extraordinary measures were necessary since the room contained millions of dollars in parts, equipment, and tools, everything needed by the mill at a moment's notice from the smallest screw to the largest electrical generator.

A tempting target for employee theft.

A concrete hall separated the building's outer wall from the freestanding metal walls, dividing the massive space into usable sections. He hustled down the corridor, trying not to attract attention. He glanced back just as the guard entered the building. He still had a fifty-yard lead but noticed the guard picking up his pace. He turned off the hall into the anteroom for the storeroom. He could now be seen through the glass cubicle. But since the man on duty knew him well, all he had to do was point to the door and the electronic bolt instantly released. He entered, never losing a step in his stride, and the spring-loaded door closed and locked behind him.

The storeroom was partially soundproofed and air-conditioned, one of the few areas in the mill equipped with those two luxuries. It was a cool, eerie, irregularly shaped space full of bays and inlets formed from the leftover square footage between the generators, the building's loading dock, and a sprawling electrical control room. The ceiling stood barely eight feet. It carried the look and feel of a library with row after row of metal shelves overflowing with tools and parts. Tens of thousands of items were precisely cataloged, tagged, and numbered, computers maintaining an accurate inventory. No one actually worked inside, people just came and went after finding what they needed and logging out.

He quickly moved to a far row of shelves and ducked behind, turning his attention back to the door.

JACKS ENTERED THE ANTEROOM.

"Did Hank Reed come through here?" he asked the attendant through a hole in the glass.

The attendant nodded.

"Where'd he go?"

"In there," the man said, casually pointing to the door.

"Open it."

HANK HEARD THE BOLT RELEASE.

He stood behind a row of shelves a hundred feet from the entrance, near the door he intended to use as an exit. He hadn't already left because he wanted to see if he could lose his tail within the maze. He knew every inch of the storeroom, often using it as a quiet spot to gather information. He hoped that local knowledge would give him an edge. Perhaps his pursuer had never been inside before.

The door shut.

"Mr. Reed, we need to talk," a voice said.

He did not respond. Instead, he glanced behind at the exit door and hoped it hadn't been locked as the shift supervisor sometimes had an annoying habit of doing.

Steps approached.

"Mr. De Florio wants to see you. No point in running. Just come along quietly."

He reached up and grabbed a two-inch washer from an open box on the shelf. Aiming carefully, he tossed it over the shelves, away from him. Metal banged against metal. The guard reacted, and he watched through the shelves as the man darted straight for the sound, the opposite direction from where he was hiding. He turned and gently grasped the doorknob.

It opened, the dead bolt not set.

Praise the Lord.

He slipped out and closed the door.

He now stood in another concrete hall, this one leading to receiving. It was there that all the equipment and supplies for the storeroom were inventoried and categorized before being shelved away. The hall was constantly rinsed to keep it free of debris and he sidestepped a stream of quick flowing water, nearly running for outside.

The barge dock was now less than fifty yards away.

AFTER SIGNING IN AT MANAGEMENT'S GATE BRENT SPRINTED DOWN the crumbling concrete road that paralleled paper machine number two. Along the way he passed the auto and carpentry shops, both in outbuildings bordering the Savannah River. He knew the pavement would take him around the building and directly to the dock.

He looked back.

De Florio stepped through management's gate and turned toward him.

THE INSTANT DE FLORIO ACQUIRED BRENT IN SIGHT HE REACHED FOR his radio and pushed the SEND button.

"Bluebird. Robin. Your position."

Victor Jacks answered, "Storeroom. In pursuit."

"Is he in sight?"

"Negative."

He knew the storeroom was a maze with a variety of exits, so he played a hunch. "Leave there and proceed outside. Toward the river."

"Roger."

He kept walking.

His quarry turned the corner a hundred yards ahead.

10:26 A.M.

BRENT CHECKED HIS WATCH.

His ten minutes were almost up. Hank should be at the barge dock any second. He had no idea what his friend had in mind, but he knew De Florio was closing in, so whatever Hank was planning had better damn well get them both out of here and fast.

He rounded the corner, the river in sight. Suddenly, to his left, Hank bolted out of the building and jumped from the loading dock. The two joined together for the last hundred feet.

"We've got company, Hank."

"Don't I know."

"De Florio's behind me."

"And another's on my tail."

"Where we going?" he asked.

"Away from here."

He shot a look back.

De Florio was rounding the corner and a security guard was exiting the building. The barge dock was a stubby concrete slab that projected twenty feet out into the muddy Savannah River. It was used mainly to off-load crude oil into three storage tanks nearby, but the company kept a small outboard tied to it for environmental testing of the river. No barges hugged the dock today.

They raced to the end of the short pier and up to one of the metal ladders leading down to the water. He looked below and saw a small boat manned by Clarence Silva.

"Get in the boat," Hank said.

He looked back. De Florio and the guard were headed straight for the dock. A redneck who three weeks ago wanted to beat the shit of him waited below. He chose the lesser of two evils and descended.

Hank slid down the ladder behind him. "Hit it, Clarence."

The engine roared to life and the boat shot out into the current.

Jon reached the end of the dock.

He pointed to the company outboard and said to Jacks, "Use that and follow them."

His associate slid down the ladder on the other side, jumped into the boat, and yanked several times on the outboard.

Brent and Hank watched while the guard tried to start the company's outboard.

"Goin' to be kind of hard without these."

Silva held up the spark plug wires and smiled proudly through his trademark corn-kernel teeth.

"I never thought I'd be glad to see you," Brent said.

"Only thing I hate worse than lawyers is them security guards."

"Clarence is a good man," Hank said. "A little warped at times, but okay."

"I take back every bad thing I ever said about you," Brent said.

Silva seemed to like that.

"Where are we going?" Brent asked.

"I've arranged for some ground transportation," Hanks said. "Clarence is going to take us downriver where it's waiting."

Brent stripped off his coat, his dress shirt pasted to his body. He yanked off his tie and stuffed it in his jacket pocket.

"Pretty damn clever, Hank. That should screw up De Florio for a while."

"What about the home front?"

"We'll have to hope they get to where I sent them. I didn't have time to check further. But I'm betting it's me they want."

"It's both of us," Hank said.

That was right, but the realization didn't make him feel any better. He couldn't decide if Hank was actually enjoying all the intrigue.

He knew he wasn't.

They motored downriver about four miles, the water deceivingly peaceful, the warm breeze like a hair dryer. Off to the east anvil thunderheads were building, blinding white above, ominous blue-black underneath starting to obliterate the morning sun. They finally turned west and navigated up one of the countless tributaries that veined the river, the meander of muddy water twining through oak and cypress. Waves of heat and humidity hovered. About half a mile inland a wrinkled dock arched out. Beyond, a tattered single-wide trailer rested quietly under a canopy of mushrooming oaks ladened with moss beards. Silva eased to the dock and tied the boat.

They climbed out.

Thunder rumbled in the distance.

"Clarence's brother lives here," Hank said. "We're going to use that truck over there." Hank turned to Silva. "Here are the keys to my mill car. You know the one. Use it till I get back. I don't think anybody got a good look at you, but you know the program, you don't know nothin'."

"Don't worry 'bout me. I won't tell 'em a damn thing," Silva said.

Brent studied the pickup, a dirty white Toyota with mud tires and no tailgate. The bumper sticker read MY KID BEAT THE HELL OUT OF YOUR HONOR KID. Why didn't that surprise him. A tan Mustang with bald tires sat next to it, a dirty American flag for a front license plate, and enough dents to have been rolled down a rocky slope.

"What's that, a '67?" he asked.

"A '66," Silva said. "My brother's."

"I need it." He reached into his coat pocket and found his keys. "There's a maroon Jeep with a cloth top parked in the front lot at the mill. Tell your brother to use it."

Silva caught the keys, then looked at Hank, who shrugged.

"My brother's sleepin' right now," Silva said. "On graveyard tonight. But I guess it'll be all right. Let me get the key."

Silva disappeared inside the trailer.

Brent asked Hank, "Where you headed?"

"To find us a place to hide for tonight. I've got a couple of possibilities."

"While you do that, I have to take care of something."

"You want to tell me?"

"It's better you don't know, just in case they find you. Have you got that copy of the list?"

Hank reached into his pocket and handed him the folded sheet. As he pocketed it, Silva returned with another set of keys.

"My brother said it's all right, what with Mr. Reed bein' involved and all."

Brent took them. "Tell him thanks and I'll take good care of it."

"You and your brother going to be able to get to work?" Hank asked, heading for the pickup.

"We'll hitch a ride."

He opened the Mustang's door and tossed his coat inside. "Hank, call me when you get a place. I'll check on the family while I'm out."

He climbed in, roared the engine to life, and raced from the trailer down the dirt lane.

11:00 A.M.

LEE SEETHED. "WHAT DO YOU MEAN THEY'RE GONE?"

He and De Florio were back in the main conference room. Hughes had finally joined them.

"A boat was waiting. The company boat had been tampered with," De Florio said.

"This is not good, Jon," Hughes said. "Not good at all."

Lee ignored him. He'd tried to get him to be at the meeting with Brent Walker earlier but the idiot overslept. "They must be found."

"I realize that. But no error on our part let them get away."

"No, just an underestimation."

"Perhaps," De Florio admitted, tone begrudging. "I'm going to review the entire files on Reed and Walker. What I had this morning were only excerpts. That information could point us on the right path to find them."

He was not concerned with particulars.

"Find them, Jon. And quick."

BRENT WASTED NO TIME GETTING BACK TO HIGHWAY 16A. BUT SINCE he couldn't be sure of where De Florio's associates might be lurking, the open expanse made him nervous. He had to make a stop at home and hoped that all the players on the other side were busy at the mill. What had Bozin written? *Jon De Florio oversees the program. There are two associates who work under him, however no one, other than De Florio, knows anything about them.* He knew where De Florio and one associate were, the problem came from not knowing where the other was located. He had to bet that person was not watching the Walker house.

He drove back into town and, instead of parking in the driveway or even on the street, he left the car a block over and walked through the neighbors' yards to his parents' house. He knew nearly all of them and no one was around at this time of day. He made it to the garage and slipped inside, locating the envelope with the originals Bozin had entrusted to him with and hustling back to the car.

He then drove out of town, turning west off the medianed four-laned highway, retracing the same route taken three weeks ago when he first returned to Concord. He moved fast, but tried to keep to the posted speed limit. The southernmost shore of Eagle Lake paralleled for a long time, water peeking in and out from among thick stands of trees. Finally, he left the lake behind, crossing the Ogeechee and entering Bulloch County, the image from the road sign—WELCOME TO WOODS COUNTY, POPULATION 12,894—fading in the rearview mirror. At the familiar fork in the road, instead of veering south toward I-16, he sped for Statesboro.

* * *

Twenty minutes later he entered downtown and headed straight to a squatty brick building marked UNITED STATES POST OFFICE. He parked the Mustang out front and retrieved the envelope from the passenger's seat. Inside, a large wall clock read 11:58 A.M. His mother should have made it to his uncle's by now.

He approached the counter and asked the clerk for an express mail pouch. He carried it to another counter and addressed the label to his former boss, the Fulton County district attorney. On the outside of the brown envelope Bozin gave him, he wrote

Please put this envelope in a safe place and keep it there until you hear from me. Tell no one about it and do not open it. If something happens to me, get it to the police immediately. I know this sounds cryptic, but you're the only one I can count on right now. I'll be in touch.

He signed his name and, into the envelope, which already contained Bozin's handwritten notes and the flash drive, he stuffed the copy of the list Reed had provided. Using the roll of tape on the counter, he sealed the envelope shut. He slid it inside the express mail pouch and gave it to the clerk, paying the overnight fees in cash.

He stepped outside.

Morning sunlight was rapidly being extinguished by black clouds invading from the east. He breathed a little easier. At least now, no matter what happened, the information would be safe. He knew he could count on his old boss to deal with the situation and, hopefully, De Florio and his henchman wouldn't think to look anywhere near Atlanta.

He needed to check on his mother and Ashley. A heavy sense of paranoia had overtaken him. Understandable, given the circumstances. So he decided to add another layer of security to the effort. It couldn't hurt. Across the street was a State Farm insurance office. He walked over and asked the lady inside if he might make a call. He displayed his cell phone and said it had died. She was friendly and understanding, allowing him to use an extension in an empty office. There, he dialed the number for his uncle Erik. To his relief, his mother had arrived. She'd also brought Ashley and Lori Anne.

"I did what you asked, son. Now, you want to tell me what's going on?"

"I wish I could," he said, keeping his voice low. "But for right now you're just going to have to trust me."

"Ashley is in a panic."

"Let me talk to her."

"Brent," Ashley said, coming immediately on the line. "What the hell's happening? Are you okay?"

"I'll be all right," he said for her benefit.

"I'm scared to death. What's going on? This could cost me my job."

"I can't go into it right now. You're just going to have to sit tight and be patient. But don't worry about your job. They'll understand."

"Is Daddy involved in this? Is he okay?"

"Yes, he's involved and he's fine."

"Brent, why can't you tell me what's going on?"

"Just keep an eye on Lori Anne. I'm counting on you." He tried to hide the edge in his voice. "Put Mom back on. And Ashley...I love you."

He hadn't said that to anyone in a long time. But he knew he had to.

"I love you too."

"Son, are you in trouble?" His mother still sounded irritated.

"You could say that."

"With the police?"

"It's far more complicated than that."

"Can I help?"

He knew she didn't understand. "Unfortunately, no. Please, just stay there till you hear from me again. Keep people around you. Tell no one you're there if somebody calls and don't let anybody out of your sight. Don't call my cell phone and tell Ashley not to call Hank's."

"Brent."

He heard the strain in her voice.

"I don't want to lose you too."

He knew what she meant and he wanted to tell her everything, but knew he couldn't. He hoped later there'd be a time and place for that. So he offered her some consolation, mixed with a twinge of hope.

"You won't."

He said goodbye and hung up.

More thunder echoed in the distance.

He climbed back into the Mustang and looked at his clothes. His shirt was soaking wet and filthy. The navy-blue pants to his once clean suit were smeared with caustic lime. His shoes, a new pair of wing tips bought only a few weeks ago, were caked in mud and dust. He needed a change of clothes. So he drove down the street and turned into the first shopping center, parking in front of a Walmart Superstore. Inside, he paid cash for a pair of jeans, a cotton pullover shirt, and a pair of tennis shoes. The jeans were okay in the waist but a little long so he simply rolled the legs and made do. Back outside, he stuffed his phone in his jeans pocket and tossed his suit into the back seat. On the Mustang's passenger's-side floorboard he noticed a soiled navy-blue Atlanta Braves cap. He stuffed it on. The cloth carried the faint smell of fish. A pair of Ray-Ban sunglasses stuck out from under the driver's-side visor. He slipped them on too and checked his watch.

12:27 P.M.

12:45 P.M.

BRENT SAT IN THE KRYSTAL AND TRIED TO EAT A FEW OF THE TINY square hamburgers he'd adored since childhood, but didn't have much of an appetite. Suddenly, his phone vibrated and he checked the display. Not a number he recognized, but the prefix signified Concord.

He answered.

"Where are you?" the voice asked.

Hank.

"Nearby. And you?"

"A house on Eagle Lake. It's a place a friend of mine has. He always said I could use it whenever. I guess this is whenever."

"You think it's safe being that close?"

"I need to stay around here. I've got a lot of people I can call on if we need 'em. Besides, there's nothing out here but trees and water."

"Give me directions."

Hank told him how to get there.

"I know where that is."

"That's good. It looks like it's just you and me."

He stared at the wall clock across the dining room. "I'll be there in a little while."

"See you then."

"You want anything to eat?"

"Hell no, my stomach's in knots."

"Mine, too. Are you on a landline?"

"Absolutely. This house has one."

"No more cell calls. These guys are not the cops. They don't have access to all the cell towers for any triangulation or tracing. But we still need to hedge our bets. Turn your cell phone off and throw it in the lake. I'll see you shortly."

He hung up and sat back in the booth.

Outside, thunder cracked closer. It would soon be raining hard.

He remembered the memorial service scheduled to begin at one. For appearances' sake he'd originally planned to attend. Hamilton Lee would certainly be there, probably leaving for it about now. Time to see if he could place the brakes on whatever Lee was planning. Slow things down. It was worth a try. So he dialed the main number for the mill, asking the switchboard to transfer his call to the CEO's office.

"Is Hamilton Lee still there?"

"He's on the way out to the memorial service."

"This is Brent Walker in the general counsel's office. Tell him I need to talk to him."

"Mr. Lee is running late."

"It's urgent. I'm sure he'll make time. He'll know what it's about."

"Hold on."

A minute later Lee came on the line. "Yes, Brent. What can I do for you?"

"Back off. We can work this out."

"I am still at a loss as to what you are referring to."

"Okay, be cautious. After all, I could be calling from the nearest FBI office with a recorder going. But I'm not. Back off, or the next call *will* be from there."

"Should I take that as a threat?"

"Take it any way you please."

And he ended the call.

3:15 P.M.

LEE AND HUGHES RETURNED TO THE MILL AFTER THE MEMORIAL service. The ceremony had been heavily attended, running longer than expected. Even De Florio dutifully went while Frank Barnard and Victor Jacks continued to search in and around Concord on the off chance their quarries had stayed in town. De Florio, Lee, and Hughes convened in the main conference room. Lee told them about Brent's call.

"Sounds like Walker's ready to turn us in," Hughes said.

"Then why are we still walking around?" Lee asked. "Get real, Larry. He was bluffing, buying time, trying to rattle us."

De Florio agreed.

"What about it, Jon," Lee said, "any idea where they are?"

338

"We've checked both their homes, but nobody is there. Reed's daughter and granddaughter are gone too. My guess is they got their families off to a safe place."

"Any chance of finding out where?"

De Florio shook his head. "We've done only minimal background checks on the families."

"What about the taps on Walker's phone in his office and the one Reed uses all the time in his break room. Anything there?" Hughes asked.

"No calls all day."

"Obviously," Lee said, "they talked with each other. That escape was well coordinated."

"True," De Florio said. "But there are a multitude of phones scattered through the mill. They could have used any one of them. Most likely, they are using cell phones."

"I didn't want to do this, as it could draw undue attention," Lee said. "But I think we have no choice."

De Florio nodded, understanding, then stepped from the room.

"What was that all about?" Hughes asked.

Lee beamed a broad smile. "I own the Woods County Telephone Company."

"When did you buy that?" Hughes asked.

"Six months ago. One of my holding companies secured a controlling interest."

"You didn't bother telling anyone."

"I told Jon. Other than that I didn't really think it was anyone's business what I bought or sold. It's actually been rather useful in his preparatory work on Priorities. You can learn a lot from a person's telephone records. All in all, though, it's not a profitable venture."

"You know the rules, Hamilton. We should have been told."

"So what are you going to do about it? It isn't two to one anymore, Larry. It's just me and you. I'd suggest you let me run things my way. We'll all be a whole lot better off."

Hughes said nothing more and sat silent the entire five minutes until De Florio returned.

339

"I was careful with my inquiries, feigning a theft situation with one of our employees. But they ran a check on Walker and Reed's cell phones. They both have service through your company. Three hours ago a call came to Walker's cell phone. From a landline. It's a house on Eagle Lake owned by a Leon Peacock. He works at the bag plant and lives in town, but built the place a few years ago for his retirement. Peacock's on vacation this week, visiting his daughter in South Carolina."

"How did you find all that out in five minutes?" Hughes asked.

"I checked Peacock's personnel file. That led me to our banking records. He obtained a mortgage from the Woods County State Bank for the construction. A call to his supervisor at the bag plant provided me with where he was and what he's doing."

"You think they're out at Eagle Lake?" Lee asked.

"We'll know in thirty minutes."

BRENT TOOK HIS TIME LEAVING STATESBORO. THE DELUGE STARTED as he reentered Woods County. By the time he reached Eagle Lake it was pouring rain and, from the look of the nasty clouds, an awful lot of moisture was going to find the ground during the next few hours.

He was still wearing the stinking Braves cap and sunglasses found in the Mustang. He hoped, coupled with the rain, he was adequately disguised from the curious view of any passing motorists, one of whom might work for De Florio. He'd destroyed his cell phone and left it in a dumpster forty miles behind him.

He snaked around the lake's east shore, passing the county boat ramp and two of the larger fish camps. He turned north at the intersection of Thrasher Point Drive and County Road 36, the north shore being the most sparsely populated section of the lake. The terrain was steep and rocky. Whole quarries had been excavated during the lake's construction. Few houses existed. The wood-sided, hip-roofed cottage he sought was nestled away from the road among tall pines, encased in heavy underbrush, nearly invisible. A pine straw and gravel drive twisted to it, the dingy white Toyota pickup parked in front. Wet gravel crunched beneath the tires as the Mustang crept to a stop.

Moisture pelted the windshield.

He quickly scampered out and banged on the front door, which Hank opened.

"It's about time. I was getting worried," Hank said. "You changed clothes."

He stepped inside and shook the water off onto the hardwood floor. "The rain slowed me and I tried to eat something. I also got rid of all that stuff."

"To a safe place, I hope."

"The safest. Even if we don't survive, it will."

"I don't like that *if* stuff."

"Neither do I, Hank, but we have to face reality. These guys are pros. Even if we go to the police right now, there's no guarantee they won't still get us. They've been killing people a long time, and have gotten pretty damn good at it."

A long blue vinyl sofa faced the rear wall. He plopped down onto the soft cushions. Through sliding glass doors, past a wooden deck, was a panoramic view of Eagle Lake, its south shore barely visible, thick woods to the west and east since the house sat in the elbow of a cove. The rain pounded the lake at a billion entry points. Lightning flashed in the distance. Thunder clamored overhead.

"Pretty place," he said, looking around the inside. "What about the owner?"

"On vacation."

"How'd you get in?"

"I know where he keeps the key."

Okay. He liked it. "The privacy should give us time to think."

FRANK BARNARD WAS WAITING IN HIS MOTEL ROOM LISTENING TO the rain when the call came from De Florio. Immediately after receiving instructions he drove straight to Eagle Lake.

Southern Republic owned a large house perched on the east shore. It was actually an extension of Hickory Row, maintained and controlled by the same personnel who oversaw all the Row's operations. The house and grounds were outfitted especially for fishing, waterskiing, and parties. Part of the accommodations included a concrete dock that harbored a pair of V-hulled outboards.

His instructions were clear. Take one of the boats and approach as close as possible to the house owned by Leon Peacock. From a map he'd already learned its location in the elbow of a cove. But by the time he arrived at the dock rain was falling in sheets, the lake pitching like the agitating cycle of a washing machine. So he vetoed a water approach and decided to head for the shore about a quarter mile from the target, on the far side of the inlet. From there, he could safely hike through the woods and observe from across the water, using the trees and underbrush for cover.

The twin engines on the eighteen-footer cranked instantly. Warm rain pounded him and, aided by his speed, pricked his face like needles. He wore camouflage coveralls, a dark-green slicker, a cap, gloves, and boots. By the time he found the inlet and beached the boat every stitch of him was soaked.

The shore was unpopulated, a steep rocky incline littered with wet palmettos, thorny vines, and ankle-deep mud. He trudged up, breasting the top of a craggy hill and cautiously peering through the trees. The house sat across on the side of the cove, on an incline, the front invisible. He assumed Victor Jacks was now nearby too. Seeking shelter under one of the bushy pines, he dialed Jacks' number on his cell phone.

"Bluebird?"

"I'm here," Jacks said.

"Anything?"

"A pickup truck and car were there ten minutes ago."

"You in position?"

"I am."

"Stay there."

He ended the call and replaced the phone in his pocket.

He checked his watch. 4:25 P.M.

The storm masked the sun and most of the daylight, making it appear much later. He crawled forward on his belly and took up a position among the scratchy brush, a clear view of the house ahead.

Rain hammered down.

He readied the binoculars.

BRENT SAT ON THE COUCH.

The rain fell harder, its soothing monotone relaxing. But his nerves remained frayed and on edge. Hank reclined in one of the chairs.

"How long have you known about Lori Anne?" he asked Hank.

"Several years."

He appreciated the honesty. "Why didn't you tell me?"

"I wanted to. But Ashley wouldn't allow it. Believe me, we had arguments on the point. But I had to respect her wishes. It's her life. I finally broke down and told your mother."

"When?"

"Just after you got back."

He shook his head. "She didn't say a word. The both of you played that one close."

"Ashley's had a tough time, Brent. Her marriages never really had a chance. She didn't love any of 'em like she did you. She was good to 'em. But if the truth be known, all three husbands knew somebody else stood in the way. You, of course, were barrelin' down the guilt road. Telling you about a daughter would have not helped a thing. And you know that."

"I still have regrets, Hank."

"You shouldn't."

"I did Paula wrong. I never should have married her."

"That's all in how you look at it. I'd say Paula didn't have to force the marriage, knowing you wanted out."

"She was pregnant."

"Was she? All we had was her word. For all you know, she could have got that way just after the wedding. Paula had her own agenda that she worked by her own set of rules."

"I can't get Paula's face from that day out of my mind. Backing out the driveway while I'm telling her *I don't love you, and I don't know if I ever did*. She cried, Hank. The first time I could ever remember her crying over anything. I didn't think stone could cry. But that day it did. It's the last image of her alive I have. The next was when I identified her body."

"Take it from a real loser, Brent. You shouldn't feel guilty. Me. I ruined a thirty-year marriage cattin' around. I have a reason to feel guilty. I asked for what I got. But there's not a damn thing I can do about any of it now. I miss Loretta every day. I hope she's happy. But I can't dwell on mistakes. It'll kill you eventually. Nobody can take that kind of pressure. Let it go."

"Loretta was a good woman. I never could understand why you did that crap."

"Me either. For God's sake don't make the same mistake I did and do more stupid things."

He smiled. Hank was trying to do what he could to make him feel better and he appreciated the effort.

"Besides, looks like I'm goin' to get a new son-in-law."

"That all depends. We still have a little problem."

"That's an understatement."

He had to say, "You realize the company used you all these years."

"I do, and the thought makes me sick. I wanted to be the big man. The one everybody looked to when they got in a jam. *Go see Hank, he'll get you out of trouble*. Right. They built a whole town to suit their needs. You couldn't have taken a crap here without them knowing how many sheets of toilet paper you used. Concord is a company town gone insane."

"They made hundreds of millions of dollars from murder. Who said crime doesn't pay?"

The rain quickened.

Brent stood and walked close to the sliding glass doors. Even under the battering from the intense summer storm Eagle Lake was beautiful. He released the lock and slid open the glass panel. Warm, moist air flooded in and mixed with the air-conditioning, fogging the double-insulated panes. He gazed beyond the railing down to the shore. A wooden dock accommodated a small skiff with a tiny outboard, a green canvas stretched over the top. Hank stepped up behind him.

"Your friend fish?" Brent asked, pointing to the boat, similar to the one he used last weekend. It was also similar to the one his father had been murdered in, and not all that far away from here.

"You know your way around this lake, don't you?" Hank asked. "Damn thing's been here thirty years and I've never set foot in or on it."

He glanced back over his shoulder and grinned. "I wouldn't recommend today for your first time."

FRANK BARNARD SPIED THE GLASS DOOR SLIDE OPEN. HE AIMED THE binoculars and two faces came into focus.

Clear and undeniable.

He dialed the phone.

"I have them."

JON HUNG UP AND TURNED TO LEE AND HUGHES.

"We located them."

Lee smiled. Hughes looked relieved.

"Kill them," Lee said. "Quickly. But carefully. With no linger-ing issues. Like the pro you are."

Jon glanced at his watch.

4:53 P.M.

Then he stood and left the conference room.

7:57 P.M.

THE PHONE JARRED BRENT'S NERVES.

He and Hank had been sitting tight for a couple of hours, mull-ing over their next steps, deciding on who to involve from law enforcement, and where. The move with Greene had turned disas-trous. They could not make another miscalculation. Whatever they did, it had to be the smart play. The house loomed dark and sullen, a lone lamp the only illumination. Hank sat on the edge of a chair. They both stared at the house phone.

Which kept ringing.

Brent stood, walked to the kitchen counter, and answered.

"Good evening, Mr. Walker."

Adrenaline shot through his body. "Who is this?"

No response.

A chill curled down his spine. Now he knew. "De Florio?"

Outside, rain was still falling, even harder than earlier. "How did you find us?"

De Florio chuckled. "You made a mistake."

His mind raced. Then it hit him. "They own the phone company?"

"A fact few know."

True. That information had not been part of the materials Bozin supplied. Which was why earlier he'd risked the calls he made. But Hank's call from the landline had been nothing but a bright beacon. Thank God he hadn't used the cell to call his uncle's house.

Hank drew closer.

Brent tensed. "What now?"

"We have unfinished business."

"Don't be foolish. Remember what I have."

"We'll take our chances."

"That could be really stupid."

"You know, I remember another time when I was out on Eagle Lake. About two years ago, I believe. August. A little better weather than tonight, but hot as hell. It was right after dawn. Perhaps you recall the result of that visit?"

Red-hot anger flashed through him. "You no-good piece of crap. Come take me on, De Florio. Man-to-man. You and me. Face-to-face. You got the guts for that?"

"Let's find out," De Florio said.

The call ended.

The phone in Frank Barnard's pocket vibrated.

He fished it out and answered.

"Proceed precisely as planned," De Florio said in his ear.

"Understood."

He beeped the phone off and turned to Victor Jacks. "Mr. De Florio says go."

Jacks yanked the telephone wire from the junction box.

He then switched on the jammer to prevent any possible cell calls from the house and they both advanced out into the rain.

Brent stared at Hank trying to calm down.

Finally, Hank said, "What do we do now?"

"What we should have done hours ago." He lifted the handset and punched in 911. Nothing happened. He tried again but it only confirmed the line was dead. It had just worked.

Dammit.

What once seemed like a safe haven now felt like a cage.

A loud crack shattered the silence.

The front window splintered as something flew into the room and struck the far wall. They dove to the floor, using the sofa for protection. On the way down Brent raked the lamp off the table, bursting the bulb, plunging everything into darkness. Two more somethings came through the windows and more glass shattered. A blast of rain and wind roared inside.

"What was that," Hank asked.

"I didn't hear any shots. All I know is De Florio's out there somewhere." He was trying to stay calm. He felt his pocket for the key to the Mustang. "Stay here. I'm going to the car. Maybe I can get them to go after me."

"Don't be an idiot."

"Listen, Hank, we don't have a chance together. We're like fish in a barrel here. Separately, one of us might make it. Once I'm away you head out back. Use the boat down on the dock or swim if you have to. Now stay here till I'm gone."

Before Hank could object he belly-crawled forward, slithering out of the great room and down a short hall toward the bedrooms. At the front door he stopped momentarily and checked the knob. Locked. At least they couldn't burst right in. He noticed a brass stand next to the door. Two umbrellas protruded along with what looked like a baseball bat. He crawled closer. It was a bat. Metal. It might come in handy, so he gripped the stem and resumed his crawl.

He found one of the bedrooms, stood, and approached a solitary window. Shoving the night table away, he unlocked the sash, popped out the screen, and, without giving himself time to be scared, leaped out onto the soaked ground. The rain drenched him like a warm shower. He hoped his exit had gone unnoticed. Luckily, the window faced dense woods on the side of the house. He crouched low and used the thorny brush to cover his path back toward the front of the house and the Mustang. No more glass had broken. But with all the thunder and rain it was hard to know for sure.

He searched the darkness ahead.

What had Joan Bates said? *"It's not always smart to be head-strong. Sometimes the smarter course is to avoid a bad situation altogether."*

Unfortunately, that was not an option tonight.

He caught movement in the dark. Had somebody moved toward the front door? A bolt of lightning flashed. An instance of brilliance confirmed the observation.

Definitely.

He headed toward the figure.

HANK WAS MAD WITH HIMSELF FOR LETTING BRENT GO. HE'D HEARD the window open and assumed Brent climbed out. It wasn't right for him to be taking all the risks. He didn't want his granddaughter never to know her natural father. And his daughter could lose a chance at happiness with the man she truly loved. He decided not to just sit huddled behind a sofa and started to crawl toward the front door. Maybe he could make it to the truck. Brent might be right. Separately they did have a better chance.

He unlocked and creaked open the front door, met immediately by a blast of warm wind and rain. He stayed low and emerged onto the porch. He used the two-by-four railing and thick wooden spindles for protection and peered into the blackness, sporadic flashes of lightning the only source of illumination. No one was in sight, the truck just a few feet away.

He found his keys and started to stand.

A figure emerged from the woods and darted toward him.

Lightning flashed.

He saw the gun. Pointed at him.

And froze.

BRENT SPOTTED THE GUN.

Not thinking there may be others concealed in the thickets, he grasped the bat and shot around the far side of the truck. His eyes were adjusted to the dark and he clearly saw the target. The man, though, was in front of the truck and couldn't see him, noise from the storm masking his approach across the graveled drive.

He cocked the bat and lunged forward.

One thrust and metal found its mark against the side of the head. The body crumpled to the mud. He stared down, bat re-cocked and ready.

"Damn, Brent. Thanks," Hank said.

"You don't follow orders, do you?"

"Is he dead?"

He bent down. Blood poured from the head wound, quickly dissolved by the rain. "Hard to tell."

"Is it De Florio?"

He rolled the body over and shook his head.

A bullet ricocheted off the hood of the truck. No retort accompanied the shot. He'd already noticed that the dead man's gun was equipped with some sort of sound suppressor. He ducked and grabbed the weapon. They bolted around the side of the house toward the lake. Just as they rounded the corner, another bullet careered off the wood siding behind him.

He aimed the gun in his hand and sent a round back with a soft pop.

"Where are we going?" Hank asked.

"The boat."

They sloshed through the mud, dodged trees, and ran for the dock.

He held on to the gun with one hand and ripped the canvas off the skiff with the other. At the same time Hank untied the boat. He jumped in and hoped to God the outboard cranked. If necessary, he'd paddle the thing. Anything just to get out of here. He pulled the starter twice and, miraculously, the motor shot to life.

"Get in."

Hank jumped down.

He twisted the outboard into gear and the skiff shot away from the dock toward the open lake.

THE PHONE PULSED IN JON'S HAND.

"Redbird is down. Possibly dead. But they are away, in the boat, headed for the intended location."

He did not react to the news concerning Frank Barnard, though he was disturbed by the possible loss of another well-trained associate. Obviously something had gone wrong. The idea had been to rattle Reed and Walker, isolate them without phones, then push them onto the lake. The house was to appear to have been vandalized, which was why rocks were used on the windows. A surreptitious check of the boat earlier revealed the outboard gassed and operational. A perfect, and apparent, means of escape. Also an easily explained theft. There was no time to criticize right now. He'd deal with any mistakes later.

"Go to your boat and follow. Stay close," he made absolutely clear in a tone Victor Jacks should fear.

"Understood. They have a gun."

Good to know.

Five hundred yards from shore, standing at the helm of a V-hull, camouflaged by darkness and the storm, Jon switched off the cellular phone.

Then he calmly waited in the rain for his prey to draw close.

351

Brent brought the skiff out of the cove and around to the south and quickly grabbed his bearings. He knew the county boat ramp lay about two miles west, an infinite number of landing points in between. He decided to head for the ramp. That area was heavily populated and the more people, the fewer chances De Florio and his goons would have to make a move. The eight-foot skiff was nearly inadequate against the stormy chop, its flat bottom taking a beating from the waves. Hank sat near the bow while he operated the outboard from the stern. He still held the gun. It was hard to see far in any direction so he navigated by his wits and the occasional help lightning provided.

"This is not the place to be in the middle of an electrical storm," Hank yelled.

"Beats the hell out of where we were."

He looked back and saw a boat approaching.

Jon patiently waited until the skiff committed to a course. Once done, he revved the 250 horsepower of the twin inboards and shot forward, its deep V knifing the water, the hull quickly planing. He left the running lights off until fully under way, then switched on the bow's red sparkler.

More than enough indication to let them know the chase was nearly over.

Jacks raced through the woods to a second deep-V beached a short way from Leon Peacock's lake house. He jumped in, cranked the two powerful engines, and roared off in pursuit of his boss.

"WE'VE GOT COMPANY," BRENT SAID, AND HE INSTANTLY REALIZED the situation. "Hank, I'm afraid we've been pretty stupid." He stared back at the puny thirty-five-horsepower outboard barely pushing them through the water. "I wondered why we weren't chased by anyone to the dock. And those guys were pretty lousy shots for professional killers."

"We have a gun."

"Not much good it will do. This is where De Florio wanted us."

"And that's him behind us?"

"You got it."

He whirled his head around and tried to find a house with lights. None was visible.

"He'll be here in a few minutes," Hank said.

"He's toying with us. He can take us whenever. We don't have the horsepower to outrun him and he knows it."

He kept searching the shoreline. De Florio was now less than three hundred yards and closing.

"We could hit the water and swim," Hank said. "Maybe he can't find both of us in this storm."

Behind De Florio, another red light was now shooting through the rain toward them.

"Looks like two of them," he yelled over the howling wind.

He was still searching the shoreline, thinking hard, when it hit him. Frantically, he scanned the darkness, wishing for lightning, which seemed foolish given his unprotected location on open water. He was rewarded with a long bolt that gave him an instant to pinpoint the location.

There. Damned if it wasn't. Just ahead to the left.

He studied the skiff and the tiny outboard. Hard to know for sure, but they just might fit.

"Get down," he yelled.

Hank gave him a strange look.

"And don't rise up."

For once, Hank did as he was told but said, "What are you going to do?"

"Even the odds."

He focused ahead on the shoreline, now less than a hundred yards away. At some point he was going to have to slow down. He'd set the bow on the last lightning strike. Another bright crackle and he refined his course.

There it was.

The opening for Brooks Creek.

Less than twenty yards away and closing.

He released his grip on the throttle and the outboard died. Seconds later the skiff shot into the blackness and slowed. He knew the gate of oak limbs was just ahead and couldn't take the chance that the top of the outboard might strike the limbs, so he popped the retaining clamp and shoved the motor off the transom into the water. He then lunged forward next to Hank, stretching himself out as low as possible. Just as he hit the bottom of the boat the limbs raked across its top close enough for him to feel their graze.

Out the other side, he said, "Into the water."

They both dove out and he kept the gun dry above. From the depth he knew they were in the pool. About shoulder-deep. He led the way toward the far bank and the tiny beach he remembered.

They emerged.

"Those limbs should slow 'em long enough for us to disappear in the woods."

Hank was catching his breath. "You don't have to tell me twice."

Brent pushed through the thickets.

Rain pounded down.

He heard the drone of an engine.

Approaching.

He stopped and looked back.

Jon saw the skiff disappear into the dark shoreline.
He slowed and cautiously approached the point where it was last seen, then followed, realizing he was in one of the creeks. He switched on the forward spotlight and saw limbs out over the water.

Approaching fast.

He rammed the throttle to neutral, then reverse. He veered the helm hard to starboard and forced the boat's port side against the water, using the hull to stop his forward momentum. The wind helped too, sweeping out of the north directly into his bow. He stopped just as the port-side hull gently kissed the oak branches spanning the creek.

That was close.

He reoriented the boat forward and searched the darkness ahead with the floodlight. He found the empty skiff, then rotated the light trying to locate its two occupants. No one was visible.

But he knew they were there.

And armed.

"Nice try, Walker," he yelled. "Amazing, I think we're in the same place where your father met his maker too. How fitting."

He switched off the running lights and the spotlight.

No sense being an easy target.

He heard the roar of an approaching boat.

Jacks saw the skiff and De Florio disappear into the shoreline. He assumed both were in a creek. Barnard had earlier briefed him on the local geography. He remembered De Florio's stern instruction to stay close. He also remembered the hole in Milo Richey's head. So he pressed the boat's throttle forward, increased his speed, and followed.

JON TURNED AND SAW THE DEEP V OF THE OUTBOARD SHOOTING straight for him. He realized screaming would be useless and cursed himself for not having more lights on. He reached for the spotlight and tried to twirl it around and warn Jacks of his presence.

No time.

BRENT WATCHED AS THE SECOND BOAT SLAMMED INTO THE STERN, apparently splintering the metal fuel tanks in De Florio's boat. The detonation was instant and horrific, gas from the other boat shortly following in another equally huge explosion that sent a blinding wave of intense heat across his face. The two boats burst into red-orange flames, scorching fireballs mushrooming up into the pouring rain. A second later the flames caught hold on the adjacent foliage and added to the inferno. In the next second both boats disintegrated, along with their occupants, searing fire turning night into day.

He and Hank shielded their faces from the heat and the flaming shrapnel thrown out by the explosion. The repercussions continued for another minute. Then the rain slowly overtook the flames licking skyward.

"Holy crap," Hank said.

Brent stared too.

And smiled.

Strange, considering he just witnessed the fiery death of two men. But one of them had been directly responsible for his father's murder. Perhaps where he was standing right now had been the place De Florio stood that August morning nearly two years before. The place where he'd waited for his Priority to arrive. Like his father did every Friday morning, living his life as a file predicted.

Then he was "processed."

Cold and impersonal.

Something to help the company's bottom line, with not a single thought given to any of the people left behind. Now the man who'd spearheaded that murderous effort was dead.

And Brent felt nothing but delight.

Five words suddenly sprang to mind.

They formed clearly in his brain and he reveled in their justice. De Florio was right a few minutes ago when he'd uttered, *How fitting*.

"That was for you, Dad."

ONE YEAR LATER

Brent followed Lori Anne out the door.

"Go get the ball and gloves," he told her. "I'll find my bat and meet you in the backyard."

He headed down the brick path into the garage to retrieve the metal bat. It was the same one used last year to down Frank Barnard. A souvenir from a rainy summer night he'd never forget.

He found the bat propped against one of the bare stud walls. Lifting it, he caught a glimpse of the same aged Florida grapefruit box that had stayed in his parents' garage since high school, brought here along with all his other belongings when he and Ashley bought their new house. He slid the box off the shelf and dropped it onto one of the waist-high benches. They were the same ones from his father's workshop, his mother insisting he take them. Inside were school annuals, trophies, and other familiar mementos along with a few new ones—magazines and newspapers collected over the past twelve months that recalled the aftermath.

He glanced at several and thought back.

By dawn on the day after that fateful Monday, he and Hank had found their way out of Brooks Creek and immediately made sure their families were safe. After dealing with local authorities, they drove to Atlanta and retrieved the original documents sent to the Fulton County district attorney. An hour's explanation was needed before law enforcement understood the full implications. He recalled trying to stay calm, speak clearly, and contain his emotions, but thoughts of his father had made that tough.

Warrants were finally obtained.

He was there when Hamilton Lee and Larry Hughes were taken into custody, a large contingent of state and federal agents participating in the arrest and subsequent search of the Blue Tower. Simultaneous with the arrest the state of Georgia and the United States seized all assets belonging to Southern Republic Pulp and Paper Company, Hamilton Lee, Lawrence Hughes, and Christopher Bozin.

Frank Barnard survived the cracked skull. But not enough was left of Jon De Florio and the man in the other boat for any positive identification. Victor Jacks' identity was ultimately learned from Barnard. A sizable amount of cash De Florio had accumulated from his years of killing was also found and seized in offshore banks, eventually added to what the government already possessed.

The final take had been staggering.

The cache included the paper mill, bag plant, sawmills, warehouses, wood yards, thousands of acres of pine trees, the Blue Tower, Hickory Row, mansions, beach condominiums, mountain retreats, tracts of real property scattered all over the world, huge amounts of cash, stocks and bonds, a fleet of trucks, heavy equipment, cars, a Learjet, all the subsidiary and ancillary businesses Lee, Hughes, and Bozin amassed in and around Woods County and in other locations, and a multitude of personal property, including some valuable collectibles.

The total value topping $5 billion.

He thumbed through a few of the newspapers and recalled the intense public debate that ensued on what to do with it all. Remembering what Bozin had cautioned in his narrative he'd argued that the assets should be returned to the employees of the company, both past and present. Others postured that they should go exclusively to victims' families. To press their claims an immediate flood of lawsuits from family after family appeared in the Georgia courts. So many that, within a few months, nearly two hundred separate pieces of litigation jeopardized the continued vitality of the company, regardless of $5 billion in assets.

But a twisted paradox solved the dilemma.

The Priority program had been carried out with an unparalleled success. So efficient that it became difficult to positively determine which employees were "processed" and which simply died from natural causes. Hiding behind the Fifth Amendment, Frank Barnard refused to testify about anything he may have personally done. Brent recalled one plaintiff's lawyer, who represented the heirs of a name Bozin himself verified as having been processed, who thought himself clever when he exhumed the body of his decedent. But the subsequent autopsy revealed nothing proving that the official cause of death, heart failure, was chemically induced. Other lawsuits experienced similar problems and, without definitive proof of causation, many foundered.

He studied a picture of himself from the *Atlanta Constitution*. A front-page article that appeared last fall when he held a press conference to postulate the plan that eventually was accepted by a federal bankruptcy court.

All the assets, both the company's and the shareholders', were returned to the corporation. Stock was then issued to all employees, both past and present. If the employee was deceased, the stock went to the heirs. Assets that weren't needed, like the jet, mansions, Hickory Row, and most of the luxuries the owners surrounded themselves with, were sold, the cash funneled back into the company, some of which was paid out as dividends to the new shareholders. By agreement when the stock was issued to each person all lawsuits were dismissed and the corporation was allowed to function, only now Southern Republic Pulp and Paper Company became one of the largest employee-owned businesses in the country.

Though it was clear none of upper management outside of the three owners and De Florio possessed any knowledge of what had been going on, the employees, who were now the shareholders, quickly demanded from the new twelve-person board of directors that they clean house. A trust factor had been irrevocably lost. So all members of upper and middle management were summarily fired. Brent had been the only person retained, promoted to general counsel for the corporation. He felt bad, those men and women in management were victims too, but little could be done to save them. The new board offered Hank the position of industrial relations manager. The employees' confidence in him was strong. But his old friend declined, preferring to remain among the ranks of the blue collars and make amends for his past mistakes.

Hamilton Lee and Larry Hughes went to prison. Frank Barnard's survival meant a witness was available who could verify at least some of what Bozin had said. A plea deal was reached with Barnard for him to testify but, ironically, once all their respective assets were seized, neither Lee nor Hughes could afford any high-priced legal talent. In the end their court-appointed lawyers arranged plea bargains. A federal judge in Savannah dished out multiple life sentences, along with additional time on a variety of lesser charges. Neither would ever live to see their release. Nor would Barnard. He was beaten to death in the Chatham County jail while awaiting final sentencing.

Which seemed fitting.

"What are you doing?"

He turned.

Ashley stood in the garage doorway. He studied his wife in her cutoff denim shorts and Jacksonville Jaguars jersey. Nearly a year of marriage definitely agreed with her.

She stepped closer.

"Remembering," he said.

She lifted out one of the magazines. A *US News & World Report* with a front-page article that proclaimed Brent and Hank Reed THE LAST PRIORITIES.

"I guess we were," he said.

"Maybe. But Bozin was actually the last."

He thought back to the old man with silver hair. A monster to be sure. But one apparently with a conscience in the end, however tiny.

"It's been quite a year," Ashley said.

That it had, and not just for him. Ashley had quit her job with the postal service and now devoted herself full-time to relief efforts organized to help surviving Priority families. She was the director of one of the largest organizations, Heirs of the Southern Republic Foundation, and he was extremely proud of her efforts. He reached over and stroked her blond hair. She drew close and they kissed.

"How do you feel?" he asked.

"Different."

She was two months' pregnant. They'd decided that one more child would be a good thing. Lori Anne had adapted well, taking the news about her biological father in stride. Manley Simmons remained a part of her life. Now "Uncle Manley," and everybody seemed fine.

"Daddy," Lori Anne said.

They turned toward outside.

"You were supposed to be getting the bat. Not smooching."

"But I like smooching."

"Could you come on now?"

He turned to his wife. "Gotta go."

He grabbed the bat and strolled toward the backyard.

His return to Concord had been bittersweet. Yet maybe a genuine good had come from years of mistakes. All he wanted now was to build a life for his wife, daughter, and new child. They lived only a couple of blocks over from his mother, on a tree-lined drive dotted with handsome Victorian clapboards and more modern brick two-stories. His house was one of the oldest, bought from a family who'd quickly left the area after the truth became known. It desperately needed attention, a real fixer-upper, but that was okay. His father had done that for him and he intended to build a home his children could depend on, too.

His mother was doing okay, enjoying her granddaughter and

looking forward to another child. His fondest hope was that she had more good years to come. They'd learned that his father had been diagnosed by a doctor in Savannah with a rare form of blood cancer. The company knew because it had access to his medical records. The treatments were going to be extraordinarily expensive so, before Brian Walker even mustered the courage to tell his wife, he'd been immediately Prioritized and killed.

Anger still occasionally seethed through Brent. But overall, he felt liberated, calm, at peace, fully in command, as though most of the taboos and delusions that had weighed him down for so many years had finally been shattered. Periodically, he ventured across Eagle Lake in the old aluminum skiff. Sometimes alone. Sometimes with Ashley and Lori Anne. Over time he hoped his children would explore all its nooks and crannies, eventually knowing the lake as well as he did. And though the explosions destroyed the overhanging limbs and made Brooks Creek forever accessible, he would never go back there. He couldn't really explain it.

All he knew was that the ghosts of good and evil dwelling within those banks were best left undisturbed.

WRITER'S NOTE

This novel of suspense had a fascinating evolution. It was first created in 1992, becoming the second complete manuscript I ever wrote. At the time John Grisham's *The Firm* was riding high, easy to see its influence on this story. But *The List* was never submitted to publishers. Its quality was simply not-ready-for-prime-time, so into a drawer it went. Through the years I'd occasionally glance at it, reading bits and pieces. The idea of a self-insured manufacturing company, located in a small Georgia town, controlling its costs through murder always intrigued me. Then, in 2010, with the enactment of the Affordable Care Act, the idea seemed to take on a greater significance. During the Covid lockdown in 2020 I decided to give the manuscript a once-over.

And the memories rushed back.

I practiced law for thirty years in St. Marys, Georgia, a small, southern town where, for decades, the largest employer was a paper mill. From the 1940s to the 1980s St. Marys was definitely a company town. By the mid-1980s I represented the local electrical workers' union (IBEW) at the mill, handling employee grievances, assisting with contract negotiations, and dealing with members' problems.

And there were many battles.

Eventually, by the late 1980s, the company decided to retain me. So, just like Brent Walker, I changed teams. Of course, that real-life paper company utilized no Priority program. No one was murdered for profit. That idea came to me one day during a grievance hearing. I wondered, What if the company didn't bother with due process? What if, instead, it just permanently eliminated any problems?

So was born *The List*.

It's exciting to finally have this story published. My sincere thanks goes out to my publisher, Ben Sevier, at Grand Central and Simon Lipskar, my agent, for believing in the novel. Also, as always, to my wife, Elizabeth, for both her constant encouragement and expert editing eye.

Southern mill towns were a peculiar institution, nearly all of them now gone. The paper mill in St. Marys closed in 2001, its buildings eventually razed to the ground. The original owner, most of upper management, and a sizable number of its nine-hundred-plus workers are no longer with us. While rewriting this story I recalled many of them with fondness.

One person, though, is still around.

His name is Richard "Larry" Daley. Hank Reed is based on him. Not in every detail, but in those that matter most. Larry always seemed larger than life. He served for decades as the electrical union's president and was the longtime mayor of St. Marys. He fought with a vengeance on behalf of his union members (and his political constituents), and was both feared and respected by the company. I learned a lot from him. There is one glaring difference, though, between Larry and Hank. In the story Hank's spouse leaves him for another man. In real life, Marlene, Larry's wife of fifty-plus years, was a saint, loved by everyone, myself included, and most of all by Larry. Sadly, she passed away in 2016. Forgive me, Marlene, but for this story Hank had to be single. Hank's love interest, though, is named Marlene Rhoden—which was Marlene Daley's maiden name.

For a locale I chose a place 150 miles north of St. Marys in central Georgia. But I patterned the paper mill there after the site that once existed in St. Marys (which I walked through many times).

Eagle Lake is wholly fictitious, though there are man-made reservoirs just like it scattered all across Georgia. The Blue Tower is my creation, but the Shrine of the Immaculate Conception still stands in downtown Atlanta.

The story of how Qin Shi tamed his enemies with luxury palaces and watched them through servant-spies is true. I came across it in 2008 while writing *The Emperor's Tomb* and incorporated it into this rewrite. For all those fans of Cotton Malone (and my other stand-alone thrillers and novellas where history plays a huge part), I could not resist adding just a dash of the past here.

St. Marys is no longer a company town. In the 1980s the massive Kings Bay Naval Submarine Base arrived and changed the local demographics forever. Over the ensuing four decades the population of Camden County grew from twelve thousand to over fifty thousand. The paper mill's closing in 2001 put nearly a thousand people out of work. That was traumatic, to say the least. I was chairman of the county commission at the time and the company was the county's single largest taxpayer. It took several years for everyone to adjust to life without it.

Thankfully, though, we survived.

Elizabeth was born and raised a few miles from St. Marys. Two of my children, two grandchildren, and most of Elizabeth's family still live there.

And though we now reside elsewhere, just like Brent Walker, rarely is that place we long called home far from our thoughts.

ABOUT THE AUTHOR

Steve Berry is the *New York Times* and #1 internationally best-selling author of nineteen Cotton Malone novels, six stand-alone thrillers, two Luke Daniels adventures, and several works of short fiction. He has more than twenty-six million books in print, translated into forty-one languages. With his wife, Elizabeth, he is the founder of History Matters, an organization dedicated to historical preservation. He serves as an emeritus member of the Smithsonian Libraries Advisory Board and was a founding member of International Thriller Writers, formerly serving as its co-president.

For more information you can visit:
SteveBerry.org
Facebook.com/SteveBerryWriter